CRITICAL PRAISE FOR *Lucy's Launderette* **BY**

Betsy Burke

"Burke's debut is frothy fun
and definitely worth a spin."
—*Booklist*

"Pick up a copy of *Lucy's Launderette*
and give yourself time to enjoy it…
you can't help but fall in love with Lucy."
—Writers Unlimited

"Burke's story charms with a shower of witty
and wry introspection. A tour de-light!"
—*BookPage*

BETSY BURKE

was born in London, England, and grew up on the
west coast of Canada. She has a Bachelor of Music
from the University of Victoria. Among the many jobs
on her résumé, she includes opera singer, dishwasher,
guitar teacher, nurses' assistant, charwoman, mural
painter, salesclerk, puppeteer, English teacher and
most recently, freelance translator. She currently lives in
Italy. Her interests include art, music, books, rejection-
slip origami, turning the planet into a garden rather
than a toxic waste dump and trying to convince her
four-year-old daughter that chocolate is not a breakfast
food. She is also the author of a murder mystery set in
Florence.

Performance
Anxiety

Betsy Burke

RED
DRESS
INK™

First edition November 2004

PERFORMANCE ANXIETY

A Red Dress Ink novel

ISBN 0-373-25068-1

www.RedDressInk.com

Printed in U.S.A.

For Sara and Salva and music-makers everywhere.

Acknowledgments

Thanks to Yule Heibel, Jean Grundy Fanelli, Katie,
David and Susan Burke, my extended Canadian family,
Helen Holubov and a very special thanks
to Elizabeth Jennings and Kathryn Lye.

Vancouver

Chapter 1

The collision was all my fault.

It had happened on the day I was making my big move. I'd walked into the travel agency that gray Monday in early October and booked my ticket. KLM Royal Dutch Airlines. Vancouver to London—Heathrow.

The woman at the agency is a big opera buff. She always asks me about my career progress and gives me special treatment. That day, she let me leave a deposit for one percent of the fare. There was no need to tell her that I still had to earn enough to pay for the rest of the ticket, because I knew I'd find the money somehow. How else could I justify all those menial jobs and forty-eight-hour workdays?

It felt so great when she printed out that little piece of paper, handed it to me and said, "Here's your flight itinerary, Miranda. I sure do envy you. I love London at Christmas."

I took a big breath and said to her, "This'll be my first time there."

Although it wouldn't feel like it. I had Londontown.com on my browser. I could tell you what was going on in every concert hall and theater in the city. I could already imagine myself strolling through Covent Garden, or grabbing a bite to eat at Bad Bob's or Café de Paris before the opera, maybe a *Carmen,* a *Tosca,* or a *Nixon in China.* I can even tell you what the weather is in London on any given day. That Monday, London had drizzle with the prospect of heavy rain.

"I'm going over for an important audition," I said.

"Oh, wow. Really? Who's it for?"

"The English National Opera. I got the letter a couple of days ago. I've got my time slot. It's January the tenth at 3:30 p.m. In the theater itself. The brand-new beautiful renovated Coliseum."

Peter Drake, the two-hundred-ton tenor who was singing Pinkerton in our current production of *Madama Butterfly,* was good buddies with everyone at the ENO, so I took advantage of his buddydom and asked him to get me an audition. And he did. Although Peter acts like a diva, he's really a very nice man. His generosity is as vast as his costumes, which could probably double as pup tents in an emergency.

"How exciting," said the travel agent, "and a little bit scary too, I'll bet. What are you going to be singing?"

"Some Handel and some Mozart. And if they want to hear more, Rossini."

"Oooo. Sounds good, Miranda."

I pulled my pink cashmere scarf tighter around my throat. "Yeah. I'll have my fingers crossed the whole way. Recycled airplane air can be hell on your high notes. And my pieces have a lot of high notes and runs. But I know it's going to be fine. I have a great teacher and I've been doing a lot of performing lately to work up to it, and I even have a technique for handling the stage fright."

"You do? What's that?"

"Well, I learned it in my Centering Group. You see, you have to give the fear a shape. So mine's a nag. An old, swayback, dirty black plug of a horse with a voice like Mr. Ed's.

And whenever it says, 'Miranda Lyme, you untalented half-wit, what makes you think you can sing this piece? Who do you think you are anyway?' I just try to push the old nag as far back in the theater as I can get it. Try to get it out through the exit doors. Although, sometimes, it's right there on the stage with you, but as long as it still has its shape, and isn't stepping on your toes or anything, the anxiety isn't too bad."

"That's a new one on me."

"It was on me, too. Four years ago."

"Well, then…I really wish you luck, Miranda."

I yelped, "No, you can't say that. It's bad luck to wish me luck."

"Sorry."

"In opera we say toi, toi. Or mille fois merde."

"Toi, toi then. *And* mille fois merde."

"Thanks. I'm so excited about being able to do the audition right there in that theater. There's nothing like standing up on a real stage where the great stars have sung and letting it rip into that huge space. It's the most incredible feeling. It's electric. It's better than sex."

She opened her eyes wide. "Really? Maybe I should give it a try."

We both laughed, then I said, "I'll be back in a few weeks to get my ticket."

I was tempted to stay and tell her about the other things that were taking me to London. Like my father, the baritone Sebastian Lyme. And Kurt Hancock, the conductor/composer who was suddenly cutting into my practice time.

Kurt hadn't been part of my strategy, but when he'd strolled into the rehearsal hall two weeks earlier to conduct the *Madama Butterfly,* all the chorus women were immediately in heat.

To be honest, he wasn't really my type. I prefer darker, heftier men. Kurt is slim, blond and blue-eyed. But there were women in that chorus ready to poison their families and run away with him, and I guess, in trying to figure out what it was about him that was making them all unhinge, I let myself be carried away by the Kurt Hancock psychosis, too.

After that *Butterfly* rehearsal, everybody went out to Mimi's, a Gastown restaurant where opera singers often showcase their talent. The place is decorated in Chocolate Box Gothic with rich dark heavy drapes and tablecloths edged with a fatal amount of flounce. It's a home away from home for the opera bunch. Sometimes the singing is really fantastic, the performances glow, and sometimes the singers leave you feeling that it might be more fun to be slapped in the face over and over with a fresh cod than to have to listen to their talent. But I guess it's a question of how everybody's feeling.

That night was a fresh-cod night at Mimi's, my fellow chorus singers all trying too hard to impress Kurt.

My defective tights had been slipping down all evening and eventually were clinging to my knees. I wanted to yank them up again without doing a striptease in front of the entire opera company, so I went looking for a private place to sort out the matter. The tiny bathroom was occupied but I opened the door next to it, which was a big broom closet, and stumbled onto Kurt.

He froze like a startled deer caught in headlights. I'm not sure what he was doing in there all by himself before I came onto the scene, but I'd heard a series of rhythmic thuds just beforehand, and now I thought he might have been punching or hitting something or someone. So I said (I was a little drunk), "Don't mind me, Mr. Hancock. This won't take long. You can go back to whatever it was you were doing in a second. I just have to take care of something." And then I hitched up my dress and tugged everything into place.

He stared at me the entire time and I stared back. Then I noticed that the wall near his foot was covered with little black crescent-shaped marks. It wasn't the first time I'd seen this sort of thing. Music training had taught me early on that pianists *never* use their hands when they have to punch something.

But then Kurt started to smile. And appreciatively, too. He looked quite sweet, even a little forlorn, and I began to get a glimpse of his charm.

I smiled back. He smiled even more broadly, then sat down on a bucket and started asking me all about myself. I told him the basics, that my name was Miranda, that I was a lyric mezzo-soprano from the illustrious cow town of Cold Shanks, B.C., and that I'd done my voice degree in Vancouver but was going to London in December to do an ENO audition. And then I added that my father also lived in London, and was a well-known baritone.

"Oh, really?" asked Kurt. "What's his name?"

"Sebastian Lyme."

Kurt stood up. "Sebastian Lyme? I have a *Don Giovanni* recording with your father singing the Don. A fine voice. A very fine voice indeed. I've seen him perform. He had great charisma on stage."

"Really?" My heart began to race.

"Yes. He did a stunning Figaro in the *Barber.* Apart from his technical ability, the man had wonderful presence. Quite exceptional acting. He had the audience in stitches. Not an easy feat."

I was nodding vehemently. More. I wanted him to tell me more. I wanted to kidnap Kurt Hancock and make him tell me everything he knew about Sebastian Lyme.

Kurt went on, "And he did an impressive *Rigoletto* for the Royal Opera, but that must have been a good ten years ago. It's a pity we haven't crossed paths… Oh, Good Lord! You're not about to cry, are you?"

I laughed, shook my head and wiped my damp eyes. "It's just that hearing about my father like that…out of the blue…"

"Heavens. It usually takes me at least a week to make a woman cry."

We both laughed and then he said softly, "So you've followed in his footsteps. Marvelous. May I ask you a question?"

"Shoot."

"May I kiss Sebastian Lyme's daughter?"

I didn't expect it but I let him because he'd really earned it. And it was a nice kiss—not too sloppy or dry, nor too deep or shallow. Maybe Kurt would never have taken notice of me if my father hadn't exalted me like that. I was no longer a nameless chorus singer but Sebastian Lyme's daughter. And I began to fall a little in love with Kurt that night because he'd said such nice things about my father. Something my mother rarely did.

We stayed in that broom closet for a very long time. He turned out to be an amazing kisser, and I started to imagine the possibilities, to think that maybe he could be my type after all. I guess he thought so too because every day for the next week there was such a huge delivery of flowers from "Admiring K to Beautiful M" that my roommate, Caroline, said our apartment was starting to remind her of a funeral parlor.

But I didn't tell any of that to the travel agent. There wasn't time. And Kurt didn't want me to broadcast our relationship. If you could call it that. After two weeks, we still hadn't made it past the intense talks and eager groping in the darker corners of the theater.

After the travel agent's, I had to get to the supermarket to buy the fruit for the dinner party I was throwing on Tuesday night, and then to work. The unpaid ninety-nine percent of the plane ticket was now hanging over me.

I admit I was very hyper and distracted that Monday after buying my ticket. My mind had also been zooming around all the other executive decisions I still had to make. Such as: should I buy the out-of-season strawberries and out-of-country mangoes and risk having Caroline rant about the exploitation of Mexican field workers? Because there was no way I could avoid inviting Caroline to the party. She was my roommate. She was three years older than me, which made her twenty-nine and on the edge of Thirties Purgatory. Apart from her political zeal, she was an okay roommate, but she did tend to hold those three extra years over my head sometimes, to polemicize everything, especially when my opera friends were around.

Caroline has a degree in poli sci. She works as a Jacqueline of all trades at the Student Union Building, but sometimes, to hear the way she talks, you'd think she were an indispensable cog in the wheels of international relations.

And she loves parties. She can sniff them out the way a pig sniffs out truffles.

Was it better to leave the pretty and exorbitant fruits and have pale, sensible and boring local varieties? The party was going to be the next evening and it was really important, a celebration of sorts, if you took the Kurt factor into account. So the dessert had to be perfect. Well, it was a cake really, but a cake that didn't look like a cake once you dressed it up with all that fruit.

The whole idea was that it had to drip with every possible tangy, sweet, sensuous decadence, the fruit literally tumbling over the whipped-creamy edges. The dessert had to look baroque and scream sex from its rum-and-cream-filled center. Because Kurt had told me he was definitely coming to the party. Definitely coming. And I'd decided it was worthwhile to impress him a little.

So I *had* to have those crazy-ass foreign fruits on that cake.

On the other hand, there'd been that dinner party six months back when Caroline had ruined everything because I'd bought a few freshly imported lychees and she didn't approve; she'd gone on and on about the oppression of Chinese growers by the new wave of pseudocapitalists, which was nothing more than a devious form of superslavery to Western consumption. There in the supermarket I started to get so anxious just thinking of that evening. It was the same kind of feeling you get while watching circus acrobats performing without a net. It made my palms sweat to recall the way my guests had slunk away, whispering their lousy excuses while Caroline pontificated drunkenly in the center of the living room.

Caroline will probably become Canada's next female prime minister. She has the hide of a rhinoceros and infinite staying power.

So as I hurried out of the travel agency and along Denman through the sidewalk mulch of falling leaves, that anxious feeling had started to grow. I passed the low green awnings of the West End Community Centre and the mute yellow deco squareness of Blenz Coffee, where the last hearty stragglers were sitting at outdoor tables trying to pretend it was still summer. They looked chilly.

Denman was getting trendier by the minute and it almost made me sorry to be leaving the city. All kinds of stores and restaurants offering empty but delicious calories were cropping up. I hurried past my favorites, Death by Chocolate, the faux-Brit Dover Arms Pub, and the rotund glass-and-brick facade of Miriam's Ice Cream and Pies on the corner of Denman and Davey.

My West End neighborhood was a jumble of architectural styles. On tree-lined streets, vertigo-inducing glass-and-concrete high-rises stood next to stout, comfortable, early twentieth-century brick and stone three-story apartments and stores. Punctuating them like a calm breath were the remnants of the earlier residential neighborhoods of old wooden houses, some painted and fixed up for the here and now, others drab and surrendering to damp rot and termites. Bordering it all was Stanley Park, and beyond that, the ocean, which was steely gray and matched the sky.

As I hurried along Davey toward the Super Value, not only were the ticket, trip, seeing my father again, the dessert and Kurt's coming to the party all whizzing through my mind,

but so was my Davey Street Song. The storefront names always made me smile. I had an urge to set them to music.

Quiznos, Panago, T Bone Clothing,
Gigi's Pizza and Steam (breathe)
Launderdog, Love's Touch,
Falafel and Shawarma,
Towa Young Sushi,
Thai Away Home.
Thai Away Home. It was like a lullaby.

As I went through the Super Value doors, I was just as nervous and excited as if Kurt had asked me to marry him. He
hadn't. But he'd said only the day before—a mere two weeks
into our relationship—that maybe, someday, later, when
things had settled down in our lives a bit, we *might* get married. I hoped he didn't mean when my breasts had settled
down to my navel. Still, I thought this was very promising,
considering the stature of the person it was coming from.

And such a combo wasn't unheard of. My singing
teacher, the renowned mezzo-soprano Elisa Klein, had, in
the last century, enjoyed a brilliant artistic fusion with her
husband, Oskar Klein. Madame Klein had been barely more
than a teenager when she met Oskar in a DP village at the
end of WWII. He'd been much older than her, and their
time together as man and wife had been more of a student
and teacher relationship. But eventually, she made her debut
as a mezzo-soprano, was applauded all over Europe and
took her place beside him as an equal. After he died, she
never remarried. Oskar had been her ideal. She had known
and sung with the greats. She'd had a significant career. The
idea of a musical marriage was enticing. Or at least, my
waking mind thought so.

The night before, I'd dreamed that Kurt and I were both
standing in a big white hall, a cross between a church and
a city hall registry, and we were getting married. I'd filled
out my part of the forms properly and I was watching his
long-fingered hands and the way they were holding the

pen. I was getting all shivery and a little crazy thinking about the way those hands were going to slide along my skin later.

The spoken questions that you usually hear in the ceremony were actually written down. Do you take this woman, and all that jazz. I looked down again at his hand hovering above the thick black ink and saw that he'd written lines and lines of gibberish. He had this half smile that he has when he's being clever. He'd written strings of nonsense words and was smirking as if he'd pulled one off.

Do you take this woman to be your lawful wedded wife?

Instead of "I do," he'd scribbled, "Spruckahaw broogie figgle foo ickle pickle beeky boo" in the provided space.

I'd woken up fast that morning, in a cold sweat, my heart thumping like a happy Labrador's tail. The dream worried me a little. There were a lot of things about Kurt's character that I still had to get acquainted with.

I was remembering all this as I grabbed a shopping cart and hurried along the aisles of Super Value. As my cart was picking up speed I was passing people casting me worried looks. I paid no attention as I wheeled around the end of an aisle and slammed into the side of another shopping cart.

Hence the collision.

The driver staggered toward the fresh-meat section and managed to catch his balance and avoid tumbling into the open freezer and flattening the chicken breasts.

He yowled with pain as his arm was mashed against the side of the meat display then he straightened up, rubbed his wrist and said, "Oh Jeeeeez." He was staring at me, first bleakly, then his face lit up. It was like the sun coming out.

I moved in quickly to touch his arm but stopped myself. "I'm so sorry," I said. "It's all my fault."

"Yeah, it is," said the man, grinning, which I thought was odd under the circumstances.

"I've hurt you," I said, although I meant it as a question.

"Just a few little fractures. Nothing major surgery can't fix."

I opened my mouth to say something witty but could only come up with, "I'm sorry," again.

He was smiling crazily.

A long embarrassed silence hung between us.

Now I'd gone and done it. I'd probably slammed into my future downfall. The guy was smiling because he was going to try to sue me. But what about when he found out that I didn't have any significant money? He'd get his revenge by creeping around in my shadow waiting for me outside my door.

Although, as potential stalkers go, he wasn't bad looking.

He stopped grinning and said in a disappointed tone, "You don't remember me, do you, Miranda?"

There was a little flutter in my stomach. I stared at him, his bulky height, the length of his crow-black hair tied in a ponytail, his scruffy jeans with the rips in the knees (boho fashion or pure poverty?), his perfect oval face, amused smile and slightly mocking eyes.

In the file cabinet of my mind, I started ransacking the faces drawer. Nothing appeared except the blank chaos of my lousy memory for faces.

There it was. The performer's curse. All those people who remember you because you had a little solo role, and they were there in the back row, but you couldn't possibly have a hope of remembering them because you were too busy concentrating on your performance. This guy had probably been in some production with me, carrying a spear, singing bass, wearing a periwig. Who could know?

He said, almost shyly, "Winston Churchill Senior High. Cold Shanks."

"You're joking," I said. He'd caught me completely off guard. I started to giggle. Cold Shanks to Cold Shanksians was one of those places that got instant tittering recognition from its citizens. Like Moose Jaw (euphemistically known as Moose Groin) or Biggar, Saskatchewan (with its sign that read, New York Is Big But This Is Biggar). We Cold Shanksians were a race apart.

"You really don't remember me," he said again. His disappointment was almost tangible.

"I'm sorry, I'm so bad with faces…"

"A few years have passed. I'm Patrick Tibeau."

The sound of his name went through me like a childhood taboo, like a decade of old schoolyard chants. There was always that weird kid at school who everyone treated as a pariah because he didn't have the same ideas as the rest of the herd, was content to eat lunch by himself in a far corner of the playing field, and stand up in class and expound endlessly on theories that only the teacher could appreciate. That was Patrick Tibeau. I really should have been more discreet but I blurted out, "Oh my God. I can't believe it. *You're* Patrick Tibeau? You've changed so much."

"You used to sing at assemblies. I thought you had a really fine voice. You still singing, Miranda?"

"Just a minute. Just let me get a handle on this. *The* Patrick Tibeau? You're a *legend*."

He was laughing now.

"The same Patrick Tibeau that set Winnie Churchill High on fire?"

He nodded. He was still laughing.

"And got sent to reform school?" I said too enthusiastically.

He stopped laughing and sighed. "It wasn't a reform school. Reform schools don't exist anymore." He seemed so instantly disillusioned with me. Sometimes, I just have the biggest, stupidest mouth in the world and can't stop myself.

He no longer resembled the geeky, spidery, scruffy-haired, beetle-browed adolescent who I remembered. This was a full-grown, credible-looking man standing in front of me.

Then I had to ask. It was irresistible. I was going to be late for work but I did it anyway. "Can I buy you a coffee?"

The chance to chin-wag about Cold Shanks with *the* Patrick Tibeau and get his side of the story was too good to be true. Tina, my best friend, also from Cold Shanks, would be emerald with envy.

"I'm in a bit of a hurry," explained Patrick.

I was frantic. He was like a prize trout about to slip off the hook. I couldn't let it happen. "Listen, Patrick." I dug my hand into my purse and pulled out a pen and an old phone-bill envelope. "I'm having a dinner party tomorrow night. It would be really great if you could come…and bring your wife…or girlfriend…or boyfriend…or whatever." I handed him the scrap of paper with my address scribbled on it.

He took it and smiled again. I noticed he had very white teeth. "We'd like that. What time?"

He was a We.

I said, "Seven. There's going to be lots of food, but bring something if you feel like it. Extra never hurts. And some wine."

"Wine. Right. See you then, Miranda. Tomorrow, Tuesday. Seven."

As I finished pushing my cart around the supermarket, I had a flash of memory. Me and Patrick Tibeau, circa age fifteen, meeting up by accident outside the tin-roof movie theater after a showing of Cocteau's *La Belle et La Bête,* walking home in the snow under a royal-blue sky full of stars and a bright disk of moon, and talking, talking, talking. Though, about what, I couldn't even remember.

Still, I was elated to hook up with someone from Cold Shanks. I hated to admit that sometimes I got bouts of hometown nostalgia, but it was true, and Patrick had cheered me up. So I thought, to hell with Caroline, and bought every fruit I felt like buying.

Chapter 2

After the supermarket, I rushed back to my Bute Street apartment. Getting it had been a coup. In a street that was quickly giving way to modern monoliths, my classic building was an oasis in the futuristic desert. The place was a stately old redbrick three-story set among ornamental plums and evergreens. Ceramic tile, yellow with a black line of trim was featured in my kitchen, but in the bathroom stood the prize—the enormous, dangerously comfortable claw-foot bathtub.

I raced up the front steps and the other two flights, went in quietly so as not to wake Caroline, and put away my bags of fruit. Then I went into my bedroom to change my clothes, tossing off my old lounging-around jeans and pulling on my skinny black Levi's bell-bottoms and a Calvin Klein men's T-shirt I'd accidentally dyed coral but thought was nice. Miracle of miracles, the dye job had come out evenly. I shoved my feet back into my Adidas, and put my old Doc Martens into my black leather knapsack along with my rumpled work apron.

I ran out of the apartment and down the front steps. Patchy dubious sunlight had started to light up the dull morning. I hurried north to Robson. The neighborhood's resident street people, who had shifted in their crannies as I jogged past earlier, had now gone, scared off by the working masses. I ran the whole length of Robson, past the restaurants and boutiques, right into Vancouver's tall bright glassy business core, thinking I'd wait before telling everyone that I was leaving. Announce it when I'd paid off the whole ticket.

Mornings, I worked at Michelangelo's. It was a spartanchic coffee shop on Pender. Michelangelo or Mike—a big burly third-generation Italian—was always immaculate with a clean white shirt, polished shoes and a neat haircut.

That morning I could see him through the plate-glass window. He was checking the plain wooden tables, straightening the wrought-iron chairs, attacking imaginary dirt and grease spots wherever he thought he saw them. Then he turned his attention to polishing the big brass beast of an espresso machine, which was his pride and joy. I'm sure it was for the ninetieth time that morning. When I came through the door he waggled his hand at me.

"Thanks for letting me come in late, Mike," I gasped.

"When have I ever *not* let you come late? Hey, Miranda. Got a story for you."

"Shoot," I said.

"See, this old guy, Italian guy, is lying on his deathbed, and while he's lying there worrying about whether he'll be allowed into heaven, he smells this great aroma of almond cookies. His favorite. So he hauls himself out of bed and with the last bit of strength left in his body, he crawls downstairs to the kitchen, and there on the tables are dozens of these almond cookies, still hot. My wife loves me, he thinks, she's done this last wonderful thing for me. And he starts to get himself over to the table. He reaches out for a cookie with a trembling clawlike hand, and the hand gets smacked with a spatula by his wife. 'Back off,' she says. 'They're for the funeral.'"

I smiled.

"That's my family all over. You want a capooch? A fast one? We're gonna be slammed again in about two minutes."

We were always slammed at Mike's. The customers moved in like an evil storm cloud. A clot of professional suits were always first, then law books from the university, and finally, old bundles of rags looking for handouts and a warm corner. My shift normally started at seven. I liked to get there early to fix myself a latte on the house and drink it slowly before total panic set in. Mike knew how to create an environment that fostered returning customers: he was sanguine and shrewd, bellowing love and peace at everybody who came in as though they were his oldest and best friends in the world.

I always went into the back room before doing anything else. At a large steel table near the refrigerators sat Grace, the sandwich lady, buttering her way into heaven. She came into work an hour before the rest of us. Soft-spoken, devout and well past middle age, with rhinestone cat's-eye glasses on a pearl-look chain and a complexion like wartime margarine, she arrived at dawn to slab together her creations and by the time the sun came out she had disappeared, making you wonder if she really existed.

She was constantly cold. Working in that dank room beside the kitchen with all that refrigeration humming away next to her meant she always wore an old pom-pom-covered rainbow sweater. It had once belonged to her mother. The pom-poms jiggled and bounced as she buttered.

Mike had unwittingly gotten a saint when he hired Grace.

Grace was still there when I entered. She'd waited for me. She slipped me a food gift in a brown paper bag and said, "Here, Miranda, honey, this is for later when you get hungry. Mike's a nice guy but he's *sooo* cheap. I know he pays you girls squirrel droppings."

I took the gift and said, "Where did Mike find you, Grace?"

"It was the Lord's doing, dear." In Grace's world, there was just the one, omniscient, celestial boss. "And Miranda…the opera was just lovely. I cried through the whole last act."

"I'm glad you enjoyed it."

"And I picked you out, too. You had a yellow kimono, didn't you, dear?"

"Uh-huh."

"Well, you looked just lovely. I've always said, and I'll go on saying until they listen, you have a special quality."

Grace was my biggest fan. Even if I was buried in the back of a hundred-voice chorus, she was there to witness my *special quality*. She got all my complimentary tickets. If I was singing anywhere, she was there in the audience beaming goodwill at me.

I stashed the paper bag in my knapsack, tied on my apron with its big print of Renaissance cherubs kissing, then went to take on the crush of customers.

My first cover was a group of men from the Vancouver Stock Exchange. Now, I should tell you, these are the kind of guys who are regularly held hostage by mirrors. They can't pass one without getting frozen in front of it, momentarily sucked in by the vortex of their own fabulous reflections.

These men swaggered in like a bunch of action-movie stars and took up way more space than was necessary. You could see it all over them, like a kind of radioactive glow. Money. Money flowing like Niagara. They loved it. It was all-powerful, the perfect aphrodisiac.

I stood at their table impatiently tapping my pencil against my pad, waiting for them to make up their minds. The Donald Trump wannabe of the group grasped my wrist and said, "I was admiring your balcony and wondered if I could lean on it sometime?" He didn't even bother with eye contact.

He talked straight to my breasts as though they were two nice people who were about to make a big donation to his favorite charity. It was frustrating.

I was starting to develop a real love-hate relationship with my breasts. Lately, they'd been attracting a lot of attention. Kurt's attention was just fine. It was the rest of it that got on my nerves. The Curse of the Mammary Glands. My breasts had been total dickhead magnets since I was fourteen.

My first impulse was to grab the poor guy by the shoulders and shake him till his eyeballs rattled around like dried peas in a tin cup, but while I was on duty at Mike's, I ignored first impulses. If I played it right, those tips would get my plane as far as Alberta.

"Waitressing is my life," I said, and flashed him a little smile. "I wouldn't think of ruining my dream career by mixing business with pleasure. Sorry. Maybe in another incarnation."

He looked a bit confused and let go of my hand. It was clear that slinging hash was *not* his idea of a dream career. But I believed that if I was going to get any enjoyment out of life at all, then I had to be Buddhist about it, and try to caress the difficult and boring bits of my day, give them a little respect, too.

I thought of that plane, taxiing down the runway, the roar just before takeoff, and I soared through the rest of the shift.

By eleven o'clock, the sun shone between billowing white clouds. I exchanged my Doc Martens for Adidas again and jogged off toward the Gastown studio where *La Chanteuse* and Matilde awaited me.

Lance Forrester, technician, artistic director and owner of the voice-over company Vox, was outside sitting on the doorstep. His forehead was furrowed and his eyes squeezed tightly shut. He was concentrating intensely on something.

This is a *really* profound mental process going on here, I thought.

Before I was near the step, he stated, "Miranda Lyme," then opened his eyes.

"Wow. Lance. How did you do that? How did you know it was me?" I asked.

"Your smell. You have a great smell. Like a bunch of freesias that have been first rained on then lightly sprayed with fresh sweat."

I was standing in front of him now. He shocked me by pulling me down onto his lap and shoving his dark curly beard into my neck, imitating a snuffling animal. "Great, great odor."

"Lance. These are female pheromones you're talking about."

"I'm not particular."

But I wasn't sure that he wasn't particular, and if he was, it was a shame. Lance was a very compelling man.

"What are you doing out here anyway? Why aren't you inside working? You know, I think this is the first time I've ever seen you in the light of day?" I said.

"I'm pale. I've become a mushroom. Summer has come and gone and I'm a nice shade of silvery white," he said.

He'd been concentrating on trying to get his marble-white skin to sop up some sun. That's what all the profundity had been about.

I ruffled his messy silver and black curls with my fingers. "You spend all your time indoors, you silly workaholic. You need some fresh air and vitamin D."

He said broadly, "Yes, it's true. I'm doomed." His voice was thick with pleasure, as though doom were something delicious, like a plate of chocolate éclairs or homemade ravioli. "How's Matilde today?"

"Hot to trot," I replied. "How else would she be?"

"Yes. I suppose she couldn't be any other way. She's the eighth wonder of the world, that Matilde," said Lance, and he led the way inside.

We went into the first studio. I pulled the script for *La Chanteuse* out of my knapsack.

"It's just the two of us this morning," explained Lance. "I think we can get the biggest scene wrapped up if we really concentrate."

La Chanteuse was an "art film" set in Paris. I'd done a little work for Lance in the past whenever there was a voice to be dubbed that had to sing, as well, but this was the first time I'd ever seen so much pork in one of our films. Or so much porking, for that matter.

The protagonist, Matilde, was an opera star who couldn't perform unless she had sex first. A lot of sex. Megasex. Unfortunately, the man she was in love with was a married pig farmer and she was forever chasing him and his salami all over Paris and outskirts. They had sex everywhere; they rolled in the pigpen mud (when his homely wife wasn't there), between the prosciutti and ham hocks, they had sex with a side of bacon watching them. Sometimes the pig farmer left his homely wife at home, dressed up and came into town to see Matilde. Then they had sex in the park, on and under the Eiffel Tower, in the corridors of the Louvre, under restaurant tables at the Plaza, on the bathroom floor and in the elevator of Matilde's apartment. It was awesome. Every time Matilde came, her screaming orgasm would swell and rise and turn into warm-ups, scales and arpeggios. Then when all the heavy breathing had finally subsided, she was away to the Paris Opera for the evening, where she washed off the smell of swineherd and gave the performances of her life.

La Chanteuse goes along pretty much like that right up to the end, until the homely wife murders them both, makes them into sausages and sells them at the local market. A bit too moralistic for my tastes but I guess there had to be human bloodshed in order for there to be a decent denouement.

And I have to confess that although it was a truly silly film, there were moments when I could really relate to Matilde's impossible obsession. I was no stranger to obsessions myself.

For a couple of hours, Lance and I stood across from each other going over and over the scenes, getting them right, wailing, adoring, whispering, grunting, panting and moaning on cue into the microphones. My arpeggios and vocal ornaments had been well rehearsed beforehand. Lance was a professional. In his dubs you never heard false notes. You never saw the mouths wagging on hours after the sound of speech had stopped. Ours was quality work. But it was a little unnerving that the actress playing Matilde looked a bit like me, with long blond hair and annoyingly large breasts, and the actor playing the pig farmer looked like Lance, a prematurely graying Greek god with iron-poor blood.

By one o'clock, I was getting hungry. My stomach was starting to rumble so loudly that the microphone picked it up. Lance looked up from the script and then at his watch.

"Nice work, Miranda. We'll have to stop now. I have the kung fu kids in about twenty minutes. You're doing a great job. Low-budget orgasms. They're such a riot. We still have four and a half of them to go before we get hacked up and made into bratwurst."

He shut off some of the equipment and came over to me, moving with the slow prowl of big jungle felines. "Just let me smell you again before you go." He pulled me into him and pressed his face into my hair. "Mmmmm."

"Lance, Lance." I felt as though I was rousing a person from sleep.

"What?" He looked up and into my eyes. A CAT scan was less probing than Lance's gaze.

"I'm a hoping-to-be-involved woman."

"Hoping-to-be-involved? Just exactly what is that supposed to mean?"

"It hasn't actually been…ah…consummated yet."

His eyes drilled me. "You poor faux-virgin. May I ask who the lucky swine is?"

"No," I said, still irritated that I wasn't allowed to name Kurt Hancock as my possible significant-other-to-be.

"No? Ah, come on," provoked Lance.

"He wants it to be our little secret. He's a high-profile guy. He doesn't want the gossip or the press."

Lance smiled and kissed my hand. "I'm sure that whoever he is, Miranda, he's a complete and utter bastard and not nearly good enough for you. I know men."

"Yes, Mommy."

"Let's kill Matilde off once and for all, okay? Can you make it tomorrow?"

I nodded.

"Oh, and remind me to pay you tomorrow."

"Pay me tomorrow, Lance. Please, pay me." I could see that KLM jet edging eastward.

This time tomorrow I would be a different woman. Yes, Matilde would have her pig farmer, but I would have been had and had again by Kurt. Finally.

Chapter 3

Off with the Doc Martens and back into the Adidas. I thought I was so smart, running everywhere and talking all my employers into working around my schedule. I was like a jigsaw puzzle. Some of the pieces were connected but the outlines still visible, and other pieces were still missing. I was not a complete picture.

I ate one of Grace's shrimp, rocket and lemon-pepper mayonnaise croissants as I power walked back in the direction of Davey Street. It was so delicious, and I was so hungry that for a moment I considered marrying Grace and forgetting all about Kurt Hancock.

I hurried through the door of Little Ladies Unlimited—a cleaning company housed in a big bleak one-story concrete block. Inside, there was just the barnlike unadorned storeroom where all the equipment was kept, and the tiny office, from which Cora, the owner, took all the client calls and kept everything running smoothly. At the end of the ranks of industrial vacuum cleaners, the other two women on my cleaning team were standing at the coffee machine.

They were having a hot debate about whether drip or plunge was better.

"No contest. Plunge," I joined in. "Now, whose husband are we talking about?"

"Coffeemakers not husbands," said Fern, smoothing down her brassy scouring-pad hair with a tiny hand. She was smiling. "And on that subject, Miranda, when are *you* going to get yourself a husband?"

"I'm only twenty-six," I said, "I'm not ready to be buried alive yet."

"Hell, I was married at nineteen," said Fern, "and I've had twenty-one great years."

"You are so full of crap sometimes, Fern McGrew," said Betty.

Betty was big and muscular, and always wore lumberjack shirts. There was something in her attitude that reminded me slightly of my roommate Caroline. Caroline was smaller, a size sixteen, so she could buy her clothes off most racks. Betty only bought hers off the racks at Mr. Big 'n Tall, but when it came to tough-assdom, they could have been mother and daughter. Betty had been a sled-dog trainer in the Yukon before she got sick of the snow and moved down to Vancouver.

Betty barged on, "'Great years,' says Fern. Miranda, get her to tell ya about the great time she had when her great husband goes and gets himself that stupid little slut on the side, and the great fights they has about it and the time he puts her in the hospital because he's broke her cheekbone with his great big fat fist."

"Every couple has its little ups and downs," said Fern, but she was looking at the floor.

Betty leaned in to confide. "I gets the word about Fern here bein' in hospital, gotta have *surgery* 'cause them little pieces of cheekbone is gonna get into her bloodstream otherwise and finish her off good-style once and fer all. So what does I do? I goes over to their place, and there's old Cliff sittin' on the couch swillin' a beer and watchin' football like butter wouldn't melt in his mouth. I hauls him up onto his feet and drags him out into the street. He's wearing just his socks, no shoes, huh, and lookin' pathetic. Then I lets the whole street know what he's done, as if they doesn't know already, and then I whacks him one across *his* cheekbone an' I sends him flyin' into somebody's recyclin' bin. The neighbors wasn't too happy about that but they wasn't gonna take me on neither. He never done it again, I can tell ya. Am I right, Fern?"

Fern nodded and said, "He's been a pussycat ever since."

Wow. Betty and her two meaty fists. Kurt would have to stay in line.

Cora came out of her office. She was a petite woman with a mass of platinum, back-combed hair in a white hair band. That day she wore tight white pedal pushers and a white angora sweater. She was in her forties but so youthful you wouldn't know it. She looked as if she'd stepped out of a Sandra Dee film. All she needed was a surfboard under her arm and she was complete.

She grinned and said in a singsong voice, "Better get going, girls. This one's a Special."

We all groaned.

Betty grabbed her loyal Hoover while Fern and I loaded up our multipocketed aprons with our sprays and cloths. Fern was on dusting, I was on bathrooms and kitchens, and Betty was vacuuming. We were like soldiers going into battle.

We hurried out to the company car, loaded the equipment into the back and climbed in. With Betty behind the wheel, we whizzed down to The Bachelor's place on Burrard. He lived on the twenty-eighth floor of a twenty-nine-story steel-and-glass high-rise overlooking English Bay.

We cleaned his place every week but today was a Special. Specials were more than just the regular Little Ladies cleaning job. They were expensive and meant we had to do anything that needed to be done. Within reason. As soon as we stepped inside his apartment, we knew The Bachelor hadn't been operating within the confines of "reason." He'd been partying.

"So what would you say's going on here?" I asked as we surveyed the scene.

"Lazy drunken slob," announced Fern.

"Barnyard animal," confirmed Betty.

To start with, The Bachelor had a round bed and not-too-clean moss-green sheets twisted this way and that. At the chest of drawers, I imagined him emptying the contents of his pockets every night, since it was covered with pennies, nickels, dimes and quarters, sticky half-sucked peppermints, condoms still in their foil wrap but well past their expiry date, and numerous crumpled bits of paper with girls' names and telephone numbers. Similar goodies sprinkled the brown-stained wall-to-wall carpet as well. The mirror tiles above the bed had some interesting spots on them, as though they'd been spritzed by quite a few bottles of fizzy stuff.

Meanwhile, the fridge held about fifty bottles of beer and a block of mold. No doubt he ordered in whenever he didn't eat out. Interesting encrustations covered most of the kitchen, detailing The Bachelor's gastronomic history for the week.

Back in the living room, there were suspicious-looking marks on his black couch. And his one weeping fig was half-dead. His shoes and socks were all over the place: on top of radiators, on the dining-room table, under the couch. One sock was stuffed into the weeping fig's pot.

In the bathroom, I figured he had a nightly struggle getting his willy to cooperate and aim into the toilet rather than all over the wall. It was probably the beer. I could be sympathetic and understanding though. Men and women have their own unique sets of problems. If I had the Curse of the Mammary Glands, why couldn't The Bachelor have the Curse of the Maverick Member?

Fern, Betty and I put our backs into the cleaning for two

and a half hours, wondering the whole time how The Bachelor's ancestors had ever made it out of the cave and into civilization.

As we cleaned, the silence was broken every so often with Betty's mutters of "Slob."

Fern said, "The poor man just needs a woman in his life. Someone to clean him up and organize him. You should have seen the way Cliff was living before we got married. He makes The Bachelor look like Mr. Neat. Now, Miranda, how about if you just add your phone number to that little pile on his dresser?"

Betty barked, "Would ya quit with the lonely-hearts crap, Fern? Miranda's doin' fine. She's gonna be an opera star and no man's gonna get in her way."

I hoped Betty was a prophet and that her words would come true. I said, "Thanks for caring, Fern. If things don't shape up by the time I'm thirty-nine, I'll get you to do a little matchmaking, okay?"

"Oh, you don't want to wait that long, Miranda. Everybody needs a soul mate."

Betty said, "A soul mate, Fern, not a middle-aged preschooler who leaves his crap all over the joint. This guy's mother has a lot to answer for."

Fern countered with, "Listen to you, Betty. You wouldn't be talking like that if you'd just get a man by your side, yourself."

"Don't need a man. Got ma dogs. And they're as good as any man ya could know."

It was dangerous territory. We knew better than to touch on the subject of Betty's dogs, or the rest of the canine kingdom, for that matter.

As I brought The Bachelor's stainless-steel fixtures back up to their original gleaming state, my imagination wandered to the life I would lead once I got to London.

My father would probably put me up. I had an open invitation, after all. I pictured his house in South Kensington, solid and white, a small garden in the back, a nice garret room with a gas fire for me on the third floor. He'd coach me on my audition pieces, give me the kind of tips that only the big singers can give you. I'd be doing quite a bit of cleaning and redecorating at his house, too, because he'd been living like The Bachelor himself all these years. He'd told me so.

He'd need me. He'd need a woman's touch around the place. When we'd spoken on the phone a few years back, he'd told me I was welcome anytime.

It had taken a lot of courage for me to make the call but he'd sounded so happy, really overjoyed to hear from me. And after speaking with him, I could have flown around the room, I felt so high. When I told my mother about his invitation, she said, "He was probably pissed. He'll have forgotten all about it by tomorrow."

And Lyle, my mother's second husband, had chimed in, "If ya gotta go 'n see him, Miranda, ya gotta go. But hang on to your wallet. And just remember, we're here for you, eh? If ya wanna talk about it afterward."

I'd wanted to fly off to England as soon as the call had ended, but I was nineteen at the time and already at university. I had no extra money and no extra time. But I knew that the day would come when the reunion with my father would become a reality.

We finished the Special and hauled the equipment down to the company car. There, I took off my Adidas and put my Doc Martens on. I badly wished I could have had a shower first and rinsed off all The Bachelor's dust. But I was on a tight schedule. Betty was nice enough to give me a lift down to the theater. She wasn't supposed to take the company car anywhere except to cleaning jobs, but she didn't care. Nobody, not even Cora, ever argued with Betty.

I ate the last of Grace's sandwiches in the car. It was Brie, speck and pickled artichokes on seven-grain bread. I looked forward to the day when I became rich and famous and would either pay for Grace to come and cook for me, or I could adopt her.

Can you do that? Adopt special spinster angels? Grace's sandwiches homed in on oral pleasure centers I never knew I had.

Betty dropped me off right at the stage door.

I checked off my name and descended into the beige bowels of the theater. Fatigue stopped me in the doorway to the women's chorus dressing room.

And then I had one of those moments. One of those insightful moments that make you so happy your skin tingles. You've arrived in your world. The one they nearly didn't let you into, the one where it's a privilege to sweat under hot lights in a costume that already reeks of another soprano, have your toes stepped on by hefty mezzos and your eardrums split by tenors who refuse to stop singing directly into the side of your head.

At the mirror next to mine, Tina, who was a mezzo like me, was applying her geisha face. I sat down.

Tina said, "Miranda. Finally. I thought you were going to be late. That stage manager would make a good prison warden. She doesn't bend an inch on check-ins."

Three red circles around your name for being late and you risked being kicked out of the chorus.

"I had four minutes to go," I said.

"That's cutting it pretty fine," said Tina.

"You going to stand in the wings tonight?" When a singer was fabulous, like our lead soprano, Ellie Watson, that's what we did. Stood in the wings and studied her, hoping some of her magic would get into our bloodstreams.

Tina nodded. "Our Madame Butterball's pretty amazing, eh? That Ellie's got another one of your paint-peeling voices. Too bad she doesn't have the look. How much do you think she weighs?"

"More than bathroom scales register," I replied.

"Yeah, she doesn't need a dresser, she needs an uphol-sterer. But I'm not just standing back there to listen to her. I'm going to gape at Kurt. I'm shoving myself under the maestro's nose so he'll notice me. I wouldn't mind studying under him any day. Under him. Over him. Any position he wants. That man is quality grade-A prime cut. He can beat my time with his baton whenever he likes."

Against all of Kurt's warning, I whispered into Tina's ear, "You're too late. He's mine."

She whipped around to look straight at me. Her voice dropped about a thousand decibels. "Kurt Hancock? What do you mean, he's yours?"

"I mean we're good friends. More than friends."

We were huddled over our makeup tables while having this whispered conversation. The dressing room was too quiet and letting the other gossip-starved dames in on the latest developments in my life would be like throwing fat juicy sailors into shark-infested waters—instant death.

"Get your face on, Miranda, and hurry up about it," Tina ordered. "I gotta have a word with you." She was as tall as me but she had an angular face and piercing, intimidating, black eyes. When she gave me orders, I obeyed.

I smeared on the white for my geisha face, then drew in the tiny pinched lips and the eyebrows. We always left our wigs until last. They were heavy and itchy. It had been a bit of a catfight when it came to the director giving out these geisha roles. There was a whale-size middle-aged singer who thought that she should get first pick of everything be-cause of seniority. What did she think this was? An office job? This was showbiz. And showbiz, as everyone knows, is the biggest dictatorship in the world. In the end, the geisha parts went to the youngest, thinnest girls in the cho-rus. Tina and me and six others.

When I finally had my costume and makeup on, Tina dragged me down the hallway and upstairs into a quiet cor-ner of the vast area backstage.

"Okay. So what's this 'friends' stuff?"

"Like I said, Kurt and I are very good friends."

"In the biblical sense, right? You mean you're screwing him?"

"Sort of," I mumbled.

"What do you mean, sort of?"

"We haven't actually gotten down to exchanging bodily fluids."

"You're kidding. What does it take to get down to it?"

"The mood's got to be right but maybe tonight. He's coming over after. I'd really like it to happen *before* the party because if he comes to the party with other people, he probably won't stay after. You know, appearances and all that."

"Why?" asked Tina.

"He doesn't want anybody to know about us because he's not officially divorced yet."

"First of all, I have to say, Miranda Lyme, are you out of your gourd? You're fucking the conductor...and he's *married*."

"Separated."

She said to the air, "Kurt Hancock, I don't know what you're up to with my friend Miranda, but you've disillusioned me. I am so disappointed. I thought you were better than that. Yet another married man screwing around."

"Well, not really, not exactly, not yet anyway..."

"Okay, and another thing. You're nearly fucking the conductor and you don't tell me? Some friend you are, Miranda Lyme."

"It's complicated. It's not what it sounds like. And I would have told you as soon as it became a fait accompli. But it hasn't yet."

"You better get moving. Only two more performances left and then closing night and he's outa here. Back to...where is it he lives? Paris?"

"London. But he's got engagements in the States first."

"So tell me about this not-what-it-sounds-like stuff. But

I'm warning you. I've almost definitely heard it all before and reserve the right not to believe any of it."

"His wife's away in Tuscany. She wants a divorce..."

"Heard it," blurted Tina.

"Just wait. If you could only see how upset Kurt is, you'd know it was for real. I mean, he must really care. It's *her* that wants to leave *him*. He's been pretty open about his feelings. They're legally separated, and now it's just a matter of finalizing."

"Uh-huh?" Tina's tone was skeptical. "So why's she divorcing him? He tell you?"

"Yeah. He said it was because he's always away. She wants someone who's there. He's almost single. Really," I protested.

Tina was silent for a long time.

"Listen, Tina. I'm going to England anyway. I bought my ticket today."

"Miranda. No. Really? You're not bullshitting me, are you?"

"I've got that audition with the ENO."

"Fantastic. Sort of... I wish you weren't going though. Where am I going to find somebody else who lets me boss them around the way you do?"

"Jeez. It's not forever. The audition's in January. So I figure, if Kurt happens to be part of the bargain, all the better. Lots of people have these tricky back-and-forth relationships. You're going to have to deal with it, too, you know, Tina. One of these days. Once you decide to take yourself seriously. Once your career gets going, you're going to be traveling a lot."

Tina snorted, "My career? Ha."

"Trust me. You have to have a couple of plans of action. I can't predict how things are going to go with Kurt. I don't want to get inside his head, I just want to enjoy the feeling while it lasts, and then we'll see. It's been ages since anyone paid so much attention to me. So right now, it's London, and the ENO, and getting to know my father again, and then

I have to be back here in Vancouver for March. Kurt wants me to sing a song cycle of his."

Tina gave me a dark look and I can't say it wasn't envy. "Nice side benefit to screwing the conductor, eh?"

I shrugged. "I had to work for it."

She glared at me. "Sure you did."

"I did." Tina had a nerve. My first big date with Kurt had been an audition.

The evening after the broom-closet incident, he'd sent an unsigned note to me in the women's chorus dressing room asking me to wait for him in the lobby of his hotel, and then to follow him up to his room at a distance. I was a bit put out by the cloak-and-dagger stuff but I did what I was told. I watched him get his key at the front desk of the Pan Pacific, then went up a few paces behind him. He left the door of his hotel room ajar, so I went in without knocking. When I came into the room, he was already seated at the piano.

Kurt had an entire suite. His rooms had fruit baskets, fresh-cut flowers, iced champagne, little chocolates on the pillow, pristine perfumed bed linen, Chinese screens, a giant claw-foot tub, a recently tuned Steinway baby grand piano and a spectacular view of Vancouver harbor.

I had to stand for a minute and take in the hotel suite. The best hotel in my hometown of Cold Shanks has lasagna carpeting to hide the spills and a series of black-velvet masterpieces and sad clown faces decorating the flocked bordello wallpaper.

Before he touched or kissed me again, Kurt asked me to sing for him. I was ready for it. In fact, I'd prayed for it to happen. I took some music out of my bag and put it on the piano. First I sang some French songs by Ravel and then some Rossini.

Without a word, Kurt then thrust a part of his song cycle at me and made me sight-sing it cold. I had to concentrate so hard I practically sweated treble clefs. Later, he made me sing it again. I must have impressed him because he was happy enough with my interpretation to promise me that I would be the one to premiere it with the Vancouver Symphony the following March.

But first, I'd have to deal with Madame Klein. She disapproved of young singers doing anything that was slightly beyond them, and Kurt's music was difficult, even more difficult than Oskar Klein's music. Oskar had been a composer in the line of Richard Strauss. The avant-garde composers of his time accused Oskar of holding back the progress of music, because his music was harmonic and harked back to romanticism. But it was singable, accessible, moving and beautiful.

As for Kurt's music, that was something else.

Kurt's music was all the fault of the composer Arnold Schoenberg and his twelve-tone row.

One day at the beginning of the twentieth century, old Arnie must have woken up, taken a sip of his good strong Viennese coffee, clutched his stomach and yelled, *"Mein Gott im Himmel,"* as an undiagnosed ulcer started acting up. Maybe if he'd been feeling good about himself and the world, he would have sat down and written some gorgeous postromantic tonal symphony.

Instead, old Arnie had a bone to pick with the world.

You have to picture a short, balding man, whose big bulging eyes were filled with a fanatical gleam as he thought, "*Ja.* I'll make all of them suffer, too. I shall invent the twelve-tone row and then they'll be really sorry."

So he uses the twelve notes that you find in an octave of black and white piano keys, lines them up in some kind of arbitrary order and calls it a tone row. Then he takes that little sucker of a tone row and sticks it everywhere in his composition, and God help you if you don't know it's there because that's the whole point of the exercise. The new big test for the musical-chic crowd—spot Arnie's tone row.

It's also been called serial music, and I can guarantee that at times it's been serial murder to listen to.

And as if that weren't bad enough, Arnie had to go and

start teaching his new approach and acquiring his disciples, Webern and Berg.

Collectively, they make up the group that I like to call the Bing Bang Bong Boys.

Imagine a cat with a really sophisticated sense of rhythm walking around on the piano. Black keys. White keys. It doesn't matter. Then imagine scoring that sound for a big orchestra. That's more or less how atonal music sounds.

I'm not saying this music doesn't have its uses. Hollywood has gotten great mileage out of it for scoring movies about stalkers, slash murderers, killer vegetables, sharks and a whole galaxy of alien predators.

Schoenberg's tone row is to music what *Finnegan's Wake* is to literature. Do you curl up with *Finnegan's Wake* when you want to have a nice relaxing read? Tell the truth now.

Okay. I know. Tonality had to go out the window. For the sake of artistic progress. It was a dirty job and somebody had to do it. And Arnie, Arnie was a guy with a real sense of mission, just the man for the job.

However, when I want a piece of serious music to curl up with, I choose something sweet and harmonic. Monteverdi's *L'Orfeo,* Bach's *Goldberg Variations,* Prokofiev's *First Symphony,* Strauss's *Four Last Songs,* Mozart's clarinet concerto. Curling up to Schoenberg and the Bing Bang Bong Boys is like trying to cling to a slippery piece of driftwood in the middle of a desolate stormy ocean.

As for Kurt Hancock's music, it wasn't that his pieces didn't have lush tonal, even pretty, moments. They did. But as soon as you thought those moments were going to blossom into a big phantasmagoric sequence of absolutely gorgeous harmonies, the composition moved into barbed and nerve-jangling Bing Bang Bong.

After I'd sight-sung Kurt's song cycle for the first time that day at the Pan Pacific, I'd wanted to shake him and yell, "Why can't you write melodic singable songs, goddammit?" But Kurt was regarded as an important composer, very much in demand, and the Vancouver Symphony had actually commissioned this song cycle to its great expense.

And when I made sneaky references to my feelings on atonal composition, Kurt had said, "What makes you think that listening to music should be an enjoyable experience, Miranda? It can be a significant, historical experience without necessarily being enjoyable."

Well…gosh…slap me silly.

Maybe, in the future, I could influence Kurt's music in some way, put a flea in his ear about accessibility.

I'd hoped our relationship would take a little quality leap that day but it didn't happen. By the time I'd finished singing, we were both late for other commitments. Though I was tentatively delirious to be premiering a Kurt Hancock composition, now that the March date was looming before me, I only had six months to make it perfect. And as I mentioned, I still had to tell Madame Klein and she wouldn't necessarily be happy about it, at all.

"Miranda…hey, Miranda. Earth to Miranda."

Tina then pinched my arm. She persisted, "I said I never thought of you as the type to audition flat on her back." But she was smiling as she said it.

"Jeez, Tina. You could have as many gigs as you want if you only spent a little *more* time on yours."

"Yeah, maybe." She grinned.

I went on, "If Kurt's still with his wife when I'm over there, fine. I'll be staying with my father anyway and we'll have a lot of catching up to do. If Kurt's not with his wife, we'll spend some time together. But he says they're on the rocks and that they're definitely breaking up. I told him I was hoping to get the audition and he said if I did, we should see each other in London, because he'd be home over Christmas. He has no engagements. They're not even spending Christmas together. That says it all."

"Ooookaay. Normally, if it were me, that is, I'd ask the guy to show me the documentation. This isn't exactly a new one, but shit, it's Kurt Hancock, so I guess I have to believe his story. I mean, would a guy with a million Deutsche Grammophon recordings to his name string you that kind of crap? I guess these things happen in life, but jeez, Miranda, why couldn't you find a man who gets right to the point?"

"I know, I know. Listen, he's going to be at the dinner party tomorrow night. He promised he'd come. But this all has to stay between you and me. If he finds out I've told you about us, he'll be mad. Typical temperamental-artist type, right?"

Tina smirked. "I'll be checking you two out at the party tomorrow. For an afterglow."

"Or a really pissed-off expression."

"I'm dying to hear what happens. I bet he's hot. You can tell by the way he conducts. You lucky bitch. I'm so jealous."

I'd been keeping the whole Kurt thing to myself for too long. Now that I'd let it leak to Tina, I felt a little less anxious. "I'll tell you tomorrow at the party. But don't get too excited. You never know what could happen."

Chapter 4

Tina Browning and I both come from the same cow town in the interior of B.C. Cold Shanks. I'm not kidding, that's its name. There used to be a big slaughterhouse there before the war. After all the cattle were butchered, a lot of the meat was put in the big icehouse before being shipped out, but the best cuts always went out first and the shanks were left over. Tons and tons of them. Hence, Cold Shanks. The icehouse, full of shanks, is gone now but the cowboys and heifers are still there.

Tina Browning came from the main trailer park, the one down by the river, and I came from a suburb that thought it was a lot better than the trailer park. Tina's last name helped her overcome the pall that hung over a lot of the trailer-park people. The teachers got it into their heads that she was a distant relation to Robert Browning, as in Elizabeth Barrett, and Tina did nothing to dissuade them.

Tina and I hated each other's guts when we were at school. By the time we had reached the age of thirteen, it was total warfare. We were always pitted against each other in the solo-voice category at every music festival. It was a take-no-hostages situation, the two of us glaring thunderbolts at each other across our parents and the audience in the Kiwanis Hall just before we each took our turn trilling out "When I Am Laid" by Mr. Henry Purcell or the "Habanera" from Bizet's *Carmen*. I always thought my clothes would give me the edge, but despite Tina's trailer-trash dresses and my mother's hand-sewn masterpieces, Tina often took first prize. Sometimes we tied though, which left us both furious.

We were a couple of unlikely prodigies, coming as we did from families where a musical background meant being able to sing along to our parents' antique record collections; the Rolling Stones or the complete opus of Dolly Parton. Tina had been named after Tina Turner if that gives you any idea where her mother was coming from. Not that Dolly, or the Stones or Tina were such bad examples. Not at all. The real trouble was, Cold Shanks just didn't have enough room for two Charlotte Church-style divas.

But then, when we both ended up by accident in the only big city we could afford to move to, Vancouver, and in the same university music department, we realized that we were very small insignificant fish in a great big pond. Everybody was so much better than us and more sophisticated and so completely at home, that we were pushed into each other's company out of pure shame.

First, it was the all-night bus ride home that got Tina and I talking to each other. Nobody ever slept on those trips. It was too uncomfortable. Going home for Christmases, Easters and half-term breaks we were often on the same 11:00 p.m. Greyhound headed into the interior. It was impossible for us to avoid each other, two mezzo-sopranos both being tortured by the same bunch of singing teachers and coaches, both being put through the wringer by the same theory and composition professors.

Tina got me on her side definitively one day in the sing-

ing master class at the U when roles were being assigned.
They'd given Tina a juicy gutbuster of a role, Azucena in
Il Trovatore, and all through the auditorium, I could see the
other mezzos visibly radiating hatred and envy in her direction. Tina stood up there on that stage in front of the entire singing department and the conductor of the orchestra,
as if she didn't give a damn, and said, "I just want to know
one thing. Does this Azucena chick get to screw the tenor
before the final curtain?"

Second, Tina and I shared one big fundamental problem. Music theory. They had it. We didn't. When the guilty
party, the only floating elementary-school music teacher in
the town of Cold Shanks, discovered early in our lives that
we had voices, she'd done her best to bang the notes into
us any old way she could, so we'd done all our learning by
ear. Written music had no more meaning than mouse prints
on train tracks for us. We had a lot of lost time to make up
for when we arrived at university. But we had something
huge in our favor:

We loved music.

I loved music so much that when I was a little kid, I used
to grab other little kids on the playground, kids I knew who
were getting more music lessons than me, and tell them,
"Sing or I'll hit you." I never stopped until I'd bullied their
whole repertoire out of them.

Tina and I missed Cold Shanks badly those first years.
We would swap stories over beer and junk food and wax
nostalgic about cowboys, big hair and big steaks. Together
we worked on self-improvement. We practiced talking like
high-brow musical prodigies and peed ourselves laughing.
The other singers in the department were so smart-ass and
vegetarian. And they were always going on about their biorhythms. I thought a biorhythm was a new kind of beat
from the Bayou.

Later, I was sorry that I hadn't known Tina earlier. That
we hadn't sat around on the porch on dusty afternoons

snapping the ends off my mother's garden green beans, singing duets. Mine had been a lonely childhood.

My mom, after leaving my father and dragging me back to Canada from England, had dated a series of losers before she met and married Lyle. Lyle had his own auto-body shop, and although he wasn't quite a loser…more of a flatliner…the first time I had a part in an opera, his comment was, "Jeez, Miranda, I'll come and see ya if I have to, but just don't expect me to stay awake while a bunch of fags in tights scream their lungs out up on a stage."

When I was sixteen, Mom and Lyle's twins were born and I was ignored. They were both boys, both blond and adorable, and both a total eclipse of my personal sun.

Onstage in the first part of act 1, we twirled our parasols and shuffled along with that knock-kneed walk that was required of geishas. I watched the conductor as much as I could without falling over my feet. I love to watch Kurt at work. At one point, he winked at me. I'm sure he did. I know every other chorus woman was convinced he was winking at her. But there was nothing to be done about it. Kurt has charm and everyone wants to be touched by it.

Now, if you don't know already, here's what happens in *Madama Butterfly*.

In the opening, the geisha dancer, Madama Butterfly, better known as Cio-Cio-San, marries Pinkerton, an American navy officer. She's only fifteen and she's soooo stupid, because if she had stuck her ear to the *shogi,* the wall screen, before putting on her matrimonial kimono, she would have heard Pinkerton blabbing on about a real American wife that he intended to marry sometime in the future.

No wonder he's so casual about his own wedding.

But Cio-Cio-San has cotton in her ears, and cotton *between* her ears, if you ask me. When she marries him, she renounces her own religion to embrace Pinkerton's Christian religion. When her family and friends find out, they all turn their backs on her.

Take a lesson, girls.

Pinkerton then boinks his bride and leaves.

And stays away for three years.

Okay, so there were no airline seat sales in those days.

Cio-Cio-San asks Sharpless, the American consul, how often the robins nest in the United States. Pinkerton promised to return when the robins next nested, so they apparently don't nest as often in the States as they do in Japan.

Nice reasoning, Cio-Cio-San.

So three years pass.

At this point, they all know what she doesn't know or doesn't want to know. Everybody's trying to talk Cio-Cio-San into divorcing Pinkerton and marrying the wealthy Prince Yamadori.

Take the Prince! Take the Prince!

But this must be looooovvvvveeeee. Because she says that although the law in Japan might permit it, the law in her new country, America, wouldn't.

Sharpless reads her a letter from Pinkerton that announces his marriage to an American woman. But Cio-Cio-San has difficulty comprehending (all that cotton between her ears) and then slowly she starts to figure it out.

Only three years too late.

She brings out her big surprise bomb, her and Pinkerton's little boy. She's named him Trouble.

Got the name right anyway, Cio-Cio-San.

Then Pinkerton and his American wife arrive in Japan, and come to see Cio-Cio-San. Pinkerton stays outside to talk to Sharpless. Cio-Cio-San, who has been hiding, wonders who this other woman is. Cio-Cio-San comes out of hiding and is polite as she and the American wife introduce themselves.

The American wife leaves and Cio-Cio-San learns from Sharpless that the Pinkertons are willing to adopt the child.

Naturally, she freaks.

Cio-Cio-San sends word to Pinkerton that he should come back by himself in half an hour and get the child.

Things go downhill from there. Cio-Cio-San gets even more freaked out and starts waving her father's dagger around. She ties a blindfold around her little boy's eyes, sticks an American flag in his hand, and when Pinkerton comes back, Cio-Cio-San makes herself into a human shish kebab and drops dead. All this before she's even reached the age of twenty.

Who says opera is boring?

Out of the geisha clogs and into the Adidas. There was no women's chorus in the last part of the opera, so Tina and I were dressed and out of the theater well before Pinkerton had moaned out his last grief-stricken "Butterfly." Tina was on her way to the Media Club for a beer with some of the techies and musicians, but I had to go straight home.

I had loads to do before Kurt arrived that night. I'd given him a set of keys to my place. Caroline could get a little bolshie with me if she found out he had keys, but I didn't care. She was paying less rent for the smaller bedroom, so I considered myself the major shareholder.

I raced up the front steps of my Bute Street building and on into the apartment. Caroline was out I quickly discovered. I gave the place a superficial cleaning. Then I took over the bathroom and set about scrubbing away all the day's grunge before Kurt arrived. I had a long hot shower, then oiled my body with white-musk scent, put on my pale blue bathrobe and went into the bedroom to wait for him. I fell promptly asleep, damp bathrobe and all.

I was woken by the sensation of warm skin next to mine. Kurt had managed to slip into my room, undress, undo my bathrobe and press up next to me without my waking up.

I pulled back and said, "Kurt." His put his fingers up to his mouth to signal no more words.

I was perfectly prepared to let our bodies do the talking. In the dim lamplight, I studied all of him. He was very tall, with slender but muscular arms and legs, longish blond hair, piercing blue eyes and intelligent mouth. He had an erection, but when I tried to do something about it, he grabbed my wrist, hard, pushed me back down on the bed and began to move all over me with his tongue, exploring hill and dale. Well, more dale than hill. And then finally, when the orgasm swept through me, I realized he'd made me come with his hands. Abruptly and frenetically, he started jerking against me and came himself in a little pool on my stomach.

This wasn't going at all the way I'd planned.

"Kurt," I said, "if you're worried about birth control and such things, I'm prepared for this, you know." I rummaged in the drawer of my bedside table, pulled out some fresh new high-quality condoms, and held them up triumphantly for him to see.

"Miranda, darling," began Kurt. "There's something I have to explain to you. And you must try to understand it. There can and will be all kinds of wonderful sex and marvelous orgasms between the two of us. But I'm a monogamous man. I will never, technically, betray my wife."

I sat up straighter and stared at him, bewildered.

Kurt took my hands in his. The tiniest hint of tears was welling up in his eyes and in his elegant British accent he said softly, "It won't be forever. You know that. We just have to be patient. Until Olivia and I have officially divorced, there will be no actual fucking."

My mind exploded, bursting into the whirling newspaper headlines that used to precede old black-and-white movies.

"SANS PÉNÉTRATION POUR MIRANDA LYME" read *Le Figaro*.

"MIRANDA LYME NON SCOPA PROPRIO" said *Il Corriere della Sera*.

"NO ACTUAL FUCKING FOR MIRANDA LYME" roared the *New York Times*.

Chapter 5

Kurt stayed the night. I forced him to. This technical glitch in my sex life was already depressing me. There was no saying what I might have done if he had left me alone. I might have tried death by mascarpone, or the lemon vodka home-embalming kit.

I was restless all night, slipping in and out of half sleep then jolting awake to stare at Kurt's motionless form and try to take in this new development. When I finally fell into real sleep, I dreamed that my bed had slid out the window and into the center of a snowy field. I was alone in it. Over the crest of a snowbank, I could hear the frantic sawing of violins, violas and cellos in a galloping rhythm, harmonies that were almost baroque but modern too. A figure appeared on the crest. It was a man. The first thing I noticed about him was his startling long black curly period wig, and as the rest of him appeared over the crest I could see he was dressed in full regalia, with a sumptuous, glittering, gold-and-black-brocade knee-length coat, huge lace cuffs, silk britches and shoes with a dainty heel. At first his face was blank but as he came closer it morphed between Kurt's face and my father's. The music seemed to be emanating from his fabulous coat.

The sounds then became visible, forming around the man into gold droplets that hung suspended on the air then floated downward like sparkling rain. I crawled off the bed and through the snow toward him and began to gather up the droplets. But I had no pockets, nowhere to put the droplets. I was wearing a nightgown, a simple white muslin nightgown of the type opera heroines wear during the mad scenes, for dementia arias. The man started to laugh. He roared and guffawed and slapped his thigh and I realized it was me he was laughing at. He wouldn't stop and I began to whimper.

"Miranda. Miranda. Wake up. You're dreaming." Kurt shook me furiously.

I opened my eyes and rubbed them. I had a moment of disorientation then said, "God, Kurt, I think I just dreamed Lully."

"You mean Lully the composer?"

I nodded. "Jean-Baptiste Lully. The Sun King's court composer."

"How very peculiar."

"He was dressed in Louis XIV period costume, but it was more than a costume, they were his clothes. Beautiful strange music was coming out of his coat."

"Too much cheese and crackers before bed, Miranda."

I ignored him. "I think I wanted to yank the coat off him, too. I wanted to wear it myself. It was gorgeous. I've got to try to remember the music…" I faced Kurt. "He looked like you, you know. And my father. Alternately."

"Good Lord. I certainly hope I'm not going to meet the same end as Lully."

"What end?"

"Well, my love, the foolish chap punctured his foot while banging time with a conducting staff, during a performance of a piece celebrating Louis' recovery from an illness. Lully wouldn't have the injured toe cut off and so died of gangrene poisoning. Silly sod."

"I think we better not analyze this one too deeply," I said.

"No, let's analyze something pleasant. Like your body." Kurt wrapped himself around me and started all over again, hands and tongue working me over until I was reduced to an orgasmic mush. After he'd finished with me and I lay there unable to move, he said, "It's all going to be just fine. Wait and see. And remember, it's not going to be forever. Find a nice little gay friend to entertain you when we're not together. That's what Olivia always did."

But from one last untouched cell of me, a shady all-knowing brain cell, a bubble of anger floated up. "I don't know, Kurt. It's all wrong," I admitted.

"It will be fine. You really must learn to be patient, my love," he soothed, and began to touch me again.

This time it was a competition to see who could make the other experience the most sensations. I did my very best but I think Kurt won. Again, I was paralyzed.

"Okay, okay, I surrender," I whispered.

My entire body felt like sluggish liquid as I poured myself out of bed and fumbled with my dressing gown. In my head, the words *it won't be forever* repeated themselves over and over. I looked back at Kurt. He was propped up on one elbow, admiring me, his face filled with happiness. How could I not believe somebody as gorgeous and talented and famous as that, somebody who adored me with all but one appendage?

At 9:05 the next morning, I was dressed and staring at myself in my full-length bedroom mirror. Pointy blue reptile cowgirl boots, La Perla tights with blue roses printed on a gray background, short jeans skirt and jacket, hair in a ponytail. Behind me, the bed, the IKEA bed I'd rushed out and bought because I couldn't entertain Kurt on my old student-style foam-rubber floor mattress, was empty.

The only trace of Kurt was the snowy battlefield of rumpled sheets.

It was important not to obsess about this new tic of his. Concentrate, I told myself, concentrate on Matilde.

I switched on the electric keyboard and sang a few soft scales, then moved on to some louder ones. When my voice was warmed up, I let loose with the kind of high notes that remind the neighbors in the surrounding square mile that there's an opera singer in the zone. Just so they didn't forget.

Sounds of ransacking from the kitchen made me stop singing. I hurried from the bedroom, increased speed down the hallway, skidding to a halt just in time to see it. Caroline had her head in the fridge. Her friend, Dan the Sasquatch, was sitting at the kitchen table. He was the hairiest individual I'd ever seen. He also had the habit of mooching around without a shirt. It was enough to put you off your food.

At my 1950s aluminum-sided raspberry Formica kitchen table, Dan the Sasquatch was smoking his strange little rollies. Caroline knew this was a nonsmoking apartment. I'd been adamant. But for some reason I couldn't fathom, the Sasquatch was The One, right down to his dreadlocks. He was the man she'd break all the rules for.

He forever rolled those little cigarettes too loose. Tiny curls of tobacco sparked and leaped out of the lit end and landed on his furry chest. I had this fear that one morning, when Caroline wasn't there, he'd catch fire and I'd have to put him out, throw water on him, stamp on him, or roll him in my favorite rug, ruining my one threadbare but lovely kilim. Or worse, that he'd burn my place down.

Not that it would have been a huge loss. Despite my craving for more luxurious conditions, all my furnishings were misfits given to me by friends on the move, or other singers off to other gigs on the other side of the country. I dreamed of a gorgeous home put together bit by bit with a sense of style and real money. But it was futile. If one of those big-city jobs came through—if I got the call from Toronto, or San Francisco or New York or London, or, the dream of all singers, La Scala in Milan—I could hardly say, "Sorry, I can't come and do your season. I have antiques now."

So most of my furnishings were classic. Classic inflatable plastic armchair. Classic stacked cardboard-box bookshelves brightened up with MACtac and ready to be closed and moved across the country at a moment's notice.

From deep in the fridge came Caroline's voice, intellectual and teasing. "Strawberries…mangoes…peppered chèvre…Brie…Camembert…stuffed artichokes…smoked salmon…caviar…well, aren't we quite the little aristocrat."

"I don't think that my food choices are quite enough to qualify me for a noble title," I laughed.

"Miranda. You're not going to eat all that yourself? Or are you on a campaign to become one of those really fat sopranos? Don't they say it improves the voice?"

"Nice if it were that easy," I said. "I could eat my way to success."

She continued, "Better hurry up and eat it or it'll go bad." She and the Sasquatch exchanged amused hungry glances.

"It's for a party. I'm having some people over for dinner tonight."

She turned to face me, crossed her arms and frowned. "Well. Thanks a lot for inviting me, Miranda. For telling me even. Very diplomatic."

"Don't be a grouch, Caroline. It was a last-minute thing. If you're around, please join us. I just thought you'd be bored. You don't really like my opera friends."

"No, but I love the food they're always stuffing their faces with."

"You come, too, Dan," I said reluctantly. Then I blurted out, "Just do me one small favor."

"What's that?"

"Don't touch anything until dinnertime. At least, let me

get it all onto a plate, let my guests see it presented, cooked maybe even."

Caroline made a face. "What do you think I am? Some kind of barbarian?"

"Yeah. A bolshie, punkophile, grunge-bucket, tree-hugging barbarian."

Caroline grinned at me and then at the Sasquatch. "I think she's got me pegged quite nicely, don't you, Dan?"

The Sasquatch said nothing. He took a drag of his cigarette and blew out a huge plume of smoke. Our disapproval was mutual. He'd never really warmed to me, either.

But I knew they were pleased. They'd scored some free trough time and a party. Caroline and her friends were artists of the low-budget lifestyle. When they weren't waving no-global placards outside an international summit, they were being "resourceful." I'd watched her and the Sasquatch work their way through the lineup at the university cafeteria, swallowing food as they moved forward so that by the time they got to the cash register, they had one measly item each to pay for. She'd justified this method by stating that half of that food went into the garbage anyway, that it was all about manipulating market values. If something could be obtained for free or with a minor criminal infraction, she knew all about it.

Caroline wasn't stupid, and although she gave the impression of ugliness, she wasn't ugly either. But the way she dressed (lumberjack shirts, frayed jeans and army-surplus boots) was a big part of her personal statement, and the statement said, "Grotty underbelly rules," which did not exactly enhance her feminine potential.

I still ribbed her about the day she answered my ad, the day she tricked me into thinking she'd be a nice dull dormouse of a roommate. It must have been the ugly tortoiseshell thick-lensed glasses (that she's never worn since), her brown hair in a neat ponytail (now her hair is always wild or full of messy cornrows), the long boring black skirt, flat sensible shoes and heap of political science books. That's what did it. I'd thought she was going to be a quiet, mature, proper little nerd, a career spinster, someone who had no life and spent all her time in the library preparing to win scholarships, so I'd never see her. I couldn't have been more mistaken.

Caroline said, "See you later then."

I grabbed my knapsack. "Later," I said, and left the apartment.

It was a beautiful sunny day, and as I walked I couldn't help but take in the gold-leafed trees and deep shimmering October sky.

And then I had a moment of panic. If Kurt and Olivia actually divorced according to plan, maybe next year at this time my autumn would be a London autumn. A Kurt autumn. He was getting under my skin in all ways but one. Except for the first big heart-crusher of my life, I'd always had a high immunity to absent boyfriends, not giving them more than a few seconds of wistful reflection once they were out the door. It was a safety mechanism I'd worked hard at developing and now Kurt had shot it all to hell.

I sank into a daydream, the one where I ask myself, "What would woman X do in my situation? For example, if her man offered her the deluxe hot dog—mustard, ketchup, chili, bacon bits, sauerkraut, mayonnaise, cheese— with everything but the dog itself, would woman X accept those terms?"

Well, that's what happens when you come from an illustrious cow town. You look around for mentors.

Such as Ellie Watson, the soprano from our production of *Madama Butterfly,* what would she do in my situation? It was a toughie. Since it was unlikely that Kurt would fall for someone like Ellie Watson, who had a gorgeous voice, and a pretty face really, but needed three airplane seats to be comfortable, but suppose, just suppose he had a thing for really big women and it had been somebody like Ellie and not me he had encountered in that broom closet two weeks ago.

Now, Ellie Watson didn't take flack from anyone. She knew exactly what she wanted from life and she grabbed it. She was from Liverpool. She'd always had the great voice, the voice with the money notes, the good high Cs. All through her childhood, she'd honed her skills by singing for money in pubs and passing the hat. Then she'd moved on to local talent nights and kept on going until she was accepted into a famous English music school where she ate, drank and breathed opera.

Ellie was greedy, in the best sense of the word. When she took the stage, she *really* took it, making everybody else seem invisible. Well, almost everybody else. Peter Drake, the tenor who sang Pinkerton, was Ellie's only obstacle. She didn't like having to share the stage with another diva.

If Kurt had proposed to Ellie what he'd proposed to me, i.e. neutered sex, she would have said something like, "No actual shaggin'? ME BOLLOCKS!" and booted him out of her bed.

In the studio, Lance was going back over the takes we'd already done. He was wearing earphones and mouthing the words along with the characters on the screen. I tapped him on the shoulder. He turned around and smiled. "It's good, Miranda. Here, listen to yourself." He placed the headset on my ears.

I listened for a few beats then said, "It's not bad, is it?"

"C'mon, sweetheart, let's bury Matilde. You warmed up?"

"Give me a minute," I said, and began to pace, first humming then breaking into scales.

Lance leaned against the wall. He was studying me. I stopped and said, "What?"

"No…it's nothing." But he was still studying me.

Then I remembered Kurt's advice from that morning. A nice little gay friend, somebody who could keep me company when he wasn't there.

"Before I forget, Lance. I'm having some people over to my place tonight. Sort of a dinner party except I don't have a big enough table, so it's perch wherever you can. I know you're probably too busy or I would have asked you earlier, but it would be really great if you could come. You have my address and my number. Come later if you like. For dessert."

I'd always wanted to invite Lance to my parties but didn't know whether they'd be his speed. I had no idea what his speed was. I'd never partied with him. I'd developed this weird intimacy with him in the darkness of the studio but I'd never seen him away from work. I wondered if he *had* a life away from work.

He nodded thoughtfully, then said, "C'mon, we're running behind schedule."

Matilde and her swineherd hurtled toward their demise, moaning, gasping, singing and generally porking their way around the rest of Paris until they were caught by the homely wife, hacked up and turned into quite a few kilos of nice link sausages and sold for a good price at the market.

When we'd finished, Lance reached out and rested his hand on my shoulder. His tone was serious. "I know, Miranda. It's peculiar work. It's not glorious and you want more limelight than this, and someday very soon you're going to dump me cold so that you can become famous."

Quicker than you know, I thought.

"But we've done a good job," he said. "We're close to finishing. I'll let you know if we have to do some retakes."

I tried never to telegraph my impatience, but Lance must have sensed it anyway, even in the darkness. In my early years in the city, the university years, I'd been so happy, so grateful to have those jobs that were somehow related to singing and got me a little closer to where I thought I should be going.

But that morning, I felt boxed in. I had the sensation of being in a cage, of suffering the same indignities as a captured parrot. Someone forced to learn words in another creature's language, on the verge of forgetting the dreams

and dialects that expressed life in the lush, raw, blazing freedom of the Amazonian jungle, now far away.

The Amazonian was the other Miranda in me. The wild,
restless, unsatisfied one, age thirteen and obedient to no
one, who heard Bach and Mozart and Brahms and Verdi and
wondered how to unlock the secrets of that music, how to
devour all the sounds in the universe, wrestle with them,
make them hers, and then pour them back out to the world.

I took a quick run over to Mike's for a double caffe latte
refresher and to check my work schedule. I'd asked for
Sunday, Monday and Tuesday off. Mike had said he'd try
to talk another girl into working my shifts but he wasn't
sure he could manage it. The other girl was Belinda, his
latest girlfriend. They'd been seeing each other for two
months and the bloom of the romance was starting to
fade. Belinda was sulking.

Mike had gone to the bank. And other than a customer,
she was alone. She slapped the customer's cappuccino down
so hard that the liquid gave a little bounce and slopped out
onto the saucer. The guy started to protest but she froze him
with a look and walked away.

I was overdue for a short visit to Cold Shanks. Even
though it was just a long bus ride away, my life had been so
busy that I hadn't been back since last Christmas.

I needed Belinda badly. I approached her cautiously. "Hi,
Belinda," I said. "How's it going?"

"Prick, prick, prick!"

"Excuse me. Did I miss something?"

I followed Belinda into the kitchen. She began unload-
ing the dishwasher, crashing everything down as hard as
possible. She was a redhead, ethereal and nervous, with short,
lank, baby-fine hair. Normally, her skin was pale and transparent, but that day, it was bright pink with anger. "I just can't
believe him."

"What's he done?" I asked.

"Mr. Smooth, eh? It's so nuts. Sooo nuts, I can't believe I'm in the middle of all this."

"So what's he done?"

"Well. In the beginning it's all wining, dining, flowers, jewelry…right?" She caught the gold chain that glittered across her collarbone and fingered it nervously.

"Yeah?"

"And you think, shit, maybe he's the one, right?"

"Yeah?"

"And then he says, 'Can you do me a little favor?'"

"Yeah?" I repeated.

"He asks me if I can give him a hand with his granny." Belinda spat out "granny" as if it were an obscenity.

"Okay," I said.

"His granny's an invalid. Prick."

"I'm not sure I see the problem, Belinda."

"She lives in the big family home, the one Mike and his brothers and sisters grew up in, right?"

"Yeah?"

"With his mom and dad and one of his sisters who's married. The sister lives there, too, with her husband and two kids, okay?"

"Yeah?"

"What he means by giving his granny a hand is that I have to spend the night there. On a roll-up cot in the same room. She can't do most things for herself. He's asking me to do night duty for an invalid. Help her to the bathroom, wash her, dress her, that kind of thing. I've done one week of it and I'm exhausted. As if I didn't have enough to do. I thought I'd be sleeping with *him,* not his grandmother. That's the whole night wasted."

"Um, you might find this hard to believe, but it's a test, Belinda. If you do that for his granny, he's yours."

Mike had scared off quite a few girlfriends this way.

"I'll end up doing it for everyone else in his family, too. I just know it. You should hear them criticizing me, bossing me around. Isn't it enough that I give a hand? But then they all tell me I'm doing it the wrong way. I can't take it anymore. But that's not even the worst part," Belinda went on. A teardrop baubled up and rolled down her cheek. "The old bag doesn't speak a word of English. She's been here most of her adult life and she doesn't speak English. The place is a total zoo." She dabbed at her eyes with her sleeves.

"It just seems like it now, but you'll get used to the way Mike's family does things."

"No...no. It's not worth it. I love him but not enough for all that."

"You're too alone in all of this. You have no infrastructure. You need infrastructure."

"Like how?"

"Well...like extra granny-sitters who have no emotional investment. Somebody who gets paid to do it. You need to wear Mike down, threaten him a little, make him realize that he hasn't got much choice if he wants to keep you. He's a typical Italian. His philosophy is to get the woman into the cave and then leave her there...to do all the dirty work. But it doesn't mean he doesn't love you."

Belinda was paying attention. "Yeah?"

"You're washing dishes in Mike's place. Don't think it'll change if you don't stand up to him. Do the words *family business* mean anything to you? It means make all the families and their in-laws work like lackies for the greater good of the family, none of whom are having any fun because they're all working too hard. Make sure you've got loads of reserves to step in and help you. And make Mike pay. He's got the money. He's been hoarding it since he was two years old."

Belinda smiled then made pathetic orphan eyes and stared at me imploringly.

I backed up a step and held up my hands. "Oh, hey, wait a minute, Belinda. Don't look at me like that. I can't help you. I'm already working overtime."

"It's nights. You're asleep most of the time. Granny takes a sleeping pill."

I shook my head.

"Ah, c'mon, Miranda. I'm sure you could use the extra money. You're not doing anything special with your nights, are you? You don't have a boyfriend…"

"Hold on a second."

"What? Now you have one?"

I backtracked quickly. "No."

"I'll talk to Mike, Miranda. He knows you. He'd never accept a stranger, but he'd accept you."

She was right.

"It'll be easy," she gushed now. "I work your mornings here so you can go to Cold Shanks for a few days, then you do this for me when you get back."

It was extortion, sort of, but I liked Belinda. And I was already picturing my plane zooming toward Ontario.

I knew a little something about Italian grannies.

During the summer between my second and third years of university, I went on a two-month work-study abroad program to Tuscany. I managed it all on the cheap, had the whole thing planned right down to the last nickel. I'd wanted to visit my father, but the pound was too expensive. Just setting foot in an English airport would have used up all my resources. And I had gigs to hurry back for.

I was primed for the romance of Florence from the minute I arrived. What I'd seen from the taxi window looked promising; medieval stone buildings, huge elegantly carved wooden doorways, outdoor cafés and restaurants with bright Cinzano umbrellas, quaint marketplaces, impossibly chic and gorgeous men. The foreign girls, tourists like me, were easy to spot. They all drifted gauzily around in loose pale cottons, looking arty, as if they'd just stepped off the set of *A Room With a View*. I quickly learned that Italian women wore tighter, darker clothes not just to look fashionable, but because the streets were narrow, and it was easy to clean the sides of sooty buildings with loose flowing skirts.

That first day, my taxi stopped in front of a large run-down palazzo just off Via de' Bardi. I was ushered in by a Philippine servant and introduced to the Melandroni family, including all the in-laws and outlaws. Each time I thought I had a handle on how many of them lived under the same roof, a new one would pop up. My job for the next three months was to "accompany" the eldest family member, Baby Melandroni.

Baby was eighty-nine years old and a Bette Davis look-alike, with crimson lipstick oozing into the creases around her mouth. "Accompanying" meant following her every demented move, repairing her wardrobe, peeling her grapes, cleaning up her accidents and making sure she didn't fall down any stairs. She insisted that I call her Contessa.

It didn't take me long to realize that I was participating in a real-life version of *The Twilight of the Gods*. The Melandronis hated, tormented and plotted against each other at every available opportunity, but were scandalized when I naively suggested they might be happier if they didn't all live in the same house.

I barely got near those gorgeous chic men that summer. I spent most of my time in the palazzo, at one window or another, sneaking peeks at the outside world. Although two of the Melandroni men lost their way during electrical storms and ended up in my bedroom, it was no consolation. They both looked like beagles and were unctuous and overeager, a product of too much noble inbreeding. Both times I had to defend myself by beaning them with the six-pound Italian-English dictionary I was trying so hard to absorb.

I was certain that all over Europe, inexperienced North American girls like me were submitting themselves to similar tortures. I had proof. Tina, for example, had chosen to do her work-study in Germany. I received a long, hysterical letter from her. It was written on toilet paper. She'd been locked into a supply closet while labor inspectors toured the hotel where she was illegally employed as a chambermaid.

It was not so much a work-study program as a ball-chain program.

The summer ended on a high note. I'd struggled the whole time to interpret Baby's ravings and finally understood that she wanted nothing more than to escape. She was being held prisoner, she told me, by her very own family, and they had taken all her jewels from her and put them in the safe in the bank, and were taking all the rest of her money, stripping her of her wealth, not to mention the last shreds of her dignity. She wanted to dress up like the contessa she was and get back into society again.

So one Sunday after lunch, when all the other Melandronis were napping after having stuffed themselves at the big meal, I got her all dolled up. I packed my bags quickly and we snuck out of the palazzo. We took a taxi to Piazza della Signoria. I deposited Baby at a central table in Caffe Rivoire, ordered her a big dish of ice cream drowned in kirsch, and left. Just before catching my train for Pisa airport (a day ahead of schedule), I called the palazzo and told the servant where to pick up Baby. I spent nearly the last of my funds that night on a pensione in Pisa. What a luxury. It had been a completely frustrating experience, but at least it had been frustrating in a new language.

Chapter 6

I stood at the bus stop, buzzing with the caffeine from Mike's, mentally preparing for my lesson. Over and over I sang the audition pieces in my head. I'd chosen them carefully. Opera management around the world was growing less and less tolerant of singers who didn't look the part. The days of the three-hundred-pound consumptive heroine were over, except in the case of the truly prodigious voices, like Ellie's and Peter's, for whom exceptions were made.

Young singers just starting out were another story. You had to fit the role, and if you were willing to do cartwheels and lose your clothes along the way, all the better.

I'd opted for something safe, with no potential for nudity. I was going to sing Cherubino's aria "Non So Più" from Mozart's *Le Nozze di Figaro* and "Iris, Hence Away" from Handel's *Semele*.

In *Le Nozze di Figaro*, Cherubino is a trouser role, a boy or man played by a mezzo-soprano. Cherubino is a youthful and buoyant, all over the place, lovesick puppy. I was pushing it, given my C-cup, but I'd bind myself up for the sake of art and a singing job.

My other aria was from Handel's *Semele. Semele* is hardly ever staged. It's a baroque opera based on the infighting of the gods Juno and Jupiter. The aria is Juno's fuming in a moment of vengeful plotting against Jupiter. "Iris, Hence Away" shows off a different style, my sung English and vocal flexibility in the middle range, as well as a character portrayal opposite to Cherubino. I tried to make my Juno dominant and alarming, a sort of Katharine Hepburn of the operatic stage.

When I'd told Madame Klein a month before that I was trying to get an audition with the ENO, she'd said dismissively. "Dis vill be a gut exercise for you, *ja?* Strange city, strange theater, people you don't know, *ja,* dat is part of de zinging experience. Und you can alvays zing in de chorus." But she wouldn't commit on whether I had a minimal chance of winning a solo role with the company.

I wouldn't be alone, though. Once I got to England, I would have my father to coach me through my pieces, prepare me, give me the inside story, let me know what my panel of auditioners really liked, on the deep dirty inside track.

But then Madame Klein had gone on to divulge one of her secrets to me, a little performer's trick, and it had been like receiving the most generous gift.

"Vhile you are zinging de phrase, in your mind's eye und ear, you gotta be also zeeing und hearing de phrase dat follows. You gotta hear two musicks at vonce."

I rode for an hour and a half, thinking about the pieces, changing buses twice, until finally I reached the homogenous streets of the city's farthest East End where Madame Klein lived. Her house was a brown stucco box in a neat row of brown stucco boxes that extended as far as the eye could see. The gardens were drab, and stumpy trees pruned to within an inch of their lives adorned the boulevard. During the winter, those trees made me think of mutilated hands grasping at the sky.

Madame Klein brought all her intensity and ambition with her wherever she lived, so that the neighborhood always seemed more impressive than before, vital and full of promise because of her.

Madame did all her own accompanying. Her arthritic hands were still able to coax subtle beauty from the keyboard. She did not want to know what was going on in her students' personal lives. She did not want to know about our biorhythms. She did not care whether our hearts were whole or broken, whether we'd just been mugged or our dog had been hit by a car the day of the lesson. There was no excuse for not singing well. Life outside the score on the music stand was a series of minor obstacles that a real singer was expected to leap over without a second thought. The voice ruled supreme.

She only wanted to know that we had studied our pieces properly and would execute them precisely as we'd been instructed. She was exacting, tyrannical, and at times, brilliant. Nothing was ever good enough for her. And she didn't need the money.

Now, there are singing teachers who make a good living buttering up egos, giving hope to hopeless cases and there are teachers who concede a compliment every so often. That was not Madame Klein. She was happy to lose students and I was desperate to keep her. It had taken me a long time to find a singing teacher who understood my voice.

Singing can be taught using various techniques. There's the Squeeze Your Buns School, in which your breathing has to be so deep that your diaphragm expands so far that it reaches beyond your buttocks—buttocks that become cramped and muscular with the effort of controlling the singing breath. Then there's the Up Your Nose School, where the soft palette has to be lifted and the sound has to

buzz in the sinuses and ring in the nasal and head cavities—
the joke being that a lot of singers have more resonating cavities than brains. There's the Forget Technique and Think
about the Music School of singing.

A good teacher believes in a delicate combination of all
these things. That was Madame Klein.

In the waiting area, I sat on a Victorian sofa whose horse-
hair stuffing prickled through the upholstery fabric, and
thought about the ENO audition, myself and Kurt, Madame
and her defunct husband, Oskar, and prepared to break the
news about Kurt's song cycle.

From my place on the itchy sofa, I could hear Madame's
voice in the studio but couldn't make out the words. There
was a staccato blast from her and then Martin, the singer
whose lesson was before mine, erupted through the door.
Martin was a tall, robust bass-baritone who also sang in the
opera chorus. He thought himself very important. Today,
he was sweating and on the verge of tears. Madame Klein
had just made him less important. He barged past me and
out the front door.

I approached her living room. Along with the lavish and
finnicky antiques and mustard-colored walls, there was a lot
of diva decor. Her walls were lined with photos of her with
her spouse, with other great artists, conductors and accompanists, in the renowned theaters and concert halls of the
world. Her recordings, awards and mementos filled the
bookshelves next to her scores.

Her coiffed silver head seemed to be drowning as it
bobbed behind the shiny black Steinway grand. She narrowed her eyes at me. She was checking my appearance like
a cattle buyer at an auction, concerned with how I was pre-
senting myself to the world. If she'd had her way, we'd all
be wearing dirndl skirts and little white blouses with Peter
Pan collars. When her perusal of me was finished, she shook
her head tragically at all my denim and leg, acknowledging
fashion defeat.

"Fräulein Lyme. Zing," she commanded, playing the exercise.

I sang.

"*Nein, nein, nein.* You bleat like a goat. I vill take your name off ze marquee. You vill never be a great zinger if you bleat like zis."

"I'm a little tired today, Madame."

"Tired schmired. You conzentrate. You breaze. You picture ze music. Und you zing."

So I did the opposite. I thought of Kurt, roving all over my body. I thought of Matilde, porking all over Paris. And I sang. I sang all the exercises and then she let me move on to some Italian art songs. After that, as a special treat, I was allowed to sing a long Mozart concert aria.

Madame Klein stopped playing and said, "Gut, gut. Not great but vee vill make a zinger of you yet."

"Madame Klein. I got that audition I was telling you about. The one with the ENO."

"*Ja?* It vill be a good experience. You get used to auditioning by doing lots of auditions."

"So I'm going to London at Christmas."

"Okay. Vhen you're dere, you go see lots of de really big zingers. You can learn someting."

"Oh and before I forget, Madame Klein, I have some more good news." I prepared to unleash the bomb, with terror in my heart.

"Vhat is zis news?"

"I'll be premiering a new song cycle by Kurt Hancock. With the Vancouver symphony."

"You vill do vhat?"

I babbled fast. "I consider it my real debut, my first important gig really. I mean, with the symphony. It's a pretty big deal. I don't count the stuff we did at university or the opera chorus or those church solos."

"You vill do no zuch ting. Zere vill be no debut."

My silence was eloquent.

"You are too young. Your voice is not ready yet."

"My…uh…voice…uh…" I was about follow in the footsteps of the baritone and let myself be reduced to tears.

"Ze music of Herr Hancock is demanding. Modern, difficult music. You do not vant to fall SCHPLATT on your pretty face." She illustrated my messy musical dive-bombing with one hand crashing onto the piano keys. "You are not ripe for ze music."

It was not the first time we'd had this conversation. If Madame Klein had had her way, none of us would have sung anywhere until we were so ripe we were rotten.

It was a vicious circle. You get a job in an opera chorus in order to have some money to pay for the singing lessons. At the singing lessons, the teacher tells you that the opera chorus will ruin your voice, ruin you for a solo career. So you're supposed to pretend you're singing by mouthing the words. But can you imagine what it sounds like when a whole chorus of would-be soloists does that?

She expected things to be the way they'd been in Vienna a million years ago. But times had changed. She didn't want to accept the fact that we were living in the world of the one-night wunderkind, that we were expected to be wunderkinder, too; that even in opera, we were part of a showbiz machine that was only too happy to suck our young juices then spit out the empty husk.

From wunderkinder to kinder tinder in one quick move.

Not that I was cynical. I believed I was ready for the opera-biz machine. It was a fact of life in the twenty-first century.

"Vhen you forget about your idea of zinging Kurt Hancock's music, ve vill talk. But now I have nutting more to say to you today, Fräulein Lyme. Shut ze door vhen you leave," she commanded, then waved her hand to dismiss me.

Still caught up in my problem, I changed buses on automatic pilot. I had to get off in the center near Granville. As

I was crossing the street, a sound floated across to me. If I had been a cat, I would have arched my back. All the hairs on my spine would have stood on end. But not for fear. For beauty. For a new enemy in the camp.

At first, it was unearthly, like a moaning ghost, and then when I got closer, I heard it for what it was, a mournful, limpid, pure soprano voice. The singer sang the hymn, "Jerusalem," William Blake's words, very slowly, with perfect control. I'd sung it myself twenty times or more in my church gigs, Sunday mornings, bleary-eyed and hungover, hanging out with any religion that would pay me to sing their top ten. I froze there on the street and listened. The singer was invisible, around another corner, and I was afraid that if I made a move, she would disappear and I would never see who she was. So I listened.

Now, with the prospect of London looming before me, the words seemed particularly poignant, especially the last part about bows of burning gold, arrows of desire, and building Jerusalem in England's green and pleasant land.

Yes, those were my sentiments exactly…I will not cease from mental fight…till we have built Jerusalem in England's green and pleasant land.

Well.

Okay.

Maybe ours wouldn't be a Jerusalem exactly. Kurt and I would have something less sacred and a little more hedonistic and spicy, something a little to the left of Jerusalem. Our own private Babylon, complete with hanging gardens and palm-waving slaves. That's where you'd find me when I wasn't singing concerts with my father.

Now that Kurt was in my life, I was starting to consider luxury, the trappings that came with the opera world, with being the desired object of a famous conductor. Gilt and plush red-velvet theaters, limousines, orchids and roses and champagne raining down on me. It was a nice thought.

When the hymn ended, the soprano began another piece.

It was "Lift Thine Eyes" from Mendelssohn's *Elijah*. I hurried in the direction of the voice, along Granville Street, past the bars, bingo palaces, strip joints, pool halls, cinemas and pawnshops. I turned a corner and under a sign that said GIRLS GIRLS GIRLS, XXX, was a beautiful dark waif seated cross-legged on a blanket with a cardboard box in front of her for offerings. She could have been fourteen or twenty-four. It was impossible to guess her age. Her face was dark and elfish, an exotic child's face.

A small group had gathered near her. Approaching that part of town, it was kind of like coming upon a single Easter lily in a field of thistles. I rummaged in my knapsack for some change. While I was unsuccessfully hunting, an oily-haired lowlife in a buckskin jacket approached her. She shook her head violently, picked up all her stuff and hurried away.

I was tempted to run after her, but I didn't. It would only be a matter of days, maybe even hours, before some other creep would get his hooks into her and have her selling her body to pay for his vice of choice. That part of town was crawling with junkies and panhandlers, some inarticulate and wasted, others fit, pompous and smart-ass, shoving themselves into people's faces with lines like, "Could you spare five dollars to assist an indigent person in purchasing an alcoholic beverage?" My knee-jerk instinct was always to cross to the other side of the street to avoid them or rush away as quickly as possible. They weren't getting my hard-earned dimes. But the girl upset me. The girl was all wrong out there.

I caught the last bus home. I still had to prepare everything for the party. I was a nervous cook. It's a fine art getting all your dishes to arrive at the finish line in the same moment, hot and crisped to perfection. So I counted on lots of cold things, hor d'oeuvres, and dishes I'd cooked the week before, stashed in the freezer and then shoved into the oven at the last minute.

I know what you're saying. What a little housewife, eh?

Well, what if it all worked out with Kurt? What if I ended up moving in? What if Kurt wanted to entertain all his world-famous friends at home? What was going to happen, for example, if he conducted a big New Year's Eve bash at someplace like the Albert Hall, and then he invited the Three Tenors over to his house after?

Even if we're just talking about a little snack, that's a wicked quantity of pasta and paella there. I've never met a singer who didn't care about food. When there isn't something coming out of a singer's mouth, there's usually something going in.

I was hoping Kurt and I would do a lot of eating out, experiencing all of London's best restaurants and bistros. And maybe I could get help in the house for some of the other big events like parties and receptions, because, on a large scale, I really was a nervous cook. He was bound to have a housekeeper, wasn't he? Somebody as important and famous as him? And separated, too? There was sure to be extra help. Maybe an au pair or two?

Although, I'd have to be careful about au pairs, screen them, make sure they were always older, fatter and uglier than me. You hear so many stories about men dumping their wives for the eighteen-year-old foreign student. Not that Kurt was going to do that to me. Wasn't his full sexual treatment, minus one point, proof of his overall fidelity in such matters?

Chapter 7

I was alone in the apartment in a state of pre-party alert. Caroline and the Sasquatch were out. I'd invited Kurt to come early, but now the afternoon was too far along to still be called early.

I reshuffled the pile of CDs. Nelly Furtado, Joss Stone, Ben Harper, Oasis, Cyndi Lauper, Simple Minds, Missy Elliott, Anggun, Lenny Kravitz, Aerosmith, The Calling, Fiona Apple, Stones, Shaggy, The Cure, *Barry White's Greatest Hits,* and a bunch of rock and roll that was so old, you could almost smell the mould growing on it. Because I like those parties where the music reminds people of another time and they start acting out their old superegos, the ones they abandoned years ago.

I happened to know that Kurt had been a flat-out fan of Spandau Ballet, Pet Shop Boys, The Cure…those kinds of groups. Back in his dubious reckless days of clubbing and eyeliner. He was a good nine years older than me, after all.

I put some Oscar Peterson on the player and checked the food again. I just hoped it all tasted as good as it looked.

Nerves had made my tongue go numb, so now everything tasted like soggy Kleenex to me.

As I was pouring myself an iced orange vodka, my favorite bottled shock absorber, the buzzer went.

I ran to answer. The voice in the speakerphone was Tina's. "C'mon up," I said.

Tina was with her new conquest, Collin.

Collin was dressed from head to toe in black leather and carried two motorcycle helmets. He was a lighting technician at the theater and a man of few words. "Life's a bitch and then you die" pretty much summed it up for him. Tina wasn't interested in a lot of words from a man. The man of her dreams was a cowboy, a drinker and a wanderer. Collin came as close as possible to a physical copy of Tina's father, except that his horse was a motorbike. You could say that Tina had a little obsession.

One day, when we were still in our third year at university, Tina stopped me in the hallway. I was on my way to the obligatory History of Musical Instruments, which, despite its potential, had turned into History of the Big Yawn for me.

"What other classes do you have today?" she asked.

"Library Skills 101," I replied.

"Skip it," she said.

"I've put if off for three years. They won't let me graduate if I don't pass it."

"Borrow the notes. You've got to come with me."

"Where?"

"To Victoria."

"Are you crazy? It's at least a ferry ride. It's money. And why Victoria?"

"I've hitched us a ride one way. I'll pay your part. We'll hitch another to get back. We gotta hurry though. Wayne, this guy in my Women's Studies class has got a truck. He's going back to Victoria for the weekend."

"Guys usually avoid those courses. What's he doing in Women's Studies," I asked.

"Studying the women." Tina smirked. "He's not as stupid as he looks."

Tina didn't waste a lot of time, so there had to be a good reason for her wanting to go to Victoria. She looked terrible that day so I figured it was serious. Her long dark hair was stringy and her face looked drawn and ash-colored.

So I agreed to go with her and we crammed into the front seat of the appointed truck at the appointed hour.

Wayne, Tina's friend from Women's Studies, appeared to be majoring in Babes and Foxes at university. He was definitely eye candy, with an Olympic athlete's body, a profile that belonged on a Roman coin and a shock of sun-bleached curls you wanted to reach out and twirl with your fingers. I imagined a lot of women were also majoring in Wayne.

He asked, "So how's life in the music department, by which I mean, any action? You girls getting G-spots attended to?"

I flashed Tina an irritated quizzical look and said, "Ouch. Forget about the prelims. Let's get straight to business." But she elbowed me to be quiet.

He went on, "I mean, are you getting it often in that department, see, 'cause I was thinking, if they were short on dudes there, of changing my major. I'm running out of inspiration in Twentieth-Century Canadian Literature."

Tina said to the windshield in a loud amused voice, "He's worked his way through the whole faculty. Students and lecturers."

"Hey. Only the babes, eh? Dudes aren't my territory," added Wayne quickly.

Tina turned to him and said, "You wouldn't know what to do with the women in music, Wayne."

"No?" He had an expression of disbelief.

"Music's bigger than any man, Wayne. And they wouldn't let you in anyway. Kazoo does not exactly qualify as an instrument."

"Harmonica?" he said hopefully.

"Don't think so," said Tina.

Wayne pried and prodded a little longer, trying to get the biological profile on all the flora and fauna of the music department.

"Flautists," he spouted enthusiastically. "All that embrasure could come in very handy."

But Tina and I acted like a couple of brick walls and he eventually gave up.

Once we'd boarded the ferry, Wayne went off to check out the babes and foxes on deck while Tina and I sat at a table inside and sipped cappuccinos. First we griped for a while about our singing teachers and then, for the longest time, we just sat in silence.

I tried to break into Tina's mood. "Wayne's really, really amazing looking," I said, "but he's…"

"He's gorgeous and he's a total hoser," said Tina, bored.

I watched the wild April ocean fracture into sapphire shards with each new gust of wind, and said, "Maybe a pod of whales will swim by and flick their tails for us."

"Hmm," said Tina. She was descending into a funk. If gigantic sea mammals impressed her, she wasn't going to let me know about it that day. In fact, she was barely there.

Tina had left the planet, something she did from time to time. She was out there drifting weightlessly in the galaxy of her personal baggage. Not that she was a space cadet. Tina had no trouble being present for singing gigs. Singing gigs were easy for her because, unlike real life, you always know what's going to happen in the end of an opera or a cantata or a song cycle. But she had other moments that were less solid.

That day I said, "Tina, you're drifting into outer space. Don't do this to me. Come back to Earth. Stay here."

"I was just thinking."

"That was not a 'just thinking' expression. It was a 'Lizzie Borden works it out' expression. You've made this trip to Victoria before, haven't you? Recently, I mean."

"What makes you think so?"

"Because you know exactly where everything is right down to what kind of coffee they make and where the stir sticks are. You know where the bathrooms are and the best seats. How come you didn't want to tell me before now? Is this about a man?"

"Sort of."

"A sort of man. Who?"

She crossed her arms and glowered at me.

"Okay, surprise me then."

We were interrupted by the call for passengers to go belowdecks. Tina gave me another grim look. I followed her down to the car deck.

Wayne showed up at the last minute, looking smug. He'd obviously scored some babe-and-fox action for later. In silence, we rode past soft hills and forest, past a long strip of car dealerships, fast-food joints and cheap motels, into the mock-English center of town. Wayne dropped us off in front of a big castlelike hotel and screeched away in his truck, laying a pungent black strip of rubber.

"Show-off," muttered Tina, then started to hurry toward her mysterious destination with such huge strides that I was nearly running to keep up.

"At least let me take in some scenery," I panted. "It's so pretty here, all the flowers, the hanging baskets." But Tina didn't answer or slow her pace. I hated her when she was like that. She made me feel so useless, closing me and everybody else out.

"Why did you bring me along if you're going to act like I'm not here, Tina?"

"Witnesses," she barked. "I need a witness."

I knew it. She was planning on killing somebody.

We'd been walking for almost an hour, uphill all the way, into a neighborhood where the trees were ancient, enormous yews and gnarled oaks, and the houses like great wooden sailing vessels, galleons for crews of fifty. Peeking through high hedges into vast gardens, I asked, "Who lives in houses like these anyway? They're enormous."

"A lot of them are divided into apartments," said Tina.

"Oh, yeah?"

"Yeah. This used to be the residential center of Victoria. About a hundred years ago. When people had servants and lawn-tennis courts. There was a token Russian princess living up here. Up on that hill there, see that castle? That's Craigdarroch Castle. It used to be the family home of the Dunsmuirs. One of the family used to invite Tallulah Bankhead up here. Old Dunsmuir made a pile with the railroad but he died a year before the place was finished. Then it was a college and then a music school at one time."

"No kidding. How come you know so much about this neighborhood?"

"You'll see in a minute."

We'd arrived at a high stone wall. We followed it until we came to stone gateposts topped with brass griffins now green and pockmarked with age. Where the gate should have been was a chain with a No Trespassing sign swinging from it. Tina stepped over the chain and started walking up the wide, weed-infested driveway. It must have once been an impressive entrance, but now it was like the cracked surface of an old riverbed. In the distance was a cluster of tall trees, a small wilderness masking the house. I followed Tina through the undergrowth and the chaos of litter. Although it had obviously been years since anyone had taken care of the property, and kids had been in there to pillage and vandalize, it was easy to see the kind of estate it had once been.

The house was massive, with foundations in the same stone as the wall. The upper part of the house was rotting wood, trimmed with the kind of Victorian gingerbread and curlicues that always made me think of haunted houses. On one side was a crumbling terrace and eight smashed French doors leading into what had once been a mirrored ballroom.

The mirrors had been smashed, too, and the effect was like looking at a person who had been maimed and blinded.

"It's incredible," I said. "It's like *The Fall of the House of Usher.*"

"The House of Browning," said Tina. There was a furious expression on her face.

"What do you mean Browning?"

"This was my grandparents' house."

"Your what?"

"My grandparents' house."

"You said you didn't have any grandparents."

"Think about it, Miranda. Everybody has to have grandparents somewhere. It's just whether they're alive or dead and your father lets you know about it."

"Your grandparents," I said, trying out the idea.

"This place belonged to my paternal grandparents. My father's parents. This is the estate my father pissed away without a word to Mom and me. If he wasn't so crocked already I'd like to kill him. They were rich, Miranda. Do you understand? My grandparents were stinking filthy rich and I never even knew they existed and they never knew that I existed. And to top it all off, my father drank it all away. The place is going to be demolished in two weeks. They're building luxury condos."

"How did you find out?"

"You know those genealogy things people do on the Net?"

"Yeah."

"Like that. It was all there. Every detail."

"Shit."

"You said it," agreed Tina.

We wandered through the stripped carcass of the house, silently taking stock and trying to imagine how each room must have been in the house's happier days.

Back in the ballroom, the black expression lifted from Tina's face. I could see she'd been harboring the secret of this house for months, hugging it to herself and trying to understand it, as if it were an affliction, a tumor. She lifted her arms and twirled three times, like an unhappy Gypsy wife giving herself a homemade divorce. She said cheerfully, "I would have held a recital in this room if I'd known it existed. I'll bet it has perfect acoustics."

She started to sing. I joined in, harmonizing. We improvised, following each other, singing whatever came into our heads, and I have to say, it sounded pretty good. We threw our notes out to the walls, walking slowly through the main floor like figures in an eerie dream. We paced and twirled and let loose in the huge abandoned house to exorcise her father's oversight.

Tina began to make changes that day. She stopped being so hard on herself, stopped calling herself trailer trash and started to become the singer she'd always imagined for herself.

On the ferry ride home, Tina was in a much better mood. "I got one more favor to ask you."

"What's that?"

"Theory homework." She unfolded a scrunched-up scrap of paper and shoved it into my line of vision. German words were scrawled on it. "I wrote the poem but it's gotta be a song, Lied in the style of Schubert. It'll be easy."

"Easy for old Franz but not for me," I sighed.

"Ah, go on. You know you enjoy it. I'll never get it done on time. C'mon. You know you can't turn down the challenge."

I was one year ahead of Tina in theory, and because she said herself that she was too lazy to figure it out, and I had done all the exercises the year before, I did her theory and composition homework for her. Pieces "in the style of" Bach fugues, Beethoven concerti, Byrd motets, Ravel arabesques. And it was true that I enjoyed the challenge.

It was unbalanced. In exchange for doing her music theory homework, I got to be her friend, witness her bad moods and endure her cruel and unusual punishments. But then, what else are friends for?

I poured out some iced orange vodka for Tina and Collin. The three of us made a quick toast to our health and knocked it back. I was a little disappointed with Tina. I was expecting her to liven things up but she sank into my couch with Collin and the two of them stayed there, exchanging gooey looks, wordlessly communicating their weird dark passion.

I moved appetizers around like chess pawns, feeling like a fifth wheel. Then I tried to break it up with chitchat. "So, Collin. You doing the next show? You doing the *I Puritani?*"

He didn't answer. He hadn't even heard me. He was deep-sea diving in Tina's gaze. A spark of envy started to flare up in me. I snatched up a platter of asparagus and scampi and ran over to shove it under their noses like an invasive mother-in-law.

Tina looked up abruptly, frowned and said, "Calm down, will you, Miranda? He'll be here."

The speakerphone went. I jumped up and ran to answer it.

"We're here," announced Kurt's voice.

"There. I told you he'd be here," said Tina.

"C'mon up," I said, then pushed the button to open the main door.

I raced into the bathroom to have a last look at myself.

My Pucci silk knit minidress (orange, brown and cream tiny swirls) was on right side out. My Frosty Peach lipstick was applied evenly, none on my teeth. I held my hand to my mouth to test my breath. Delicious orange-vodka mouthwash scent. My pointy brown shoes with pointy low heel were both shined, both on the right feet. My hair was up in a topknot with a shank pulled through and hanging down, sixties go-go-dancer style.

I was as ready as I'd ever be.

As I was about to go out of the bathroom, Tina appeared in the doorway then came in, closing the door behind her. In a whisper, she said, "You never told me what happened, by the way. I was waiting for your call so I could hear all about your big night. You did have a big night, didn't you?"

I blushed to a deep fuchsia and said nothing.

"That good, eh?" she said.

"No, it's uh…"

"Oh. Oh, I see. That BAD."

"No. It's like this…"

And then I told her about the full sexual orchestration minus the one instrument.

Her face went as blank and cold as a tombstone, and then her jaw muscles clenched slightly. I waited for the explosion. "I hope you told him to get lost. That coward. Listen, Miranda. Forget him. He's a rich, famous, talented piece of crap."

"But it's not like that. Can't you see it means he's faithful to the person he's officially with? He's just got principles, that's all."

"Principles? It could mean he's just plain old kink-o-rama, Miranda." But she could see I wasn't going to be convinced. "Sure, right. Well, thanks for filling me in. Something Kurt Hancock is NOT doing for you, might I add."

"It won't be forever," I said.

"It's deranged." There was another long pause. "Listen, Miranda. There's been a little gossip around the chorus…"

"What a surprise," I said sarcastically.

"I wanted to tell you what I heard but I don't really know…"

"What? What did you hear?"

"Well, it's…uh…"

There was a banging at the bathroom door. Collin's voice on the other side said, "Finish the committee meeting, would ya? Gotta take a leak."

Tina shook her head. "Kurt will be at your door in two

seconds. I don't want to spoil your party with dumb gossip. I'll tell you some other time."

We filed out of the bathroom and into the living room.

I was dying to know what she'd heard but I rearranged paper napkins and tried to look as though I were above gossip.

There was another moment of silence and then her voice, at first tiny then getting louder, trickled out in a mock country-and-western whine, "I'm a lonely ole olive who's got no pimento, no, ain't got no pimento…jest a dyin' ter git stuffed…"

"Oh, shut up, Tina," I said.

"Yes'm, ma'am." But she continued crooning. When she was being like that, I almost preferred her bad moods.

I made a last frenzied check of the apartment, whizzing around like a hornet that had just been swatted. Tina sniped in the background. "Jesus Christ, Miranda. You'd think you were entertaining the friggin' pope. But it's only Kurt Hancock, or should that be Kurt HAND…COCK."

"Shut up, Tina," I hissed.

"Miranda Lyme, would you stop jumping around? You're driving me nuts. You know why you're so nervous? You're not getting enough pimento in your diet."

"Enough what?" asked Collin.

"Nothing," I said.

Tina went on, "If I had some Xanax with me, I'd force it down your throat."

Collin settled back into the couch and said, "Can have some of mine if she likes. Or I got a little Golden Glory if she wants to try a different kind of buzz."

We both stared at him.

He shrugged, pulled a Baggie full of multicolored pills and capsules out of nowhere, and said, "Okay, so Golden Glory's not your ideal hit, I got some Pepper Kitten and some Moonbeam. Hey, but it's okay, man, they're…like… herbal…natural."

Tina snapped, "Natural, Collin? That's good. That's really good. That's like saying, 'Here eat some of these berries I picked in the woods. I don't know what they are and I don't know what they're called but they won't hurt you. They're natural.'" She looked at me and went on in her best Dolly Parton voice, "City boys. Don't know their nature from their asses."

Collin shrugged again and put the Baggie away. "Hell, Tina. All my product is top quality and tested by yours truly."

The Baggie didn't really surprise me. Tina had mentioned that Collin was a walking drugstore and supplier to the stars. There was usually enough nervous singers' energy up on that stage to light up the city of Vancouver, and Collin could always be counted on to give their stage fright an extra little wallop.

Outside my door, in the hallway, there was a sound like thunder and cackling hyenas. It crescendoed at my door. The buzzer went. I was about to answer when Tina got up and said, "No, I'll open it. You don't want to look too eager. Actor's task. Do something unimportant and try to look like you don't care. Go fiddle with a nutcracker or something."

I did as I was told and went to hide in the kitchen. A second later, I could hear the door open and Tina say, still in her Dolly Parton voice, "Maestro. And Peter. And Ellie. Y'all brought your entourage. C'mon in." I could hear her add, "Care for a *stuffed* olive, Kurt?"

They'd all arrived at once, the entire upper echelon of the opera crowd. They poured into my living room. Kurt immediately went over to the most comfortable armchair (a Salvation Army bargain with an Indian spread thrown over it) and sat down. He radiated kingliness and apart from a little nod and raised eyebrow in my direction, he was playing the role of the conductor who didn't really know the hostess (me!) all that well.

As if we'd never fallen on top of each other into that very chair and tumbled off and rolled around the floor where his

Timberlands were now so casually planted. But I knew how fussy he was about his own rules and I was willing to play the game. I ignored him right back.

Kurt was so stupid. One minute he risked being seen alone on the street or in a restaurant with me, the next he was ignoring me at *my* party. Surely everyone must have known about us by then.

Tina kept going up to him with platters and making remarks like, "*Cock*…tail sausage, Kurt?"

The two heavyweight stars, Ellie Watson and Peter Drake, had headed straight for the buffet, chirping with joy at the sight of all the food. They dug right in and within minutes, their enormous arms were intertwined and they were feeding each other tidbits like the most embarrassing of lovers.

I stared at them, my jaw sagging a little, then I went over to them and said, "But I thought you two hated each other. Don't you?"

"Aye, we do an'all," said Ellie, and looked at Peter. The two of them giggled fatly. "An' we especially hate each other when those media wankers are around. They can't wait to catch us with a cobb'on," she added.

"But your fights are famous. You're so awful to each other. Always," I protested.

"I think we give our public their money's worth, don't you? Another little shrimpy, Smellie?" said Peter.

"Oooo aye, Petie. Mmm, looovlay." Then she turned to me. "Looovlay nosh, Miranda, just loovlay."

"Thanks."

I left them to their piggy heaven and went back to Kurt.

He was being entertained by the first violin, Iris, a sloe-eyed divorcée with a whole bunch of problems that took the form of her teenage children. I snuck in behind her and eavesdropped as she complained to him. "You know what the conversation was with my daughter and her friend the other day? I mean, these are fifteen-year-old kids. And they're saying to each other, 'Who's your lawyer?' Your lawyer. Okay, so, yeah. My fifteen-year-old daughter totaled the car. And worse, she just walked away from the accident. They said it was like a kind of amnesia. But it's not her that's paying *her* so-called lawyer, it's me."

"Bloody hell. Teenagers, eh?" said Kurt.

I wondered if Iris knew that Kurt himself had been the worst sort of teenager, giving his parents snow-white hair before he'd hit nineteen. He listened to Iris as if he'd been Mr. Conservative Golden Boy all his life, and not the little juvenile delinquent that he'd really been, getting pissed and stoned out of his mind with his prep-school buddies, defacing statues and tormenting pigeons in most of London's finer parks.

One day, if our relationship ever got off the ground, I would have to talk to Kurt about children, inform him that we would have to wait until we were both very, very, very sure.

Not that there was any chance of an unwanted pregnancy at the moment. Dammit.

Over Iris's shoulder, I made a face at Kurt. A flicker of a smile crossed his lips then he ignored me again.

A wave of anxiety washed over me.

It wasn't going at all the way I'd planned.

I went over to talk to a pair that Tina and I secretly called the Meow sisters. They weren't women, but a couple of chorus tenors named George and Brandon. It was amazing how much they resembled felines. George was dark and Brandon was blond, and they were both sleek, preening and self-absorbed, always, always landing on their feet. Not only did they share candlelit meals and household linen, but also a taste for extreme and ruthless dissing. In the whiny voices that had earned them their nickname, they were heartily bashing away at a restaurant they'd recently visited.

"Glop," said Brandon. "It was glop with a garnish."

"My filet mignon was filet of work boot, if it's any consolation, and the waiter was rude. But a nice little piece, I have to say. What he needed was a good whipping," said George.

"George. Brandon," I whispered. "Have you two no shame? Don't you ever NOT do it?"

"No, Miranda. Never. We are filters of style and good taste. We do it for the good of posterity," said Brandon.

"To improve the quality of life for generations of morons all over the planet," said George, elegantly sipping his wine.

I watched George watching Kurt go out on my tiny balcony with the concertmaster. Then he said in lowered tones, "Now, tell me how you managed to get the maestro to your party."

I would love to have told him how I'd extorted the promise out of Kurt, threatening to broadcast our relationship all over town if he didn't show up. But I said vaguely, "Everyone was invited. I'm surprised that he actually came."

"Well, I happen to know he's having an affair," said George smugly.

"Oh, really?" I tried to look surprised. "And who's the lucky woman?"

"Who said it's a woman? The details still have to be verified, but I'll have the goods soon enough. My smut detector says he is definitely fooling around."

I was relieved and disappointed. Kurt and I had been fairly careful. But I knew the center couldn't hold, that I would quickly get tired of careful, of always looking over my shoulder, of making our ridiculous separate exits and entrances.

"Hey, what's going on here? Who were you talking about just now?" Our conversation was butted into by Marian, a chorus soprano who was nudging middle age, slightly hysterical about it, and definitely in bad denial. Her hair was cut short in that look of ordered choppy chaos, and dyed white blond. She dressed like a teenager, in lowslung wide flare jeans, her bare midriff showing off lax and accordionated skin, her tie-dyed top stretched obscenely over her sagging bust.

It's hard to tell someone that gravity is a force to be respected, but Marian needed to be told. You got the feeling that Marian was plotting something, an escape into another more youthful dimension, and that the bland conservative husband and daughter she always left at home were not part of her plan. I had the idea that Marian wanted her plan to include Kurt though, because she'd been throwing herself in his path ever since he'd started conducting in Vancouver. He'd even complained to me about her.

We were interrupted by Tina. She tilted her head toward the far side of the room and said to me meaningfully, "You've got more guests."

There was Patrick Tibeau standing in my kitchen area. In one hand, he was holding a bottle of wine, and in the other, he was holding the tiny porcelain-skinned hand of one of the most beautiful women I'd ever seen. She was petite, with short dark hair and large aquamarine eyes. Wolverine eyes.

I went over to them. "Hi, Patrick. Glad you could come."

Patrick didn't let go of the little hand as he made the introductions. "Miranda, this is Evie Marcelle, my girlfriend. Evie, Miranda Lyme."

I knew then I should have said to Patrick when I had run into him in the supermarket, "By the way, Patrick, if you're planning on bringing the world's most beautiful woman, would you please make her wear a paper bag over her head and have her stand in my hall closet for the duration of the party?" but it must have slipped my mind. Instead, I mustered what I thought was a very cheerful "Hi, Evie," plucked the wine bottle out of Patrick's hand and directed them to the living room and the buffet. People were filling plates and eating, perching awkwardly or just standing.

I realized I needed more chairs so I grabbed my keys and headed down to the basement and the storage lockers. I had six folding chairs parked behind all my junk. I waded through the dusty mess and started to shift boxes. It took me at least fifteen minutes to pry them all out and wipe them down with a rag. I looped them over my arms and staggered back up the stairs toward my apartment.

I was proud of myself. The noise that resounded through the hallway was the noise of a successful party.

I staggered back into the living room with the chairs and set them up. It was then that I noticed that Kurt was no longer on the balcony. He wasn't in the living room, either. I thought, aha, he's waiting in the bedroom. I'm supposed to read his mind and go in there and then he'll ambush me and… I was building up this nice little fantasy as I approached the bedroom. Everybody's coats were heaped up on the bed. He wasn't in there, either. No one was.

And then I had a dismal thought.

I began to burrow through the coat pile like a dog looking for a favorite bone. Jackets and scarves flew everywhere, but Kurt's long brown leather coat with the suede collar and hip little pocket buckles was nowhere.

Then I checked the rest of the apartment.

He was gone. And Ellie and Peter had gone with him.

Tina, anticipating my disappointment, came over to me. She said, "Peter told Kurt that it was time to go."

"He what? Well, who does he think he is, anyway? Just who is Peter? Just a tenor," I snapped.

Tina said, "He's *the* tenor, Miranda. You know what tenors are like. Sopranos are a dime a dozen but you can't afford to upset the tenor, especially not if he's as famous as Peter."

"Oh, right. Good. Fine. Why don't we just do away with female singers altogether, like the good old days, and go back to using *castrati*. Here, line up some men and I'll do the honors." I brandished a cheese knife.

Tina ignored me. "Then Ellie agreed that they might as well get out of here because once all the cashews had been picked out of the mixed nuts, there was no reason to stay."

"Oh, Jesus. I can't believe he went with them. He didn't even stay half an hour. That is so infantile, letting Peter and Ellie decide for him."

"I told you he isn't worth it."

I was frustrated after all the trouble I'd gone to, and I was going to say so, but all that came out was a croaking sound.

Tina had an I-told-you-so tone. "Listen to you. It's getting you in the voice. Now, isn't this just the kind of thing Madame Klein is always warning her singers about? Not letting your private life interfere with your voice?"

"Yeah. Madame Klein wants us wrapped in cotton batting and put away for concerts and performances."

"She'd prefer it if we lived in a convent and were allowed out on a day pass just for singing lessons."

I said, "Well, Oskar died a long time ago. She probably doesn't even remember what love is like."

I went over to the buffet and poured myself another vodka. At that moment, the buzzer sounded. I ran to the speakerphone and picked it up hopefully. Maybe he'd come back. He'd only left because he'd forgotten to bring me a nice gift, some flowers or chocolates or diamond bracelets, and of course he'd rushed out to make amends.

"Kurt," I said breathlessly.

"It's Lance," said the voice at the other end. "Who did you think it was?"

"Oh, Lance. I…ah…said…flirt. I was telling my friend she's a flirt."

"Miranda," said Lance's voice, "are you going to buzz me through this door or are we just going to chat on the speakerphone all night?"

"Yes, yes, sure, sorry. Apartment 306, third floor. Come up."

I was pleased that Lance had come and went out into the hallway to wait for him. After a minute, Lance appeared at the top of the stairs, not out of breath at all. Not that he was old. He was only thirty-four, a year younger than Kurt, but some of my younger, chubbier opera friends had arrived at the top of my stairs huffing and puffing.

"Miranda." He came up to me with his smooth walk and pulled me into him. He looked good, in veteran chic khakis, trimmed beard, long curly hair and white-skinned Greek-looking face. For a flash, I wished Kurt could be less uptight and British, and more like Lance.

"You look good enough to eat," he said.

"Don't torment me, Lance. Come inside and help me drink everything wet."

"Hmm. Problems?"

"You could say that."

"Is it something to do with that bastard you're involved with?"

"How did you know about… ?" I smiled. "You almost got me."

"Give me points for trying. You're upset."

"You're not supposed to be able to guess."

"It's written all over your face."

"Is it?"

"That's the face of a frustrated woman."

"Well, it's nothing a little more vodka can't fix," I said.

A group had formed around Patrick Tibeau and Tina. Tina was gesticulating wildly and provoking him, throwing out old Cold Shanks names and locations. It was logical. Patrick Tibeau was *the* Patrick Tibeau.

Lance leaned against the wall with a beer in his hand and listened with a concentrated look on his face. I drifted over toward the armchair which had just been vacated and sat down.

Tina was laughing and waving her hands and Patrick was leaning into her desperately trying to explain something through his laughter. "No, no, you've got it all wrong, Tina. Now just let me start from the beginning. I was making a film…"

"That's what they all say," laughed Tina.

"No, it's true."

"A likely story," said Tina.

"All I needed was a backdrop that would look sort of Palladian and pastoral. There was that bit of white wall near the school's entrance and some reasonably elegant bushes. My girlfriend was playing…"

"Your girlfriend?" squealed Tina. "You had a girlfriend? We always thought you were one of those dorky wieners who was heavily into solo sex."

Patrick was laughing and wincing at the same time, then said, "Just let me set the record straight on that count. Mary was older than me by at least eight years, and divorced."

Evie, who had been miles away, looking out the window and fingering a glass of red wine, came crashing back to attention and said, "Mary? You never told me about a Mary."

Patrick sighed. "Sorry, forgot."

"Forgot?" Then she laughed. It was that melodic self-assured laugh that the world's most beautiful women often have.

"The film I was making was pretty awful, now that I think about it. A typical first effort. Gotta start somewhere. Fortunately, nobody's ever going to get the chance to see it. It was about a woman who's going crazy, sort of a *Juliet of the Spirits* meets *American Beauty*." He grinned. "I thought I was being so surreal. I had this scene. I was set on having a lot of torches and greenery. The torches must have sent out some sparks, and man, does the sap in those bushes burn. Then some of the burning stuff started to fly around and the roof caught fire. I told Mary to run, just get out of there. It would have been very bad news if they'd found her at the scene of the crime, so I stayed to try and put the fire out but wasn't too successful. Nobody believed it was an accident."

"Gee, Patrick, it's too bad it *was* an accident," said Tina, "because we all kind of liked your seriously criminal image. But the older-woman part. Now, *that* restores some of your allure."

He was looking up at the ceiling as he spoke, his eyes glinting black. "Mary. I haven't thought about her in a while. Mary is one of those experiences that I've sort of locked away in a corner of my mind. She was important for me."

Evie smiled again and gave Patrick an almost maternal look.

He went on, "There was something about what she projected, her longing, that inspired me to start making films. I needed an actress and Mary needed someone."

I half stuttered, "But you were only about…what…sixteen?"

"Yeah. I was always encouraged to go with my feelings. My parents were quite liberal about it. They pretended not to know. But it must have been a grueling time for them."

"Well, it's only a little illegal. Old Mary was robbing the cradle," I said.

"And I shall be eternally and deeply grateful," said Patrick with a nice lecherous smile.

A pair of hands rested on my shoulders. Lance was standing behind the armchair. I looked up at him. He seemed so serious, as though he had a terrible secret to divulge but couldn't.

"So that's when they caught you and put you in the slammer," said Tina.

Patrick laughed. "Right."

As they bantered, Lance's hold on me got tighter.

"So what was it like, Pat? Wearing the striped pajamas, I mean?" asked Tina.

"Tina watches a lot of Cartoon Network," I informed Patrick.

"Yeah, right. Striped pajamas and tin cup. They sent me to a kind of outdoor-survival program. It was like Outward Bound with a few more cultural features. It was really hard at first, but now I realize that it was the best thing that ever happened to me. That's where I met my first important teacher, the one that got me to make films in a serious way. If I'd known it was going to be so useful, I would have burnt down Winnie Churchill High the day I set eyes on it."

"Winnie Churchill was pretty awful, wasn't it?" I said.

"The best thing about it was finding ways to escape from it," said Tina.

"Escaping Blackmore, you mean?" said Patrick.

Tina and I sent up a whoop of recognition.

"The vice principal. You have to wonder if he got any real work done. He used to drive his car through the surrounding neighborhood during school hours looking for escapees and victims," I explained.

"And smokers," added Tina.

"Tina and I always had music festivals to sing in. That was one legitimate means of escape," I said.

"Actually, I did a lot of extra music festivals in Bogus, B.C.," admitted Tina.

"Yeah, I invented some myself."

Patrick said, "I saw you girls sing a few times. You were both quite good."

"You did? We were?" we chimed in unison, always grateful for any extra ego buffing.

"Miranda's going to be a star," said Lance solemnly.

There was an awkward silence. The mood in the room had changed instantly.

Caroline and the Sasquatch had arrived. Like a pair of big bluebottle flies in the ointment, or in my case, flies in the spectacular rum-and-cream cake with the hyperglobal and transgenic fruit.

Caroline had changed out of her lumberjack shirt and now had on a pair of ripped stressed jeans and a skimpy T-shirt with Che Guevera's face plastered across her tits. And the Sasquatch had made the polite gesture of putting a clean snood over his dreadlocks. I only hoped he would be able to keep his shirt on during the party.

"Hi, Caroline. Dan," I said flatly. "Get yourselves a drink."

What else could I say? With Kurt gone, I felt like the captain of a sinking ship. Might as well make the most of it.

Somebody had changed the music. The rhythm picked up and some cramped dancing started. I was heading down the road to Liquid Oblivion, so it didn't matter much to me that there seemed to be a kind of jungle drum among Caroline's friends, a native telepathy that transmitted the address of any free lunch going. Because after half an hour or so, they all started to show up.

Just before my blood alcohol went stellar, I counted a total of four more dreadheads, two shrub babes, three droopy-sleeved dropouts from grunge boy bands, thirteen nose studs, eight tribal tattoos and twelve more random body mutilations.

The very last fragment of memory from the party that shone out through the haze was when the people started to spread out and a lot of them had migrated into my bedroom. One of the dreadheads was standing by my bookcase reading out the title of each book and nearly choking with laughter, giving his little critique of my choices.

"Love stories. Romances," he howled and sneered, "Chick lit. Wedding pornography."

Patrick had come into the bedroom just in time to hear the comments. "You don't think love is important?" he asked.

"Love is a crock," said the dreadhead.

"Well," said Patrick, "it depends how you define it. How big or small you decide to make it."

I had no idea what he was talking about.

Patrick went on, "You think politics, for example, has nothing to do with love, but isn't it all the same story in the end? It's just a love story between a man and his country. Or a man and his position of power."

"Or between a boy and his favorite nude beach," piped up George on entering the room.

"We're not forgetting you, George," I said as the coats on the bed begged me to stretch out on top of them.

"Between a village tribe and its sacred mountain," said Patrick.

"Between a girl and her box of chocolates," came Tina's voice.

Patrick went on, "It's a pretty big word. Who knows when it's the difference between love and desire or possession. Maybe there is no difference. Once we've obtained what we desire it transforms, maybe we don't care anymore. So having it means losing it at the same time. But one thing I'm sure of, it's all about some kind of passion, about obtaining and hanging on to what we love or think we love. The thing that makes it all so complicated is the reaction from trying so hard to obtain or keep the love object…at least, that's the way I see it."

"You've had enough to drink, Pat," said Evie, taking the glass out of his hand.

But everyone else was nodding vigorously. Except the dreadhead. He was pouting like a kid who'd just lost all his marbles in one round.

After that, it all got a bit blurry.

Somebody suggested that we all get out of the apartment and go dancing, and by then I wasn't interested in limiting the damage. We left Caroline, the Sasquatch and friends to devour all the food, then we piled into cars and taxis and headed down to Anastasia's.

At least, I think it was Anastasia's.

I had a vague recollection of bodies gyrating and extremely loud music, of glittery exotic women and the sound of tiny bells. Anyway, those were the images that were roving through my dreams just before I woke up.

When I opened my eyes the next morning, I was in my own bed and facing a set of broad male shoulders that definitely weren't Kurt's.

Chapter 8

I watched the back and shoulders rhythmically move up and down indicating a deep sleep.

"Omygod, omygod, omygod," I mouthed mutely to myself. Hard as I tried, I couldn't remember what had happened the night before.

My tongue felt like the hallway carpeting in a rent-by-the-hour hotel and I was stiff all over.

I started to touch my body. I wasn't naked, because my clothes were digging into me in the strangest places. I lifted the covers and looked down at myself. I was wearing orange chiffon see-through pants with a gold spangly belt. There was a broad expanse of bare stomach. A string of tiny bells circled my waist. I had on a low-cut push-up bra covered with large gold sequins.

And then I saw what it was supposed to be.

A belly dancer's outfit.

When I tried to edge off the bed, I jingled. The body on the other side of the bed groaned and rolled over to face me.

Oh. My. God.

Who was this guy?

Gorgeous, a gorgeous stranger.

Where had I picked him up?

And what had we done?

The body stiffness and the generally hungover feeling did not promise good behavior.

And then, as if things weren't bad enough, I could hear voices from somewhere outside my bedroom door. One of them was Caroline's and the other was a man's. But it wasn't the Sasquatch speaking.

It was Kurt.

Oh. My. Double. God.

He must have let himself in with the key.

I jumped up from the bed, flew to the closet, shoved my feet into a pair of black boots, pulled my long red trench coat over the belly dancer's costume and belted it tightly, then zipped out of the bedroom closing the door very, very quickly. I nearly bowled Kurt over in the hallway.

"Kuuuuurt," I sang out.

I had him by the elbow and was shoving him toward the front door, babbling fast. "I was just on my way over to your place. C'mon, let's go out for breakfast. I'm absolutely starved. Famished. There's this great new place just down on the corner, two seconds from here."

He didn't have a chance to protest because I just kept pushing him, talking, chattering mindlessly all the way out to the street.

"Famished," I repeated. "Wasn't it a great party? I thought it was a real success, all considered. The best parties are when the police have to be called. I thought all those people would never leave. What time is it anyway, Kurt?"

"Twelve-thirty," he said dryly.

"No wonder I'm so hungry."

"Miranda?"

"Yes?"

"Do you realize you're tinkling?"

"Oh…ah…yes…it's a…surprise. For you."

I stepped back into the deep recess of a doorway, undid my belt and allowed him a peek at my belly dancer's costume.

He grinned broadly and I have to say he looked very enthusiastic. "I hope you're planning on performing a little *Salome* for me."

"Oh, definitely," I said.

At the restaurant, I had to keep up the pretense of being famished. I got Kurt talking about his early life as a childhood prodigy. It was one of his favorite topics and he talked about it as though it were one of the wonders of the modern world. He expounded while I tried to remember the details of the night before and exactly how the stranger had ended up in my bed. But hard as I concentrated, it just wouldn't come into focus.

I'd ordered a huge breakfast to keep the lie going. The waitress brought it and set it down before me while my stomach roiled and rose. The eggs on the plate stared up at me like a pair of accusing, runny, hyperthyroid eyes.

And then, through my private fog, I heard Kurt say, "It looks like Wayne."

That was the stranger's name. Wayne.

I sat bolt upright and glanced quickly at the restaurant entrance. "Who?"

"I said it looks like rain. Do wake up, Miranda, darling. You're a bit of a dozy cow today."

After I'd mushed the entire breakfast around my plate without actually eating any of it, Kurt paid the bill and suggested that we go back to my place. All I wanted to do was get Wayne out of my bed then die the agonizing death of the profoundly hungover.

So I told him, "We won't be able to do anything."

"Why not?"

"Caroline's having a committee meeting for her THA group."

"THA? What's that?"

"Tree Huggers Association," I said.

Kurt was British. What did he need to know about tree huggers?

I went on, "They're hard-core shrubbies all of them. With a mission to change the world. We'd hardly feel comfortable with a roomful of Trotskyite green granola heads spilling their guts and spouting shrub policy just outside my bedroom door. We'd have to pretend we weren't in there. We wouldn't be able to make any noise, and that wouldn't be any fun, would it?"

"Mmm. Perhaps not," he said.

Again, it came down to Kurt's long list of sneaking-around etiquette. It was okay to be seen in restaurants. Singers and conductors were always having business meetings in restaurants. It was not okay to be seen going in and out of apartments or hotel bedrooms. Not together, anyway.

"Look," I said. "How about if you head right back to your hotel and I'll wait twenty minutes then join you there."

I knew what his reaction would be. He was so uptight about any whiff of scandal that he went for it.

It was the first time I'd ever stood him up. I watched him go, and then I ran home. On the way, I tried to get Wayne in focus.

We'd met up at Anastasia's. That was it.

It was coming back to me. Tina had pointed him out last night on the dance floor at Anastasia's and said, "Hey, that's Wayne from our first-year English class." I didn't remember him. Then she said, "You must remember him. Wayne was majoring in Foxes and Babes."

The memory of the rest of the night and the deed itself just wouldn't come.

When I entered my bedroom, Wayne was still sleeping. He hadn't budged.

I carefully pulled back the covers. It was impossible to ignore his assets. He had a body that was so hard you could bounce tennis balls off it. His curls were even more sun-

bleached and enticing. And he had that general air of good
health and eagerness that promised a very good time. With
a pang of regret, I gripped his shoulder and shook him hard.
"Excuse me, excuse me. Wayne. Wayne. Wake up. You have
to wake up. RIGHT NOW."

His head shot up, eyes wide open.

"It is Wayne, isn't it?"

"It is indeed," he yawned. "Hi…uh…uh…babe."

Hmm. The greeting of a man who couldn't remember
the name of his pickup.

I tried to be diplomatic. "Listen, I just want to know one
thing. Did we do it or not?"

He laughed. "We still gotta get it on, babe." He reached
out and traced a delicate circle around my exposed navel.

"Right," I said, shivering slightly.

"Sure, sweetheart. I didn't think it was fair to take advantage of a girl who was definitely shit-faced. And I mean plastered right out of her skull. Like, now you see her, now you
don't. I thought we'd have more fun if we waited till we had
our energies back. Got any OJ in the house?"

He lunged across the bed in a halfhearted attempt to pin
me down. I pushed him away impatiently. Something very
scratchy was digging into my skin inside my bra. I reached
in and pulled out a folded twenty-dollar bill.

"Love the costume, girl. Can't wait to take it off you, sequin by sequin."

"That…ah…um…would be…" I couldn't say I wasn't
interested, so I left open a tiny window of opportunity.
"Okay," I said. "And I'm really looking forward to it, too,
Wayne, but there's a hitch."

"What's that?"

"First you have to tell me my name."

He sat up and looked at me incredulously. "Hey, babe…
that's not…"

"Not fair? Is that what you're going to say?"

"Well…"

"I think it's pretty fair."

"Aw, now listen, sweetheart."

"All you have to do is tell me my name."

"Um…" His expression became serious and determined. "Monica? Patty? Ashley? Courtney?"

"Oh for crying out loud, do I look like an Ashley or a Courtney?"

"Well…"

"Out. Out of my bed."

I felt very humble that night at the theater. Kurt was mad at me. He avoided my gaze and behaved very haughtily.

The other chorus members told me it had been a great party, and that they had especially enjoyed the last part when we'd all stormed Anastasia's and then I'd just gone out to find the bathroom and come back dressed in the belly-dancing outfit. Apparently, I'd stolen it from the closet where the costumes were kept for the drinks waitresses who worked there. Then I'd gone on to do some very provocative dancing on top of a few tables, and started to collect ten- and twenty-dollar bills as I moved through the gathering audience and the men had tucked them into my clothes.

According to Tina, it was somewhere at that point that Wayne had attached himself.

And I didn't remember any of it.

Oh. My. Triple. God.

That was it. No more parties for the next decade. And no more booze. Ever, ever again. I'd been lucky to get off lightly but my alter ego seemed to have a life of its own. I couldn't handle it.

I had to look after myself.

To prepare my body to be given to music.

One more night like that and I'd be giving my body to science.

After I'd washed off all the stage makeup and changed into my street clothes, I lingered in one of the bathroom cubicles until everyone else had gone. Then I left the theater and walked toward my bus stop. A taxi was creeping along beside me. When I reached the curb to cross the street, its back door opened and an arm reached out and yanked so hard at my coat I nearly fell sideways.

"What the hell do you think you're doing?" I yelled into the taxi.

In the back-seat gloom, I could just make out Kurt. He ordered me to get in. I did as I was told.

I was now facing a very angry-looking man. Even though it was dark in the taxi, I could see that he was that nice shade of apoplectic purple.

"Where were you? I waited all afternoon," he bellowed.

Fatigue and hangover made me seem calmer than I was. I said, "I couldn't make it. Something came up." It wasn't a lie. That afternoon, just before I fell into my bed, most of the contents of my stomach had come up.

In his best conductor-as-world-dictator tone, he went on, "I asked you where you were. Now answer me."

"I'm sorry. But there was an emergency. And besides, you said you would come to my party. I expected you to stay. You left practically before you got there. You shouldn't have bothered taking your coat off."

Kurt's words came fast and cool. "You wanted me to come. I came."

"Oh, thank you for blessing us with your presence, Your Royal Highness. While you're up there chatting on your direct line with God, put in a good word for me, would you? Your word is so much more important than mine." I made bowing and groveling motions in his direction.

"Would you bloody well stop doing that? I just wish to know how you could take your actions so lightly, Miranda? Do you realize how precious my time is? I can't afford to waste it. Not a minute of it."

"Don't lecture me, Kurt," I snapped. He sat back a little in his seat, surprised. "I'm upset, too, okay? I made a beautiful cake and you never even glimpsed it. And I'll have you know it was full of politically incorrect fruit, too. But you didn't stay long enough to see it. You didn't even stay long enough for the sausage rolls to get warm."

His rigid mouth softened into an amused smile. "Now you're the one that's overdramatizing the whole thing."

"I don't think so."

He sighed. It was a truce-declaring sigh. "Come now, Miranda, my love. Calm down. We only have two more days before the closing. Let's not waste them." He was trying to pull me into him but I was resisting. And then I let him close his arms around me. He whispered, "Nobody said it was going to be easy."

"Kurt, there's something I have to tell you."

"What's that?"

"Madame Klein doesn't want me to sing your song cycle."

"Ah."

"She says your music is difficult."

"Does she indeed?"

"I hate getting on the wrong side of her."

"Miranda, my love, I was under the impression that you were going to audition for the ENO and take London by storm."

"I am."

"Well, what Madame Klein thinks will make little difference at that point. You'll be moving into another world."

But it did make a difference to me.

It was long after midnight when Kurt left. I was in the kitchen making myself a cup of chamomile tea when the buzzer went.

"Caroline's thoughtless friends," I grumbled aloud.

Maybe I was being a little unfair. I'd found the apartment spotless the morning after the party.

"Who is it?" I growled into the speakerphone.

"Miranda? It's Pat. Patrick Tibeau."

"Oh." I was in my bathrobe and feeling antisocial. "Come up."

Perplexed, I went back to my mug of chamomile tea. I flung the soggy tea bag into the garbage and took a sip. It was too late for polite social visits. What did Patrick want at this hour?

His knock came a minute later. I went and opened the door.

He had one hand rested against the top of the doorjamb and it was the first time I noticed how really tall he was. His dark hair was loose. He was wearing ripped jeans again and an old denim jacket. His face was slightly damp, as though he'd been jogging, but his expression was relaxed.

"Hi, Pat," I said.

"I know it's late, Miranda, but…"

"Do you want to come in?" I stepped aside.

"No, I won't come in. I was out for a walk and noticed that your lights were still on."

"A walk at this hour?"

"It helps me focus my ideas."

"What does Evie think about that?"

"She's at home. Focusing on sleep."

"Sensible person," I said. "I hope she enjoyed the party. I couldn't tell. She wasn't very talkative."

"I'm not sure she likes it out here in Vancouver. She's an easterner. It's hard for her to adjust. People are more laid-back here. She says they don't seem very dynamic."

"Some people are so laid-back they appear to be part of the vegetation, but apart from those, I'd say the rest of us were pretty energetic."

"You know, it's funny. It took me a while to get back into living in a place with a decent climate and amazing scenery. It was like a guilty pleasure at first, like I didn't want to give in to it because it would distract me from my work. I think Evie's still feeling that. She's still stuck in some practical East Coast mode."

"Just tell her it's possible to get the work done and enjoy the scenery, too. Does she *have* some work, by the way?"

"She's got a few auditions lined up."

My stomach did a little flip. "Auditions? She's not a singer, I hope. We don't need any more competition."

He laughed. "Don't worry. She's an actress." Then he held up three videotapes. "Look. I don't want to keep you. I just wanted to leave these for you. This one on top is the most recent. It's a documentary. The others are fiction." He handed me the tapes.

"Uh…"

"You mentioned when we were all at Anastasia's that you'd like to see my films."

"Oh…uh…right."

He smiled. "You don't remember, do you?"

I grimaced.

"You *were* a little inebriated," he said.

I could feel myself turning scarlet. "You want the truth?"

"The truth's a wonderful thing," he said, holding back a smile.

"Patrick, I was blitzed. I am *never* going to drink again. I swear."

"That's a shame," he said, "because you did this fantastic dance of the seven veils with some paper napkins." His face rounded into a grin. "I didn't know opera singers could move like that."

I winced. "Could we just pretend that I was rehearsing for something? I feel like such an idiot."

"Don't worry, a little bender from time to time helps let off steam. You obviously had some hard-core belly-dancing issues lurking in your subconscious just waiting to rise to the surface."

I smiled.

"Anyway, Miranda, I don't want to keep you. I just wanted to drop those copies off. Gotta go. Let me know what you think of the films."

He was already backing down the hallway at a run, and by the time I started to say, "But I don't know how to get in touch with you," he was gone.

I shut the door and took the videos into my bedroom, where they would be out of reach of Caroline and friends. In my room, I had a small TV and video machine that I used for hashing over my recorded performances. My tapes were all neatly arranged on shelves inside my walk-in closet, out of harm's way. I deposited Patrick's videos next to mine.

Just before I switched off the closet light, I noticed them. My black Missoni shoes. My best, irreplaceable, recital shoes.

They lay on the floor in the corner of the closet, out of their special bag, like a pair of crippled children. Somebody, and it must have been somebody with a lot of strength, had broken off both heels and stuck them inside the shoes.

I could feel a numbness spreading through me. Who would want to do a thing like that? It could have been anyone, given that the entire world had been through my apartment the day before.

When I finally fell asleep, I dreamed I was at a party with hundreds of people. I didn't know anyone. I began to wind my way through the crowd, searching for something, but I didn't know what it was. Everyone, men and women alike, was wearing a brand-new pair of black high-heeled Missoni shoes.

Mike got to me early the next morning, as I was choking down a cappuccino before hitting the floor. "I'm surprised at you, Miranda. In all the years I've known you, this is the first time you ever been late without tellin' me you would be."

I hustled into my apron and Doc Martens. "Really sorry, Mike."

"Yeah. Try to be on time. I can't handle the morning alone."

"I said I was sorry."

"Well, Grace isn't here either today. Off sick. No sand-wiches."

"No sandwiches?"

This was serious.

"So what's wrong with her?" I asked.

"She didn't say."

As long as I'd worked at Michelangelo's, Grace had not been sick a day, nor had she ever played hooky. It put me in a strange mood all morning. The display counter was dismal without her sandwiches.

Out on the floor, the guys from the Vancouver Stock Exchange were snapping their fingers in my direction. I sighed and went over to take their order. The Donald Trump wannabe held up a fifty-dollar bill and said, "This'll be your tip if you leave me your phone number."

I smiled and quickly reeled off the number of a seedy but popular massage parlor that I'd memorized for customers just like him.

I raced from Mike's down to Granville and caught the bus to Broadway. Up the dark, narrow stairwell of the Holistic Cooperative, my Centering Group was already into the third phase.

I'd gotten involved in the Centering Group in my second year of university, when I'd started to suffer from terrible stage fright. I'd suddenly become acquainted with the black maw of terror that arises when a performer has something to lose. I had to get emergency help.

The group's leader, Chi Narnia (don't ask me—she chose those names herself when she was rebirthed) taught us how to find an island of strength and clarity in demanding situations, and draw positive experiences toward us. I was so desperate I would have tried anything to stop having stage fright—prayers, drugs, animal and human sacrifices. As it turned out, Chi Narnia's approach involved the least bodily harm all round *and* it worked. My anxiety nag had been born. It had a shape and a voice, and could be corralled.

Chi Narnia said to the group, "Trust. You must feel the trust spreading through the room. Keep your eyes closed and feel the trusting vibrations of the person next to you."

Chi Narnia was a large-boned woman in her thirties. She had a full red mouth, short curly black hair streaked with gray and large dark eyes. You wouldn't say she was pretty, but she was attractive. She was always serene and slightly smiling. It was unnerving. Nothing was going to change her world.

I put my knapsack on the floor and joined the standing circle of people.

She said, "Now take two steps forward and one back, two steps forward and one back. Feel the rhythm, one two one, one two one. Now start to take bigger steps, keep your eyes closed and let the circle move." As we were doing this little step dance, Chi Narnia kept the rhythm with tiny cymbals attached to her thumb and forefinger.

And then I had just the kind of thought you weren't supposed to have while you were doing any of Chi Narnia's exercises. I imagined somebody quietly sneaking in off the street, rifling through our purses and making off with all our valuables while we were all prancing around in a circle doing the Big Blind Dance of Trust. I couldn't get the picture out of my head and started to giggle uncontrollably.

"Miranda," said Chi Narnia, "share it with us."

"Just a nervous reaction. I've been very stressed lately," I explained.

"It didn't sound like that."

"No, that's all it was," I insisted.

"All right. Trust. Everybody feel the positive vibrations, the trust spreading all around."

We moved on to phase four and were told to spread out on the floor and imagine ourselves on a warm sunny beach, stretched out on the white sand, little puffy clouds in a clear blue sky, the waves washing in and out, seagulls crying over-head, boats gliding on the horizon…

When I woke up, the entire group was walking around, putting on their coats and getting ready to leave. As I strug-gled to my feet and rubbed my eyes, they all stared at me accusingly, as if I'd done something awful, committed some act of desecration. You know. Like drawing a mustache on the Mona Lisa.

Outside the Holistic Cooperative, I waved down a taxi and headed toward the Pan Pacific. It was time to face the music. At least Chi Narnia's warm sunny beach had left me rested for my rehearsal.

I have to confess, I was a little nervous about the upcom-ing session, and having to sing Kurt's opus.

The elevator came. I stepped inside and rode it up to Kurt's room. When I knocked at his door it was ages before he opened up. I began to worry that he might have some-one else in there, some other soprano with better breathing apparatus, if you take my meaning. Because one thing you can be sure of in this business is that there will always be somebody with better breathing apparatus waiting in the wings to take your place.

When Kurt opened the door, his face was long and pen-sive.

"Kurt. Is something wrong?" I asked.

"I was on the phone with Olivia. It's a jolly good thing we have no children. We're…attempting to do this thing civ-illy."

I just nodded and pretended to be serene. It was impor-tant that we all get along, Kurt, Olivia and I, because there were going to be those awkward moments when we all showed up at the same restaurant or concert or art exhibit and would have to at least *pretend* to be on top of the situa-tion. There was no reason why we couldn't all be adult about it? Was there?

Without another word Kurt sat down at the piano and began to play the dreaded introduction. I was as ready as I would ever be. Singers get used to warming up any old place. They're forever humming and lip-buzzing and clearing sinuses in taxis and buses and subway trains, in hallways outside audition halls, resembling outpatients who've strayed from the local psychiatric ward. I was no exception.

I managed to follow the score and come in at the right place. That in itself was an achievement because the opening was very chaotic, a clash of dissonant chords and constantly changing rhythms.

The text to the song cycle, which was called *La Città di Pietra* (The Stone City) was about life in the vast metropolis of London. The poems were written in Italian, by a famous contemporary poet buddy of Kurt's named Guido Castracani, and there were all these observations; of how lurid and colorful the characters on the street were, and how mighty and wet and dank the Thames River was, and how deep and inhuman and sinister the underground was, and how gloomy and endless the rain was, and how mysterious and depressing the fog was. A bit like an Italian version of Eliot's "The Wasteland."

It made me think that Guido Castracani must have been one hell of a homesick Italian when he wrote these poems. Kurt's music reflected Guido's mood quite well. It was gloomy on a grand scale.

Kurt was constantly saying that *Città di Pietra* was a work in progress.

As I positioned myself smartly against the piano (I'd taken pains to match the piano with my gray cashmere sweater with the thin yellow stripe along the edges, an item I'd ripped out of some other woman's hands at the Holt Renfrew sale), I was aware of something expectant in Kurt's face. He was waiting for something from me but I didn't know what. And then as I started to sing, and he started scribbling annotations with his right hand and still playing the bass line with his left, it came to me. He was letting what he heard suggest ways to help him correct and finish writing the end of his piece.

He said again, "I'll remind you, Miranda, that there will be some revisions."

Revisions, my breathing apparatus.

"Not the night before the performance, I hope." I couldn't tell him that I wasn't exactly a quick study. "You know I need time to work it into the voice, Kurt."

"I know. We'll schedule more rehearsals as soon as the piece is finished definitively and I'm satisfied with it. You're doing rather better than I expected," he said, and before I could ask him to go over the section that was all in the middle range—the most uncomfortable part of my voice—he was dragging me toward the tub.

After the Saturday-night closing of *Madama Butterfly,* we took a chance and spent the night together in Kurt's hotel room. I realized it was only the second time Kurt had actually stayed with me all night. Usually he crept away when we'd finished working each other over.

He was the noisiest sleeper I'd ever shared a bed with. He seemed to do a good portion of his conducting and composing in his dreams. That night he sang, and hummed, and conducted with both arms (I had to avoid his sweeping blows all night). He even bellowed at an imaginary percussion section that they had no rhythm and that he would have every one of them sacked before the next rehearsal.

All in all, it was a terrifying experience.

But then if you want to be with a man, you learn to put up with his little quirks, don't you?

Kurt had an early plane out for Dallas where he was conducting some Vaughan Williams and Orff, and I had a lot of things to do before I caught the evening Greyhound for Cold Shanks, so we were forced to say goodbye in the hotel elevator before making our separate exits.

"When will I see you again?" I asked, trying not to sound whiny.

"Sooner than you think. I'll be taking another look at my schedule. There may be some changes. And I'll call you. Often." His face softened and he gently traced a line down my cheek.

"Of course you will," I said. "Because if you don't, I'll call you at home in London, and Olivia would really love that."

He flashed me a warning look.

"Just joking." But I wasn't quite.

He squeezed me tight and gave me a quick kiss before the doors opened, then acting as though he'd never seen me before in his life, he hurried off toward his waiting taxi.

The staff at the front desk weren't fooled at all. They smirked at me knowingly. I just shrugged at them as if to say, "I know, I know, it's ridiculous but he insists that we keep up appearances."

As if they weren't wise to every single moist and sneaky move that went on in their establishment.

Chapter 9

It was Lyle Alcorn, my mother's second husband, who met me when I tumbled off the all-night bus from Vancouver at six-thirty on a dark icy Monday morning. Belinda had stuck with our agreement—she was working my shifts at Mike's and when I got back, I'd be on nonna duty. Meanwhile, the ride had played havoc with my body. Stiff with fatigue after a night of tortured twisting to fit the seat, I was grateful not to have to wait around for a lift.

Lyle's slightly bumbling, oxlike presence took me by surprise as he whipped my heavy carryall out of my hand. He made it look as if it were filled with air. "Hey, Miranda."

"Hey, Lyle."

He gave me a little one-knuckle thump on the shoulder. I knew it was hard for him. He was not a hugging or kissing guy except with my mom and their twins. For the rest of the world, he was a hide-in-the-basement-rec-room-with-a-beer-until-they-go-away kind of guy. He'd managed to win me over in the early days by avoiding me unless I spoke to him first, and his crowning strategy was in not trying to be a father to me and not trying to adopt me. He'd come out of himself a little since then, but he still felt more at home with his toys—car engines, spark plugs, vise grips and table saws—than he did with human beings.

Lyle resembled most people in the town. Cold Shanks had a race of tall, wide-beamed, sunburned, blue-eyed men and women with abundant straw-colored hair. It was as if a whole crew of Norse sailors had been shipwrecked by magic in landlocked Cold Shanks a century or two ago.

I climbed into Lyle's latest toy, a red Honda minivan, and we pulled out of the bus station, heading in the direction of the suburbs and the long, low white house where my mother and I had moved when I was eleven, when she'd married Lyle.

"So, Miranda," said Lyle, his voice thinning out like a worn thread unraveling. "Guess yer doin' all kinds'a singin', gettin' real famous down there in the Couve, eh?" Talking about the opera world still put him under pressure.

I decided to cut to the chase. "I'm going to England, Lyle."

He flashed a worried look at me. "Yer mom won't be too happy about that."

"I know. Don't tell her. I'll tell her myself when I've paid for my ticket..."

"If you need some money, Miranda..."

"No, no. It's okay. I have an audition there in January. I'm getting the money together."

"That mean you might be movin' there? If they like you at the audition, I mean?" Now there was alarm in his voice.

"Only if things work out. If it's worth my while. I have to be back here in March for a concert anyway."

"So you gonna see him? See yer father?"

"That's the whole idea," I said.

Lyle was silent for a while, then he let out a huge sigh, and I thought he was going to say something more, but he didn't. He was quiet all the way home. In the carport, he got my carryall out of the van, we tiptoed into the sleeping house and he put my bag in my old room.

"Thanks, Lyle."

"Sure," he said, and disappeared.

I slid, fully dressed, under the white candlewick spread and rose-covered eiderdown of my old bed. Within seconds, my father was standing at the foot of it. I assumed he'd done a conjurer's trick, making himself small to fit in the trunk I kept there, and then waited for the right moment to pop out. He was dressed in commedia dell'arte costume, as a tatty Harlequin trying to be Rigoletto, but the colors of his costume were soiled and faded, shades of rust, olive green, rose, and gray-blue. The fabric was torn. The makeup on his face was thick and smudgy, making it impossible to see his real features.

"Sebastian?" I said.

He struck an overly theatrical court-jester pose.

I tried again. "Daddy?"

"Are you the new soprano?" he sang at me, and immediately I paid attention to the underlying music, which danced and flashed in greens and pinks, like the northern lights. He's singing a new opera, I thought. I wonder who the composer is?

"I'm your daughter. I'm Miranda. Don't you recognize me?"

"We've been waiting, waiting, waiting for the soprano all goddamn morning," he sang, crescendoing angrily. "We'll have to go on without her. She is an obnoxious diva. She will get the treatment." He made more exaggerated gestures with each phrase.

Whatever was he talking about? The treatment? I began to have my doubts.

"Who are you anyway?" I yelled. "Take off that makeup and show me who you are."

"I am the great Sebastian Lyme," he boomed. The orchestra hiding somewhere under my bed played thunderous sounds that looked like huge purple thunderbolts.

"I want to see who you are. Take off that makeup right now," I insisted.

"It's not in my contract," he sang.

"You're an impostor," I said.

He turned his back to me in a stage huff and refused to sing another note, so I waited and listened to the orchestra. The sound grew warmer and warmer. I grew warmer and warmer until I was broiled and sweating.

I opened my eyes. Sunlight was pouring through the window making everything aggressively pink and striking my face and bed with an intense heat.

I yanked off the covers and lay there, listening.

After the dream, the silence seemed abrupt. I was no longer used to the quiet of grassy suburban streets, nothing louder than the rustle of the last leaves in the wind and the occasional saw buzzing in the distance. I'd grown accustomed to the West End background noise of honking and cussing downtown drivers, the roar and the crash of the Dumpsters, the clacking heels of people coming home from the clubs after a long night.

I stretched out as far as I could on the narrow single bed. The odor was so familiar. It was the odor of plotting my future.

I stood up and started to vocalize right away. As soon as my voice was warmed up, I pulled out all the stops. I don't know what it was about Cold Shanks, why I had to be so belligerently the singer. When I was at home I reverted to some crucial moment of childhood. I pushed and pushed at every point until I was sure my mother would want to slap me. Because at least if she gave me a slap, I would be getting something definite from her. My mother had become so indefinite lately.

At a pause in my vocalizing, I heard a quiet shuffling outside my bedroom door, then some sniggering.

I waited.

Then came more scuffling sounds.

I opened the door quickly.

My twin half brothers were standing there, two identical blond heads, two identical imp faces attached to identical skinny ten-year-old bodies, a collection of scrapes and scabs and bruises and week-old dirt. My brothers had names, Darryl and Danny, but since they were always switching places with each other to cover their crimes, they were more like one person divided into two entities, and everybody just called them The Twins.

One of the twins, and to this day I'll never know which one, held up an economy-size bottle of something they gave to the dogs for worms and said, "That's a real bad bellyache you got, Miranda. Should we call the ambulance?"

"Yeah, should we call the ambulance? Or should we call the veterinarian?"

"Yeah, the veterinarian. Ya sound like a sick hound." They collapsed in spasms of laughter, delighted with their genius.

"Do I know you?" I asked. "Now wait a second. Somebody somewhere told me I had some brothers, but you know what I think?"

"What?" they said in unison.

"I think you're not really my brothers. I heard you were both adopted. But only temporarily."

The two of them looked at each other, suspicious.

I went on, "You see, Lyle and Mom aren't your real parents, you know. The police brought both of you and gave you to Mom and Lyle to keep until your real parents get out of prison. If my calculations are correct, their sentences should be up as of yesterday. They're probably on their way over here right now to take you back to their slum to live with them."

Their two bratty faces started to fill with panic and one

screamed out, "Mom…Miranda said the police brought us…"

They ran off to verify.

I took my time showering, then I got dressed and sauntered into the kitchen.

My mother was at the sink, shoving toothpicks into an avocado stone with thin red-knuckled hands. My mother was a small thin nervous person, with a shock of blond frizz for hair.

"Avocados are cheap to buy, Mom, and buying them is quicker than growing them," I said.

"Oh, Miranda, I wish you wouldn't tell the twins that they…" Her voice trailed off into nothingness. It had been a couple of years since I'd heard my mother finish a sentence.

"The twins need to be told," I said. "Just what are they doing at home on a Monday anyway? Shouldn't they be at school? They sure don't look sick to me."

"Lyle and I have decided that homeschooling might be…"

"Homeschooling?" I squawked.

"They're very rambunctious and the teachers at their school…" Her voice drifted away into nothingness again.

"You don't have to tell me. The teachers can't handle them, right? They've swung from every rafter in the school building, blocked every toilet, done everything they possibly can to make themselves persona non grata."

"It's not that they can't handle them, it's just that…oh…to hell with these stupid…" She dropped the avocado stone in the garbage and wiped her hands with an air of finality.

"What was that you just threw in the garbage? Science class?"

"We were going to try and grow…you know…so that they could see…"

"I think the homeschooling's a bad idea, Mom. Those twins are gonna kill you."

They'd already taken away the ends of her sentences. Who knew what they would take next?

"Well, really, Miranda. They're not going to be kids forever. In just a few years, they'll…"

"Grow up?"

"Of course. You were just like them once. You don't remember but you were exactly…oh…"

"Pay no attention to me, Mom. I'm sure you wouldn't be doing it if you didn't have good reasons. I thought I'd go for a little walk."

"Bundle up. It's cold out there. Your snow boots are in the cupboard by the…and your parka is somewhere…"

"Thanks, Mom. I'll find them."

Downtown Cold Shanks was built in a flat valley. On the outskirts, the river wound through the countryside and the big trailer park where Tina had grown up wound along the river. The valley was locked in on one side by mountains and on the other by the river, beyond which stretched the endless flat miles of grassy grazing land. Cold Shanks had hot dusty summers, cold snowy winters, rattlesnakes and wolves.

The changes since my childhood weren't many, just the recognizable chain stores and fast-food joints you find everywhere in the world, and the new mall, which seemed to be the highlight in everyone's lives these days. But except for those, the place still looked so much the same that it felt like déjà vu whenever I came home.

When I stepped outside, it was sunny and crisp. I strolled along wide suburban boulevards admiring the big leafless trees. It took me half an hour to get to the center of town by foot.

I came to the main street, two rows of low brick buildings with fancy cornices that gave it a hint of big city but weren't quite enough to keep it from looking like the frontier cow town that it was. The main street was trapped in time, stopped somewhere in the sixties. Alongside the banks and insurance companies and other less interesting businesses, there was Muriel's Boutique, a fashion challenge that was heavy on glitter and light on taste, the Golden Galleon Grill, whose owner dressed as a sea captain and had never seen the sea, and the Hair Fair where Cynthia, Tina's mom, worked as a manicurist. The kind of hair that came out of that place was mammoth and put Cold Shanks on the map as the bouffant capital of B.C. There was Lyle's place, The Auto Stop, with its same old yellow-and-blue sign, touched up every few years. Then there was the Little China Emporium, whose owner, Mrs. Yee, peddled kids' toys, wicker baskets, bolts of cloth, oriental jewelry and ghost stories.

That day, I wasn't stopping in any of those places. My mission was to walk by the big picture window in the front of the RCMP station and try to catch a glimpse of Brent (without him seeing me do it), and more importantly, make sure Brent caught a glimpse of me. You know what they say—living well is the best revenge—and I thought I was doing a fine job of getting my revenge by living well down in Vancouver.

I'd had a few boyfriends but Brent was my only heartcrusher to date. I first set eyes on him in Zeppo's. Zeppo's, in my high-school days, was a coffee-bar-cum-club that held talent nights. Brent played his own compositions and accompanied himself on guitar. We all thought he was very hot, with his tall dark presence, his bass voice and his saddog songs about being a loner and movin' on and all that sort of nonsense. And it turned out to be nonsense, too.

I should have wondered at his sudden appearance on the scene. Here was a guy who claimed to have grown up in Cold Shanks but who none of us had ever seen around before then. Who wonders about those little details at age seventeen? We all agreed he was a hunk in August, and when he showed up in my grade twelve English class in September, he was still a hunk but now he was accessible. None of the girls could ignore him because he was just so sure of himself, so much more mature than the other guys. He actually had something that passed for a beard.

I sang at Zeppo's, too, crossover pieces, jazz that would show off my voice. One night, after all of the talent had been sharing coffee and cheesecake at a table, Brent offered me a ride home. I can't say I wasn't squeezing myself closer to him and willing him to get personal with me, so when he offered the ride, I leaped at it.

In front of my house, in the car (an antique Buick that Lyle's automotive eye could not ignore), we got into a big round of kissing. It turned out we had an audience. When I got inside the house, Lyle said, "Cars are great things. A guy's gotta have wheels and a big back seat. They're like…who he is." Then he chuckled knowingly and I just wanted to die.

After that, there was no more parking. The next time Brent gave me a ride home, he and I drove straight into the mountains where he relieved me of my virginity (something I'd been eager to get rid of at the first reasonable chance) in a little mountain refuge he said belonged to an influential uncle. When he took me home, I got him to let me off around the corner.

Our conversations, the rare times that we had them, were so weird, I should have figured it out. He said he was always looking for a party, then he'd get this serious sexy look on his face, make his voice even deeper and say, "You know what I mean? A really, really good party." I wondered what the hell he was talking about. What was he into anyway? Whipped cream and two-headed cheerleaders?

I wanted to say, "But I'm your party," but I stayed silent, because silence was another of the earmarks of my relationship with Brent. He hardly ever talked to me. For a while I consoled myself that he was communicating through his songs, which he sometimes practiced in the cabin. He had a pleasant enough voice, and he played okay, but I'd begun to feel that there was something missing. I let myself think that the songs would be enough, but after a couple of months, the long silences between the songs started getting to me. I would probably have dumped him eventually if he hadn't dumped me first, but I would have suffered afterward.

He did the dumping in a spectacular way, announcing it to me in the locker bay at school so that my homeroom classmates, the most ruthless audience in the world, could hear every word.

I learned that the day after he'd broken up with me he started taking other girls into the mountains, girls who knew where the better parties were happening, I guess. And then he started dumping them, too, at the rate of about one a week, and I'd see them mooning through the hallways at school, looking slightly suicidal.

Brent kept on singing at the talent nights at Zeppo's. I wasn't so impressed anymore. The sight of him made me so mad that I just had to react in some way. I got together with the Nuclear Heads (a group of dweeby computer pals from school), who synthesized some background rock for me, and we put together a song for one of the talent nights at Zeppo's.

The piece was called "Brent, Us Girls All Know That You're for Rent," and I dressed up in gash-and-trash punk fashion and half screamed, half spat the song at him from the platform. A lot of people came up to me afterward and said they enjoyed it and that I should switch my style, that the song had real feeling. It wasn't much on melody, but feeling was the *one* thing it did have.

Brent didn't seem particularly angry or moved one way or the other and I decided that he didn't have emotions, that he was, essentially, a lizard.

And then one night, Mom and Lyle were watching the news and Lyle yelled out to me from the living room, "Hey, Miranda, come here and see this. Isn't that your old boyfriend there?"

They were running a news item on a bust that had been made on an ecstasy lab. It turned out that the Nuclear Heads were also good at science and had found a way to supplement their weekly allowance. Well, you know how it is. All that computer technology and equipment is expensive when you require the best.

There was Brent on the news being herded into the back of an RCMP vehicle. But the connection didn't fit because the Nuclear Heads had never really taken to him or let him into their circle. And a week later, there he was back at Zeppo's again with some lame story about the influential uncle and no charges pending.

It hit me hard. His songs had always lacked sincerity and in the newsreel his acting innocent was just as bad. The part that really offended me was that except for the fact that the Nuclear Heads had given me a hand copying videotapes and burning CDs from time to time, I didn't see how Brent could have thought I was into ecstasy in the first place.

In the news story, when they raided the lab, you could see all the substances that went into those designer drugs. Half of the bags containing the raw ingredients were marked Corrosive. Now, why would I want to swallow toilet cleaner before going to a party?

Brent had used us all, the slimy narc.

So it was vital that every time I came home, I passed by the RCMP station. I could sometimes spot Brent there stuck behind a desk taking care of paperwork, and I took note of how he was looking. I always made sure to slow down in front of the big picture window so that he could see my carefree stride and my aura of excitement, the signs of the great life I was leading as a single girl down in the Couve.

Brent's hairline was receding quickly and although he was still under thirty, he already had a beer gut and a sour expression on his face. Now, you wouldn't think that in this day and age a shotgun marriage could still happen, would you? But according to Lyle, who serviced all the RCMP vehicles, Brent had pushed his luck and seduced the seventeen-year-old daughter of one of his superiors a couple of years after the ecstasy escapade, and now he was unhappily married with three kids, all a year apart in age.

It did my heart good.

That night after dinner while we were washing the dishes, I said to my mother, "Anyway, Mom, have you been working on it?"

"Oh, you mean the…?"

"Yeah. Can I see it?"

"Oh…yes…I just have to…"

My mother fussed a bit longer, this time with a white viscous living sponge that she used to make yogurt.

"Oh, God, you're still feeding Eric." Eric was the sponge's nickname. Now, I just have to say that the trouble with live health food and the reason I never bother with it is that it can really put a damper on your social life. You might find yourself having to say, "Oh, no, sorry, I can't spend the weekend with you in the Bahamas. I have to get home to water my bean sprouts and feed my yogurt culture."

"It's better than…" started my mother.

"Yes?" I said.

But she had fizzled again.

She put the milk away, dried her hands and started toward the basement door. I followed her down to her sewing room.

On the tailor's dummy was her latest masterpiece, a dark red velvet off-the-shoulder evening gown with a floor-length gored skirt. I'd brought the fabric to my mother the previous Christmas and shown her the picture of what I wanted. She'd worked on it bit by bit whenever she found a little time and it was a perfect copy. This was the definitive concert dress, and I'd decided that it was the dress I was going to wear when I sang Kurt's song cycle.

"Mom, you're wasted here. This is fantastic," I said.

"Try it on. I still have to finish all the…"

She unzipped the two zippers and I stepped carefully into it. She did me up. "Miranda, you've lost some…"

It was a little loose on me. This was the kind of dress that needed to be tight to stay up. The only alternative to gaining weight was to glue it to my body.

My mother said quietly, "There's nothing wrong, is there? Is everything okay down there in…is there something you…?"

"Want to tell you about? Everything's fine, Mom. And I do eat. It's just that I've been really busy lately."

I ought to have told my mother all about Kurt, but I sensed she wouldn't approve. She never came out directly and talked about it, but I got the feeling that even after all these years, she still had a bitter taste in her mouth over her experiences with opera people, and in particular, my father.

When my mother was eighteen, she went off to England, determined to work as a costume designer in theater. When she found a job as a seamstress with the Inner London Light Opera Company, it seemed like a dream come true.

For a little while.

My father, who was the company's lead baritone, and a good ten years older than my mother, began to notice the fragile blonde who measured him for cloaks, britches and codpieces, and stitched him up when he got carried away onstage and ripped his costume.

It wasn't long before they were married, living in a two-room flat in Holland Park Road, and expecting me. Four years later, my mother left my father. She told me the age difference was what finished it, but I didn't think that was the whole story. There was a lot she wasn't telling me.

Throughout my childhood and adolescence, I collected bits and pieces of my father and tried to put him together into a whole person. He was in a large trunk at the foot of my bed in Cold Shanks. The trunk contained newspaper clippings, reviews of my father's performances, photos of him in costume, little doodles, letters, notes and old programs, things he'd scribbled while talking on the phone, or drawn on the back of a coaster at the pub, or sent to my mother from abroad.

The old record jackets of my father's vinyl recordings were windows to his world. As a child, I studied them for hours, imagining myself walking into the picture and up to the tall, square-faced, bearded, dark-haired baritone. He was at his best as Don Giovanni. In the recording, he had all the qualities of the dissolute, reckless rake, and the scene where he opens the door to the Stone Guest—Death—and is dragged into hell for eternity, was a dark musical revelation that made my skin prickle all over.

My mother knew I had this stash. I'd taken everything she had of my father and hidden it in my room, and she'd never said a word about it.

I was ten years old when vinyl started to go out of fashion. I panicked. I could see my father slipping away from me. It was the Nuclear Heads who rescued me by converting the old records into CDs.

I was convinced that any talent I might have originated with Sebastian Lyme. All the music that was in me came from him. I spent hours and hours holed up in my bedroom, listening to my father's singing voice and resenting the day my mother left him.

I planned to have him back.

We would sing together.

The marquee would read Sebastian Lyme, baritone, and Miranda Lyme, mezzo-soprano. We would come to be known as an important musical family.

And maybe things would work out with Kurt, too. It wasn't out of the question. Maybe Kurt and I would have our musical fusion and I would improve the pedigree of our musical family with Kurt's contribution. If his genes ever managed to collide with mine, that is.

Chapter 10

Three days later, I was rested and back in Vancouver, standing on the doorstep to Michelangelo's family home.

I'd talked to Belinda on the phone earlier and she and I had decided she needed to be much harder to get. She was already trying out a new job managing another restaurant and hadn't told Mike about it yet. She was going to cut off all work ties and obligations and then deliver her ultimatum to him. She was going to tell him, "Either we have fun when we're together or it's nothing doing. And that means nights, too."

Mike's home was on the edge of Shaughnessy, the central part of well-to-do residential Vancouver. It had taken his family three generations to move into that neighborhood and break more than one housing bylaw. You could see that the original building, a simple two-story wooden family house, had been modest, but the additions had given it the look of a Roman villa squatting on a kerchief of land. Any potential for garden had been asphalted over and replaced with Doric columns, enormous ornate fountains, terra-cotta urns and concrete lions. Mike's entire extended family had been accommodated, and now it lived like the Melandronis, all huddled together in the same fortress, screaming and ranting at each other.

It was Mike who opened the front door that Thursday evening. He looked embarrassed. The men in his family didn't usually go to the door when the bell rang. That was a woman's job.

"Hi, Mike."

"Come inside." He frowned. "Belinda said she had something important come up. Thanks for offering to help out."

"No problem, Mike. You're all right with our price?"

"Yeah, yeah. Don't worry about it. Me and my sisters been alternating for all these months and we're worn out. I figured Belinda wouldn't mind…you know…watchin' Nonna…but," he said, his face screwing itself into a confused scowl.

"She does."

His scowl tightened.

"You could get yourself an old-fashioned Italian girlfriend," I said. "She'd know exactly what to do."

"Naw," said Mike. "That would be a known quantity. Boring. C'mon. She's this way." He led me along the frighteningly spotless hallway of the house to a modern addition that jutted into the backyard.

"Nonna's rooms," he said, opening the door. We entered the blackness.

It reminded me of that old joke—how many Italian/Jewish/Polish/Russian/Greek grandmothers does it take to screw in a lightbulb?

None. They'd rather sit in the dark.

It took my eyes ages to adjust.

Mike had gone over to a corner of the room and was huddled over a tiny woman swathed in black cloth. He shouted at her, "Nonna, the girl's here. Her name's Miranda. She's going to stay with you in the night."

"*Fammi vedere,*" said Granny. *Let me see.*

I stood in front of Granny.

"*Carina,*" she said. "*Meglio di quell'altra.*" *Cute. Better than that other one.*

Then she looked back and forth between me and Mike and said, "*Quando vi sposate?*" *When are you two getting married?*

Then Mike shouted, "Now, Nonna, this isn't Belinda. This is Miranda. You'll like her. She's a singer, Nonna. An opera singer."

"*Opera lirica?*" said Granny, almost suspiciously.

"*Sì, signora,*" I said.

The old woman started to sniffle. She rummaged in all that black clothing, found a white handkerchief and started dabbing at her eyes.

"*Opera lirica,*" she repeated. Then she began to sing a line or two from *La Bohème* between sobs.

I kept my goal brightly in my mind. That silver jet moving through the skies toward London. The Atlantic passing underneath.

Granny stared at me, her glaucous brown eyes at first not seeing and then suddenly clearing and nailing me. She reached out and grabbed my hand, stretched my fingers and flattened them with inhuman strength to look at my palm. Then she studied it carefully. After a few seconds, she began to sob again and clasped my wrist so tightly I had to wrench it away from her.

I stared at my own palm. "What do you see in there?" I asked her in Italian.

But all she could do was sob.

Aiuto! It was going to be a long night.

When I got home the next day, Caroline said, "Your Brit friend, you know, the old one with the snotty accent, kept phoning."

"Caroline, he's only in his midthirties," I protested.

"I know. But he acts like he's a hundred and thirty-five. So he's the one with your *key*." She grinned and wiggled her eyebrows. "I told him I didn't know where you were. I finally had to put the answering machine on. It's full of messages from him."

"Thanks, Caroline," I said.

My sleepless night on the roll–away cot next to the snoring Granny hadn't been for nothing after all. With each message, Kurt had left the number where he was staying, which meant he'd left it about ten times. I quickly dialed.

"Dallas Hilton," said the voice at the other end.

"Kurt Hancock, please."

"I'll put you through."

The room phone rang only once then Kurt's voice said, "Yes?" He sounded distant.

"It's me, Kurt. It's Miranda."

"Miranda. Where were you?"

"Oh, just out partying."

"I see." His tone went from suspicious to bright. "Miranda, I'll be in San Francisco next month. The third weekend in November. I'm conducting two Rossini evenings. I think you'll rather enjoy these singers. Do fly down and join me. I do miss you so."

And? And? Okay.

I could live with just being missed for the time being.

"I miss you, too," I said.

"Then you must come," he said.

"I'll have to look at my schedule."

"Make time. Do it for me."

"I'm not sure, Kurt. I have a budget. I can hardly hang glide down to San Francisco."

"Oh, Lord, silly girl. I'll have a ticket left for you at the airport."

"No, Kurt, you shouldn't—"

"I insist."

"Well, in that case, I can hardly say no, can I?"

"No, Miranda, you can't. I'll see you in November."

The following night, Friday, Tina and I met for drinks in the stain-glassed, ivy-covered comfort of the Sylvia Hotel bar. We were just in time to get the last table with a good view of freighter lights flashing over the black water in English Bay.

"Guess what?" I blurted. "I'm flying down to San Francisco to stay with Kurt for two nights."

Tina took a swig of her beer. She tried to look unimpressed. "When?"

"Third weekend in November," I told her.

"What about work?" she asked.

"I've talked to Mike and he's rearranging the schedule and the Little Ladies don't have any cleaning that weekend so I'm okay."

"Miranda, your brain just sprang a leak."

"What?"

"Your timing is perfect," she said. "Right smack in the middle of the last *Puritani* rehearsals. Remember? They moved them forward."

"Oh shit, oh shit, oh shit."

"Get the maestro to write a note to the principal excusing you from school."

"Tina," I protested.

"I'll cover for you. I'll tell them you've got something. Rabies or strep throat or measles or the plague or dementia. Don't look at me like that. No. It's okay. I'll cover for you."

"Thanks, Tina... Now, tell me that thing you were going to tell me about Kurt."

"What thing?"

"C'mon, Tina, that gossip thing."

She lit up like a jukebox, electric with the information. "Okay, yeah. Now this dirty little tidbit comes from the other side of the country. Remember that Garcia chick who use to sing second sop with the chorus about three years ago?"

I nodded.

"Yeah, well, she still stays in touch with Brandon…"

"George's Brandon?"

"The same."

"Go on."

"She's in Montreal now."

"So?"

"Kurt had a Verdi *Requiem* gig, I think, something with some chorus and soloists and the Garcia chick was doing the soprano solo I guess…although I can't picture it. She has a voice like fingernails on a blackboard and she looks like a dancing pig onstage…"

"Just tell me, will you?"

"So she said that he had got real cozy with the mezzo…"

"He who? Which mezzo?"

"He Kurt. Her Jane."

"Oh, for crying out loud, Jane who?"

Tina went on, obviously enjoying torturing me, "Jane the mezzo, who is not a plain Jane at all, according to the unreliable sources. According to Brandon, who got it from the Garcia chick, who got it from Jane the not-so-plain mezzo, the word is that Kurt Hancock is all over the place."

"What do you mean by that?" I was starting to get an unsettled feeling in my stomach. I was imagining everything, right down to whipped cream and two-headed cheerleaders.

"One in every port. *So* cliché."

"WHAT?"

"He's got a harem," said Tina, arching one eyebrow.

I laughed.

Tina said, "The unreliable word is that he's got one in every town and that he likes to keep them all down. You know. Faithful to him and him alone. Well, you know what these big-shot opera types are like. They've all got their little friends, whatever town they happen to be in. They want their entourage, their harem. They collect women. Some of them collect men and women and whatever weird beast the cat drags in. You're Kurt's Vancouver slave girl."

"That's pretty funny. I know where I can find the costume."

"You don't know that you are, but you are. Really."

"Get off it, Tina. That's just so stupid."

"Maybe it is, maybe it isn't. How do you know what he's doing when he's wherever he is?"

"Dallas and then Chicago."

"Well, how do you know?"

"Well, Tina, for your information I've got miniature microphones planted all over his hotel room and in his luggage. Why is it so important that I know his every move?"

"It's only those in-and-out movements you want to know about. They're the ones that count."

I shook my head and downed my vodka and tonic. "I know he's not doing anything he shouldn't be doing. I know it because I love him. And that means I trust him. I know how you feel about men, Tina. But that doesn't mean everybody else feels the same way. Or acts the same way. I'm determined to make this thing work. I've never wanted anything so much in my life. So ask me about it after San Francisco, okay?"

"Well, you've got it ass backward if you ask me. It ought to be that you trust him because you've sicced a detective on him so you know for sure he's not doing those things. But have it your way."

"I hope I do," I said.

"And there's one more thing," she said.

"What's that?"

"There's a good reason he's leaving you with that empty, hollow sensation."

"What?"

"Paternity suits."

I choked on my drink.

"That's right," said Tina. "And not just one. That's the reason his sperm isn't going anywhere near an egg that doesn't have a marriage contract soldered to it. You do know that his wife has mountains of money, don't you?"

"Kurt told me. But he says it doesn't make any difference."

"Like hell it doesn't. Anyway, seems his DNA is in big demand. He was tricked a while back by some of his slave girls. They must have used the old pinholes-in-the-condom routine…"

"I don't want to hear any more. Jesus, Tina. It's *chorus* gossip. On their own, they're okay, but en masse they're a garburator for petty news items. No story stays intact for a nanosecond."

Tina shrugged. I could see that she didn't want to let me have this one. If I didn't know her better, I would have said that she didn't want me to be happy.

Weeks later and the rehearsals for *I Puritani* had begun. Each production brought a whole new team—new stage director, new conductor, new costume and set designers, new soloists—and there was always the wild rush for the chorus and orchestra (the only constants) to get acquainted with everybody. It was a love-them-and-leave-them world by virtue of the high turnover. I had been lucky to meet Kurt and it was Boris who made me realize it.

Boris, the new stage director of *I Puritani,* lay his head back down on the table and closed his eyes. He appeared to be sleeping. Boris was yet another British director foisted on us by the opera management. He wasn't Russian at all, but the son of militantly socialist parents from Clapham. He had carrot-red hair that sprouted in bristly tufts, not just from the top of his head, but from other parts of his body: ears, nostrils. knuckles, wrists, back and eyebrows. He looked like a human toilet brush.

It was the first of a series of extra technical rehearsals and we were supposed to be Puritans on the battlefield rescuing our dead and injured. Boris's head shot up from the table. He was now awake and screaming, "More snow, more snow, more smoke, more bloody effing smoke."

It may have looked like a freezing winter up on that stage, with all that dry ice smoke and Styrofoam snow, but thanks to some distant designer's obsession with Bertolt Brecht's approach to stage detail, we were wearing heavy wool capes over our wool jackets and full-length wool skirts. The lights brought the temperature to at least forty degrees Celsius up there. Sweat poured off our faces, stung our eyes and soaked our costumes.

"I said BANDAGE, not BONDAGE, you cretinous fools," roared Boris.

Tina and I were cast as a couple of Florence Nightingale types.

As the scene opened, we were kneeling side by side with our heads down, attending to a patient.

"Tina," I whispered. "Are there horses in this production?"

"*Fidelio*, yes, *Aïda*, maybe. This *Puritani*, no," she whispered back. "Why?"

"I could have sworn I saw a black horse in the wings."

"Naw, that's just fatigue you're feeling."

When our cue came, we trundled across the stage with a stretcher to rescue George, our next wounded soldier. We were supposed to treat his wounds then carry him offstage, first making a tricky detour through the other flailing casualties and down to center stage.

Tina and I put down the stretcher, grabbed George's ankles and wrists.

"What a lead ass," muttered Tina as we loaded him in.

George kept shifting his weight in the stretcher and squealing, "Oh fuck, oh fuck you're going to drop me."

There was a lot of dramatic battle music going on at this point and Tina said to me without moving her mouth, "Miranda, could you just put a bandage over that stupid trap of

his, please? George, you and your fat ass amount to a friggin' deadweight and if you don't be quiet and stop squirming around, I'm going to drop my end. In a real battle they
would have rolled you in the nearest ditch and run for it."

George's indignant squeals got louder. "You bitch. I can
feel myself tipping. Get me out of this thing. You're going
to drop me. You're going to hurt me. I've got a bad back."

Boris's voice blasted through the din. "Would the corpse
in the center-stage stretcher kindly SHUT UP? You birds
have my permission to slap him senseless. You in the
stretcher, whoever you are, you have just expired. You are
DEAD. KAPUT. MORTO. DEFUNTO. Do you under-
stand? And that goes for the rest of you who are supposed
to be corpses. Now those of you who are supposed to be
wounded, act wounded, and those of you who are supposed
to die, shut up and DIE, the poxy lot of you."

"Another day, another dollar," muttered Tina.

The Mark Hopkins Hotel. Number One Nob Hill.
I'd made it. Fantastic!

Kurt and I were having an early dinner in Top of the
Mark before he had to conduct that evening. I was dressed
in the periwinkle-blue raw-silk Laura Biagiotti cocktail
dress my mother had copied from an *Elle* magazine and tiny
diamond earrings my mother and Lyle had given me for
graduation. Kurt whispered in my ear as we entered the
restaurant, "Miranda, darling, you look fabulous."

At our table, I kept whirling around and staring at the famous people dining (*pretending* to dine—they all sipped Per-
rier water and nibbled on the world's most expensive lettuce
leaves). Every three minutes I'd lean toward Kurt and say,
"My God, isn't that…and isn't she…"

For a while, Kurt was amused but when my stargazing
went on and on, he said, "Bloody hell, Miranda. Would you
bloody well stop gawking? You're making a bloody specta-
cle of yourself." But it didn't matter a bit to me because it

was a case of an eye for an eye and a tooth for a tooth. Kurt was famous, too, and other people were staring at *him,* and he was with *me.*

We were definitely making progress.

"Do stop behaving like a schoolgirl and eat your oysters," said Kurt. "I had them specially brought in for us." He sounded like a weary father trying to get a reluctant daughter to eat.

How could I break it to Kurt that I was a Cold Shanks girl and that the only oysters I'd eaten up till now had been rolled in bread crumbs and fried. I didn't want to hurt his feelings. He'd gone to so much fuss and spent so much money. And normally I'm quite a food pioneer, willing to go gastronomically where no man has gone before. But I have to draw the line at *raw* oysters.

These oysters he'd had specially brought in were raw, quivering, and looked like huge blobs of snot on a half shell. And I didn't care that they were supposed to be an aphrodisiac (for all the good it was going to do us), there was no way I was going to let one of those slimy mollusks slither down my throat raw. For all I knew, they still hadn't given up the ghost and were going to go into their final death throes in my stomach.

So I filled up on champagne and bread sticks, and when Kurt got up to talk to some musician across the room, I scooped a couple of oysters into the napkin and hurried to the ladies' room where I deposited them in the garbage and kept the empty shells to display on my plate.

This is really living, I thought. Tipping fresh oysters into the ladies'-room garbage can at the swankiest joint in town.

As soon as Kurt stepped out on the podium at the theater that evening I knew something was horribly wrong.

In a box all to myself, before the curtain went up, I'd been having a great time daydreaming. All the lush theater decor had me revved up and I'd been trying to imagine opera reality in the seventeenth and eighteenth centuries, in those days when it had been a real circus.

Back then, the theaters were like casinos-cum-bordellos where the public ate, drank, laid bets on the singers and got lucky. The boxes had curtains and the audience would ignore the parts of the opera they didn't want to hear and draw back the curtain to hear their favorite singer, and boo and hiss the others.

And these singers. They trained for hours a day, racing up and down scales, perfecting trills, improvising vocal acrobatics. They were amazing.

But the most amazing singers were the male sopranos. Castrati. Castrated men. Thanks to some biblical reference about women having to stay silent in church and not being permitted to speak, the powers of the moment extended this to singing, and practically every kind of female vocal soloist was prohibited from performing in public.

Castrati became the important singers. People started to develop such a craving for this high powerful sound that there was a huge traffic of eunuchs all over Italy, and especially in Naples, which had become a hub of male mutilation.

It was a gamble though, like training racehorses. Hustlers bought orphans or poor children, paid for the castration operation, then hoped the children would grow up to be opera stars and earn them back their investment. Needless to say, the streets were filled with dirt-poor tone-deaf men who spoke in high squeaky voices.

Take a note, boys. Trying to shut women up can be hazardous to your health.

Although I'd arrived after the opening, Kurt had conducted the same program of Rossini two nights before, and I'd heard it had been a huge success. Tonight, he stepped onto the podium, and I just knew that everything was askew. He didn't raise his baton right away, but stood there immobile, his hands clasped in front of him, staring into a corner of the pit as though he was searching for something.

Whatever it was, it never appeared. He stood like that for whole minutes, then finally, when the suspense grew ridiculous, he raised his baton in a fatalistic sort of way and launched into the music.

A thrill ran through my spine. I imagined the day when it would be me up there in the all-Rossini program, Kurt conducting. I knew these pieces. I'd studied them and listened to all the recordings available. That night, the sound was thinner than it ought to be. Something was definitely missing.

I looked my program over carefully. There was a credit for a guitarist, but there was no guitar in the pit. I'd just figured it out when the singer's voice petered out. For ten horrifying seconds I could see the tenor struggling to remember where he was in the music. But then he regained his footing and carried on and probably most of the audience never knew the difference.

Kurt was going to be furious. A musician's no-show was something he wouldn't tolerate.

When the concert was over, I resisted the urge to go backstage. Earlier at Top of the Mark, Kurt had told me, "Wait for me in front of the theater. I have to talk for a few minutes to one of the singers, but then we'll be free."

I walked up and down in front of the theater but when more than half an hour had passed and there wasn't any crowd left to mill around with, I decided to go and look for Kurt.

I was let in by the custodian at the stage door. The theater must have been nearly deserted. As I came closer to the corridor of dressing rooms, I could hear the sound of smashing glass. I tiptoed along toward the sound and turned the corner. The door to the conductor's dressing room was ripped off its hinges and dangling at an angle. Through the crack, I could see Kurt. There was broken mirror glass everywhere, detritus, loose papers and torn books, overturned chairs and pushed-over shelves. And he still hadn't finished. He appeared to be doing some major renovations, making two dressing rooms into one. Because the hole he was kicking in the wall was growing larger.

He never saw me. I backed away quickly, and then from the start of the corridor called out, "Kurt? Are you here?"

He appeared suddenly around a corner and hurried me out of the theater. "Miranda, I was just coming to look for you. The bloody guitarist was caught in a traffic jam coming over from Marin County. Why don't they think? He should have left earlier. Fucking idiot. He ruined the performance."

"I didn't think it was so ba—" I started to say.

"Hush. Not another word, Miranda."

That night, his wordless campaign continued. He was grim and determined as he wrestled me to the bed and gave my body a working over. I kept hoping he'd forget his half-baked chastity vows, get pulled into the heat of the moment and consummate, consummate, consummate, but no. It seemed as though Tina might be right. And that got me thinking. Was I nothing more to him than a potential paternity suit?

I flew back to Vancouver two days later.

Just before my departure, in the San Francisco airport, Kurt kissed me and told me he'd call soon.

From Vancouver Airport, I went straight to the Little Ladies headquarters, garment bag and all, and spent the afternoon scrubbing brass fixtures and huge marble bathtubs in a Shaughnessy mansion.

Fern started right in. "So, Miranda, San Francisco. I'm so envious. Me and Cliff were there in…what was it? Oh, seventy-nine. Just loved the place. Did you get to see the Golden Gate Bridge and Fisherman's Wharf and Chinatown and all those places?"

"Yes, I did, Fern."

After Kurt's bout of temporary insanity, he charmed me all over again by becoming the perfect gentleman, showing me the city from the back of a limousine, with a magnum of Brut and my father's impossible-to-find *Don Giovanni* recording playing in the background.

"Oh, and Alcatraz. Did you see that? My Cliff loved Alcatraz when we visited it."

"Then ya shoulda' told him to stay if he liked it so much," said Betty.

"Now, Betty, Cliff's much better now. You know that."

"I don't doubt it," said Betty, standing up tall and blowing on her knuckles.

After the Little Ladies, I headed to the theater where the last technical rehearsal for *I Puritani* was being held.

"Feeling better, Miranda?" asked the stage manager as I checked off my name at the stage door.

"Oh, much," I said.

Down in the dressing room, Tina's first question to me was, "So, did it happen?"

I shook my head.

She grinned maliciously and mimed rocking a baby.

After the rehearsal, I took a cab directly to Mike's place and Granny.

Granny was waiting for me, eager. She insisted on reading my palm again. I let her stare into my hand and handed her Kleenexes as she started to weep.

"Would you please tell me what you see in there?" I asked her in Italian. But she wouldn't. She shook her head and launched into another copious bout of weeping.

When I finally had her calmed down and organized in her own bed, I lay in the roll-away cot next to her, trying to sort out my confusion, trying to apply some of Chi Narnia's centering lessons.

"Visualize what you want for yourself then reach out and caress it." Easy for you, Chi Narnia, I thought. You're not trying to consolidate a relationship with a temperamental conductor who lives on another continent and is taking his sweet time divorcing his wife.

Chapter 11

I was going to murder Tina.

She'd gone ahead and told.

I was on my way back from my very last singing lesson with Madame Klein. How else could Madame have known?

Tina'd blabbered to Madame Klein that I had no intention of withdrawing from the debut of Kurt's song cycle. And she must have told her the rest.

Madame Klein's precise words had been delivered softly, compassionately, in a tone I'd never heard from her before. "I feel zorry for you, Fräulein Lyme. You haff no idea vhen tings are going gut. Who is ze teacher here? You or me? Vhen I tell you you are not ready for zometing, I haff my gut reasons. You tink it is enough to schtup ze conductor to haff a career? You are no zinger of mine. Adieu, Fräulein Lyme."

I stumbled out of Madame's studio the way I'd seen so many of her singers stumble out of there before me. Crushed and humiliated.

On the ride back to town, I went over the moment again and again. Tina was the only one who knew, the only one who could have told her. As I got off the bus, my anger was interrupted.

It was that soprano voice again, wafting through the streets, carried on the wind. The sound was pure liquid gold gliding effortlessly up to what we in the business call the money notes, the high Cs and C-sharps, and soaring down to a solid chest voice. If only I had a voice like that, I wouldn't need Madame Klein.

The voice was singing a very improvised and embellished version of "Swing Low, Sweet Chariot." I followed the sound. It just pulled me along. Although I was late for my centering session I couldn't stop myself. My brain said I had to hurry south, but my feet kept going north, all the way to Robson Square. This time there was a small crowd surrounding the girl. I pushed in closer to get a good look at her.

She had long dark straight hair, fine features with startling violet-blue eyes and skin that was somewhere between olive and coffee. She sat cross-legged on a small blanket halfway up the steps to the law courts, a hatful of change on the ground in front of her. Her eyes were focused on the people around her and her body was relaxed. She seemed completely at peace, something I'd seen in very few young performers.

All the singers I knew were full of ticks and tension; they were as rigid as wooden soldiers, or as frenzied as hyperactive preschoolers, or like charging bulls in a ring, or had clenched jaw syndrome, or their eyes skittered like the eyes of a spooked horse, or they had hands that turned into lobster claws and shoulders that gave them that Hunchback of Notre Dame posture as soon as they stepped onstage.

This girl was so natural, she made me feel both peaceful and exhilarated at the same time.

The crowd was growing larger. I stayed for a long time, five songs' worth, and when it looked as if she was about to give up and leave, I dug in my purse for all the spare change

I could find. It amounted to just under ten dollars. Other people were putting money into her hat. I stepped up and put mine in and said, "That was really good."

She said, "Thanks."

What I really wanted to say was Who are you? Where do you come from? Where did you learn to sing like that? How old are you? How do you live? Where do you live? Are you living on the street? Are you okay? Is there something I can do to guarantee that nothing will harm you or your voice? But I didn't know how to say it all without sounding like a psycho.

She smiled, picked up the hat and left.

I Puritani opened a week later.

The final dress rehearsal the night before had been a disaster. But it was okay, because dress rehearsals are supposed to be a disaster. That way the cast is scared into making it right on the night.

Elvira, the soprano heroine, had, without knowing it, worn a chair, which had attached itself to the back of her gown, for most of the big wedding scene. There had been so much smoke and snow in the battle scene that we couldn't see the conductor and coughed and groped and tripped our way around the stage, missing almost half of our cues.

But it all paid off.

On opening night, the audience loved us, and they especially loved the staging with all the smoke and snow to such a point that when it was over and the singers and conductor had taken their bows, the audience called out Boris's name and stamped and roared for ages.

When the curtain finally came down, Boris just shrugged and said, "The public. What do they know?"

We took off our makeup and costumes and got ready for the after-party. I waited a while then looked around to be sure most of the other chorus women had left.

I confronted Tina. I'd avoided confronting her for a week,

afraid I'd say something I'd later regret, but I couldn't hold back any longer.

"You told," I whispered.

"What are you talking about?" But she was biting her lip and looking away, a sure sign she was covering up.

"Madame Klein. She knows all about me and Kurt," I said.

Tina blushed a deep red. "I swear I didn't say a word."

"But you did have some kind of conversation with her. Nobody else knows about us."

"Listen, Miranda, she had a newsletter on the piano when I was at my lesson this morning. I didn't really get a good look at it, but it was probably the symphony newsletter announcing the next season. All she did was ask me if it was true that you would be singing. I couldn't think fast enough so when I didn't say anything she just took it as a yes."

"But she knows I'm sleeping with him."

"Sleeping's a good word for it. Screwing it isn't." Tina rolled her eyes.

"You know what I mean."

"I didn't breathe a word, Miranda. She's not stupid, you know. I'm sure she just guessed by looking at you. You haven't exactly been yourself lately."

How could I make them all understand that it wasn't that way at all? I was finally waking up. This *was* my real self.

The opening-night party was held at a little Indian restaurant near Broadway. I made the mistake, right at the beginning of the party, of biting into the hottest thing in the buffet and wondering for the rest of the evening if I would have to have my tongue amputated.

Everyone except me was in high spirits. The soprano dumped ice cubes down the front of Boris's pants, Boris used some incredibly filthy language to describe the soprano, the tenor and the bass had a high-C competition in the men's bathroom with everyone laying bets and the bass winning, and George, using a tablecloth in place of a handkerchief, did an imitation of Pavarotti.

It was a dull evening for me, though. I stuck to soda water that night. Having finally been dumped by Madame Klein and missing Kurt as I did, I couldn't trust myself. There was a gorgeous Indian waiter giving me the green light all night. I couldn't risk getting pissed out of my mind and waking up in my bed wearing a sari and staring at the shoulders of some beautiful Bollywood male who would then offer to teach me all the positions in the unedited *Kama Sutra*.

When I got home after the party, I couldn't sleep. I'd grown used to the sound of the snoring granny and now that I had a night off, I was having trouble sleeping in my own bed. My own bed reminded me of everything that wasn't happening.

I went to the closet and pulled out one of Patrick's tapes. I slid it into the video machine and pressed play.

A Tom Waits song accompanied the credits. The film was called *The Other Street*. I let it play for about two minutes and then, when I realized it was going to be a documentary about homeless people, I changed my mind and turned it off. I'd watch it later when I could give it my full attention.

Grace was back at Michelangelo's. She was sitting in her usual place, slapping on the butter and mayonnaise and the Dijon Poupon, making sandwich art. She seemed a little thinner and her complexion was doughier than usual, but she was cheerful.

I wanted to hug her but didn't think she was a hugging sort of person. "I'm so glad you're back, Grace. What was it anyway?"

"Oh, just one of life's little setbacks, Miranda, dear."

"But you're better?"

"I'm just fine, bless the Lord."

That morning, Michelangelo's was superslammed but I was happy. It gave me a sense of reassurance to see Grace's sandwiches lined up in neat little rows in the display. Cappuccinos were flying. The caffeine buzz was jacking up everybody's personal volume.

Screaming over the noise was out of the question for me, so whenever I had to be heard, I took an operatic approach, and pitched my voice up so that I was almost singing my questions to the customers. It was the only way to save my vocal chords on days like that. So there I was, practically making an aria out of, "Would you like cinnamon or chocolate sprinkles on that, and whole or partly skimmed milk?" to a tableful of law students, when I saw a face smiling at me from the table behind them. It was Patrick Tibeau.

I finished taking their order and went over to him. He looked very good that day, as if he was dressed for business, in an upscale charcoal-gray high-necked shirt and pressed pants. His hair was loose, gleaming black and down to his shoulders.

He stood up, towering over me, and touched my arm. "Hi, Miranda, I didn't expect to run into you here. Nice apron."

"Florentine cherubs," I said, "kissing."

"I can see that." He sat down again. "I didn't know you worked here."

"Until I get the big call from La Scala or the Met, I'm working here."

"Perfect. This is a neat place. Good coffee. Great atmosphere."

"Have you tried the sandwiches?" I asked.

"No."

"Try the sandwiches," I said. "They're fantastic. They're orgasmic."

Patrick's expression became deadly serious. "I'll take ten, please. To go."

I started to laugh and then choked on my own saliva. I tried to speak. "I'll…bring…you…one…to…try…" I sputtered. I couldn't stop coughing and choking.

Patrick jumped up, put his right arm around my waist from behind. He slid his left arm under my left arm and lifted it up, then raised my chin with his hand. My choking stopped but his arms lingered there. "You okay?" he asked. "Or do I have to give you the full Heimlich?"

"I'm okay now. Thanks. My God. How embarrassing. Choking like that."

He let go of me and sat down. "I'm ready for you. I have an aunt who chokes on her food every time I see her. I have to Heimlich her practically once a month." He became deadpan again. "Now, how about that orgasm?"

"Will that be with or without mustard?" I asked.

But as soon as I'd said it, he was standing again, and wincing slightly. "Oh, no, cancel that order. Some other time. I'll see you, Miranda. There's Evie now. Gotta go."

Evie had just come through the doorway and was walking toward us, using the men who had fallen at her feet as stepping stones.

Okay, that's an exaggeration. But I'm not exaggerating when I say that every man in Michelangelo's was fiddling with his zipper and belt buckle and panting and mopping the floor with his tongue.

Late on a Friday afternoon near the end of November, I received a call from Lance. "Miranda, honey, *La Chanteuse* opens tonight at the Ridge. You have a night off, don't you? The theater's dark tonight, isn't it?"

"Yes. *I Puritani*'s closing tomorrow, Saturday. But we're free tonight."

"I think we both want to be there tonight for Matilde's North American debut."

"Oh wow. That's exciting. It was so fast. I thought it would be years before the movie came out in English," I said.

In a gangster voice, Lance said, "Matilde is one fast broad. I think you should invite your friends."

"You mean get a group together?"

"Of course, Miranda. Maybe we're not the stars, but I think we gave a good enough performance to deserve to have a noisy and irritating little crowd at the showing."

"Okay, we can get a group together but let's not tell people right away that it's us, okay?"

"Not tell them? What are you talking about, Miranda?"

"Don't tell them that it's our voices."

"Why not? *You* gave a great performance." He paused and said quietly, "Miranda. You're not ashamed, I hope?"

"Ashamed of what?"

"Ashamed of being part of a Lance Forrester dub."

"No, I just want to see if they can guess it's me."

"Now," said Lance, "change of subject. Are you going to bring your man? I'd love to meet him."

"My man?" I asked.

"The one you're not telling me about."

"I'm not sure…"

"Yes, you are. The creature you're in love with. The one who grunts in monosyllables and whose knuckles drag along the floor."

"Oh him. He's…uh…busy tonight."

"Busy?"

"He's out of town on business," I said.

"Aluminum-siding salesman," said Lance.

"Not likely."

"Carney. Operates the Tilt-A-Whirl throughout the Midwest."

"When hell freezes over."

"Pink-flamingo manufacturer," said Lance.

"Cold. Ice-cold."

"A tiny hint?" said Lance.

"I can't," I said. I already regretted having told Tina.

"See you at your place. I'll pick you up in an hour," said Lance, and rang off.

Caroline was out so I retreated to the bathroom. It became a think tank, a practice room and a theater. Where do you think most great singers got their start? In the bathroom mirror, of course. Where else could you find that great echo? Where else could you steam your sinuses for hours on end?

My greatest performances had taken place in the bathroom. I'd often thought that if auditioners would just put a big claw-foot tub full of hot water and some nice bathroom tile up on the stage, they'd hear the best singing ever.

Lying there in that enormous tub, I tried to imagine what a soprano would do if she, by some impossible fluke, couldn't do music. If she became deaf overnight, for example. The concept was beyond my grasp. Few of us were Beethovens. Matilde would be all pork and no voice. And me?

Inconceivable. Strip away the music and what was I left with? Waitressing, cleaning houses and granny-sitting. Ouch.

I'd expected Lance to come in his old Volkswagen van. He arrived at my door dressed in leather and carrying two helmets. "Do you have a warm jacket?" he asked.

"Oh shit. A motorcycle. You ride a motorcycle. Why didn't I know that? After all my blabbing on and on about it, you come on a motorcycle. Why are you doing this to me? Do I have to?"

He nodded, leaned forward and gave me a light kiss on one cheek. "It'll be a breeze."

Lance knew how I felt about motorbikes. In the darkness of the studio, I'd told him that they scared me, that I thought Tina was crazy to spend so much time on the back of Collin's bike.

At the time, Lance had just said, "Sometimes confronting your fears can be very exciting." And he'd smiled through that dark beard and I'd wondered what he meant. Now I could see that it was impossible to say no without looking like a complete baby.

I got my navy-blue leather jacket from the closet and followed him out of the apartment. I let him fasten the helmet on me, then I climbed onto the back of the motorbike and clutched him for dear life.

When I saw my friends in front of the Ridge, I said, "Oh my God."

Standing out in the little group of Tina, Collin, George and Brandon was Peter Drake.

"What is it?" asked Lance.

"Peter Drake is here."

"The…uh…THE Peter Drake the tenor?" said Lance.

"The same."

Lance looked pleased. "I'm going to enjoy this."

I was already feeling a little shaky from the ride and the five made me feel shakier.

Peter came toward me, singing my name so the whole street would know he was there. "Miranda. It's a treat to see you again."

"You, too, Peter. Are you in town for a gig?"

"Some Messiahs in Seattle next week. I thought I'd come ahead of time and pal around in Vancouver. Any word on that audition? I told them that if they valued their working lives they'd better give it to you."

"They did."

"Lovely. We may see you in London, then."

I nodded. "I hope so."

The rest of the group was giving Lance the third degree so I finally veered them onto another topic. "Anybody know what this movie's about?" I asked.

"I read the French reviews. The film's set in Paris," said Brandon, full of authority.

"J'adore Paris," said George.

"Fine opera house. Nice acoustics," said Peter.

"When were we there last, George? It seems so far away and long ago. Like a dream. We stayed in that fabulous little flea pit on La Rive Gauche," sighed Brandon.

"Four years ago," said George.

"You should enjoy this film then," said Lance, smiling. "It takes in all the major tourist attractions."

Peter, Collin and Tina laughed through most of the film while George and Brandon seemed mortified. I don't know what they expected. Probably *Last Tango in Paris* meets Merchant and Ivory. I hadn't seen so much cringing from the two of them since we'd gone to see an all-nighter of *Alien 1, 2* and *3*.

About five minutes after *La Chanteuse* started, George and Brandon went into shock. When they weren't screwing their eyes shut at the sight of pig's blood, they were cringing at the sight of straight sex.

"Oh, ick. That's an awesome amount of mammary gland, isn't it? What's she trying to do? Suffocate him?" said Brandon.

"Just be glad this film isn't in 3-D. Or IMAX. Can you imagine all that female flesh just coming straight at you? " said George.

"Although the pig farmer's not bad, not bad at all," said Brandon.

"I know. But how can he stand it with that WOMAN?" whined George.

"But her notes, George, her notes. You have to admit she has fabulous notes," said Brandon.

"Yes, Matilde's notes are very good. I'd gladly have sacrificed children for soprano notes like that," sighed George.

I thought it was funny that nobody recognized my voice right away, but then I had made it a little deeper and breathier with a slightly generic European accent. I thought it made me sound more sophisticated.

When the credits rolled by at the end, everyone scolded me.

"Miranda Lyme, you coy little bitch, that was your voice."

"Yes, it was. And Lance's."

"Fairly good notes," said George, a little begrudgingly.

"Not bad for a soprano from the provinces," agreed Brandon.

"Brava, Miranda," said Peter.

On our way out of the movie theater we got stuck waiting for other people in the aisle to move. From the row behind us, I heard a voice call, "Miranda? Miranda? Over here. Behind you."

I turned around. It was Chi Narnia, waving at me. She was wearing a pair of mukluks and a coat that looked like an inside-out polar bear. I don't know how she did it, but on her, whatever she wore always looked daringly fashionable.

"Hi, Chi. Nice coat."

She pushed her way through the people until she was at talking distance. "Miranda, I forgot to tell you last time. I'm going to be organizing some extra sessions for some of the people who can't—"

She stopped talking and all the color drained from her face. I turned around to see where she was staring. Evie and Patrick were coming out of the row on the other side of the aisle.

I waved and called, "Hi, Patrick." Then I quickly added, "Evie."

Patrick saw me and smiled. But then he stopped smiling and looked right past me. He was staring at Chi Narnia and she was staring at him. They started to move toward each other slowly, as though in a daze.

"Patrick," said Chi Narnia.

"Mary," said Patrick.

Chapter 12

"Who's Mary?" Tina asked me.

"The cradle snatcher," I whispered.

"Which cradle... Oh... His first big lay? That one?"

"Yeah, that one...I think," I murmured.

"Shit," said Tina.

"Shall we all go for a quick one and toast the *La Chanteuse* voices?" asked Peter loudly.

"Yes," said Evie, too quickly.

At the Media Club, I watched the group with fascination. After the basic introductions, Evie gave Patrick and Chi Narnia a few nervous glances then went to get herself a drink. Chi Narnia said to Patrick right away, "Chi Narnia is my name now. I'm not Mary anymore." But that didn't stop the two of them from moving into a soft corner and holing up to talk with so much urgency you would have thought the end of the world was at hand.

When Evie found out that Lance was entirely responsible for the English version of *La Chanteuse* and had a studio of his own, she took a gulp of her white wine and changed tack. She was wide awake and interested, paying attention to his every word. Not that he was giving away anything that I didn't already know. Lance was a genius at not talking about himself. It was maddening. I was sure, that with all those people there, he might let something slip, and make references to three ex-wives, his fire-eating male companion, the favorite horse he had buried in his backyard. Anything.

But nothing doing. The man was like a bank vault.

I'd even tried doing a Google search on him, and his studio's home page had come up, but not a word about his personal background or his private life. There was a long list of credentials for all the dubbing and film work he'd done, and some beautiful graphics, and that was it.

And I also watched Evie. But the way one watches expensive tropical fish in a big fancy blue tank. At a cool distance. There was something I hadn't noticed the other times I'd met her. The other times, she'd always had a man to play to.

But now, as the evening wore on, Patrick was still talking to Chi Narnia, all the other guys were getting up to talk to people they knew on the other side of the club, or they'd gone to play pool. When there was no male paying attention to her, Evie got a dull look in her eye, as if the lights had gone out in her head, as if her power source had shut down. The company of women wasn't enough to keep her interested. And then as soon as a man looked at her again, she shone. It was scary. It made me feel as though I didn't exist.

Tina had noticed it too. When we met up in the bathroom, she said, "That Evie chick is deep-dish strange, with a tough crust and too much ice cream on top."

I was standing on a stage wearing a belly dancer's costume. I was supposed to be singing in an opera but I realized in a panic that I didn't know which opera it was and that I was one season behind everybody else. I didn't know the music.

I begged the conductor (who looked just like Kurt) to let me have a copy of the score. He handed it over but it was covered in childish crayon scrawls and blobs of black ink. I decided I would fake it and improvise my way through the opera. I started to sing and walk around the stage, guessing at the blocking, making extravagant gestures. The audience was laughing. I looked down at my costume and saw that I was naked. My singing voice wavered and then started to ring like a telephone.

I struggled awake and looked at my clock. It was six in the morning. I had to leave for work in forty minutes. I hoped it was Kurt.

I staggered out to the hallway and picked up the receiver. "Hello?"

"Miranda?" It was a man's voice but not Kurt's. A desperate-sounding voice.

"Who is this?"

"It's Patrick."

"Patrick… It's six in the morning."

"I know. I'm really sorry."

"Is everything okay? Your voice sounds strange."

"Could you come over here?"

"Sorry? Over? Here where?"

"I need your help."

"What with? It's six in the morning."

"I didn't know who to call. Please come, Miranda. I just live around the corner. It's important."

"Well, yeah, okay."

Well, that's how it is. When a fellow Cold Shanksian calls, we respond.

He gave me the address and we hung up. I pulled on my clothes and put on my Adidas, got my keys and hurried out to the address he had given me.

His building didn't look residential at all. It was an old gray concrete warehouse. It gave me the creeps. But I centered myself to attract positive energy and rang the buzzer.

Patrick's voice answered, "Evie?"

"No, it's Miranda."

"It's open. Come up to the top floor."

I went up the four flights of stairs and knocked on the only door at the top. Patrick opened up. He looked destroyed. "Miranda. Thanks for coming." He stepped aside for me to come in. When I saw his place, my stomach sank.

"You've been vandalized," I said.

"Not exactly. Come into the kitchen. I'll make you a quick coffee. I think there's still an unbroken cup."

It was a long wide warehouse room converted into an open-studio apartment and obviously the place where Patrick did a lot of his work. Every possession had been used as a shot put or javelin, hurled or tossed across the floor, all except for some expensive-looking video and film equipment that was neatly set out on shelves and a long table. There was broken glass everywhere. Torn books, mutilated and slashed clothing and broken dishes were strewn around the floor.

While Patrick was in the kitchen, I continued to survey the scene. The bed at the windowless far end of the room was soaked. At its center, on top of the covers, was a bunch of battered pink roses and a large broken glass vase. Near the bed, a small trail of fresh blood dots went from a broken window to the door.

Patrick seemed nonchalant when he came back and handed me a cup of black instant coffee.

He put his cup down and rubbed his face with his hands. "She must have cut herself. We have to find her. We have to find Evie. Her cellular's turned off."

"Evie? Evie did this?"

He nodded. "I was stupid. I can't believe I was so stupid. But seeing Mary like that out of the blue… I've been up all night talking to Mary. I just came in a few minutes ago and found all this." He shook his head.

"You mean this isn't the first time Evie's done something like this?"

"I should explain."

"It sort of speaks for itself," I said.

"She's a little unpredictable."

"I'll say she is."

Patrick ran his hands through his hair. "She can go for months without noticing a thing. And then some woman will offer me a piece of gum and she'll go completely ballistic. She has a temper."

"That's an understatement." My mutilated Missoni shoes came to mind. "I hope I'm not going to get home and find rabbit stew bubbling on my stove and Evie with a carving knife in my bathroom."

"The damage is usually contained. She doesn't touch my equipment. She has *some* sense of priority... I mean, Christ...I've always used her in my films. And I said, I would use her in my next film. I'm not sure that I want her in all of them, forever and ever, amen, though," said Patrick.

"Do you mind if I ask a personal question?"

"Ask away."

"How long did you say you'd been together? Two years?"

"Two years, three months and six days."

"But who's counting? Right?"

He smiled a twisted little smile. "We have an...an open relationship. Except that it's always been open on her side. I'm usually so busy with my work, I don't have a lot of time for other things. You can't expect a beautiful woman to resist all the temptation that comes along. We're only young once, right? So I tell her 'Carpe diem. As long as you're careful.'"

"Uh...sure."

"Well, then I have a little connection with some woman. As I said, it doesn't have to be anything much at all. Just a moment, a word, a stick of gum, and Evie freaks, she flips out, and I can't see her face anymore."

"If I hadn't seen the state of this apartment I never would have guessed."

He laughed. "Well, that's the idea. I have to believe that everything's fine. And usually it is. I have to convince myself. It looks like I convinced you too, eh?"

"And then along came Mary," I said.

"Along came Mary." His shoulders went back and his face relaxed, became beatific. "God, it was good to see her. It was like a breath of fresh air. I feel like I've been living underground."

"You mean as in stifled?"

"I didn't say that."

"Okay."

He looked up at me and smiled. His expression was sheepish, like a kid about to confess some tiny crime. "Yeah. Well. Maybe a little. Stifled."

"What are you going to do, Patrick?"

"That's the sixty-million-dollar question," said Patrick. "I can't leave Evie. I love her."

"You know what, Patrick?"

"What?"

"The way you said that makes it sound like a taped message."

He nodded. Then he shook his head. Then it looked as if he might start crying. But he just stuck his hands over his face and rubbed. Then he rolled his head to stretch his neck in all directions, as though he was trying to ease a chronic pain.

"Just leave all this mess and come to my place," I said.

"But I can't…"

"Yes, you can. Just leave it. It's not going anywhere. When she comes home, she'll find it all here waiting for her."

He looked at me as if I was crazy. His face was drained of color.

"Come *on.*" I tugged on his arm and made him get his jacket.

He obediently followed me back to my place. He seemed too tired to resist. I prattled on and on. About getting some rest. About how everybody needs a little break from their lives. About how it was hard to think when you were under the influence of certain people.

When we got to my place, I took the quilt off my bed, brought it to him and said, "Now listen, Pat, just stretch out here on the couch, forget about Evie and when I get back, we'll talk about this."

I felt so motherly that I even made him a cup of Ovaltine before I left. I don't know why, but somehow, it was like I was soothing a part of myself.

Evie came looking for Patrick at Michelangelo's that morning. She had a discreet professionally applied bandage around one of her hands. As soon as she walked through the doorway, my hackles rose. I could see all the men in the place drooling and craning their necks to get a look at her. They obviously didn't see her as I did—Miss Destructive Bitch of the Decade—but as a poor delicate sparrow with a broken wing. I had an urge to give her a hard kick in the shins, help her really get into her role of wounded beauty.

"Hi, Miranda. You haven't seen Pat around, have you?" she asked sweetly, as if she hadn't just broken an entire service of crockery.

I stared straight into her wolverine eyes and said, "Nope. He hasn't been in here this morning."

"Well, if he comes around, would you tell him I was looking for him? Tell him to call me on my cellular?"

"Sure I will, Evie. If he comes around."

The Little Ladies were doing The Bachelor's place that afternoon.

I was tackling a nefarious clump of burnt brown crud that seemed to have exploded and welded itself to the stove and the side of the fridge.

I yelled to the next room, "You see, Betty, the way he talks, it's like he's saying out one side of his mouth that he loves her, and out the other side that she's driving him crazy and he has to get rid of her."

Betty yelled back, "Ya wants me to take her on?"

"She's half your height and half your weight, Betty. I don't think it would look too good from the onlookers' point of view. But thanks for the offer."

From the hallway, Fern added her two bits. "But they've been together for two years. Maybe they can work it out."

"Listen to her," said Betty. "If Fern was married to Jack the Ripper, she'd still be sayin' we can work it out. Some people."

"I figure it must be like alcoholics," I said. "If Patrick doesn't want to help himself, there's nothing anybody can do. But then, he called me, didn't he? It's like confessing your drinking problem, having somebody else see the mess."

When I got home that night Caroline came out of her room. She was looking confrontational. "You didn't tell me at the party that your friend was Patrick Tibeau."

"Is it important?" I asked.

"Well, duh. *The* Patrick Tibeau?"

"I don't see what you're getting so worked up about."

She had her mad-lecturer look. "He's *only* one of the most important new indie filmmakers in North America. Or didn't you know that? He's been all over the press lately. He was just short-listed for a prize at the Venice Biennial. Did you know that?"

I shook my head.

"The arts pages love him. They're very excited about his work. They're saying that he's a young Atom Egoyan."

"A young… Really? So?"

"Do you know who Atom Egoyan is, Miranda?"

"Um…"

"Or have you ever actually *seen* any of Patrick's films?"

I was waiting for her to shine a hot lamp in my face, pull out a cattle prod.

"I…uh…yes." I'd watched two minutes of one. It wasn't a lie.

She went on, her voice getting louder. "Patrick Tibeau doesn't look like his pictures at all. That's why I didn't recognize him the other night. He woke up at about two this afternoon and I was making some tabbouleh and soy cutlets. He came into the kitchen and made a comment about eating low on the food chain and I asked him who he was.

"When I found out it was *the* Patrick Tibeau, I gave him some of my lunch. Don't look at me like that. Believe me, I wouldn't have done that for a couple of your opera species there. Some of your friends are way overnourished, you know what I mean?

"We had this long talk. I mean…it's like…that man is old beyond his years and so well informed on a number of issues. He's politicized in exactly the right direction. We talked about everything. I still can't believe it. I mean, Dan was talking to him at the party but he didn't have a clue that it was *the* Patrick Tibeau. It's like the most amazing coincidence because we were discussing his films the other day, in terms of European influences versus the Hollywood schlock mill. And his girlfriend," she went on, "you know that's Evie Marcelle? I thought she looked familiar when she was here the other night. There was a long article about the Patrick Tibeau and Evie Marcelle team in the Globe online."

"The certifiably strange Evie Marcelle," I muttered.

But Caroline wasn't listening to me. "I'm planning to organize a seminar at the SUB auditorium and get him to talk about his work. Do you have any idea how much he's done in his twenty-seven years? I'm just flying so high. And he only lives round the corner."

"Wait for an invitation before you go visiting," I said, raising my voice to match hers.

"You don't own him," said Caroline.

"I'm covering your butt, Caroline. Evie's his girlfriend. Read into that whatever you want."

"So what?"

"So, she's insanely, pathologically jealous."

Caroline sat back and scrutinized me. "Really? Just exactly how pathological?"

I told her all about Evie turning into Godzilla and trashing their apartment. Then I added, "I think he's afraid Evie will slit her wrists or come gunning for him if he leaves her. I know it ought to be none of my business but I'm still wondering why he phoned me to come over and see. I felt so sorry for him when I saw that place and the way he looked, so I invited him back here."

Caroline frowned and said, "That is so pathetic. It makes me sick when people use emotional blackmail. Everybody loses in love at some point in their life. It's inevitable. My mother used to do that to my father, threaten to stick her head in the oven. He wanted to leave her because he couldn't even go into our *bathroom* without her thinking that he was fooling around on her. I told her she needed to get therapy, that she was driving him away all by herself."

"So what happened?"

"He left her and she stuck her head in the oven, we pulled her out just in time and made her get professional help," said Caroline.

"Oh my God, Caroline, I didn't know that. I always just assumed you had two regular parents."

"I make a point of not talking about it. I don't know anybody who has two regular parents. Maybe they're out there but I don't know them. That's life. Some people just don't want to be helped."

And then the phone rang.

Chapter 13

When I put down the receiver I was hyper with happiness.

There was so much to do. I only had two weeks to get organized. The opera wasn't a problem. The next production had an all-male chorus. But I had to let Mike know, and Cora down at Little Ladies. And I had to pick up my ticket and say goodbye to friends and my family.

Kurt wanted me to stay with him over Christmas. Stay at his house. I told him that I'd probably be staying with my father, that we needed to get reacquainted. I'd tried my father's number a couple of times over the last year and had only spoken with an answering machine, but it was definitely my father's voice, and even if he was out of town, I'd track him down eventually. So Kurt's offer was timely after all. It would be a good chance to find out what living with him would be like.

"Mom, it's me."

"Miranda."

"I'm going to London. I've got an audition with the ENO."

"I know. Lyle…"

"I asked him not to say anything."

"Oh, for heaven's sake, Miranda. Lyle's…he's…"

"I'm flying out a week before Christmas and I'll be back in early February."

"Where will you stay?"

"I was thinking…"

"Miranda, if you go to see Sebastian, you be careful. I don't want you to get…"

"He's my father, Mom. And he can help me."

"Miranda, don't rely on him. Do you have enough money? Lyle and I are sending you some…"

"I have enough money."

"I'm sending you some anyway so…it's better…just don't…oh, Miranda…I don't like the idea…"

"It's doable, Mom. Really, it is. Singers fly back and forth across the Atlantic for work all the time."

"The *great* singers fly… Oh Miranda, oh, London…is so…" Her voice sounded tired and heavy. "Be careful. Just be careful of…"

"I'll call you as soon as I get there, Mom."

Tina had me to a farewell dinner at her place. Her apartment was near Oak Street in a neighborhood of brand-new characterless duplexes. Her place was spacious and bright, with all the mod cons, gas fireplace, dishwasher, garburator, jade-green wall-to-wall carpet, washer, dryer and one of those vacuum cleaners built into the wall. She had two bathrooms and a rented upright grand piano in the spare room, where she taught singing to anyone who was willing to pay. Tina couldn't play the piano any better than me. She made her students hire accompanists and then pretended she was Madame Klein. She made quite a good living at it.

I sipped cheap wine while Tina clattered around in the kitchen. I did an inventory of everything in her living room.

She was collecting at a dangerous rate. A couple of big once-empty wall spaces were now filled in.

"Tina? What are you doing?" I called toward the kitchen.

"What do you mean, what am I doing?" she called back.

"You're buying art. I recognize this artist."

"It's Joe Average," said Tina. "He's a local. His art is on a Canadian stamp. Good, isn't it?"

"What? You can't collect Joe Average works, or any other works for that matter," I said.

"Can't what?" she yelled.

"Can't collect artists."

"Why can't I?"

"Your career, stooopid."

She appeared in the doorway. "Career? Right now my career resembles the water swirling out of the kitchen sink."

"It's just a temporary lull. All this stuff weighs you down, Tina. You've got to be ready to go when you get the call."

She sighed. "The only calls I'm getting lately are telephone sales pitches trying to get me to buy frozen foods in bulk. And I might even do it. I'm sick of living the way I lived with my mother. I want everything I own to weigh a ton. Then if I have to move, I'll hire a real big van. But where am I gonna go? Collin likes it here."

"Collin? Collin? You'd stay here for him?"

"You're a fine one to talk. You're going to London for Kurt."

"No, not for Kurt. For London itself. London's practically the center of the music world. Next to New York or Milan."

"I wish you weren't going," said Tina, serious. "Don't go."

I sighed. "Don't say that to me. Just don't say it. Now, what's for dinner?"

She smiled diabolically, went back into the kitchen and brought out two plates.

"Oh my God. That's it?" I said.

Glaring up from the plates were servings of bright yellow Kraft macaroni dinner, creamed corn from a tin and spaghetti squash. It was exactly what we used to eat during our university days. As a joke.

"The Infamous Yellow Meal," said Tina.

The night before departure, I organized a last-minute bon voyage party.

Everybody came except Patrick and Evie, who were never home when I passed by their place. I'd tried their number and left numerous messages on their answering machine, but I guess they either hadn't heard them or weren't in town. Out of Cold Shanks camaraderie, I stashed Patrick's tapes in my suitcase, thinking they might come in handy for those homesick moments.

Everyone else was at the party. Tina, Collin, George, Brandon, Lance, Mike, Belinda, Grace, Betty, Fern and Cora. And of course, Caroline, the Sasquatch and the Free Lunch Brigade. By then I'd learned the hard way that no party was complete without them.

Soul music throbbed on the stereo. A case of Asti Spumante and a dozen huge pizzas were supplied by Mike. Grace got a little drunk and started dancing a highland fling to "I Heard It Through the Grapevine." Then she came over to me, took her Saint Christopher medal from around her neck and put it around mine. "Give 'em hell, Miranda. And always remember to put this little guy on," she said, and collapsed into a chair.

"Will do, Grace," I said.

Mike boogied up to me next. "Now, Miranda, the thing about London is, don't drink the coffee…unless it's an Italian place, then you're okay. Other than Italian places, they got this stuff they call coffee, but it's not really coffee, and they ask you if you want it white or black. Real strange."

Belinda said, "Don't listen to Mike. He was there a hundred years ago. The coffee's improved since then."

"You callin' me old, girl?"

"Old and decrepit," Belinda teased. Mike went after her.

Lance was sitting at the aluminum table, nursing a beer. I went over and sat down beside him. "No Spumante?" I asked.

"Too sweet." He sat back in his chair, expanded his chest and gave me a Cheshire cat grin. "London. Well, I have to say, Miranda. You have my full admiration. And envy. Will you write to me? E-mail me? Send me notes in bottles?"

I held my glass up high. "I will, Lance. Tell me which beach and I'll make sure the bottle washes up right there."

He leaned forward and hugged me. "Please botch the audition, Miranda. I'm afraid you won't come back and where will I find another Matilde. Please come back soon, Miranda."

"Will do, Lance."

Then Betty, a one-outfit woman in her usual lumberjack shirt, came over and settled herself into the chair on the other side of me. "Gotta have a word with ya, Miranda. It's about London, eh? See, when you're over there, and ya happen ta go by one of them royal palaces, an' if ya happen ta see that Anne woman, you tell her fer me, them bull terriers are a tricky breed, got mean an' nasty in their blood, can't help themselves fer attackin' kids an' dogs. It ain't their fault. It's the owner gotta be damn careful with them, eh, otherwise yer gonna have more than one dead corgi on yer conscience, right?"

"Will do, Betty," I said.

Fern, in a sparkly gold sweater, made up for Betty's lack of glitter. She said, "Now, Betty, Miranda doesn't want to go getting involved with royal dogs. It's royal *men* she needs to meet."

Cora joined in. "That's right. Miranda, when you get to London, check out the clubs. There's some great ones there. Oh, to be single again. I had the greatest time in that city about twenty years ago. The last thing you want is to be alone in London, so get out there and party."

"Will do, Cora," I said.

Then Caroline came over, yanked a slip of paper out of

her pocket and said, "Before I forget, Miranda. You have to look up these people. Really cool cross-genre musicians. They can do anything. I met them at a jazz festival in Montreal last summer. We all shared a bottle of Southern Comfort and got a little wild together. Then sick as dogs. Well, hell, nothing like puking your guts out in unison to form a tight bond of friendship, right? But, really. Go look them up."

"Will do, Caroline," I said.

George and Brandon were the next to offer advice. "She has to go to Neal's Yard, George."

"And the Pharmacy."

"And she has to see that new Queen musical."

"And the *Phantom,* Brandon. She must see the *Phantom.*"

"Oh, George, the *Phantom*'s passé. *Mama Mia!* That's what she has to see."

"I'll see it all and let you know," I told them.

Then Collin and Tina came over and Collin said, sotto voce, "Listen, if you need a little something to calm you down for the flight, don't hesitate to ask, Miranda. All my product's high quality."

"Thanks, Collin, but I'll be fine."

Then Tina said, "Most important of all, make sure the maestro uses that baton of his properly when you're over there. Know what I mean, Miranda?"

"All too well, Tina."

It was overwhelming to think that I was actually, finally leaving the next day, and when I went to bed that night, I dreamed wild horses; black, snorting, restless, with fear in their eyes.

London

Chapter 14

My city!

As I stepped off the plane and took a deep breath, I knew I had come home. The air was strange yet familiar. I could almost taste the buildings and streets, those places from a deep forgotten memory; Buckingham Palace, Piccadilly Circus, The Strand, Whitehall, Kensington Park, the British Museum, Portobello Road, Highgate Cemetery, Trafalgar Square, Kew Gardens, the National Arts Centre, the West End, the Royal Albert Hall.

All waiting for me.

I spotted Kurt right away. He stood out in the crowd at the Arrivals gate with his long black overcoat and his Nordic-hero good looks. I approached him with the long-flight wobbles coursing through my body. He lifted my carryall and suitcase out of my hands and said, "Miranda, my love, you look positively the worse for wear."

Well, what did he expect? After a nine-hour intercontinental night flight seated next to a middle-aged divorced giant whose spittle flew when he spoke and whose mission

in life was to distribute his abundant dandruff over the entire planet?

"Nice to see you too, Kurt," I said.

He put down my bags again. "Sorry," he said. "I'm very
glad you're here. I'm absolutely thrilled. It's super. You've no
idea." He kissed me on my dry cracked jet-lagged lips right
there in public, in the International Arrivals, and I thought,
now we're getting somewhere.

"Follow me, my love." He picked up my bags again and
walked briskly in the direction of a sign that read Way
Out. I thought it might be a hangover from the swinging
London days, Carnaby Street, the Fab Four, Mary Quant
and Twiggy. Now all we needed were signs that read Cool
and Groovy. I hurried after him, out to the car park. The
sky was a low mass of brownish gray cloud and a cold driz-
zly mist mingled with exhaust fumes. Elixir. Perfect English weather.

Kurt was walking toward a navy-blue Jaguar. I froze. A
rush of adrenaline ran through me and then the old terror
that I'd kept at bay for so long, the nag of anxiety leaped
forward, looking completely out of place in that parking lot.

Look at the car, Miranda, said the nag. What if you aren't
up to it all?

Anybody can get used to money.

"Oh, yeah?" nagged the nag.

But I'm Sebastian Lyme's daughter.

Big deal. When was the last time you saw your father in
the flesh? When was he ever any help to you?

He's my voice. He's what my voice is all about. I inher-
ited it from him. Now leave me alone and let me enjoy this,
just a little.

You're a twenty-six-year old soprano, one of a million just
like you, who doesn't know anybody in this town, except
Kurt, and who knows what he's about?

I broke up the game of mental tug-of-war and followed
Kurt to the car.

Kurt put my luggage in the back. When I mistakenly started to get into the driver's seat, Kurt smirked and then like a gentleman, pointed out the passenger seat and helped me in. Then he climbed in himself, started the car and pulled out quickly.

"Watch out," I blurted, "you're on the wrong side of the road." And then I remembered. "It's not the wrong side, is it?"

"Foolish little Miranda."

"I'm not little."

"No, you're not." He reached across the space between us and palpated my right breast.

As he drove, I stopped short of flattening my face against the window to take in everything passing by, the English world of brick red and kelly green, the gray-and-brown-brick row houses, the Dickensian pubs and shops squeezed in beside modern glassy high-rises, the dense, teeming world at the center of the universe.

"Good flight?" asked Kurt. He didn't wait for an answer. He pushed a CD into the player and fooled around with the knobs and buttons until a blast of sound filled the Jaguar. It was the last movement of Beethoven's *Ninth Symphony*. He allowed me a few minutes of listening before he lowered the volume and said, "We recorded this last year. What do you think?"

"Well. The soloists are great. They could strip the varnish off a table. And the orchestra's pretty good too, but the conducting sucks," I said.

"Lovely to have you here," he said. "My stroppy little colonial." He turned and gave me a full-throttle smile and I panicked because he should have been looking at the road. It was full of speed-crazed lunatics.

I was aching to ask him about the state of the Olivia business. I avoided the subject though. I had one eye on the maniacal traffic, and the other on the scenery, the intricate wedding-cake facades flying by, and then a glimpse of the wide mud-silver Thames River snaking into the distance as we rode over a bridge.

I filled him in on all the music gossip from Vancouver. We chatted about opera nepotism and nasty music-management deeds until he pulled up in front of a four-story Victorian mansion surrounded by fussily manicured box hedges and small oaks. It took me a second to get my bearings. The house was huge, a mansion of redbrick with a white-pillared porch, numerous turrets, iron railings, big stony lintels and Victorian gothic weather vanes.

"Very…interesting…house. What neighborhood is this anyway?" I asked.

"Putney," replied Kurt.

"Putney? I've never heard of it. Is it famous?"

Kurt seemed a little offended. "Good Lord, it's as well known as any other part of London, I suppose. Actually, it's considered to be quite chic. Let me see now. Dick Turpin wandered these parts, plundering and pillaging, and ravaging maidens."

"Talk on, Maestro."

He smiled, leaned forward and gave me a long kiss. "Why? Where did you think I lived."

"I was hoping you'd live in a famous neighborhood, where I could bump into somebody, a place like Notting Hill. You know, Hugh Grant land."

"Hugh Grant," he laughed. "Is that what you wanted? Were you hoping to meet Hugh Grant, you foolish thing?"

"Why? Do you know Hugh Grant?"

Kurt frowned. "I'm afraid he's out of the country filming at the moment," he quipped. Tugging my bags out of the boot (imagine calling the trunk of the car the "boot"—it was going to take me a while to get the hang of being half English), he instructed, "Do come inside and we'll get you unpacked. I imagine you'll want to take a bath and rest a bit."

He opened the front door then ran inside and disappeared, then quickly reappeared. "Had to turn off the alarm.

Always remember that, or you'll have armed guards crawling all over you, if you should happen to come in by yourself and forget. I'll show you how it works. Oh, and I've given the help some well-deserved time off."

He winked at me as he said this, as if I'd be pleased.

Time off for the help sounded like very bad news for me. I hoped he didn't think I was going to do all the cleaning. From what I could glimpse from the door, it was clear that the enormous house was filled to the brim with beautiful antique dust collectors. In the entrance hall, which was painted a shiny aubergine color and studded with small botanical prints, I could see into the living room. It was a huge warehouse of a room, jammed with ornate claw-foot furniture and bric-a-brac shelves lining the terra-cotta walls. Beyond that was a dining room and large conservatory extending into the garden.

Antique silver pieces cluttered every table and sideboard. Think of all that buffing and polishing. Art filled every bit of wall that wasn't bookcases or china cabinets. There were enormous oil paintings in heavy gilt frames, portraying gloomy English landscapes, groups of people on horseback dressed up for fox hunts, and spaniels with limp mallards and partridges in their mouths.

"Interesting decor," I said.

"Olivia did the interior decorating. It's one of her passions."

Olivia? The paintings had to go.

But there was great potential, definitely great potential. And a little feng shui wouldn't hurt, either.

I followed Kurt as he hauled my suitcases up stairs that were carpeted in a dark burgundy shade. On the second floor he set them down and said, "Now, where shall we put you?"

My heart sank.

My expression must have given me away because he started to laugh and said, "Miranda, my love, don't look so bloody solemn. It's just that there's rather a lot of Olivia left in the master bedroom. She hasn't taken away all her things yet."

"But I thought you said you were legally separated."

"She left in rather a hurry."

"But she will be taking them away?" I ventured.

Kurt sighed and said in a resigned tone, "As far as I know, yes, she will. Otherwise we might have some jolly good fun tossing all her gear on a bonfire out in the back garden."

I smiled.

"Now, let's do this. You can put your clothes in the larger guest room. There's oodles of closet space there and it has its own bathroom. You can have a little rest in there now but of course you'll be spending the nights in my bed, won't you?" He grabbed me around the hips, pulled me close, kissed me, then let me go.

That was what I wanted to hear. I only hoped he wasn't going to be conducting and firing musicians in his sleep. And I hoped, I hoped…

"Now *do* come along, Miranda. We do want to get you organized before next century."

Jet lag made me too weak to do anything more than follow Kurt around like a newborn duckling. He ushered me into a bedroom at the end of the lemon-yellow hallway and began to open closets and drawers to show me where I could put my things.

"I'll leave you to it then," he said. He left me, shutting the door behind him.

The guest bedroom was a deep French blue. On the blue telephone, I called my mother to let her know I'd arrived safely. I was already chilled to the bone and the color made me feel even colder.

The adjoining bathroom was French blue, too, with all the accessories in the same color, a series of marine etchings all in blue, little blue starfish and shell-shaped soaps, blue bath-oil beads, blue towels, blue toothbrush glass, blue scales for weighing myself after all that airplane food and putting myself in a blue mood. I turned on the enameled blue hot tap and almost expected blue water to come gushing out.

Then I went to get undressed. I pulled off my traveling clothes, climbed into the tub, stretched myself out in the hot water and thought, Sorry, Olivia, but all this blue has *got* to go.

Kurt shook me and whispered, "Wake up, lazybones. It's teatime."

"I was hoping for something stronger than tea," I yawned and threw off the blue-striped duvet.

"Teatime means dinner, silly girl. Get dressed. We're going out. What do you fancy? Indian? French? Vietnamese?"

Kurt made the final decision. He picked a little Chinese place in Soho where we ate chicken almond, shrimp in black-bean sauce, fried seaweed, drank sauvignon and flirted shamelessly. I thought I looked very chic that night, even though the jet lag made me feel a little as though I'd been hit across the head with a plank.

I was dressed in a cream lace patchwork skirt with a cream-colored and very revealing cashmere V-necked sweater and flat-heeled beige cossack boots. My coat was camel hair, gorgeous, and nobody needed to know I'd bought it for sixty percent off in the army and navy sale. Kurt alternated between feeding me morsels, looking me predatorily in the eye and staring at my cleavage V. It might mean a sacrifice but I could learn to live with that pampered feeling.

After dinner, we walked through town. It was a couple of weeks before Christmas and there were hordes of shoppers and fashionable-looking people to stare at. We walked all the way to Harrods. The Christmas windows were lit up and in motion, and as we stood there watching the fairy-tale theme (and I tried to imagine what kind of gift Kurt would be giving me), a few flakes of snow fell from the sky. The whole world seemed to be glittering and full of promise.

And as soon as I was over my jet lag, I would go and

look up Sebastian. I would be his Christmas present and he would be mine.

When we got back to the house, snow was falling heavily.

Kurt led me up the stairs and into the master bedroom. It was a room that Olivia had obviously taken great pains with but it made me think of the Spanish Inquisition, from the huge portraits of grim consumptive ancestors right down to the damask-draped centuries-old four-poster canopied bed.

Kurt undressed me slowly, paying attention to every inch of my body. I was so sure. I thought, Now, this is it, tonight's the night I'll be ripping open those little devils in foil packets.

No such luck.

Afterward, as I lay there in the disappointing half-baked afterglow, I couldn't stop myself from whispering, "Kurt, when are we going to have the normal boring old-fashioned kind of sex? I promise I won't get pregnant."

"You won't…ah…you know about those."

Those?

"I took it for chorus gossip," I said.

He was silent for a long time and seemed very far away. "Two paternity suits haven't helped my situation with Olivia. I confess…I was stupid and careless… I…"

"Don't worry, Kurt. I understand. You're at the center of things all the time. I've seen the way women push themselves at you. But now, what about us? I have no intention of having children. Not for the next decade at least. I've got a career to launch. And I've got munitions." I reached for the box of high-quality condoms and held it up.

"So you do." His expression was gentle. "This business between Olivia and I is nearly finalized. Perhaps tomorrow night…"

"Do you really mean that?"

"Yes, I suppose I do."

He sounded a little morose. His voice was the voice of a lost man, a man at sea. But it didn't matter to me in the least.

Hallelujah choruses exploded in my head.

In the middle of the night I was wide awake on Canada time. I lay there staring at the ceiling afraid to get up in case I woke Kurt. Kurt had been fairly quiet in his sleep with only occasional outbursts of something that sounded like, "F-sharp, you tone-deaf clods. You're flat."

Finally, I climbed out of bed, tiptoed out of the bedroom and downstairs into the living room. I switched on lamps and went over to the sideboard where at least ten photo portraits of the same dark-haired Roman-nosed woman framed in silver smiled a superior smile at me.

Olivia.

It had to be.

There was Olivia at the seaside. Olivia in evening dress and diamonds. Olivia in ski wear. Olivia trying to look denim casual against the side of a building (the bank where she kept her mountains of money, I imagined). Olivia at a costume party dressed as Cleopatra. Olivia in fox-hunting garb on the back of a horse in front of an enormous country estate. Olivia dressed from head to toe in something that looked an awful lot like fetish leather. She wasn't naturally beautiful, but even from the pictures, I could see she had plenty of the kind of style and gloss that only money can buy.

I tiptoed back upstairs and into the big bed. After half an hour or so of listening to Kurt's ravings, I finally fell asleep.

The next day a blanket of snow covered the ground and weighed down the boughs of the topiary trees and shrubs in Kurt and Olivia's fussy garden.

Kurt brought caffe latte and croissants and jam on a tray and we ate breakfast in the four-poster bed. We finished up by licking each other's fingers and then the little sticky places on our bodies where jam had fallen.

I had to admit that the bed was growing on me a little.
The rest of the room would have to go, though.

Kurt then decided that because there was all that snow
(laughable by Cold Shanks standards but I humored him),
we were going for a walk in Richmond Park.

When we got there, it was so cheesy, just like a bad movie.
We made snow angels, then we chased each other across the
stretches of patchy whiteness, startled the stags in the park
and got them running and stampeding, kissed each other at
the center of a big field as the wind came up and started to
freeze us to death.

And then we went to a pub to get warm and eat lunch.

As we sat there nursing mulled ales, Kurt said, "You've
been practicing, I hope."

I grimaced at him. "Oh, of course, Kurt, I sang in the airplane bathroom all the way across the Atlantic."

"You know what I mean."

"Let me land," I said. "I feel like I'm still flying through
the air. My ears haven't stopped buzzing."

"I thought we might rehearse the song cycle this afternoon."

I looked at him aghast.

Madame Klein had this thing about singing and snow and
it was well drilled into me. You don't taste snow, you don't
turn your face up to the freezing sky and let snowflakes fall
on your tongue. You don't roll around on the cold ground
or run through the brisk damp air with your throat uncov-
ered. You always wear a scarf. Plus, you don't drink warm
beer on snowy days before singing. You don't drink at all,
in fact. And you don't lose a lot of sleep with a man in a
four-poster bed on the snowy night before you have to sing.

Good thing Madame Klein was so far away.

So that afternoon, we climbed the stairs up to the
fourth floor. Kurt opened the door to one of the rooms
and ushered me in. It was a studio with yet another baby
Steinway grand piano (there was a full-size Steinway

grand in the living room downstairs too). This room had its own turret and was where Kurt kept equipment, tape recorders, computers, extra keyboards. He locked himself away up there to do his composing, like some modern-day Merlin.

He went straight over to the piano. The score to his song cycle was already laid out, ready to be played.

"I wouldn't mind warming up, Kurt. I can't sing this thing cold."

"Warm up then," he said.

"Go away then," I said.

He got up reluctantly. At the door, he said, "I'll be back in fifteen minutes."

I began my scales very quietly. For the first time in my life, there was an odd sensation as I sang, as though I was fighting my whole body. I tried centering, moving my jaw, relaxing my neck and shoulders, visualizing the notes, expanding my breath even further to support the sound and keep the pressure off the vocal cords.

When Kurt came back in, I was less worried about his piece than about making a decent sound. As he played, I labored to keep that dragging feeling away and keep the sound afloat. I had a couple of moments of jet-lag stupidity in some of the major Bing Bang Bong sections but Kurt didn't seem to notice. He made a few annotations here and there but he didn't do as much erasing and scribbling as usual.

Toward the end, there was a long-held high note, and I wanted to show him I was in good enough form to show off. I held the note long after the accompaniment had stopped but it nearly killed me.

Kurt made an approving face and said, "Nice note, Miranda. Shut the door behind you when you leave, would you?"

"How did it seem?"

"It seemed passable. I actually do believe..."

"What?"

He nodded his head slowly and said, "I believe that the piece is finished."

"Just like that?"

"I made the corrections I needed to make. Let's just sing it through one more time."

Oh sure, and let's just haul the Titanic *to the ocean's surface while we're at it.*

"Do you mind if I mark?" I asked.

He gave me an odd look. "Mark if you must but I'd rather you sing it as it was meant to be sung."

I obeyed, and I've never worked so hard in my life.

When the last note had stopped ringing and silence filled the room, I expected his opinion, a critique or a compliment, but instead he said, "Oh, by the way, Guido might be dropping in tonight. He wants to meet you."

"Guido?"

"The author of the text you were just singing. Guido Castracani."

"Oh, that Guido."

The poor homesick Italian who hated London.

Kurt looked at his watch. "Now. You go downstairs and do what you like while I transcribe the corrections to the computer. Then we really ought to pop out to Sainsbury's. The cupboards are rather bare."

There were three cars in his garage, the Jaguar, the Jeep, and the brand-new Mercedes-Benz. He asked me to choose which one I liked and he'd let me drive. I chose the Jeep but I was terrified. I aged a whole year in half an hour, getting us there on the wrong side of the road, with Kurt white-faced next to me. But if I wanted to live in London, I'd have to get the hang of it.

At Sainsbury's, we wheeled our cart around the aisles, grabbing every kind of impractical and politically incorrect goody to eat, no fear of Caroline popping up to lecture me on the cruelty of bursting geese's livers for pâté de fois gras, or the frivolity of buying prepackaged Brie and sorrel soup from France and wine from Italy and passion fruit from Israel. Kurt said to take whatever I felt like getting so I filled the cart up with so many delicious and exotic things that they were rolling and tumbling off the top. Kurt paid with a credit card and didn't even flinch when the cashier told him the total, three hundred and seventy-one pounds and forty pence!

It was all so promising and domestic. This is what it would be like to be married to him, I thought.

Kurt insisted on driving home, and when we got back from the supermarket there was a man waiting on Kurt's front porch.

"There's Guido now, old love," said Kurt.

Guido Castracani was in his midforties, tall and broad-shouldered with thick neatly trimmed salt-and-pepper hair, green eyes and a trimmed mustache and beard. His clothes, pressed gray slacks and heavy olive-green sweater, were tidy and chic and fitted him perfectly. He had style. He must have been a totally breathtaking knockout in his younger years, but now, despite the style, he looked like a man who'd lived too hard. His eyes were pouchy and red-rimmed and he was dragging on his cigarette as though he wanted to get every last particle of tar and nicotine out of it.

Guido opened the car door first for Kurt and then for me. As I got out, he said, "At last. I have been out here freezing my balls off for the last twenty minutes. And now I finally get to meet the new girl, La Miranda that I have been hearing so much about." He made a little bow and kissed my hand. I wanted to laugh but I said, "Hi, Guido. Nice to meet you." The Melandroni men had been heavily into hand-kissing, too.

I wasn't pleased with what he'd said about me being the new girl though. I went straight over to Kurt, gave him the evil eye and whispered, "I'm not supposed to tell anybody about *us* but it's okay for you to go blabbing to this guy about *me?*"

Kurt brushed me off. "Guido and I are old friends, or rather, comrades in adventure."

Adventure, my breathing apparatus. Whipped cream, two-headed cheerleaders, harem girls, and swapped wives in fetish gear. It wouldn't have surprised me. Guido wasn't wearing a ring and there was no little ring-wearer's trench on his finger, but Kurt had once told me that he was married.

We all went inside and while we put groceries away, Guido chose a bottle of wine from Kurt's extensive wine cellar and opened it. Then he proceeded to stand over it like a protective bulldog, saying, "Nobody touch it. We cannot drink it yet. It must breathe."

Kurt took out some Carr's Water Biscuits and Camembert and we started to nibble. After ten minutes of Guido moaning about his writer's block (his wife's fault) and watching the wine breathe, Kurt said, "Oh bugger it, Guido, give us a drink then." Guido frowned, muttered something profane in Italian then poured the wine into three huge beautiful crystal glasses.

"Ah, Brunello di Montalcino," he said, swirling it in the glass and savoring its bouquet.

Then Guido and Kurt sat back in their chairs and started talking about soccer—or football as they called it here.

Now, it's not that I dislike sports, not at all, not if we're actually playing them. But talking about them and not actually playing them bores me to tears. So as soon as the two men started talking World Cups, Ronaldo and Beckham, I slid into a coma. It seemed as though I was in it for days, but when I came to, famished, only ten minutes had passed.

I finally interrupted them to say, "Do you two realize it's well past dinnertime? Would you guys like me to make some pasta?"

Both of the men looked at me as if I'd suggested that they eat deep fried grasshoppers.

They shrugged and looked indifferent. "If you're hungry, make some for yourself," said Kurt.

"Well, yes, I am hungry so I'm making some. And I'll make a little extra just in case you happen to change your minds…" They ignored me and went back to arguing about soccer players.

I opened cupboard doors in the enormous white and stainless-steel kitchen until I'd figured out where everything was. I put on a pot to boil, then I poured olive oil into a pan, simmered loads of parsley, garlic and hot pepper, and finally put in a tin of baby clams. The smell was so good that I could almost see them both drooling. When the spaghetti was cooked, I sloshed it around in the pan with the clams.

I set out three plates and we ate the pasta and drank the wine and both Guido and Kurt had two helpings. Then they sat back holding their stomachs and looking at me as though I were no longer Miranda Lyme but someone else, someone far more important. Like the Queen.

"I didn't realize you cooked, Miranda," said Kurt.

"Well, if you'd stayed at my party that night…" I snapped.

"Let's not cry over spilt milk, shall we?" he snapped back.

"Perhaps La Miranda would like to do a little pub crawling," suggested Guido.

"Yes, please, can we? I'd love that," I said. "That sounds like the perfect London kind of thing to do. Are there any good pubs in Notting Hill?"

We called a cab and piled in. Guido kept calling me "Bella" and finding excuses to press against me. He'd started earlier in the evening when I'd been clearing up the dishes, and later, getting in and out of the car, going through doorways, crowding around the table at the pub.

That night was a blur of wood paneling and dark smoky walls, of raucous laughter and jostling, elbowing bodies with the damp wool and expensive aftershave smell. When the pubs started to close, we moved on to clubs.

At the last club, Emporium (somebody's Greek fantasy complete with gushing fountain and go-go guys and girls dressed all in white), Guido said to Kurt, *"Bella fica ti sei trovato, Kurt."* I guess he didn't realize I actually understood a little Italian, that I wasn't another one of those singers who faked it. The first things you learn in a new language are always the worst things, the swearwords. What he'd said loosely translated as, "Nice set of female genitalia with legs you've found yourself, Kurt."

I remembered another little tidbit from my indentured slavery in Florence and I said to him, *"Te e tu mai, testa di rapa."* Which loosely translated from the Tuscan vernacular meant, "You and your mother, you turnip head."

He choked briefly on his Pernod and water, and then he threw back his head and roared with laughter. He was very polite and well behaved for the remainder of the evening.

It was three in the morning when we had the taxi drop Guido off at his house in Kensington.

"Be nice to Guido," said Kurt, when we got back to the house. "He's my friend. He and his wife are going through a rather rocky moment. They may be splitting up and if they do, it's going to be an acrimonious divorce."

"I'm not surprised. He kept feeling my kneecaps under the table, or didn't you notice."

"Oh, good lad, Guido. He's done most of the preliminary work for me then, hasn't he?" said Kurt, smiling and sliding his hands beneath my skirt.

It was four o'clock in the morning when we climbed the staircase in Kurt's house. Tonight was the night. He'd promised. We both undressed and stood in the double shower stall of the rose-colored bathroom off the master bedroom. Under the streaming water, we touched and kissed each other. My skin was so sensitive, I was ready to come just at the thought that finally, Kurt and I were going to do it right. We both stretched out on the canopied bed, touching and kissing some more, and as I reached for the little foil packets that I'd stashed in the drawer of the bedside table, the phone rang.

"Bloody hell," said Kurt, climbing over me and off the bed. "I'll take it in Olivia's study." He bounded out of the bedroom and down the hall.

I still hadn't had a chance to snoop through the whole house. Kurt had barely left me alone for a minute. Olivia's study would definitely have to be surveyed for renovations.

I slid out of bed and went into the hallway. At first, I could only hear the rise and fall of Kurt's voice in the distance but not the words. I moved a little closer to the study door, which was ajar.

Now I could make out all Kurt's words. "…you're sure? I don't want a repeat of the… I have been… I swear… for what it's worth… you have to be sure… this isn't just one of your… I know, yes I do know… I know you do… and I do too." The last few words were spoken tenderly. I raced back down the hall and into bed and tried to keep my imagination from hurtling out of control.

When Kurt came into the bedroom his face didn't have a trace of tenderness in it. He looked cool and businesslike, the way he looked at opera rehearsals. He didn't meet my eyes. He went over to his closet and started to pull out suits and shirts.

"That was my agent," he said as he tossed clothes onto the bed and wrestled with suitcases.

"At four-thirty in the morning?"

"It was urgent. He wants me to fill in for another conductor who has just broken his arm. It means a number of closely booked engagements around Europe for the next few weeks. I'd rather looked forward to our little holiday at home, but work is work. One can't always say no."

"Fantastic. We can see Europe together."

"Miranda, my love, I've *seen* Europe. I want you to stay here."

"But Kurt…"

"I want you to see how it feels to be here when I'm not. I'm so often away. It could be a useful test. You might use the opportunity to act as lady of the house. It can be harder than it seems. Olivia complained endlessly when I was away. And I'll leave you the keys to the Jeep. You will take care and not wrap it around Nelson's Column, I trust? Also, I have a few musical jobs I'd like you to do for me. I'll show you right now. I would have done them myself but it looks as though I shan't be able to. I'll be getting a seven-thirty flight to Amsterdam so we've got to be quick."

He made me put something warm on then he dragged me all the way up to his music studio, where he turned on the computer. "Now let me show you how to find the score for *Città di Pietra*. You do know how to use a mouse, don't you? Oh, don't look so wounded. Now, when you have the whole thing up, it's like a spreadsheet. You like it, do you? I had this software specially designed for me. You do this to separate the parts. Click here and here and here. They have to be checked against the handwritten score, separated, printed, then checked again and sent to Vancouver. The address is here. It's not actually as difficult as it seems. The software does all the work. And don't worry if you bugger up on the first go. I've made a couple of backups.

"Here's the address of the printer here. He's in the area. You just put all the separate parts on CD and take it to him. And here's the type of paper I want used. Ask for Nigel. He knows what to do. You won't bugger it all up then, will you, my love? It's horribly expensive so you do want to get it right. Now can you manage it all?"

It was a bit daunting but I was flattered that he was putting so much trust in me. "Of course I can manage," I said. "What do you take me for?"

He smiled that sweet forlorn hapless smile that

charmed so many chorus women all over the world (and some of the men), making them trip and fall over the hems of their costumes.

"Make yourself at home, and have a wonderful time. And practise, practise, practise, and the next time we work on the piece, I'm sure it will be perfect."

I nodded. I'd go over the house thoroughly too, and make plans, big plans for wiping out Olivia's personal signature and putting in my own. It wasn't the only house I had to worry about either. Kurt also had something modernly rustic in Cornwall, a huge estate in Kent (I'd leave that alone except as a place to deposit the other awful antiques—didn't want to tamper with history) and a cottage in Ireland for tax purposes.

But then it occurred to me. "Kurt, I'm going to be here alone at Christmas. Alone on Christmas *Day*."

"I know, Miranda, my love, I know. And I'm dreadfully sorry about that. But we just couldn't foresee it, could we now? And it is *rather* an overrated day, don't you think? All that fanfare and nonsense over one bloody silly *baby*. Chill a nice bottle of Brut and make believe I'm here with you while you're getting pissed. Stiff upper lip now."

But my stiff upper lip was quivering and I turned away so that he wouldn't see. I wanted to say, "Kurt, if it weren't for the one bloody silly *baby*, the world wouldn't have all that bloody wonderful sacred music," but I kept quiet.

He went downstairs to finish packing his bags. He seemed so happy and enthusiastic about having to fill in for this conductor that I began to worry that I might be involved with a bad workaholic and not a man.

"So when do these engagements end?" I asked. "When will you be back?"

"Oh, in several weeks, I should imagine," he said.

"But what does that mean exactly?"

"Several weeks. It depends on the recovery of the person I'm replacing."

"And just who is this other conductor that you're replacing?"

He looked quickly at his watch. "Good Lord, is that the time? Come along with me now, Miranda, I'll show you how the burglar alarm works."

I obeyed. What else could I do? I didn't want to turn into another Olivia before we'd even gotten started. Olivia had obviously been a demanding, obsessive harpy.

After he'd showed me how to activate and deactivate the alarm, he caressed my cheek and said, "Listen, Miranda, just in case anybody should pop by, like one of our nosy neighbors, I think it would be best if you told them you were the house-sitter. Bloody hell, don't look so tragic. It's just a useful little lie. So that we can break our news in our own good time. You haven't been in the limelight much in your short life, but I have, my love, and these things must be carefully planned, organized by my agent and PR people so that the paparazzi don't have too much of a field day. There's some cash in the main desk drawer in the kitchen and important phone numbers in the leather-bound book next to the kitchen phone. Now chin up."

He was holding my chin in his hand and gave it a little upward nudge. Then he leaned in and kissed me, a lingering warm kiss that would have to tide me over for far too long. Outside, a taxi honked its horn. He whispered, "I'll call you," and disappeared into the cold night.

I wandered around the huge empty house, then went into the downstairs den and turned on the TV. Kurt had satellite, so I played channel roulette for a while but nothing interested me. I went upstairs and yanked the rose-colored satin quilt off the four-poster bed. It still smelled of Kurt. Breathing in his scent for a while, I wrapped the quilt around myself. Back downstairs in the kitchen I opened cupboards and rummaged until a huge bag of Lindt chocolates were located, which I'd put in the shopping cart the day before. I took the chocolates and the dregs of a bottle of Grand Marnier and retreated to the conservatory to watch the dawn.

When the sun came up, there were a few seconds of rich mandarin sunlight over the opalescent landscape. But then everything clouded over. The snow turned to rain and made the yard beyond the window glass patchy and slushy, gray and disappointing. When full daylight finally came, the world outside seemed like a misty heap of muck. I retreated, climbing back up the stairs and into our empty bed.

Kurt roared at me to dance faster. He was dressed as a pasha and had a huge bulging crotch in his billowing pasha pants. Instead of a baton he brandished a whip. Dancing in the air behind him were hundreds of photographs of Olivia, and she was laughing at me from each and every one of the little silver frames.

"Faster. Dance faster. Allegro, Miranda, molto allegro. Fortissimo," bellowed Kurt. I sensed I would be rewarded if I did as I was told, but I wasn't quite sure how. As I danced, I realized I had two heads. I looked over at my other head, which grew out of the right side of my neck, and there was no doubt about it; the other Miranda definitely looked smarter and wiser than me.

"Tell me what you know," I demanded.

"You know it too," said my other head, "it's just that you're too stupid to know that you know."

I grabbed the neck of my other head and started to squeeze with both hands while my other mouth croaked out, "Stop, stop choking me. I'm you and you're me, you silly moo…"

When I woke up, it was dark again. The bedsheets were twisted all around my body and my neck. I untangled myself, crawled out of the bed and into the rose-colored bathroom. I stared at myself in the mirror.

There was only one Miranda Lyme head staring back at me, thank God.

I went downstairs and confronted Kurt's stereo system. It was an enormous complex thing with millions of controls so that you could have music anywhere in the house. I programmed it for the rose-colored bathroom off the master bedroom, choosing a version of *Die Walküre* with Birgit Nilsson singing Brunhilde. Then I went back upstairs and had a long leisurely bath filled with rose-colored bath oil.

By the time I'd had some coffee and dressed—black jeans, black turtleneck sweater, Doc Martens and my camel-hair coat—I was feeling much better about everything. I had slept through an entire day and the following night and it was now seven o'clock in the morning.

I was ready to take on London.

Chapter 15

When I emerged from the subway near Hyde Park, a regiment of red-jacketed uniforms and brass instruments was marching by, almost as if they'd known I was coming and sent a welcoming committee.

First I went to Buckingham Palace and tried to irritate the busbied sentry in the sentry box (he was truly amazing, made of wood). After that, I went to the Tate Modern and took in sculptures that looked like white stones, and white stones that looked like sculptures, kitchen utensils that looked like sharp art in primary colors, and primary-colored art that looked like kitchen utensils. I walked through the Christmas crowds in Carnaby Street, Leicester Square, Tower Records, Piccadilly Circus, and along the elegant gray crescent of Regent Street, past the windows full of expensive woolens. As the light seeped away and damp cold turned to freezing cold, I headed toward Victoria Station and home.

And then, at around seven o'clock that evening, as I was heating up my gourmet TV dinner in the microwave (lemon veal and potatoes Romanoff with snow peas and julienned green beans), the doorbell rang.

I ran into the hallway. Through the stained glass of the front door, I could make out a female silhouette. Maybe it was Olivia, back from Tuscany, come to tear out my hair and scratch out my eyes. Feeling a little jittery, I opened the door. On the doorstep was a woman in her midthirties wearing a long black mink coat, long black leather gloves, a black mink hat and pearls. Under her arm was tucked a dog that resembled a cross between a rat and a fox.

She gave me an up-and-down once-over and then said, "Err, herrlerr," which translates from British Upper Crust to regular English as "Oh, hello." She seemed much too calm to be Olivia and besides, she wasn't the woman from the living-room photos.

"Hi," I said.

Then she looked lovingly into the little dog's eyes, "Oh, I say, Poozie, it's the colonial. Shall we ask her to invite us in?"

Behind her in the street, a chauffeur at the wheel of a black Rolls-Royce kept the engine running.

"Do come in," I said.

From now on, Kurt's friends were my friends. Unfortunately.

"Can I ask you something?" I said, looking her straight in the eye. Since I was the colonial, I'd act like a colonial.

"Err, yerrs."

"Who are you?"

"We're Judith, Olivia's cousin, aren't we, Poozie?" she said to the dog. She swept past me through the hallway and straight into the living room to the drinks tray, where she picked up a decanter and poured herself half a tumbler of scotch without even putting the dog down. She took a dainty swig and said, "And you are…?"

"Miranda."

"Lovely to meet you, Amanda." She offered me the tips

of her black leather fingers as some kind of a handshake, then with a flourish, she spread herself out on the couch and arranged Poozie on the cushion next to her. "Kurt must be over the moon to have you," she said.

"Ah…to…um…*have* me?" Kurt must have blabbed to her too. It was nice to know that everyone was taking our relationship so well.

"Darling, Amanda, you've no idea. It's such a huge relief."

"It is?"

"We were all so terribly worried."

"You were?"

"Oh yes, you've no idea. Olivia was positively neurasthenic about it. But now that you're here, we're all feeling much, much calmer." She gulped down the rest of her drink. I half expected her to hurl the empty glass into the fireplace, but she set it on the coaster and stood up. "I must dash. I simply had to pop by and meet you, Amanda. We'll see you again very soon, won't we, Poozie. I may be around to pick up the post. Ta-ra." She swept out the front door and into the back of the Rolls. She gave me a little wave just before the car whizzed away.

I shut the door and went to reheat my dinner.

That night I went online.

My email to Tina was:

Crack open the beers and have one for me. The word is that me and Kurt are an accepted couple. Olivia's cousin Cruella De Vil came around today to empty the scotch bottle and tell me they're all relieved that I'm here. Can you believe it? The house is huge but is a bit of a baroque nightmare. Will have to hold big garage sale. Plenty of spare rooms here for when you want to come and audition for the English National Opera—tell Collin he can come too if he wants to. Maybe Kurt can find him a job.

To Lance, I wrote:

Dear Lance, I'm not famous yet but am doing my best. Hope you're not working yourself to death out there in the Colonies. If it turns out I stay here forever, will you come and visit me? I'd love to see you.
Matilde

My message to Patrick read:

Hi Pat. I'm in London, England. I tried to return your tapes but nobody was home and they ended up in my suitcase and now they're here with me. Sorry about that. I'll mail them to you. I hope you've been able to solve that "little housekeeping problem" you had.
Miranda Lyme
P.S. Merry Xmas

The next morning, I woke well before five. I was lying in bed and despairing that I would never get off Canadian time and on to British time, when I heard the sound of a man half singing half screaming outside in the garden. It was a vaguely familiar sort of scream. I listened a little longer then recognized the aria "La Ci Darem La Mano" from Mozart's *Don Giovanni*. It was sung in a crackly drunken baritone that was a little off-key. The Italian was perfect, however.

"La Miranda. Where is La Miranda?" shouted the voice up toward the bedroom window.

I went over to the window and peeped through the rose-and–brick-colored damask curtain. It was Guido. "Are you there?" he shouted. "If you are there, Miranda, please open up and let me come in. I am a poor cold wet bedraggled shell of a man and I wish to warm my hands and feet."

As long as it was only his hands and feet.

I opened the side pane of the casement window and

called down. "Guido, what are you doing out there at this hour?"

"Crying over my lost youth," he slurred. *"Non amo che le rose che non colsi, non amo che le cose che potevano essere e non sono state...."*

"What?"

With one hand over his heart and a pained look on his face, he tried again, "I only love the roses I did not pick, I only love the things that *could* have been and were not..."

"Please don't be so dramatic, Guido. Go home."

"I cannot go home. My wife will not let me in."

"I don't believe you."

"She is not alone."

"Oh, dear. That sounds serious. Don't you have somewhere else to go?"

"I always come here when she locks me out," protested Guido.

Kurt's was a big house, and if I got desperate, I could always bolt the bedroom door.

"Oh, all right," I said. "I'll come down and open the door..."

"Bellissima Miranda."

"But you have to promise me that you'll behave."

He made an elaborate bow.

I ran downstairs, turned off the alarm and opened the door. Guido smelled like a brewery. He stumbled past me and into the kitchen.

"Do you also make espresso as well as you make pasta?" he boomed.

"I might be able to rise to the occasion," I said.

I got out the Italian Moka espresso maker, loaded it up with coffee and put it on the stove. He sat in a kitchen chair and wrestled himself out of his coat, muttering and cursing at it.

I struggled to think of something safe we could talk

about. "So now, Guido, are you planning to do any other pieces with Kurt apart from *La Città di Pietra?*"

Guido immediately went from drunk to sober. He sat up straight, his green eyes suddenly wide and clear. "Oh, well, yes. The opera." He said it in a tone that implied the entire world knew all about it.

"Opera? You and Kurt are writing an opera?"

"He has not told you about it?"

"He ah…no."

"Povera piccola Miranda."

I fiddled with cups and spoons and the sugar bowl so that I wouldn't have to look him in the eye. If he'd told me Kurt had a new girlfriend, I would have felt less hurt and betrayed. "What's it about?" I ventured.

"Oh, the usual things," said Guido softly. "Men, women, love, strife, death. It is not particularly original."

"You're just trying to be nice."

"Clearly, he has not talked about it to you."

"No."

"I am sorry. It surprises me. I should not have mentioned it. That was very careless of me," said Guido.

"It doesn't matter," I replied sulkily. "It's only going to be another piece of Bing Bang Bong anyway, only much, much longer and with a larger orchestra, costumes and a stage director."

"A piece of what?"

"Bing Bang Bong. Atonal music, Guido."

"I would not know. My ear is for the words, not so much for the music."

"You're joking."

"My collaboration with Kurt is very complicated. It is partly out of friendship but also there is another bond. I cannot really hear his music."

"But you were singing *Don Giovanni* outside," I laughed.

He gave me a tiny knowing smile.

"That's a good one," I said. "You're being nice again. Now tell me. I'm curious. Where did you and Kurt meet?"

"When Kurt came to study in Torino, quite a few years ago now, maybe fifteen. I was teaching language to foreign students at the university while working on my thesis, twentieth-century Italian populace poets. My mother was English, which was useful for handling foreign students."

"Your English is very good."

He smiled. "Yes. And Kurt was one of the foreign students taking those terrible language classes. He was still just a child, you know, wet behind the ears and already conducting concerts there."

"I know. He's quite the prodigy."

Guido paused then said quietly, "Then I committed a large error."

"Sorry?"

"I made a mistake. I took Kurt home for dinner one night."

"That sounds like a hospitable thing to do. What was wrong with that?"

"Olivia was with me back then."

"Sorry?"

"Olivia was living with me in Torino when she and Kurt met."

"Oh. I see...I think... Are you telling me he stole her from you?"

"Stole her...I do not know. What is a man supposed to do? Beat his breast like a gorilla and snatch the woman away from his rival? That would not be civilized. I loved her but she chose him. Maybe it was because they were both English and homesick. I do not know. He had youthful energy. He won that match. And it was a long time ago."

"Not that long ago. You're talking like an old man, Guido."

"There are days when I feel ancient. But in the end, it is better to collaborate with your enemies. Know them."

He tapped his forehead and then sat there looking like a beaten dog.

After a minute of silence, I said, "If you're trying to get me to feel sorry for you, it won't work."

He smiled. "You women. How will we ever understand you?" He shook his head.

I observed him for a moment and then said, "Guido, can I ask you a personal question?"

"Ask me, Miranda. I am at the mercy of your corn-flower-blue eyes and red-velvet mouth."

"Are you still in love with Olivia?"

"That is a very good question and one I would rather not answer."

"That's sort of romantic," I said.

My heart soared. I wanted Guido to go off to that part of Tuscany where Olivia was rumored to be hiding out, and whisk her off with him to a distant place that was well out of harm's way.

New Zealand would be good. Or perhaps the South Pole.

"You are so young, *cara* Miranda. Enjoy your youth. Do not take love seriously. Just live and enjoy." As he said this, he was ogling my breasts as though they were cookies to go with his coffee.

"And your wife," I said abruptly, interrupting his reverie. "What about her? Does she know that you're still in love with Olivia?" I asked.

"Judith? I have no idea. I am sure she does not care what I think or feel."

"Judith? Her name's Judith? A Judith came around here yesterday. She said she's Olivia's cousin."

"Yes. Judith is my wife."

If you can't be with the one you love, marry her cousin.

I said, "This particular Judith had the mink and the pearls and the Rolls and the little dog…"

I could see I'd offended him. Guido stood up and began to bluster. "Olivia and Judith come from very wealthy families. An artist should always have at least one wealthy patron. Freedom from financial worries is necessary in order to create." He made a sweeping gesture with his arms. "You are a singer. You should know about patronage and if you do not, you should learn."

"So really, in a way, you and Kurt are family."

He made a sort of harrumph sound that passed for a yes. He slumped back into the chair and looked so miserable that I poured out his coffee for him and even stirred in the sugar.

There was no doubt about it. As far as relationships went, I was now playing in the big messy league.

Looking up Sebastian was weighing on me. Why, in all these years, hadn't he looked *me* up? Or had my mother warned him off somehow? All of a sudden I was scared.

It was easy to put off the visit. I had Kurt's song cycle to get in order. The next few days were spent in Kurt's music studio playing with his composing software and getting the hang of it. He was right. It wasn't as hard as it seemed. I had to check that the transcribed computer score was the same as the handwritten one, then separate the parts. In fact it was so easy, I took *La Città di Pietra* apart three times just for fun.

The original score was copied and saved separately in case anything got lost in the process. The amazing thing about the software was that it played back, in the indicated instruments, everything that was written on the virtual manuscript paper. You didn't have to know how to play an instrument in order to hear the music you'd written.

So naturally, when I realized the software had this great playback feature I couldn't resist fiddling and twiddling with the sounds. I saved all the parts in another file and started making "corrections" in Kurt's original score, just for kicks. I didn't change anything in the solo soprano voice, but in the underlying accompaniment, I raised and lowered notes to create slightly sweeter sounds and harmonies, still leaving in enough dissonance to give the overall impression of atonality. Then through the bass line, I carefully threaded in the notes from the melody line of "Girls Just Want to Have Fun." You couldn't actually hear it because it was so heavily camouflaged. But I would know, and that was the important thing.

I clicked on Save As, gave the file my name and turned off the computer.

On Christmas Eve day, an icy wind swept away all the remaining clouds and left a clear blue sky. I had a long lonely brunch of porridge with cream and brown sugar and then some crispy bacon. My favorite comfort food with a light sprinkling of despair.

Things weren't going at all the way I'd planned.

After I'd finished eating, I went for a walk. Putney high street was a frenzy of last-minute shoppers. Happy people with families to go to and a big meal to share.

I kept saying to myself, it's just a day, a day like any other day. If you didn't know it was Christmas, you'd be fine.

What is it about Christmas that fills people with so much expectation? What do we think is going to happen? That some divine power will give us the gift of all gifts?

Maybe.

We've had the childhood Christmas and now we've graduated to the adult one. It goes well beyond diamond bracelets. The trouble with Christmas that year was that I wanted what a lot of people wanted; that somebody wonderful would invest me with an entire universe of their love. The very same universe that the Baby represented. That wasn't asking so much, was it?

I wandered aimlessly, looking into shop windows, watching the couples link arms, exchange kisses and hurry off to their wonderful enviable lives.

Night began to fall at around four-thirty in the afternoon and the dusk was illuminated by street lamps that were at first a beautiful rosy-peach color then turned to orange when real night fell. By the time I started back towards the house, the sky was glittering with stars and the eerie orange streetlights.

That night I tried calling Tina, but all I got was her answering machine. And then I tried calling Caroline to check on the apartment, but my own voice answered, telling me I couldn't come to the phone but that if I would leave my name and number, I'd get back to me right away.

Chapter 16

At eight o'clock in the morning on Christmas Day, I began my wait for my "Merry Christmas" phone call from Kurt. I was open to other possibilities as well, such as a doorbell ringing with an FTD florist bringing me dozens of red roses, or a huge box of chocolates, or that diamond bracelet that never seemed to arrive. I waited all day, listening to music, drinking decaf coffees spiked with brandy and topped with whipped cream and nutmeg, and pacing.

It was not going at all the way I'd planned.

That evening, Guido, Judith and an older blue-rinsed birdlike woman with the same dress sense as Judith appeared at the front door.

When I opened up, Judith pushed past me with everyone following her into the living room. When we were assembled, she pointed to me and said, "This is Amanda, Aunt. She's Canadian."

"Ooo, a colonial," said the aunt, clapping her birdlike hands together. "How are you finding it here, dear? Guido suggested we pop by. He thought you might be lonely."

Guido shrugged in a way that suggested it hadn't been his idea at all. I smiled weakly and Judith poured out huge drinks for everyone. I noticed that Guido was wearing a wedding ring that evening. It was all very confusing.

Then Judith said to the little dog, "Oh, and we're ever so delirious about the news, aren't we, Poozie? Did you know, Aunt, I talked to Olivia yesterday, she'd just been to Gucci in Via Tornabuoni and bought all sorts of fabulous things…"

The aunt said, "I adore the Florence Gucci, but the Ferregamo and Luisa are better. And how is Olivia doing? The last time I saw her she was furious about another of Kurt's little misdeeds."

It was strange. They didn't seem to care a bit that I was in the room. In fact, they behaved as though I weren't there at all. Except for Guido, who kept casting worried looks in my direction.

"Well, she's called off her legal pit bulls and that's something. She was quite prepared to pull out the major artillery, not having done a prenup, but now it seems it's no longer important. There's a new arrangement apparently." Judith then stared straight at me. Or maybe she was staring straight *through* me. It was hard to tell.

I gave her a nervous grin. She looked away as if she hadn't seen me. "She only has one thing on her mind at the moment. She tells me that she and Kurt are trying to have a baby. Isn't that just so typical of Olivia? One minute the world is black, the next she loves us all. And now a baby. How god-awfully trite she can be at times."

"Someone must continue the line, Judith dear," said the aunt. "And I don't see Olivia as a candidate for immaculate conception."

Judith burst into a strange nasal honking laugh. "Err, yes, Aunt, quite. Harn, harn, harn…" It seemed as if that laugh of hers would never finish.

Guido's face was in his hands.

I drank the rest of my gin and tonic in one gulp. There was no feeling in my fingers. I was going into shock.

Guido said, "Come with me into the kitchen, Miranda, I would like an espresso. She makes a very good espresso, Judith."

"Oh, clever little Amanda," said Judith.

As soon as we were in the kitchen, I turned on Guido. "You knew. You knew he was there with HER and you never said a word."

"I knew nothing certain until now. They were going to separate. We all knew that Olivia was starting to have second thoughts but we did not think anything would come of it. It seems she has changed her mind. She is aging and wants a child. It happens every day. Aren't you women always saying that it is your prerogative to change your mind? Now, are we going to have this espresso?"

"I'm the house-sitter. That's what Judith thinks, isn't it?" Tears were now falling down my face and into the jar of coffee. Guido's expression was odd, as though he couldn't decide whether to console me or yell at me. "That was what they were all so relieved about. Someone trustworthy to stay in the house to make sure the family silver and horrible paintings don't get stolen."

"You should not have found out this way," said Guido. "But do not lose your head. None of us must lose our heads. There is too much at stake. You will still be singing Kurt's piece. He has told me that he is very keen for you to perform this piece in Vancouver. There is an incentive program in your province giving grant money to composers who encourage local performers. And the performers must be born in your province and under thirty. Kurt was worried about the cycle but quite glad to have found you. He mentioned that your father was a singer too, and one he admired. So you must think about your professional relationship. Kurt is very good and very well connected and as a singer, you need him. You would be foolish to throw him away for personal reasons."

I was completely numb. I concentrated on getting my fingers to close the espresso maker but didn't manage it.

Well after midnight, I was still waiting for Kurt to call, so I could tell him what I'd heard. And he could deny it and tell me that Olivia was delusional, that she'd taken too much ecstasy in her youth and saw Swiss postal boxes whenever she opened her eyes. But the call never came.

At four in the morning, I dialed my home phone number in Cold Shanks. The line was free and after four rings Lyle picked up. He was tanked.

He said, "Hey, Miranda, you should be here. We're all gettin' merry here on the rum and eggnogs, eh?"

Everyone took their turns talking. My mother came on the line and gave me her rundown. "Oh well, the tree's just beautiful with a new set of oh…and we had a big tur…Danny, get down off the…and then Sal and Bud came around with their…oh, they really can be funny as a crutch when they're not…Darryl, I have told you fifty million times, you're going to lose your priv…and Tina dropped around to say…Danny, stop annoying the…"

"Mom? How was Tina? I haven't heard from her."

"Oh yes, well, she was saying that…oh Darryl, put that down and stop terrorizing…well, of course you can…I didn't say you couldn't talk to your…well then come and talk to…"

The phone was snatched away from Mom, and Darryl came on the line, "Hey, Miranda, guess what I got a mountain bike and so did Dan and we rode over to the creek and there was this dead deer there it was so gross it looked like a ball of slime and then we went and ate all Mom's shortbread cookies she was so pissed off and Dan's a pig he ate nineteen of them…"

How I envied him. It had been years since a deer's carcass had been enough to make my day. I didn't need to speak to the other brother. It would have been like listening in stereo.

My mother came back on and said, "Miranda dear, be careful over there in…"

"I will, Mom." And then I surprised myself by saying a little thickly, "I miss you." There was a short silence and my mother said, "Of course we all love and miss you too."

We both said goodbye at the same time and hung up.

Half an hour later I was still sitting next to the phone having a hard time realizing that staring at it wasn't going to make it ring. I considered rifling through the address book in the kitchen, finding a number for Tuscany, and phoning Kurt, having it out directly. But I was afraid I'd get Olivia or that I'd rage and sputter like a cartoon Tasmanian devil and not make any sense at all.

I went upstairs and online, thinking that maybe Kurt would have been enterprising and thought about sending me an e-mail instead.

There were two messages for me.

Hi all,
I'm out of the office for the next few weeks. Will be back in early Feb. I'll be picking up messages from time to time.
Lance Forrester

Dear Miranda,
First of all, Merry Christmas. Don't worry about the tapes. Watch them. I'd still like to know what you think. What are you doing in England? It was a surprise to get your message. You were there one day and gone the next. I dropped round your place a couple of weeks ago and your roommate told me you were on a plane headed east. Will you be coming back and when?
As for my "little housekeeping problem," it's getting worse. I'm glad you saw it. It made me do some hard thinking. I've got this feeling I'll be cleaning house pretty soon. I don't know how yet but I'm sure there's a way. Only painless suggestions, please. I'm too much of a coward to deal with

heavy fallout. You know, you maybe wouldn't think it, but I'm still a sensitive kind of guy after having been in the slammer and all that.
Let me know how you're doing over there.
All the best,
Pat

The next day, I rode the tube to South Kensington. Sebastian's street was full of elegant four- and five-story houses, some redbrick with white trim, a Dutch look to their facades, others all white and reminiscent of genteel Regency paintings.

In my hand was the one direct communication I'd had from Sebastian, apart from the phone call, in the form of a letter—well, a note really—which had been folded and fingered and stroked and mauled by me to the point that its texture was like soft chamois.

It was written in a nearly illegible hand and read:

Dear Miranda,
I was glad to hear from you and learn that things are going well for you in the music world. We old singers keep busy as the winter season brings more engagements, not just in London but in the North as well. If you should ever happen to be in the area, do look me up. It would be lovely to see you again. I apologize for having waited so long to write.
All the best,
Sebastian

Over the years, I'd been able to read so much into one simple paragraph, but now, standing in front of his redbrick house, it seemed like nothing more than a polite note from a perfect stranger.

I approached the front door, lifted the brass knocker, a lion's head, and banged loud and long.

The door was opened by a small woman in her early fifties with coiffed black hair. "Yes?"

"Is this the residence of Sebastian Lyme?"

"It was."

"Oh, dear. Has he moved?"

The woman peered at me inquiringly and then smiled
sadly. "I think you better come inside."

I stepped into the hallway. To my left was an empty room
with a parquet floor, white ghost impressions on the wall
where pictures had hung and a cold fireplace.

"You're Miranda, aren't you?" said the woman.

"Yes. How did you know?"

"Sebastian told me about you. It's very lucky you caught
me in. I'm Doris, by the way. We expected you sooner. Years
ago, actually. You should have come sooner."

I was expected? Fantastic.

She led me toward the kitchen at the back, talking the
whole time. "We've put the house on the market. You're
lucky to have got me at all. I just came up to London for a
last few days here before we have the movers come."

"I left some messages on the answering machine for Sebastian."

"Yes, I heard those. I'm afraid I didn't know how to get
in touch with you, or I would have done right away. As soon
as it happened."

"As soon as what happened?"

She bit her lip. "Oh dear, what a cock-up. I was sure
you would know...ah, but you don't, do you? Oh, dear.
Why would you? Although it was in the papers...three
months ago."

"I'm sorry. Know what?"

"Sebastian had a heart attack... Oh, my dear, do sit down.
You don't look at all well. He'd grown absolutely enormous,
you know...would you like a glass of water? No? I knew
when I married him that his health was not good but what
can you do? Both of us were a certain age and we wanted

company. The drink certainly didn't help but of course that got so much worse when he began to have problems with his voice… I told him…teach…you can teach. You have so much to offer. But Sebastian was used to being a star, you see. It was very hard, practically from one day to the next, to have your voice and then have nothing. He did rather go downhill, losing himself in food and drink…I worried dreadfully about his heart, but then at our age it's hard to change… I have some pictures around here some- where…yes, there we are. Let me show you. This is him when we got married. Goodness, that was about seven years ago. He hadn't put on the last five stone yet. Lord, it was a nightmare. His attack happened in an upstairs room and it took six paramedics to move him down the stairs, but it was no good. When they got him to hospital, he was gone. You can be thankful that it was all rather quick. Are you sure you wouldn't like a glass of water? A whisky perhaps?"

"A whisky," I murmured.

Chapter 17

It was like a punch in the stomach. I stared around me, numbly, and then I started to sob with huge lurching breaths. Doris waited patiently, then handed me the glass tumbler.

"He was only in his fifties, though," I sobbed.

She nodded. "It happens. Sometimes I think he just lost the will to live, didn't care if everything went to the devil." She sighed. "He could be so witty and charming, when he was able to pull out the best of himself. I do miss him terribly." Her eyes glistened with tears.

Doris began to fiddle with the photographs again, as if looking at them would bring Sebastian back. My father was a strange kind of a ghost in his last years. There were his dark eyes—I still recognized them—but haunted and unhappy in the long sagging gray-bearded face of a tall obese man. He was gone, and with him, my hopes and plans.

The four-year-old in me was bereft and cheated. He'd gone and died before he'd given me the chance to know him, to be his daughter again. The hazy old images, the few memories I'd clung to, were damaged, like snapshots left out in the rain. My father had suddenly stopped tying my shoe. I had no more red candy pills in my toy doctor's kit to put in my father's mock-serious mouth. The old folk song we used to sing together had stopped before the last verse:

I know where I'm going/ I know who's going with me/ I know who I love/ But the Lord knows who I'll marry…

Doris told me I could sit there as long as I liked, until the shock had passed, but the scene felt strange. I mumbled my thanks and left my father's house. It was a biting gray day. I wandered through Holland Park and sat down on a bench near the sleeping flower beds. Freezing tears streamed down my face and once, a passing couple asked me if I was okay.

"My father died," I gulped.

They nodded, understanding, and walked on.

I was confused and upset. I was a fraud. I hadn't really known my father at all. I had no right to cry like someone whose father had shared a lifetime with them. Anger surged up, mixing with the sad emptiness. I was furious with my mother for leaving England in the first place, furious with Sebastian for not coming after me, not pursuing me and teaching me his singer's secrets, furious with Kurt for lying to me and not being there when I needed him, and furious with myself for arriving too late.

That night, back in Kurt's studio, I played a middle C and prepared to sing AH. My voice started to resonate and then SCHPLATT, it just quit. Not unlike Madame Klein's description of my career, the voice just seized up. It felt as though awkward little swellings like small chewed pieces of apple were permanently stuck on my cords.

I was losing my chops.

I went over to the computer, turned it on and found the file for *Città di Pietra*. Then I had another thought. I clicked on my "Girls Just Want To Have Fun" corrected version of the piece, separated it into orchestral parts and put it on the CD for Nigel the printer. I would take it around to him the next day.

In that moment, I was tempted to hunt for Kurt's opera but I still had a few tiny slivers of principle remaining in my being. Besides, I was sure it would be as I'd told Guido, a longer, dressier piece of Bing, Bang, Bong.

After that, I defragged the computer. It was relaxing to just sit and stare at those little cells of color eating their way down the screen.

If only there was a way to defrag my heart.

Later, I went online and sent a message to Tina asking where the hell she was, and then I sent another to Patrick. On the tube back from South Kensington, I'd given his situation a little thought. It had saved me from having to think about all my problems. And I'd come up with an idea.

I wrote:

Dear Pat,

I hope life is treating you well. My life is taking a strange turn. I'd hoped to meet my father but he died three months ago. And now I have this audition to sing and I'm not sure what I'm doing here. All my plans seem to be shifting from one day to the next.

I thought about your housekeeping problem. You need to make yourself extremely unattractive. Manure under the armpits is a good start. Generally not washing makes an interesting impression on most women. And losing ambition is good too. Women don't like men who lack ambition, and that includes the ambition to get out of bed every morning. They don't like jealousy and possessiveness either. Hope this is a help.

Miranda

Kurt's call came at two in the morning on New Year's Eve. In the week and a half that had elapsed between his departure and his New Year's phone call, I had cried and screamed at every wall, every inanimate object in his house, venting all my feelings. By the time I got his call, I was hoarse but calm.

"Miranda, so sorry about the hour, my love, couldn't get away. We played a big New Year's concert here tonight."

"And where's here?" I asked.

"Frankfurt. It really was tremendous. Apart from the fact that it was the usual fare, *Die Fledermaus,* but an excellent cast, a rather stunning Adele…"

"Oh yes? How did you manage to do it?"

"Manage to do what, my love?"

"To get from Florence to Frankfurt and back to Florence so quickly. You must have the latest in the new line of *Star Trek* transporter beams."

"What are you raving about, Miranda?"

"You and Olivia, Kurt. Judith said the two of you are trying to have a baby. That's an interesting new twist to the separation agreement."

"Bloody hell, that Judith. She is such a bloody prying cow…I'm so sorry, Miranda. I would have told you very soon. I just didn't think that over the Christmas season…"

"Kurt…how can you just change your mind like that? It makes me think you never cared for me…" I tried, unsuccessfully, to hold back the tears.

"I did care…I *do* care, but Olivia's my wife. She wasn't completely convinced about this separation and I wanted to cover every contingency…"

"I was a contingency plan?" I blubbed.

"Miranda, you're not going to go all weepy on me…"

"You bastard. Kurt. Bastard, bastard, bastard."

I heard him sigh. "Yes, I suppose I am rather a bastard. Do forgive me. It's rather important that we consider our professional relationship, you and I. I still want you to sing my piece for me. In fact, it's essential that you do."

"That's what Guido said. But you know what? It hurts," I wailed.

"Steady on, old girl. I'm sure it does. But you're a tough old thing, Miranda. You'll survive. You'll be fine, I'm sure. Listen, while we're on the subject of the house, we'd like you to stay there a little longer. Olivia and I intend to stay on in Tuscany, and we really would prefer to have somebody in there. Our neighbors had the most dreadful moving-van burglary. They emptied the house out. We'd like it if you'd stay on another five weeks. Until the middle of February. If you have any trouble changing your airline ticket, let me know, my travel agent is very competent. So try to enjoy yourself a little. See London. Get those parts printed out. We still have the piece to perform in March. And there may be others. Oh, and do remember to put on the alarm when you go out, Miranda. Have a good New Year's. And good luck on the audition."

"Don't say that, Kurt," I shouted. "You can't say 'good luck'..."

I heard a click on the other end.

I stood there trying to remember how to breathe. How did the drill go? In and out? Out and in?

New Year's Day.

ENO audition: less than two weeks away. With my head still on the pillow I tried my singing voice. The sound that came out was that of a cigar-smoking, whisky-drinking frog's croak. Along with swollen vocal cords, I also had a cold. The famous London fog, a dangerous brew of chimney smoke, car and factory exhaust, railway soot and honest mist had finally gotten the better of me. So I spent the day alternately crying into Kleenexes and coughing and honking like a Canada goose. But it was going to be all right, I told myself. I'd sung through colds before.

I took the pillows and duvet from the blue room and moved out of Kurt and Olivia's bedroom and into the downstairs den, which had a very comfortable brown leather couch and a big TV screen.

As I was sipping hot honey and lemon and flicking around the channels, a fragment of a Tom Waits song made me pause. Then came the opening credits, slightly familiar, and the title The Other Street. I laughed a gravelly laugh. They were showing Patrick Tibeau's documentary.

This time I stuck with it. It was a series of interviews with some of Vancouver's more savory homeless people. Each person got to have their say. How they'd ended up on the street. How they survived there. What plans they had, if any. And you knew Patrick was behind the camera asking the questions even though you never saw him.

Patrick had managed to make Vancouver's grottier back streets seem somehow romantic and evocative. When the sound track wasn't made up of scary silences, he'd used some great music choices. Jazz, pop and serious music. Manipulative, yes, but then what are sound tracks for if not for that?

But when the camera moved in on the haunting girl soprano, *my* girl soprano, with her incredible glowing olive skin (despite the crappy street diet) and those violet-blue eyes, I nearly fell off the couch.

What came out of the interview was that her name was Biba. She didn't have a last name and she didn't know how old she was. Her real family were Yugoslavian Romany. She was a Gypsy. Her adoptive parents, who'd been with the Canadian Diplomatic Services in Rome, had taken her in as an emergency intervention when her case first came up. They did it as a favor for a friend and because they had no children of their own.

Biba talked about her early life in a detached tone, in a voice that had no trace left of her other countries. Hers had been a case of physical abuse, beatings, starvation, cigarette burns on her skin, in short, endless torture. Biba was taken away from her Romany mother in Viareggio and installed with the Canadian foster parents. They spoiled her rotten. She had everything a child could wish for. And she was never punished again.

When her Canadian foster parents moved back to Alberta taking her with them, Biba ran away to Vancouver. She said it was hard being with her own people but that it was also hard being with Gaj—people who weren't nomads. She wanted to be near the sea. She said the sea reminded her of Viareggio and her real mother, who she missed. She missed her torturer.

Patrick asked her how it was that she knew so many hymns and spirituals and she said that her Gaj parents had encouraged music and that she'd sung in church. Sometimes, she still sat at the back of churches during the service to learn the pieces, then slipped away before the service ended.

Then Patrick asked her if she remembered any Romany music. She said that it had been a long time ago and she wasn't sure if she could still remember, but then she started into this eerie lament full of sliding quarter tones and slithering minor-key oriental rifts. A shiver ran up my spine. The sound was pure gold.

And then she said, "Everything's okay when I'm singing. When I'm singing is the only time I feel good. It's like I'm safe. I have no problems. I wish I could always be singing."

I dragged my feverish body upstairs to the computer and sent an e-mail to Patrick.

Dear Pat,
I've just seen *The Other Street*. It's really great.
Where is Biba? Do you know her well? Do you know how to get in touch with her?
Love, Miranda
P.S. How's the housekeeping going?

Then I fished Pat's tape of *The Other Street* from my suitcase and played Biba's interview and the Romany song over and over.

The next day, my voice was no better. There was no question of practicing. I went to the computer, opened up Kurt's fancy software and tried to transcribe Biba's song. It was a difficult, near-impossible task because I didn't have notation for quarter tones, but trying helped me take my mind off my other problems. After I'd put down something that resembled a melody line, I wrote an accompaniment for it and let the software play it back. And I have to say, it wasn't bad. It wasn't bad at all.

The following morning, I felt a little better so I muffled up and went into the city. It was biting gloomy weather but I had cabin fever and was sick of being in Kurt's house, of being surrounded by his and Olivia's possessions.

The first thing I did was go to Canada House and sign my name and Kurt's address in the guest book. Then I went to the National Gallery and gazed at Monet's *Water Lily Pond* and Leonardo da Vinci's *Virgin of the Rocks*. But the Virgin and her plump Child reminded me of Kurt and Olivia's little baby-making project, so I hurried out of there.

I saw a lunchtime recital at St. Martin-in-the-Fields, a soprano singing an all-Purcell program.

Henry Purcell had been a Londoner, too, one of the few English composers of the period to write an opera. But poor, poor Henry. He'd died too young. Only thirty-six. The rumor was that his wife locked him out on a cold night and he'd developed pneumonia, which eventually finished him off.

Henry was one of my favorite composers. At a time when the famous soloists and castrati were embellishing pieces beyond all recognition, Henry took the situation in hand and wrote out the embellishments himself, as if to say, "There, try and ruin that, you flagrant embellisher!" And you could tell he'd been a singer himself, even if it was only as a choirboy, because his music sat so nicely in the voice. He painted pictures with music.

As I listened to the soprano singing, "Music for a while/shall all your cares beguile," I could almost see the harmonies and their spectrum of colors. And there was this wonderful ostinato bass line. The bass line was like a charmer's snake, winding and hypnotizing and beguiling the audience.

At the end of the concert, I left the church and walked around the city, feeling hollow and sad. With my defective voice, it was as though a gift I'd been given had been taken away again viciously. My voice was the only thing I had. I didn't play any other instruments well enough to be accepted, to be allowed entrance into the magic circle of real musicians.

If I couldn't make music, you might as well push me into the river.

But I also realized something else in all my musings about Henry and my other favorite composers. Here was this whole club of extinct geniuses who'd leaped across time to lend me their music, these composers who were now taking their music back again, and do you want to know what they were?

They were all men.

Days later, I stood in the wings of the Coliseum stage and waited my turn. I'd been stupid. Whatever had made me think I'd be the only soprano there? The wings teemed with taller, glossier, cuter, younger, more self-assured sopranos than me. All waiting their turn. Pacing in their Chanel suits and Gucci shoes. Mouthing the words to arias that were far more ambitious than mine.

The odor of dusty velvet, old paint and hot lights that had once been an elixir now terrified me. The nag was back, right on my heels. I concentrated on taking big breaths, holding them for a long time, then letting them out counting to sixty. My voice had worked that morning when I'd gone through my pieces, but now my throat was parched and dry. I couldn't focus on the music and my roles. Instead, I saw a desert full of horse-shaped mirages snorting nearby.

I was first on the list. Somewhere out in the theater, my name was called. I swallowed, smoothed down my conservative curve-hugging knee-length black dress, walked out onto the stage and handed the accompanist my music.

"'Cherubino—Non So Più?'?" he asked in a tone that implied he'd played it fifty times that day and couldn't bear to play it one more time.

I heard someone say, "Miranda, how are you?" I peered out into the theater in the direction of the voice but the lights were in my eyes and too bright to see anything. "It's me. Peter. Peter Drake."

"Oh, hi, Peter." I was no longer anonymous.

"Miranda is Sebastian Lyme's daughter," said Peter to someone beside him.

"Oh, is she really? Well, Miss Lyme, your father is a fine singer. We haven't seen much of him lately though."

How tactless. How could they not know? I bit my gums and then my lower lip. I tried to tell them, "He's...uh... uh..." But it was better not to say it if they didn't know. It was better to try to keep him alive a few minutes longer. The adrenaline was coursing through my body, making me light-headed. The black nag was lurking close by, stomping and whinnying.

Peter's voice asked, "What are you going to sing for us today, Miranda?"

"'Non So Più?' and 'Iris, Hence Away.'"

"Fine," said Peter's colleague. "When you're ready."

I nodded at the accompanist.

The music started up and I sang Cherubino's words, *"Non so più? cosa son, cosa faccio..." I don't who I am or what I'm doing...*

Truer words never sung or spoken.

The nag was there on the stage beside me, growing bigger and bigger.

"Or di foco, ora sono di ghiaccio…" Now I'm on fire, now I'm made of ice…

Precisely.

The nag was looming huge, a great big black Trojan horse, with the enemy in its belly.

I headed for the next phrase and a high note. Not a very high note, though, just a G.

"Ogni don…"

And that was when it happened. The word should have been *donna* but instead of a beautiful ringing G there was nothingness. My voice just climbed up and committed suicide at the top.

The accompanist smirked at me, ready to start again, but all I could do was mutter, "I'm sorry. I'm sorry."

I grabbed my music and ran right out of the theater. And consequently, right out of my life.

Chapter 18

Peter called the next day offering apologies and sympathies. He was the one who'd suggested that I get professional help. I was a singer without a voice, any voice, which, loosely translated, means a nothing. He gave me the name of a voice doctor who worked in a preventative clinic near Holland Park. I booked my appointment, telling the secretary that it was an emergency, and two days later, I was sitting on a little stool facing Dr. Singh. He clasped my tongue in a piece of gauze, clamped my knee between his knees, slid a tiny camera into my throat and asked me to sing AH.

Up on a TV screen, my vocal cords vibrated like two strips of dubious bacon.

Dr. Singh was from New Delhi and had a very gentle manner.

"There is potential for some little disturbance in this area here," he said, pointing to an imperceptible danger zone with a long pointer. "This is where perhaps you could develop an annoying inflammation."

Where were all those enormous applelike lumps that were driving me so crazy?

He let go of my tongue and slid his knees away from mine. "Presently there is nothing serious there. But I think you are not really so ill here." He touched his throat. "You are perhaps ill a very tiny small part here—" he touched his forehead "—and a very large part here." He touched his heart.

Then he led me over to his desk and sat me down. He smiled a warm, brown, bald-headed smile and said, "You know, I once had a great-aunt (he pronounced this "ont") who was in love with a soldier posted to India, a Scotsman whose home was in the Orkney Islands. Of course, my aunt's family thought this was most unacceptable. 'You will be blown away by the dreadful cold winds there and forced to live among those savage imbibers of Scotch whiskey,' they told her. She was not to marry and go off to this barbarian northern wasteland where her life would surely be nothing but cold weather and suffering. Well, later my aunt married a countryman from New Delhi and her life was warm weather and suffering. But after that first broken heart, whenever she was upset, she would lose her voice. Perhaps, Miss Lyme, you are also a little upset."

I nodded and bit back tears.

"Perhaps it is a person, an intimate person, who has made you sad, who has let you down in some way?"

I nodded again.

He smiled and nodded back. "This is not uncommon. And if this is so, then you must now be a soldier. You must be strong and go into battle. This person who has brought sadness into your life must be your adversary, a worthy adversary. And you must match them move for move. You must be a better soldier, a general… Depression is the child of procrastination."

"The problem is, I have an important piece to debut in a couple of months."

"Ah, that *is* a problem. Well then, here is one little happiness." He wrote out a prescription for some serious medicine, steroids, just to show that he didn't take my complaint lightly. "It is best, as a precaution, to rest the voice. Using it will only aggravate. If you have engagements in the next month or two, it is good to call them off. That way you will be sure you have done your very best. And please try not to talk if you can avoid it."

I raised my eyebrows. He smiled and shrugged.

"That is the voice also. But if you must talk, pitch your voice higher and softer," he said. "And here is another happiness. These will help you." He wrote out a list of books for me to read and handed it to me. "Be well, Miss Lyme, be serene. You are young and beautiful. You have the whole world waiting for you."

I left his office feeling bewildered but happy, as light as air, and slightly in love with Dr. Singh.

That afternoon, equipped with Caroline's addresses, a bottle of wine I'd picked up at Harrods food hall, my *London A-Z* and a thread of a speaking voice, I took the tube up toward Hampstead Heath. I didn't want to risk taking the Jeep all that way on the wrong side of roads that I didn't know.

On first glance, the neighborhood seemed quite nice, rows of tall brick terraces nicely restored. But then I turned the corner onto the street I was looking for, and it was like being on a set for a film about the WWII bombing of London. Narrow derelict houses, several missing a roof, others a front door, still others missing sections of outer wall, lined the street like a mouthful of rotting and broken teeth. The cramped gardens were filled with weeds, broken bottles and crushed beer cans, fast-food containers and cigarette butts.

Unfortunately, there were signs of life. In the paneless windows all along the street, blankets and sheets and old torn pieces of fabric were nailed across windows as makeshift curtains.

I was getting my first taste of the famous London squats.

Caroline had been so insistent that I look up these friends of hers, that even though my instinct was to run back to the plush solitude of Kurt's house, I gritted my teeth. I needed to make contact. Solitude was getting to me. I was afraid that if I spent any more time alone, voices in my head would start telling me to paint my body blue and streak Buckingham Palace.

The house number I was looking for was one of the less derelict buildings. Some attempt had been made to keep the front garden neat, and there was glass or plastic in nearly all the windows. I banged on the navy-blue front door.

It was opened almost immediately by a tall skinny boy dressed in jeans and a very wrinkled blue shirt. His feet were bare on the dirty gray splintery floorboards. He had short blond porcupine hair and a startled look on his face, as though I'd just woken him from a deep sleep.

I made a start. "Hi, um…you don't know me…"

He smiled crookedly. "Man. Come on inside. It's friggin' cold on this doorstep," he said in good Canadian.

I stepped into the freezing hallway. "I'm looking for Clint, Rosie and Morris. Caroline gave me their names. Caroline Fisher? From Canada?"

"No shit? You're a friend of Caroline's? Hey, man, that's so cool. Rosieee," he yelled into the dark dusty upper regions of the house. "Rosie, Morris, get your asses down here. We got a guest. I'm Clint, by the way." He thrust a long bony hand at me and I shook it.

"I'm Miranda. I'm Caroline's roommate. Um, I studied music in Vancouver and she thought…"

"Her roommate in Vancouver, like in British Columbia, Canada?"

"Yeah. Vancouver."

"Vancouver. Skookum. Very cool." He scratched his head violently then called out again, "Rosie, get down here, you shameless hussy. Morris, you deviate. Get out of bed and get your carcass down here."

"I brought some wine," I said limply, and handed him the bottle.

"Hey, whoa. You didn't need to do that. But…like… thanks, man. Hey, c'mon into the…parlor." He twisted his mouth in mock Englishness to say the last word.

The "parlor" had been painted in a bilious green paint that was now peeling away, giving the walls the look of reptile skin. The room was completely bare except for some mismatched pieces of old carpet and a single light-bulb dangling from a dangerous-looking tangle of wires that had been illegally run through a crack in the window from outside.

"Pull up an armchair," said Clint, and plopped himself down on the floor, cross-legged.

I did likewise, cringing for the fate of my camel-hair coat.

"Hi," said a woman's voice. I swung around. A tall part-African woman wearing jeans and a huge pink turtleneck sweater leaned against the doorjamb.

Clint stretched out his arm and said, "Hey, Rosie. This is Miranda. She's Caroline's roomie in Vancouver. She's a musician."

"Well, not exactly…"

"No shit," said Rosie, straightening to her full six feet. "Welcome to our hovel."

Well. At least she had no illusions.

"Caroline said I should meet you guys because you're in music, too."

"S'right," said Clint.

"What sort of music?" I asked.

Rosie said, "We went to the University of Toronto. That's where we all met. But we've been jamming around London for quite a while now, almost a year. What would you say we were, Clint? Jazz? Pop? Alternative."

Clint shrugged. "A little of everything. Whatever. Doesn't matter about the label. People love us to pieces. So what brings *you* to old Londontown, Miranda?"

"Um, well, I'm a singer and I was invited for the holidays by a conductor friend."

"No shit? What kind of singing?" said Clint.

"Opera mostly."

"Right on," said Rosie. "So, Miranda, are you planning on doing some auditions while you're here?"

She'd hit my tender spot and I temporarily lost my mind. Maybe it was being around those few seconds of cozy Canadian accent, but it just came pouring out of me. "I came to spend the Christmas holidays with this conductor…who was supposed to be my…well, he's married, you see…I mean…I got this cold and my father died and I had this audition and now my voice isn't working…and my boyfriend, I should say, my ex-boyfriend…I mean, that ex-boyfriend jerk conductor and his wife…" And then my voice just seized up and no more sound came out.

Fortunately.

Rosie and Clint exchanged the kind of glances you exchange when Martians have landed in your front yard.

Clint said, "Hey, girl. You need some hooch."

He stood up and handed the bottle to Rosie, who took it away to some other dark part of the house. She came back a few minutes later with the bottle opened and some interesting mismatched carnival-glass goblets. She poured out the wine and said, "Here's to your health. Drink up."

"Maybe Miranda would like to see our music room," said Clint, grinning and wiggling his eyebrows.

I nodded.

Rosie said, "Follow us. And if you're squeamish, don't look too closely at the rest of this slum dwelling."

I was starting to get the feeling that Rosie wasn't too happy with her accommodations.

The "music room" was up two flights of rickety stairs. On the first-floor landing, Rosie pushed open one of the doors and I caught a glimpse of color; flaming chiffons, bright scarves and Oriental silk dressing gowns. The bed was heaped with colorful clothing too, florals and stripes and pastels. Across the window was draped a heavy blue velvet curtain with gold tassels, creating a theatrical effect.

"Morris," said Rosie. "Morrie, wake up, I need your key."

The mound of clothing on the bed parted like the Red Sea and a figure sat up in the middle of the heap. At first, I thought it was a woman, but then knew it was a man when he stood up in a yellow silk nightgown and two scrawny, hairy and definitely masculine legs stuck out below. He went over to a dressing table, flung a few scarves aside, found the key and handed it to Rosie.

When he saw me, he stepped back with his hand to his heart, then said in a soft voice, "You gave me such a start whoever you are." Then to Rosie he said, "Ten minutes and I'll be up too."

Another open door gave me a glimpse of what must have been Rosie and Clint's bedroom. A double mattress with green duvet on the scrubbed and bleached bare floorboards, a paraffin lamp and an old wardrobe painted white with green trim. It was a spartan oasis.

As we climbed the next flight of stairs, Rosie said, "That's Morris. He's very delicate, but he plays like nothing you've ever heard."

When we reached the third floor, there was a door bolted shut with three large padlocks.

Clint handed Rosie a key and she opened each padlock.

"Dodgy neighborhood," she said to me over her shoulder.

The music room, in contrast to the rest of the squat, had been cleaned up and made pleasant, even if the temperature was arctic. The floorboards and walls had been thickly painted white and the window was solidly blocked off from the elements with heavy plastic and duct tape. There were five kitchen chairs of different designs also painted white, and then there were the instruments; a double-bass case leaning in one corner, two acoustic-guitar cases, a mandolin case, a violin case, two different kinds of accordions out of their cases. There was a set of vibraphones, an electric keyboard and numerous drums, bongos, and miscellaneous percussion instruments. There were flutes and pennywhistles and recorders and harmonicas, and a sax gleaming in one corner. There was also a space heater connected to the bundle of dangerous-looking wires that passed through a hole in the window plastic. The whole room had a pearly light. It seemed like a great place to practice. No distractions of any kind.

"Wanna hear something, Miranda?" asked Clint. "We're workin' on a new piece. We'll bounce it off ya, eh?"

"Sure," I said.

Rosie turned on the space heater and Clint started to take the double bass out of its case and tune up. The door opened and Morris came into the room. Morris made all his moves as though slightly pained. His hand was often on his heart, as though he were some kind of fluttery southern belle who was always on the verge of fainting. His face constantly had that cringing tension in it, as if he were about to get jabbed by a very long hypodermic needle. Perhaps life itself was like a jab for him.

The makeup he was wearing was full metal jacket, just right for doing battle in a beauty pageant. He wore gold stud earrings in pierced ears and shoulder-length fine brown hair combed straight. He had on base, cover stick, eye shadow, mascara, lipstick and rouge. His shirt was shiny cream with frills along the cuffs, and his pants were brown velvet flares. Over it all, he wore a long embroidered sheepskin vest. The overall effect was stunning and slightly sixties, except for the Boy George makeup job.

And then Morris went over to the electric keyboard, switched it on and started to play. In that moment, I didn't care what gender he was or how many pounds of makeup he wore, just as long as he didn't stop playing. After a few minutes of warm-ups, the three of them moved seamlessly into a love song, a jazzy ballad, Rosie's big warm voice took over, and I was infatuated with the three of them.

Before I left we made an appointment to meet at the Black Satin Club in Richmond. They were playing a gig there in a couple of weeks.

Caroline was right. They were very fine musicians.

Chapter 19

That night I checked my e-mails. There was only one. It read:

Dear Miranda,
Great to hear from you. Really sorry to hear about your father. I want to thank you for the housekeeping advice. It's put a damper on my working time, and my side of the bed is turning into a malodorous ditch, but it seems to be helping. And Mary says she's visualizing it for me.
Glad you liked *The Other Street* tape. Biba's around but there's a hitch. You may not know by looking at her, but she's very, very street-smart. That's part of her past. Quite a voice she's got. Am I to understand that you'll be coming back soon? Because I'd really like to see you again. I promise I'll take a bath first.
the best,
Pat

Still no word from Tina though. This was not good, given her track record of bad moods.

On an impulse, I picked up the phone and dialed her number. It rang and rang. Even her answering machine was turned off.

It was Biba's voice. When she came into focus, I could see that she had six undulating arms and tiny cymbals on her fingertips. Her arms were as long and thin and dark as licorice strands. Her feet were cocked and angular, moving in Balinese-dancer style, but I knew she was running away. Under her voice was an exotic chiming with other chorus voices intertwined. Biba was now running fast, with Gypsy ease, running on orange and red flames, faster and faster until she leaped into the air and flew in an arc. The music continued. I could hear it all perfectly, each note and the underlying instruments, and I thought as I listened, now *that* is great music.

I could see that the flames were made with moving fabric, the way fire is represented in Balinese plays. A second later, there was fluttering blue silk for water, too, and watery music. A child's choir sang angelically off in the distance.

I realized then that I was on my stomach, groveling on a floor. I wanted to join in with the other singing voices but I couldn't stand up, and every time I opened my mouth to sing, I got a mouthful of dust. I lay back down and watched.

Other people from my life made entrances. My mother came on and sang half of every phrase then walked off in a huff. My little brothers bounced around the stage like rubber balls, singing in shrill little voices, then bounced off again. George and Brandon were there at the sidelines, commenting on the action with scathing lyrics in a tenor duet. I sensed that Kurt was creeping up behind me and was about to commandeer the conducting, but I didn't want to look at him. I wanted him to go away. I covered my ears and half croaked, half screamed, "No," before waking myself up.

★ ★ ★

I was excited. I hopped out of bed and ran upstairs to Kurt's computer to write down the music that Biba had been singing in my dream.

Somewhere between fooling around with Kurt's software, transcribing Biba's song, listening to the music in the Hampstead squat, taking Dr. Singh's advice, and thinking about poor old Henry Purcell, I'd been taken over by another spirit. Without knowing it, I'd decided to be a warrior.

I would write my *own* opera.

It was going to be tonal, theatrical, it was even going to be pretty in places.

I could already see the musical elite shaking their heads and scoffing.

Miranda Lyme writing a—what did she call it?

A folk opera?

A world-music opera?

I could hear their laughing and guffawing, their making fun of my hackneyed old forms. I confess that I was worried about what they were going to think, all those guys in the magic circle. But I also knew I'd have to learn to stop caring.

Make way, boys. Miranda's musical dinosaur was coming through.

The Black Satin Club was pulsating. It was an old cinema converted into a club, slick shiny blacks, carnation pinks, slices of chrome, the see-through dance floor a landing pad for contraband, a myriad of illegal substances. I shimmied between the sweaty bodies and moved closer to the front, feeling the rhythm of the music. Totally contagious.

Up on the stage, Morris was decked out in a gold lamé shirt, black velvet jeans and gold ankle boots. Clint had on the same clothes as the last time I'd met him, and Rosie was wild in a black leather halter minidress, knee-high black leather boots and an ornate wide silver filigree collar.

They'd had to come up with a name for themselves, so at the last minute, they'd jokingly called themselves the Pemmicans. Their sound was as chewy as their name. They played a heavy synthesized reggae beat with trickles of improvisation from the other instruments that Clint and Rosie alternated with voice, and Morris's magic hands seducing the keyboard, making us all think that those inanimate black and white keys were a crying, groaning, whining, laughing live sexy creature. And then there were Clint's and Rosie's amazing vocals, sometimes soul, sometimes hard rock, sometimes lyrical folk. Edgy. Very edgy.

After the first set, I went backstage to say hello to them and gush like a preteen at her first rock concert. I couldn't believe myself, repeating over and over, "You guys are just so great." But they seemed happy enough to see me and told me to stick around till the end.

When the evening was over, I went to join the rest of their fans hanging around backstage, waiting to get a piece of them.

We all sat around talking about their performance. When they wanted to leave, Rosie asked me if I'd mind helping pack up their stuff. I helped them load their instruments into their battered ex–ice cream truck, which was still pervaded with the odors of vanilla wafers and chocolate sprinkles.

They climbed in. Morris gave me a little flutter of a wave as Rosie started the van. The engine coughed a few times then died. Rosie's yell of "fuckin' junk heap" echoed down the street.

I'd brought the Jeep, knowing I'd be out late and didn't have too far to drive.

I ran over to the driver's window and shouted up, "Listen, you guys, why don't you load all your stuff into my Jeep and come back to my place for a drink."

They looked at each other. Rosie said, "It's late. Then we'd have to get home from yours. And we'll have to call somebody to do something about this heap of crap."

"You can stay over. Then worry about the van in the morning," I offered.

They continued to exchange glances.

"There's plenty of room, and there's central heating and cable TV. I'm there all by myself and I'm getting sick of it. And there's plenty of food too if anybody's hungry." I was definitely begging.

"Right," said Rosie without consulting the others. She jumped out, opened the back of the van, pulled out the double bass and said, "Point the way." The other two looked at each other, shrugged and started to unload, as well.

When they saw the shiny top-of-the-line Jeep, they gave me curious looks. "It's not actually mine," I said. "It belongs to a friend...it's his house I'm staying in...well, not actually a friend, an ene... Well, no. I'm supposed to look at him as a worthy adversary, according to Dr. Singh."

"Ohhh," said Rosie, suddenly understanding. "One of THOSE."

"So does this dude whose place you're at have a name?" asked Clint.

"Kurt Hancock."

They all stared at me slack-jawed.

"No fuckin' kidding," said Clint. "Wow."

"The golden boy of British music," said Morris. "Good work, Miranda."

We drove in near silence all the way to Putney. Occasionally one of them would say, "Kurt Hancock, eh?" and then chuckle. When we arrived at the house, they all climbed out and looked up at the Victorian monstrosity with expressions of awe. As we approached the front door, I half expected them to cross themselves and genuflect right there on the cold doorstep. They behaved as though they were entering a temple, a shrine.

I had to set them straight. "Now listen, you guys. Let me just say one thing about Kurt Hancock before you come inside and help me make good use of his house. The guy is a first-class, big-league hosehead fuckup."

Rosie made a mock-shocked face, then laughed and said, "Well, hell, don't mince words, Miranda."

"Shit," said Clint.

Morris winced and looked as though the sky was about to fall on him.

I unlocked the door, turned off the alarm, and we all went into the living room. In my best imitation of Olivia's cousin Judith, I said, "Drinks everyone?"

I took their orders. Morris sipped a Manhattan then went straight to the piano, opened the lid, and with his unimpressive stubby chubby fingers, began to play Debussy. There were images of rushing water and rose petals and moonlight and starlight and some new scintillating entity floating in the middle of the room. The inside of Debussy's head perhaps.

"How does he do it?" I whispered to Rosie. "Why isn't he touring the world as a concert soloist?"

"He did," said Rosie. "Morrie was playing the Chopin F-minor concerto when he crumbled. He was in Chicago at the time. Clint and I rushed down there as soon as it happened. We nearly had to bring him home in a body bag. He needs a buffer from the world. I guess Clint and I have sort of taken on the job. Somebody has to. We just all hit it off at music school and can't seem to separate. Morrie's very fragile but he's recovering. Being in London has helped. I don't think the venue much matters, as long as we're all making the music we want to make and sticking together. Times are changing. I'm big on the crossover. Gotta break down the barriers. The attitudes at music school nearly drove me nuts. I was going to be an opera singer, too, you know, and there were some really great people at the school, great teachers, great students, a lot of great people. But there was also an awful lot of broom handle up an awful lot of butt."

I grinned. I knew exactly what she was talking about.

"Morris seems permanently heartbroken. Does he have someone?"

"Like?"

"A boyfriend or a girlfriend or someone?"

Rosie laughed and shook her head. "He's celibate. He tried sex once but said it was too physical for him, not nearly as sensual as the things going on in his head. He lives almost completely in his head. Except for his little flair for fashion. That's his biggest physical manifestation. That and his fingers on the keyboard."

We all got a little drunk that night and I showed them the house. Everything. I hadn't intended to open so many drawers and closets, but when we got into Olivia's things, Morris got this ecstatic look on his face and ended up giving us a fashion show with all of her best designer items. I laughed so hard I did damage to my ribs.

After that, I ran the water in the double hot tub in the rose-colored bathroom, poured in rose-colored bubble bath and insisted somebody try it. Clint started to tear off his clothes with Rosie protesting, but then she disappeared after him.

And that's how Rosie and Morris and Clint came for a night and stayed three weeks. I was so happy to have them there filling up the house with music, and they were happy to take a holiday from their freezing squat. The house was so big that it was impossible to get in each other's way. And it was good to be with other people who spoke Canadian.

I told them to go ahead and use Kurt's home studio, and they made a CD of their music to sell during their concerts. And I have to say, it wasn't bad.

We prepared big meals together, and then afterward they helped me play through what I'd written. They were just sketches, musical ideas for arias and ensembles, but they were growing.

When I showed them Biba's interview on the tape, Clint said, "That is one hot damn voice."

And Rosie said, "Gold, pure gold. So you actually know Patrick Tibeau? How cool."

"Yeah. It's not just the voice. I should say the voices. It's the stories. Like Biba's story. That's the libretto I'm working toward. It's all right there in the singer, the woman, the girl. Like you, Rosie. Your story."

Rosie grimaced at me. Her mother had been a teenager from Cameroon, cleaning houses in Toronto when her white employer (and well-known local politician) got her pregnant. Rosie's father helped out with expenses because her mother was tough enough to threaten blackmail. So they'd had quite a nice life as single mother and daughter with Rosie's father secretly paying the way.

"Or…or," I said, "how about this, Rosie? We could have you play God in my opera."

"You gonna have God in your opera? He should be a bass, shouldn't he, with a long white beard?" said Clint.

Rosie groaned. "Climb out of your little tiny mental box, Clint, and look around you."

"Well sorr-reeee for living," said Clint.

I said, "No, I was thinking, maybe, God as a black house-cleaner type of woman."

Rosie grinned. "Why not? Just as long as it's not my story. My story's a bore. There are other better stories. You just have to dig it all out of yourself and narrow it down. It's easy. It's finding the right words and notes and then getting them all in the right order."

"Sure."

She sighed. "Don't use my story. My story's really just about my father being a typical man. Men. Becoming a father is a piece of cake. Like falling off a log. Staying a father is the problem for most men."

"I can't wait to see what kinda kids Rosie and I are gonna turn out," said Clint, grabbing her around the waist. "They're gonna look like a buncha Licorice All Sorts."

Rosie swatted him and pushed him away. "I don't know why I put up with you," she said.

"I do," said Clint, grabbing her around the waist again.

"Foul beast of a man." But she left his hands where they were. I felt a pang of envy. They had each other. And Clint's physical appearance had improved. Rosie had talked him into doing all his laundry at Kurt's house and the baths had taken off a little of his squat patina. But even though he ate mountains of food, he still had that famine-relief victim look about him.

During the second week of the Pemmicans' stay, the doorbell rang one morning just before eleven. I ought to have panicked but I didn't. I was feeling bold, in the warrior mode, as ordered by Dr. Singh.

I had already dealt with Judith twice by just not answering the door. She'd coo-cooed and tut-tutted outside to her dog Poozie but after a few minutes gave up and went away. Guido, too, had been around one more time, and I'd let him in because the others had been out at the time.

Guido had been in a horrible woman-hating mood that day, obviously wanting something from me and I'd made an excuse about having to go out and buy obscure female products at Boots, implying that even if I'd wanted to, it was a no go. I'd hustled him out of there almost as soon as he'd arrived.

I crept across the living room to see a silhouette in the front door. It was a male. And not Guido.

I went and opened the door.

The sun was shining brightly behind the man and it took me a minute to recognize him, but when I did, I blushed right into the heels of my Doc Martens.

Chapter 20

"Lance."

"Miranda." He looked delectable, his skin dusky and tanned, emphasized by the white linen shirt poking out from under his black overcoat. His hair was a tangle of gleaming silvery-black. He looked like a designer pirate.

"What are you DOING here?" I stood there on the doorstep, staring in disbelief and pleasure.

He leaned rakishly against one of the porch's white support pillars. "I was on my way back from a little holiday in the Maldives. Found your name at Canada House and thought I better drop in and make sure you weren't misbehaving."

"I'm not misbehaving at all. Unfortunately," I said, feeling my features cave in at the thought of Kurt. "How long are you here for?"

"I have one night here. My plane to Vancouver's tomorrow. Is the great man here?" asked Lance in a tone that suggested something much smaller than greatness. "I was afraid he'd answer the door and then tell me that you couldn't come out to play because you were all his."

"He's in Tuscany."

Lance raised his eyebrows.

"With his wife, Olivia. They're trying to have a baby." On the last syllable, my voice seized up into a choking cough.

Lance shook his head. "I always said he was a bastard. Didn't I?"

I invited Lance to come in.

The others were still sleeping. They'd played a late gig the night before.

Lance strolled into the living room, looked around at the decor and said, "Interesting mausoleum. Where's Morticia? Out in the greenhouse chopping heads off roses?"

"It is a little…heavy, isn't it?"

Lance sat down on the sofa. "Come here," he said.

I moved closer.

"Right over here." I moved closer still.

He reached out for my hand and pulled me into his lap. Then he buried his face in my hair. "I've missed that Miranda smell."

I pulled away. "Lance?"

"Yes?"

"Does your mommy know you're here?"

He narrowed his eyes to slits and after a long silence said, "No," in a tone that worried me.

I jumped up and straightened my hair. "I'm starving. Are you hungry, Lance? I was just about to make lunch."

"No, don't make lunch," he said.

"But I'm hungry."

"I'll buy you lunch in town. At a restaurant."

"That's the best suggestion I've heard this year," I said.

"This year is only a few weeks old."

"Even so. Listen, how do you feel about driving? Do you know how to navigate in this chaos they call London?"

"Let me see. I've driven in Athens, and New York and Cairo and Los Angeles and…"

I grabbed the keys to the Jeep from the coffee table and tossed them in his direction. "Here, Lance, catch. You're driving."

Lance took me to Zilli Fish, behind Piccadilly Circus. I had prawns and sole, and something with such hot curry in it that I thought my head was going to burst into flames. I had to drink a whole jug of water to douse the fire. After that we both had vanilla ice cream and then Lance said, "Let's walk over to St. James's Park."

It was already three-thirty in the afternoon when we left the restaurant, and it was a perfect sunny, windy kind of winter day, with scudding clouds and patches of icy-blue sky. We strolled arm in arm along the wide avenues of bare trees, and I said, "Now tell me all about the Maldives, Lance."

"Well, the water was very clear, very warm, very blue and very wet."

"I'm not sure if that's the part I want to hear about."

"What part then?"

"Did you go alone?"

He laughed but didn't answer my question.

"You're the most frustrating person on this planet. Tell me something I don't know about you, Lance. And that could be almost anything."

"Tapioca pudding. I can't stand tapioca pudding. It looks like fish eggs and glue and it tastes like school paste."

"How would you know what school paste tastes like?"

"I was a very hungry boy at school."

"Ah, now we're getting somewhere," I said.

"And my appetites weren't just limited to food." As he said this, he turned to face me and ran a finger gently across my lips.

Now we were *really* getting somewhere.

I said, "Oh no? Tell me more about your appetites."

"Let's not talk about *my* deprived childhood. Let's talk about *yours,*" said Lance.

"Mine? It's hopeless. I'm not me anymore."

"What does that mean?"

"I'm not Miranda Lyme the singer at the moment. I shouldn't even be talking to you. Doctor's orders. I'm not supposed to use my voice. It's gone. My singing voice is gone. I start off okay, and then I sort of hit a bump in the vocal road and everything just freezes up."

Lance seemed to be considering this seriously. "What are you going to do? Voices are tricky things."

"I'm not sure. I'm trying not to think about it. I have other projects."

"Such as?"

"I'm…um…writing an opera."

He stepped back and scrutinized me. "That's a new one. Do people do that? Just wake up one day and say they're writing an opera?"

"It's not as sudden as that. It's been creeping up on me for a while. I just didn't know it."

"Are you equipped for something like that? Writing an opera sounds like a very big complicated project that requires a particular talent."

"I don't know. How can I know if I don't try? I didn't do *too* badly in theory at school."

"Uh-huh," he said.

Lance didn't seem convinced at all, and that irritated me.

But then we were distracted by birds. They'd begun to swoop in masses from one tree to another, in their frenzies of flight before sundown. Lance surprised me again by closing his arms around me and kissing me on the mouth. For a long time, since knowing him perhaps, I'd wanted him to kiss me. But now that it was happening, I felt as though the world had tilted sideways and I was going to fall off.

And then he said, "C'mon, weren't you going to show me Harvey Nichols?"

* * *

On the ground floor of the swank store, everything was chic and lit brightly with clean lines and great colors. There were all those purses and perfumes and emergency beauty products for the oversmogged and overpartied person. The products had the wildest names, like "Shag Me Till The Cows Come Home."

Well maybe not exactly like that, but similar.

Lance treated me. He told me to pick out something so I chose a Dolce & Gabbana blouse.

When we got back to the house it was almost 10:00 p.m. and Rosie, Morris and Clint were out.

We were in a frivolous mood. At Harvey Nichols, Lance had practically bought himself a whole new wardrobe. I'd acted as fashion consultant for him, and then, when we'd finished buying clothes, he'd got me drunk in one of the Harvey Nicks's bars. As the designated driver, he'd been quiet, sipping soda water and watching me while I got silly.

When we arrived back at the house, he put all his bags down in the front hall and without another word, pressed me up against the aubergine wall and all those stuffy little botanical prints and kissed me again. Still in a clutch, he moved me into the living room and we were on the couch. We slid to the floor, all the cushions sliding with us, and carried on kissing there for a while. Then Lance's hands were under my coat. In seconds, he had worked my coat and sweater off my body, kneading, as if me and all my clothes were soft clay.

Then he took off his coat, reached down and lifted my T-shirt over my head.

Then his sweater was off.

He was undoing the top button of my jeans.

I heard a zip and it was as if I'd been slapped.

I pulled away and whispered, "We better stop."

Lance stared at me.

"We have to stop this, Lance."

He was bewildered. "Why?"

"I'm just not sure."

"You don't need to be. You know the old maxim? If it feels good, do it?"

"That's my point. I'm already confused enough. If we do this, my life is going to be *so* complicated."

He moved a strand of hair off my face and whispered, "It's only sex, Miranda," as though sex were the simplest thing in the world.

"Then that's exactly why we have to stop, Lance. Right now."

Lance sat back on the couch. There were several minutes of silence and I couldn't think of any smart or right thing to say.

"Lance, talk to me. Don't be mad."

"You have no idea of the kind of signals you've been giving off all these months, Miranda. And the kinds of scents. My olfactory has been going haywire with you. You've been driving me crazy. You still are."

"I didn't know. I wasn't sure what I wanted to happen between us. But now I know. I want us to be friends."

"Friendships can have interesting variations. And you know it. You can't tell me you haven't been feeling it, too," said Lance.

It was embarrassing to admit that he was right. "I've been feeling it, too. And I guess that's the problem."

"I don't understand why it has to be a problem."

"Maybe you can do it, but I can't. I'm handicapped that way. First of all, I'm just feeling so burnt over Kurt. I've gotten complicated overnight. I'd be thinking of everything you're trying to hide from me. Right away. Right from the start. I wouldn't be able to enjoy it at all because my mind would be racing ahead always wondering if there was going to be more…or if you loved me enough…or if you were about to dump me. Don't you get it?"

"Can't you look on it as therapy? Isn't getting burned all the more reason to get up and running, wouldn't you say?"

"No. The bottom line for me is…"

"What?"

"We were supposed to be friends. Or at least friendly colleagues. Sex changes everything. Everybody knows that. I'd have a really hard time being relaxed with you or working for you again. And I'm not sure I want to give that up."

"Miranda, Miranda." He was shaking his head.

"And there's another thing."

"What's that?"

"I know almost nothing about you, Lance. You've never, ever told me anything about yourself. I know nothing except that you dub films, you ride a motorbike, and you like to eat school paste."

"We're all entitled to our privacy. Everybody has to have their little secrets."

"There. You see? You're doing it again."

He smiled mysteriously. "Give me a hug, Miranda. Just a friendly hug."

We fell asleep side by side amidst the cushions on the floor, holding each other. In the middle of the night, I opened my eyes to see Morris standing over us with a blanket. He smiled his sweet pained smile, whispered, "Go back to sleep, Miranda," and gently covered us both.

Before Lance left the next morning, I made him promise to go on being my elusive friend and colleague, and to look up Tina when he got back home, and let me know what the hell was going on with her.

That night, Rosie, Clint, Morris and I sat down on the big leather couch in the den to watch one of Patrick's other tapes.

I shoved the tape into the machine and pushed play.

"So what's it called?" asked Clint.

I read the title on the box. *"Silent Heart."*

"How can a heart be silent? That would make its owner dead, wouldn't it?" said Morris thoughtfully.

Rosie hushed us all. "Everybody be quiet and let's just watch it, okay?"

Silent Heart was Patrick's first really successful indie film, according to Rosie, who seemed to know all about it. It was about a guy who was obsessed with a beautiful girl who he could only ever glimpse at a distance. Basically, the hero was a stalker, but he was a type you sympathized with, like Patricia Highsmith's Tom Ripley. Patrick took you so far into the stalker's mind and soul that by the middle of the film you were not only rooting for him, you were hoping the girl he was stalking would get her just deserts. She didn't, of course. Patrick was subtler than that.

I suppose the fact that the girl was played by Evie Marcelle biased my opinion a little. But Patrick had captured her perfectly on film. Rosie, Clint and Morris all agreed, Evie Marcelle came across on-screen as a beautiful monster.

Easy gig, I thought, all she had to do was play herself.

The other tape was a CBC interview with Patrick after he'd been short-listed for an award at the Venice Biennial.

It was the first time I really got a proper look at him at his proudest, and I have to say, maybe the camera was a lying fool, but it sure made Patrick Tibeau look good up there.

After the film, I went online and sent Patrick a message.

Dear Pat,
Just saw *Silent Heart*. Very good. And very interesting the way Evie comes across in it. What's the word on the housekeeping situation?
Love, Miranda

His reply bounced back almost immediately.

Hey, Miranda,
Just got your e-mail. Glad you liked *Silent Heart*. As for Evie, she's gone. I still can't believe it. Just like that. I came home two days ago and she'd finished packing all her stuff. She told

me there was no love left anymore and that she was leaving. It was like a bad country-and-western song. She seemed okay. Actually it seemed like she couldn't wait to see the lurid, reeking back of me. I smelled pretty bad those last few days. Thanks for the advice.

Evie's found somebody else, a local producer with real money. The thing that amazes me is how fast she found him once she decided to make her move.

Mary's been a big support through all of this. She and I are heading to L.A. tomorrow. I've got some meetings down there and she wants to go on to Santa Fe. Are you going to be staying in England permanently?

Pat

Good question.

I'd thought seriously about staying too, of finding work and not letting a botched audition, or a dead father, or people like Kurt or Olivia or Judith chase me away. London was as much my city as theirs. But with all the wrestling and grappling I was doing to pull an opera out of myself, and understand its technicalities, and with all the distractions Rosie, Clint and Morris had given me, I hadn't bothered to change my original plane ticket.

I realized my project was going to take every resource I had and that most of what I had was back in Vancouver. London could wait.

And there was also Lance's e-mail.

Dear Miranda,

When are you coming back to Vancouver? You don't want your friend Tina to get all the action, do you?

Lance

My plane was leaving in two days. After the Pemmicans moved out, I used the time to clean up Kurt's house and make a copy of his composing software for myself, and a copy of all my work. Then I called up Guido and gave him my news. He understood. He'd been fairly honest with me. I still needed a pipeline to Kurt—he wasn't going to go away just like that.

But I still felt as though I were leaving like a thief in the night. I told Guido that he and Judith could worry about the house now, that he could pass the message on to Kurt. I'd be seeing Kurt when he came out to do the song cycle.

Then I made one last trip over to the Pemmicans' squat to make them promise to meet me later that summer in Vancouver. If everything went according to plan there would be an opera to perform. Rosie told me they'd been thinking about Vancouver for a long time, thinking about moving there. Clint was a head case and couldn't feel the cold but she didn't think she or Morris could take another year in London or the squat.

The last thing I did was call my mother to tell her I was coming home on schedule. I could almost hear her relief singing down the telephone lines.

Vancouver again .

Chapter 21

When I opened the door to my Bute Street apartment, I thought I'd made a mistake. It was somebody else's place. It had to be. And then I recognized the aluminum leg of my vintage kitchen table peeping out from under a lacy white tablecloth. Similar pristine fitted covers hid the couch and the big old armchair, and there was a distinct odor of Lysol in the air. There were bouquets of fake flowers all over the front room and my kilim rug was missing. I went down the hall and opened my bedroom door.

I felt just like Baby Bear. Like all *three* of The Three Bears. Somebody's been sleeping in *my* bed.

When I found Caroline, I was going to kill her. If Caroline still lived there.

There was a lacy cover on my IKEA bed, and enough stuffed toys to populate Belgium. The walls were plastered with vapid spineless prints of pastel couples walking into sunsets on smooth stylized beaches. In my mean-spirited jet-lagged mood, I could only hope a big tidal wave was rising around the next bay and about to wash them away. All my other stuff, the contents of my closet, my cardboard boxes full of books and musical scores, were gone, replaced by a chest of drawers and a white fake French provincial vanity with a huge lacy flounce all around it.

I banged on Caroline's door, and when I didn't get an answer, I opened it. The fusty, grassy, patchouli odor was familiar. There were the same grunge clothes tossed over chairs, on the bed, over the top of the closet doors, shoes everywhere. Posters of no-global events from around the world filled the walls along with Che Guevera, Gandhi and Karl Marx; jazz- and rock-festival brochures and other more ominous political flyers were strewn everywhere, her huge bookcase was sagging under the weight of all her books, and the big brass ashtray was full of roaches.

Well, at least it was the same old Caroline. And living up to her same old reputation, it seemed. A minute before going through my door, I'd been so grateful to her for introducing me to the Pemmicans that I'd actually wanted to see her, compare notes, find out how she was and thank her. Now I just wanted to throttle her.

I went into the now-spotless and Lysoled bathroom and tried to wash the jet lag from my face. Goldilocks's beauty products were lined up in a neat row inside the medicine chest, fruity harmless perfumes for children, baby shampoo for her golden tresses.

It was early afternoon by the time I'd found what I needed in my suitcases, changed my clothes and left everything there in disarray, in the middle of what used to be my living room. The little sun I'd seen on landing earlier had disappeared behind a cloud and now it was a cold February day. I headed for Tina's place. Hopefully, I wasn't too late and could help her get a handle on her life. Or whatever was happening.

I rang the buzzer. Tina's voice over the speakerphone said, "Collin?"

"No, it's me, Tina. Miranda."

"God. Oh jeez. Great. Miranda... Come on up."

I got a shock when I saw her.

When she appeared at the top of the stairs, I thought she was somebody else. A movie star.

She had new hair, a shiny black shoulder-length blunt cut that looked even more dramatic with the dark red lipstick and black eye makeup she was wearing. Her usual jeans had been replaced by maroon leather pants and a knee-length black leather coat.

I stood and gaped at her.

She laughed breathlessly and ran down the stairs, dragging me out the front door and locking it. "Come with me, Miranda. I'm going to town." She laughed again.

"So, are you two...?"

"No. We're not...but sometimes he still comes around. I asked him to detox just after you left. He wasn't too happy about it and didn't really try, so we're just friends now."

"Well, he was kind of a drugstore with helmet, two wheels and a degree in theater."

"Yeah, it's like, the great sex we were having just fizzled away. He stopped getting it up, couldn't even care if he did or didn't, and I told him he was turning into litmus paper, popping all those pills, and that I wasn't sure if I wanted an important relationship with someone who was just one big walking altered state. I mean, his sweat was starting to get this really strange smell to it. You could get a contact high just breathing the air around him. But he didn't do anything about it so I got busy."

"Busy? Like how?"

She grinned. I'd never seen her look so beautiful. "Like everything. You were right about the singing gigs. I'd been letting things slide for too long. Let me see now, I've got a full recital at the university in April. Got in touch with some of the old gang and we've thrown together a program of cabaret songs. Schoenberg, Benjamin Britten and some Kurt Weill. Should be hot."

"Wow."

"Yeah, and I've got a bunch of auditions lined up. Talking a CBC recital, too. Some Mahler. You going into town, too?" I no longer knew where I was going so I nodded and said, "I tried calling you when I was over there but you were always out. You didn't answer my e-mails, either."

"Sorry, Miranda. I've just been so busy."

I could hear the tables turning in my head.

"Lance said something about you getting all the action."

"Oh my God, that was embarrassing. Your friend Lance came around here and Wayne and I were having a big day between the sheets… Don't look at me like that, Miranda."

"Wayne the hoser?"

"Yeah." She grinned. "I'm on my way to meet him now. Between his bod and Collin's mind, I just about get a whole man."

"You're seeing them both?"

"Uh-huh. Don't look so shocked. A woman's gotta do what a woman's gotta do. Anyway, Lance said he'd seen you in London. I knew you were okay." Then she looked at me, squinting. "You didn't fuck him, did you?"

I mumbled, "No." Then I said much louder, "No, no. I was tempted but I didn't."

"Don't do it."

"Why?"

"He's gay," said Tina.

"How do you know? I thought he was maybe bisexual."

"Hmm, I don't think so. He came around here with his companion. Steve. Guy works as a waiter at the Fairmont Hotel."

"Oh jeez."

Tina let one corner of her mouth rise into a smile. "Close call, eh? Now tell me about Kurt."

"Kurt? He's in Tuscany fucking his wife."

"Ouch."

"Technically, you could say I shouldn't be upset because

technically, nothing ever happened between us. And now they're trying to have a baby."

"Oh yuck. Put that way, all the fun goes out of it. How disgusting. How gross. I'm sorry, Miranda. Now will you let me do it?"

"What?"

"Say I told you so?"

"C'mon. You thought Kurt was hot, too. At the beginning."

"I did. At first. But those telling details always speak for themselves. He's a kink-o-rama."

"Yeah, and now if it goes according to plan, there's going to be a little kink-o-ramette in his life," I said.

"Keeping him awake for nights and nights on end…"

"Pooping its diapers every hour on the hour…"

Tina said, "Screaming its head off for no reason at all…"

"Regurgitating those cottage-cheese splashes all over his concert tux…"

"Emptying the flour and sugar containers all over the living-room rug…"

"Then the kid'll grow up," I said.

"And get zits, and be rude to its parents, and start doing drugs and stealing cars and getting girls pregnant or getting pregnant itself…"

We both began to smile.

"It's wonderful news, isn't it?" I said.

When Tina and I got to town, we dropped by Michelangelo's Coffee Shop.

As soon as Mike saw me, he threw his hands in the air and bellowed, "Miranda, what the hell ya doin' here? Nonna predicted you'd be comin' back but not so soon. Ha. Come over here and lemme see ya. Wanna know what else she predicted?"

"No, absolutely not," I said.

"You hungry? Somethin' for you an' your friend? On the house."

"We want a couple of Grace's best sandwiches. Croissant, Brie, speck and rocket."

Mike shook his head. He looked grim. "Grace hasn't been in, Miranda. We gotta new sandwich supplier. Pretty good. Not quite like Grace's but pretty good."

"So where is she?"

"Grace's not doin' too good, I'm sorry to tell ya."

"She was fine when I left," I said.

"She tell you that? She's quite a lady. Didn't want you to worry." He smiled with a sad little twist at the corner of his mouth.

"She said it was just one of life's little setbacks. Those were her words. I thought she must have had the flu or something."

"She's sick, Miranda. Terminal sick. She's been sick for a while now. A couple of years back she had some chemo but I think she doesn't feel much like fightin' anymore. She's in the unit. I'm amazed you didn't notice before you left. She's been goin' downhill for a while now."

I used breathing technique, pushed down on my diaphragm to stop myself from crying. "Too wrapped up in my own stupid problems to realize," I said.

Mike hurried off for a customer who wanted to pay.

Tina stood up and went to get us a couple of lattes and some of the new person's sandwiches. When she came back, she set the cups and plates down and said, "Actually, you don't mind if I eat both of these, do you, Miranda? I'm so hungry I could eat a horse and the cowboy who's riding it."

Mike came back over again and sat down at our table. "I went down to see Grace at lunchtime today. She asks about you whenever I go, your news, if we've heard from you. You should go and see her."

"I'll go today," I said.

"No, go tomorrow. She gets real tired, eh. She's not takin' anything. Her request. I don't know how she's handlin' the pain, but she is, goddammit…she and her God, she says, god-dammit." Mike looked up at the ceiling and said, "Sorry to take you in vain."

"I'll go first thing tomorrow." Although I was in shock again, I asked, "So how's Belinda?"

Mike mumbled, "Belinda and me are gettin' married."

"You're what?" I said.

"I told her, why fix it if it ain't broke, an' she told me she'd be seein' me around, so in the end… Maybe you'd like to sing at our wedding. It's in two weeks."

I said, "Yeah, that would be…no…I can't…maybe my friend Tina here could. She's really good. Much better than me. Tina? Tina?"

Tina had been so engrossed in her sandwich, she hadn't heard a word. "What?"

"Do you want to sing at Mike's wedding?"

She made her "I don't do weddings" face. Mike's eyes opened wider.

"She'll do it," I said.

"Yeah, okay," said Mike. "Listen, Miranda…"

"Listen, Mike, I was wondering if I could come back…" We'd both started to speak at the same time.

He looked apologetic and said, "I gave your job to Belinda's sister. Belinda told me she wasn't doing any more free-bies, and no extras, unless we made the big move. She said she'd go back to nights with Nonna, but I had to give her sister the job and a raise in pay. And she keeps all her tips. Those two chicks are fleecing me big-time," said Mike, grinning. "I'm really sorry, Miranda. I gave it to her because they all told me you definitely weren't comin' back, that you had decided to stay permanently in England."

"All who?" I asked.

"Your friends."

Tina stopped chewing. "Don't look at me like that, Mi-randa, I've got nothing to do with this."

"My friends? Which friends?" I squawked.

"That hippy chick who you share a place with, for one," said Mike.

"CAROLINE?" I shrieked.

Everybody in the coffee shop turned and stared.

"Yeah, her. She called me to tell me 'specially."

Mike sighed then got up and went back to the counter that he'd been buffing when we'd come in.

Tina said, "Listen, Miranda, don't sweat it. It's just a waitressing job. You've still got the opera chorus for April. Oh, and by the way, I don't do weddings."

"You have to do it. Because Mike and Belinda are friends and I'd really like to and I can't and it'll be a blast. It'll have the best food in the world and lots of dancing and single men who don't have anything to do with opera."

"Hmm, yeah, maybe when you put it like that."

"Listen, Tina, I've got to ask you another really, really big favor…"

After leaving Tina in the center of town, I hurried toward the Little Ladies office. When I got there, the warehouse was almost deserted. All the Little Ladies were out on jobs.

I walked through to the main office. Cora was inside, concentrating on paperwork. I approached her door and knocked.

She looked up and exclaimed, "Miranda. What are you doing here? You're supposed to be in England."

"Hi, Cora. I'm back." I smiled, but a bad feeling was coming over me.

Cora looked stricken. "I'm so sorry. I've already hired a new girl to take your place. They told me you weren't coming back."

"Who told you?"

"Your roommate. She phoned up to say that you wanted the information passed on. I'm really sorry, Miranda. I won't be hiring for another couple of months, but if anybody quits I'll call you right away."

Winter was making itself felt in Vancouver too. The air was damp, freezing and salty and I could feel it right down to the bone as I trudged back to the center of town to catch a bus. The scent of snow blew down from the mountains. There was that other underlying scent of fried onions and roasted chestnuts coming from fast-food joints and street vendors. Every time another gust of wind blew, people would take a step backward, slightly daunted, and pull their scarves up. A group of teenage girls wearing just their skimpy T-shirts and raccoon eye makeup giggled at me and sneered as they passed by. I wanted to tell them to put on a coat, a sweater, to put something between themselves and the cold hard world.

I felt old beyond my years.

There I was, Miranda Lyme, the nothing, waiting for the eternal bus in damp freezing downtown Vancouver; my sandwich angel was dying, I had no more boyfriend, no more waitressing job, no more cleaning job, no more voice and no more bed of my own to sleep in.

I started to giggle, my hysterical, bottom-of-the-barrel giggle. The raccoon-eyed girls in T-shirts joined in.

Chapter 22

I turned my key in the lock. There was music coming from Caroline's bedroom but her door opened as soon as I stepped inside the apartment. I went into the front room where my open suitcases were still spread across the furniture.

She followed me in and I could see she wanted to explain herself but before she could say a word, I muttered, "Caroline. What's happening here? Who did you give my bedroom to?"

She was already making placating gestures with her hands. "Wait, Miranda, before you jump all over me, just chill out. Let's talk about this."

"You rented out my room," I whined. "I never said anything about renting it out. I told you I was coming back. Well, here I am. Back. And right on schedule."

"This is all really confusing," said Caroline. "You want some tea? I've got an explanation. Or at least I think I have. Shit. This is all such a mess. When I saw your stuff around the room, I didn't know what to think. Some last-minute change of plan? Right?"

"Wrong, Caroline? What did you *think* the plan was? I told you before I left what the plan was. It was six and a half weeks unless I let you know otherwise."

She walked toward the kitchen. "I have to have some tea, special blend. For stress headaches. I'd rather have a joint but Cassie might arrive and call the cops."

"Cassie?"

"The girl I rented your room to." Caroline was rubbing her eyes. "I don't get it. It's a total bummer. Complete screwup. I just don't get it."

"What's there to get? I told you I'd be back around the beginning of February and you went and rented my room out to Goldilocks."

"Yeah. Ha. That's funny. Goldilocks. More like Little Bo Beep… Okay, now, wait, look. This is what happened. Remember just before you left, Patrick Tibeau was here and we got talking about his work?"

"Yes?"

I was getting a bad feeling.

If Caroline and Patrick…?

Naw.

Judging by his last e-mail, Patrick still seemed to be hooked on his old girlfriend, Mary. Alias Chi Narnia.

Caroline said, "Well, then I wanted to organize that event at the Student Union, get him to speak, right? So I went over to his place. He was just like so laid-back, a real human being. Really available, if you know what I mean. We got all hyped discussing what we would do. Technical stuff, what he'd talk about, which films we'd show, the dates and times, etcetera. And he told me to come back later in the week, that he'd look at his schedule and we'd firm things up— Hey," she interrupted herself. "He's working on his next project. I'm sure that whatever it is, it's gonna blow some minds. Really. You know he's done some documentary work as well as fiction—on street people? Yeah, I was asking him how he got his inspiration and he said all you have to do is look around you, get a sense of the place you're in. He said he'd even thought about doing something on that famous Stanley Park case. You know The Babes in the Woods?"

I nodded.

The Babes in the Woods case. In the fifties, the skeletons of two children were found in Stanley Park, Vancouver's big urban park. They figured they'd been there since the forties. At first they thought they were the remains of a boy and a girl, but DNA testing revealed that they were both boys. Along with the remains was a fur coat that had covered the skeletons, two leather WWII children's flying helmets, two lunch boxes and one woman's high-heeled shoe. Someone said they had seen a woman in a fur coat carrying a hatchet go into the woods with two children and come out without them, but by then some years had passed. They never found the guilty party. The case is still open.

Caroline said, "Yeah, but then he said he had something more personal in mind. He says it's going to be a love story. He's probably working on the screenplay now as we speak. I'm sure it's going to be radical. All his work is. He said he'd let me interview him when it gets close to release time. I'm going to be doing it for the *Straight*."

"He talked about all those things with you?"

"Yeah, and Evie Marcelle was there, too. She didn't say anything. She was so quiet I was starting to think she was a bit of a bonehead. She was just listening. Anyway, the next time I went back there, so we could confirm, she was there again, but acting very sociable, offering me coffee and stuff. So when I was finished talking to Patrick, and I was leaving, she told me to wait and that she had to go out herself and would walk partway with me. Well, it was sort of flattering…you know, like, hey, I can say to my friends, 'When I was chatting with my friend Evie Marcelle the other day…' So we went a little way together and she gets all panicky and says, 'Oh my God. Pat forgot to tell you.' I asked her what and she said, 'Your room-mate. Miranda.'"

I stared at Caroline, the bad feeling getting worse. "What did she say about me?"

"She said that you and Pat had been exchanging e-mails and that you wanted him to pass the word on that you wouldn't be coming back and that we needed to let all your employers know, and so on. And I asked her if you'd said anything about your apartment, and she said you'd be ar-ranging to have all your stuff shipped to England... Don't freak out... I was really careful. I put all your stuff in the locker downstairs... Now that I think about it, it's weird that you didn't tell me yourself, right?"

"God, Caroline. I would have phoned you if I'd wanted to tell you something as big as that."

"I'm really sorry about all this, Miranda. But you know, Evie Marcelle, she's like...up there in the public eye. Fa-mous. Why would she make stuff up?"

"I told you before, Caroline. She's psychotic."

"She didn't seem like it at all. She seemed so normal and well balanced. Really nice."

"That's why she's the actress and you're not. I knew she liked to step on the occasional head, but this is ridiculous. She seems to have it in for me."

"I don't like being used, either." Caroline frowned.

I slumped onto the sofa. "What about my chorus job with the opera? Did you give that away as well?"

"No," Caroline protested. "Gimme a break. It was a fluke about the others. I was just going to give it one try and pass on the information to whoever I could reach that day. The line at the opera office was busy so I didn't bother try-ing again. You know, I *did* have your interests at heart when I was doing all this, Miranda. I thought you'd ap-preciate getting your rent back for these months. It's not good business to leave a bedroom empty anyway when you're paying rent."

I was exhausted. It took all my strength to just say, "Evie Marcelle, that little…" and then my voice buckled.

Caroline leaped up. "I just hate that feeling of being had."

"One consolation, though," I choked. "Pat told me they'd broken up."

"Hey, you okay? Wanna glass of water?" asked Caroline. I shook my head.

Caroline said, "I haven't seen him since he gave his talk at the Student Union, which was a phenomenal success, by the way. I don't know what's going on with him now."

"He wanted to leave her, and he finally did it," I said.

"You know what I'd really like to do? I'd like to go out there and find that Evie Marcelle, and then I'd like to thump her. And then she wouldn't be the beautiful Evie Marcelle anymore. She'd be the loony chick with the broken nose. But I can't because it's against my principles."

I laughed. "You sound just like Betty, the woman I work…the woman I used to work with."

"Oh yeah?"

"Yeah, she's all for thumping people to settle a dispute… The big problem now is, where am I going to sleep tonight?" I said.

"This fuckup is my fault. You can have my bed," said Caroline. "I'll sleep on the couch."

Caroline's fuggy, animal-lair bedroom? I quickly said, "No, no. That's okay. I'll sleep on the couch tonight. Then I'll have to dream up something else. So tell me about Cassie."

Caroline rolled her eyes. "Well, you know how it is when you put up an ad. You usually have to take whoever answers and she happened to be the best of a bad bunch. There was another guy interested but he had really shifty eyes and a parakeet. I hate that squawking noise they make. It does my head in."

"What's Cassie when she's at home?"

"She's a secretary. She has about as much imagination as a head of iceberg lettuce. She's a thirty-one-year-old virgin and she's got a thing for her boss, and I'm sure she's going to die with a thing for her boss, because from the sounds of it, he barely knows she's alive."

"I saw the bedroom. Pretty bad. An eleven-year-old's bedroom."

"Yeah. Gag me with a Smurf. But I gave the room to her because I knew she'd be tidy. I didn't know she was going to do all the cleaning single-handedly, though. She's got tins of food lined up in alphabetical order in the kitchen cupboards. You know the type...? Hey, Miranda, want a beer? Dan had some temp work delivering for a brewery. The beer's only two days past the expiry date. He brought me three cartons. It's got a limited life span. We gotta drink it."

Caroline went to get a couple of bottles. She put a Bobby McFerrin CD on the player and we started to drink.

"I went to see your friends in London. Rosie and Clint and Morris."

"No shit?"

"They're great. Great people. Fantastic musicians. I really want to thank you for putting me on to them. They kept me from going crazy."

"Well, hey. Great. I don't have a franchise on the people I know."

"They helped me get started on my opera."

"Your opera?"

"I'm...don't laugh now...I'm writing an opera."

Caroline made a mock-surprised face and then said, "Right on. That is so cool. You go, girl."

I laughed again. "They might come out in a couple of months and help me put it on."

"All right. I'd love to see them again. Hey listen, I've got a singing voice like a crow and they didn't let me onstage in school because I tripped over things, but I'm a good organizer. If I can do anything to help, count me in."

"Thanks, Caroline. I'm not sure what I'm getting myself into, what it all really means yet. I guess I'll find out. I

don't have a job and I can't pay you any money, but I'm
sure I'll need people when the time comes. I'm thinking
of summer."

Chapter 23

The corridor was empty and I hurried along it until I came to the right room. I entered cautiously. I'd expected to see Grace hooked up to a million machines, but there was just her, smaller and whiter than before, being consumed from the inside, wracked with pain. A television droned on in a high corner but Grace was concentrating on another program. The program of preparing to die.

"Grace?" I whispered. "Grace? Are you awake?"

Her eyelids opened slowly, as if they weighed a ton each. It took her a minute to focus before she recognized me.

"Miranda."

I pulled up a chair and took her hand, the hand that had buttered and sliced forever. "I feel so...so stupid...that I...that I didn't know. Why didn't you tell me you were..."

"I didn't want to upset you." Her voice seemed to be coming through a heavy fog. It took all her strength to speak. "I'm ready, Miranda. Now talk to me. Quickly. I want to know it all. Tell me about London."

I began to babble, the whole story, everything from Kurt

and Olivia right down to meeting the Pemmicans and my opera. I thought she had drifted away but when I began to talk about the opera, she said, "You have grace, Miranda, like my name. It's a gift from heaven. Don't waste it…you mustn't waste it. Now, what's your opera about, from the beginning to the end."

I wasn't sure at all about Grace's concept of heaven but I hoped against all hope that Grace was right and I was wrong, that there *was* her kind of heaven somewhere. Because there were a few people I wanted to meet with up there. My father, for starters. Not that I was sure that he'd be let in. Or me either. I was like Groucho Marx and clubs. Would I want to be let into a heaven that would include a person like me?

"I don't want to talk about me anymore, Grace." By then I was swallowing hard, fighting back tears.

"Please…" whispered Grace.

The day flowed into night. I was afraid to leave. I stayed near her bed, taking short walks and grabbing coffees from the machine down the hall, then going back to hold her hand for a little longer, slipping in and out of sleep as she slipped in and out of consciousness. I'd already blown it with my father. I had no intention of blowing it with Grace.

There were other visits while I was there, from Mike and Belinda, and people from Grace's church. But the unexpectedly quick end came while I was alone with her, dozing at the side of her bed, and when I shook myself awake, she had gone, leaving just that peaceful expression, and her rainbow pom-pom sweater draped over the chair near her bed. I slid the sweater into my knapsack.

And her death would have been terrible, really terrible, except that just after that, I swear, and I know it sounds crazy, but I swear I felt this huge warm spirit filling the room and I knew it was her.

It was there during those two days in the hospital, talking to Grace, that I began to pull the threads together. In being forced to talk about my ideas, my opera, for a woman who was only going to hear about it then and there, I had to put in my best, everything I thought that Grace, now arriving at the end of the line, might want to hear.

The next day, at the memorial service in Grace's little Baptist church, her friends surrounded me as soon as I arrived.

They pushed forward, telling me, "You have to sing, Miranda. It's what she would have wanted." I shook my head frantically but they wouldn't pay attention to my protests, my pleas of laryngitis. "It doesn't matter how it sounds," they said. "It's what Grace wanted. However it comes out will be fine."

So in the quietest voice imaginable, I stood up there and sang, an octave lower than it should have been, "Oh, happy day…" When my voice faltered and disappeared, and my throat tightened up with tears, the whole congregation jumped in to save me, to pull me forward. They belted it out blissfully and I found my voice again and was carried along by them, going somewhere with them. Grace, even from her special place in Paradise, never stopped encouraging me.

Chapter 24

On the bus heading to Cold Shanks, I watched the damp green turn to patchy white snow, and the snow grow deeper as we moved inland. I'd only let my mother know I was coming just before boarding the bus. But she'd sounded relieved. I tried not to think about Grace, and how stupid I'd been not to realize sooner.

And then there was my apartment. Cassie had turned out to be a dumpling of a woman, thick glasses, short blah-colored hair and enormous thunder thighs. To make matters worse, she dressed like a Girl Scout leader, big-hip and thigh-swelling knee-length culotte skirts, sensible shoes. Her voice was high and chirpy, à la Alvin and the Chipmunks, like she'd just swallowed helium. She took her soap operas very seriously and her evening's entertainment was to catch up on the soaps she'd taped during the day while she was at work. Between programs she went into ecstasy over ads with fluffy kittens and rolls of toilet paper. She was going to be hard to dislodge.

Caroline was apologetic all evening and knocking herself out for me, and it was hard to get used to. And then Dan came over, and even his tree-hugging misadventures as an agro-agit dreadhead made a pleasant contrast to Cassie. I mean, who would you choose to spend the evening with? Dan the Sasquatch, who was trying to save rain forests—the natural habitat of sasquatches? Or Cassie, whose major after-dinner social activity was to floss her teeth in the living room while we all looked on?

My mother met me at the bus station with her Chevy station wagon. I noticed she had the snow chains on.

"How're you feeling, dear? Was the trip...oh look, there's Mrs. Eisel, she is such a...did you manage to sleep on the...oh, shoot. I forgot to buy the purple onions for the..."

"Don't start the car, Mom."

"Why?"

"I want to talk to you about Sebastian."

"Ah...okay...how did it..."

"He's dead, Mom."

A small ghost of a sound escaped her lips.

"It was a few months ago. He had a heart attack. He'd lost his voice and then started binge eating and drinking..."

"How did you learn this?"

"His widow, Doris, told me."

"I see."

"She seemed nice, Mom."

The car was still stationary. My mother gripped the wheel tightly and looked ahead, immobile. Her transparent Scandinavian looks colored quickly when she got emotional. The tip of her small sharp nose turned slightly pink. "You know, it doesn't really surprise..."

"It all went wrong," I said. Our breath was frosty even inside the car, and the windows were fogging up. My mother reached forward and began to furiously wipe the windshield with a rag.

When she'd finished, she turned and faced me. "Miranda, people like that are hard to help. I didn't tell you about it when you were younger because I didn't think it was fair to…"

"You should have helped me more."

"Helped you?"

"Helped me get to him sooner. If we just could have met, maybe I could have helped Sebastian somehow.

"Now it's all a big mess. It's all gone wrong. I still don't know how you could have left someone like my father and ended up with someone like Lyle. Haven't you ever thought that our leaving might have helped push Sebastian Lyme over the edge?"

"You really don't remember anything, do you?"

"Like what, Mom?"

My mother was angry now. "I had good reasons for leaving your father. It was one of the hardest periods of my life. When we came back here, there was another long bleak period after him and before Lyle, a continuation of the other bleak period I lived through in England with your father. Things didn't get better until I met Lyle.

"Don't you remember me taking in all that sewing after we came back from England? In that sordid little apartment over the Hair Fair? You could smell the scorched perms right through the floor. You really don't remember, do you? I had to sleep in the living room. On a bed made up to look like a couch. There was only the one bedroom and I gave it to you. And the awful old cracked linoleum in the kitchen? And that horrible stained bathtub? That was our life here before I met Lyle.

"And as for your father, Miranda, I wanted a man in my life who wasn't going to squander the rent money on booze, who wasn't going to say he was going out for five minutes and stay away for five days, who wasn't going to pawn my diamond scatter pin, my string of pearls and the opal pendant left to me by my great-aunt Prue. And that man was Lyle, not Sebastian Lyme. Lyle's a good father and a good husband, and maybe if you'd give it some thought, you'd realize that you are where you are thanks to him. Who do you think paid for all your extra music lessons, your entrance fees for the competitions, your university fees? Not me. They weren't free, you know. I wanted a proper family. A proper home. I couldn't have done it without Lyle. And don't you forget it for a minute, Miranda Lyme."

It was the longest speech she'd made in years. I should have applauded but I was tired, jet-lagged and jobless. All I wanted to do was cry. Nobody could accuse me of not knowing the value of money. So I did the same as her and stared straight ahead.

After we'd driven a dozen blocks and reached the edge of town, my mother turned the wrong way off the main road.

"Why're you taking this road, Mom? This is the mountain road."

"Oh, I've got a meeting with another woman from my weaving guild. We're putting together a booth for the spring fair. You don't mind coming…"

"No, no." I did but I'd been humbled. I sank back into the seat. Cold Shanks, if nothing else, was far away from the lion's share of my problems. Or, at least, that's what I foolishly believed.

We climbed higher and higher up the precarious mountain road and turned off into the dense forest. After another five minutes, my mother turned again onto a narrower unfamiliar salted dirt road. "Where are you taking us?" I asked.

"You'll see."

We bumped along over the bad road through even denser forest, a fairy-tale forest of untouched giant evergreens. We came into a clearing and in front of us was a sprawling light-colored log house. Beyond that was a lake, half-frozen over with a thin glaze of ice.

I climbed out of the car and followed my mother to the front door. It was opened by a small dark woman with an oval face.

"Hi, Nora," said the woman to my mother. "Now let me guess. This is your daughter."

"Miranda," said my mother. "Miranda, this is Jeanette. She's one of our star weavers."

"There's quite a resemblance between the two of you," said Jeanette. "Come on in, both of you. I thought Luc was going to be here today, but he had a client down in Penticton."

My mother whispered, "Her husband does something with computers. I still haven't understood what. Software or something."

The interior of the house was fantastic, with a huge living room and picture window overlooking the lake. The room was filled with big comfortable furniture for dreaming the day away, woven wall hangings and original modern bright paintings. A delicious sweet baking smell filled the house. Jeanette disappeared and came back with a tray of coffee mugs and cinnamon buns. Then Jeanette vanished again and returned with an armload of woven masterpieces. There were shawls, skirts, jackets and throws in beautiful colors and weave combinations.

"Your mother's been sewing my bolts into some very classy clothes. They've been selling like hotcakes the last few years at the local craft fairs."

I drank coffee and ate cinnamon buns and they talked Weavers' Guild business for a while.

Then Jeanette looked at us both and said, "So okay, now, Nora? Miranda? You girls ready for a sauna?"

"Oh, yes, great," said my mother.

It seemed like a good idea. Maybe they also had a hot tub tucked away there. It was right along the lines of the kind of self-pampering that was advised for girls who'd just been dumped by boyfriends and employers. But as it turned out, it wasn't going to be so much of an after-the-fall pampering type of experience as a Siberian Gulag type of experience.

"The sauna's down at the edge of the lake," said Jeanette as she and my mother stripped off their clothes and pulled on bathing suits. I shrugged at my mother. What was I going to wear? But she was a step ahead of me. She pulled an old Speedo of mine from her bag and tossed it to me. It was so worn it was nearly transparent.

Jeanette said, "After the sauna, you have to roll in the snow or wash yourself with it. Of course, in the summer it's nice because we dive into the lake."

I guess she noticed my appalled expression. This was one of those situations—like accidentally stumbling into a nudist colony—where anyone not joining in looked like the dork.

Jeanette went on, "It's very invigorating. You have to try it at least once before you say you don't like it. You'll feel like a new person."

Those were the words that convinced me. Although I didn't really need to *feel* like a new person. I needed to *be* a new person.

I pulled on the swimsuit and accepted the bathrobe and rubber clogs that were offered to me, then followed the two women outside and across the snow down to the lake where a wooden building was giving off steam.

"It should be good and hot by now," said Jeanette, opening the door. We stepped into the outer room. I took off my bathrobe and hung it up, then followed the women into the heat of the sauna itself. The room was thick with steam and it was hard to see at first. I could make out another form lying across one of the top benches. It lifted its head and said in a deep male voice, "Hi, Mom."

I peered through the steam and when it cleared a little I let out a tiny gasp. "Patrick? What are you doing here?"

"Miranda?" he laughed. "That should be my question. I live here. Some of the time, that is. This is my parents' place. I guess you've met my mother in all her glory."

As he said this, he sat up and openly and happily gazed

at my body in the nearly invisible swimsuit. I gazed back. Then both of us grinned and laughed.

And I have to say, the view was not bad, not bad at all. Patrick was a little bulky but there were solid muscles under the padding.

After the first shock of finding Pat in the sauna had worn off, and we were all engaged in the business of sweating en masse, a strange, languid, unexpected euphoria came over me. I felt glad just to be alive, to be in my skin, to be in the company of other sweaty but good people. I closed my eyes and let the heat go around and through me.

"Come on, Miranda," said Pat. "You don't want to stay in too long the first time around." He must have seen my eyes closing dangerously. He came over to my bench and offered me his hand. I climbed down and let him lead me out into the cold and before I knew what was happening, he was rubbing snow all over me and himself. The sensation of having my skin touched was already foreign and I was mortified as his snow-filled hands moved deftly over me. If he noticed that I was paralyzed under his touch, he pretended not to. He hustled me back inside to the little outer room and helped me into the bathrobe. He pulled it tight around me, reached all the way around me and tied my belt into a neat loop, then smiled and said, "I'd rather be untying this than tying it up but I guess it's the wrong moment."

A shiver of excitement went through me.

My mind was fighting my body. There had been Mary, and there had been Evie, and who knows who else there had been in between, and now there was Mary again reincarnated as Chi Narnia, but somehow, the idea of all those other women just wasn't bothering me enough that day to ruin my euphoria.

Jeanette invited my mother and me for lunch and I could catch Pat's approving expression on the sidelines. The meal began with mulled wine and different cheeses and olives and grilled peppers, and then went on to mutton stew, salad and homemade scones. Jeanette looked at her plate of mutton stew and then over to Patrick and said, "You're not eating."

"You put yellow squash in this. The one food I can't stand is yellow squash."

"Patrick, you are such a fusspot sometimes," said Jeanette.

"Yeah, you wouldn't think a guy who'd been sent to the Devil's Island penal colony would be so finicky about his food," he said, grinning at me.

His mother frowned. "I wish you wouldn't make jokes about it. If the justice system hadn't been so—"

"Give it a rest, Mom. Miranda, my mother doesn't like me making jokes about it because she thinks I was falsely accused. But actually, it *was* me that burned down the school even if I didn't set out to do it. I sort of get a little buzz thinking about it."

"Patrick! If Luc were here…" hissed Jeanette. I was getting the feeling that Pat's reform-program days had been more painful for his parents than they had been for him.

"Mom, I'm pulling your leg. It was the best thing that ever happened to me and you have to start living in the present and accepting it. Things couldn't be going better. And that's thanks to the program."

"What about Evie?" asked Jeanette.

"I know you liked Evie, but now that she's gone, I feel like I've been sprung from a cage…"

Jeanette looked at me and said, "That girl was completely lost when she came up here. The *one* time she came up here. Boy, she thought she was really roughing it. And I provided a week of maid service. I couldn't wait to see the back of her."

Patrick was serious, staring at his mother. "I had no idea you felt that way about Evie."

"My dear child, Patrick. When you have children of your own, you'll realize how hard it is to be a parent." He was going to say something but she cut him short by gathering up dishes and taking them into the kitchen.

After lunch, Jeanette and my mother went off to Jeanette's workshop.

Pat and I sat in front of the fire in the big living room. He made me try some lavender wine that he'd made himself. It wasn't nearly as awful as its name suggested, but quite good once you forgot it was made from flowers that are usually reserved for soaps and perfumes.

He sprawled on the couch opposite me and fixed me with his coal-black eyes. "So now, Miranda, just exactly what were you doing in England anyway? I was never clear on that."

"I went over there because of a man," I said.

"Aha."

"I guess the fact that I'm back and in Cold Shanks tells you how badly it went."

"Well, now. The scenario could go a lot of different ways. He could be joining you later to meet your parents. Or he could have come with you and is right now out buying a little plot on one of the Gulf Islands so that you two can build yourselves a log cabin and raise goats. No?"

"No. Not this guy. He's English. From London. Mr. English Culture personified. And he did happen to be married. Still *is* married."

I tried to keep my features bright but they sagged immediately at the thought of Kurt.

"That always adds a peppery little zing to the situation, but I'm sorry it didn't work out," said Patrick. "Anybody I know?" he added.

"I don't know. He's a conductor. And composer. Kurt Hancock."

"Oh, really? Kurt Hancock? Well, that's pretty interesting."

"Yeah. I wish I could say I dumped him because he had lousy hygiene but he dumped me."

Patrick grinned, nodded his head slowly and said, "I really want to thank you for that little suggestion. It was just so simple. I added some nice extra touches to the manure under the armpits."

"Like?"

"Oh, munching on raw onion and garlic around the clock."

"Yecch."

"Very healthy. They say garlic does great things for the immune system," he laughed.

"What else?"

"A few dead fish hidden in inaccessible places."

"No, seriously."

"I am serious."

I was giggling.

"And just lying in bed for days on end watching the Shopping Channel or the Weather Channel is a real turn-on for the babes, too. Evie finally showed me her real self."

"What was that like?" As if I didn't know.

Patrick said, "I don't want to cast a shadow on all that went before, all the good parts, but what really threw me for a loop was how cold she was, how completely unemotional she was when she finally decided to leave. I would have preferred another of her scenes. It would have convinced me that she had at least felt something for me. Maybe a tiny part of me didn't want to be on the losing end. It shouldn't have surprised me that the man she left me for and moved in with, she'd already been screwing for weeks. But it *did* surprise me. More than usual.

"The thing is, Miranda, I've just been so busy for these last couple of years that when I realized that there was a big problem, the idea of dealing with it seemed like something that would require more energy than I had at the moment, so I didn't. But *not* dealing with it was the answer in the end. I got a lot of practical thinking done while I lay around and pretended to do nothing."

And then I said, "Pat, I've got to tell you what Evie did."

After he'd listened to the whole story, he sighed heavily and said, "Miranda, why don't you do this. Take my keys back with you and use my place."

"No, no, it's nice of you to offer but I couldn't do that."

"Oh, yes, you could, Miranda. I'm partly to blame."

"No, you're not."

"Go on."

"I don't know."

"Please, use my place. And you can clean up the dead fish while you're there."

I grimaced.

"Just joking. I hosed it all down the day she moved out, then I called in the shaman to kick out all the bad jinn."

"Uh-huh," I said.

"She won't come calling."

"No?"

"No, and she doesn't have a spare key. I changed the locks after she left, so you don't need to worry about that. Listen. For the most part, I'll be up here to work on my screenplay and do a little carpentry for my mom. I've got a couple of trips to L.A. so I'll pass through town then. But nobody will bother you. You can practice your heart out. I imagine you have roles and concerts and gigs to prepare for and things like that."

"I…uh…would have had. Normally. I guess you could say I'm branching out in a different direction."

"Different from singing?"

"I've been having some vocal problems."

"That's hard when you're a singer. What kind of direction?"

"I'm writing an opera."

He laughed. "Oh, really?" He reached down into a large magazine rack that was beside the sofa and began to feel around for something.

"I can see you're amused," I said.

He pulled out a video camera and trained it on me. I made a face but he said, "Just ignore the camera. I'm practicing. I don't think I've ever met anyone who was writing an opera. It's a first for me."

"Yeah, it's a first for me, too."

His face stayed hidden behind the camera. "What's your opera about, Miranda?"

I started to giggle. "I'm embarrassed to say."

"Why?"

"Well, you gave me the idea. Indirectly. And now I don't know whether or not I'm stealing from you."

"Sorry. You've lost me."

"It sort of revolves around the Babes in the Woods case."

He looked out from behind the camera. I watched him let the idea sink in. He said, "The best world is the one where ideas are shared. I, for one, like my competition to surprise and excite me."

"You were talking to Caroline about using what's around you."

"Yeah, Caroline. She's quite a lot of fun."

"She is?" I said, half-shocked.

"You don't think so?"

"I guess I haven't really been too fair with her. She's a bit too political sometimes."

"Scratch her ranting socialist surface and she's fun. She's sincere, too."

"Yeah. Maybe."

Patrick was back behind the camera. "The Babes in the Woods is quite the evocative little story, isn't it? I can't wait to see what you're doing with it."

"I don't know, Patrick. I don't know what it's going to be like. But I'm going to finish it, and maybe it'll be bad or insignificant or mediocre, but then I'm going to go out there and find some singers and get down on my knees and beg them to sing in it, and then find some techies and a theater somewhere and I'm going to damn well get it performed. Because I can't live without music. I came to this conclusion in London that men have cornered this market too long. There are so few women composers. Of serious music, I mean. Why is that? It's time for opera to rear its female head. If I can't be part of that other opera party, I'll throw my own instead."

He put the camera back in the magazine rack, cocked his head to one side, looked at me hard, then came over and sat close to me on the couch. "You know, when you put it like that, I have no doubts that you're going to do everything you say you're going to do." He surprised me by leaning in, sliding an arm around my shoulders and kissing me on the forehead, like a priest giving me his blessing.

Our mothers' voices snapped us out of the comfortable, warm and slightly drunk embrace. Patrick stood up, went over to the fire and poked a log until sparks shot out.

Jeanette and my mother were in the living room now.

My mother said, "I really have to get moving, Miranda. I left the twins with Sal and you know how she gets when they…"

I had another jolt of memory. "Patrick. Biba," I blurted out.

Patrick nodded slowly. "You asked me about Biba in your e-mail. Yeah. Let me think about it. It's a bit tricky."

"I need to find her…"

"Miranda…we really need to get…" My mother's voice was picking up that hysterical edge.

"Coming, Mother," I said.

"How much longer are you up here for?" asked Pat.

"Just a couple of days. I've got to get back to Vancouver and find some more work."

"Let me get you my keys," said Pat. "I'll be back in and out of town for the next few weeks. We can talk when I'm down there next."

In my mother's sewing room, I fingered the crimson velvet evening gown and said through my streaming tears, "It's beautiful, Mom."

"Oh, Miranda, please don't cry into the dress. You'll ruin it. Velvet is so…"

"But it's all gone wrong, Mom. All my plans. I was supposed to premiere Kurt Hancock's song cycle in March and now I'm going to tell him I can't do it. I've got this problem with my voice and it won't go away. I'll never get through the piece. I'll have to tell the composer I'm pulling out. I'll have to tell Kurt…"

"Um, Miranda…um…this Kurt…"

Our eyes met. I realized in that moment that my mother knew everything there was to know about Kurt.

"Doris, Sebastian's last wife, told me that my father started having vocal problems and then he lost his voice completely and look what happened to him. He just went right downhill. What if it's hereditary?"

"Don't be silly…"

"Music's my life. I'll die without music."

"*Now* you sound like Sebastian Lyme. He was always overdramatizing. Oh, Miranda, don't you know that old expression? There are plenty of ways to skin a cat? You could do something related that uses your knowledge. You could teach."

Now I *really* felt like crying. I wanted to say, I don't want to teach. I want to be in the inner circle, but I knew better and kept quiet.

"I'm too young to teach. I don't have any experience."

"That doesn't seem to stop a lot of teachers. What about Tina? She teaches."

"Tina likes teaching. She likes being a dictator and bossing people around, pretending she knows it all. But she's also good at it. I'm crummy. I can feel things but I can't describe the sensations in a way that makes sense to other people."

"Well…"

"I can't explain it, Mom. I have to *have* the music. I have to own it. It has to be inside of me. That's why I thought I would try to write."

"Oh, now, that's a good idea. You could write articles about music. You could review concerts."

"No, Mom. Music. Write music. I'm trying to write an opera."

"You're trying to do what?"

"I'm trying to write an opera."

"That's an unusual…that's remarkable, Miranda. What a good idea. Will you let me hear some of it? What's it about?"

"It doesn't matter. I don't know if it's awful or wonderful. Sometimes I feel like I know exactly what I'm doing with it and other times I don't have a clue. It's all just way beyond me."

"I wish I could help you, dear, but music isn't really…"

"It's probably crap. It's probably just total shit and no one will ever want to put it on."

"That's not a very positive attitude. When you talk like that, I don't recognize you, Miranda. I really don't. What's happened to you?"

I wanted to say, Kurt Hancock happened to me. But it was better not to say anything.

That evening I sat at the piano in the living room and tinkered with my opera score, correcting, trying out new ideas. When I looked up, Lyle was standing behind me. He'd been so quiet, I hadn't heard him coming.

"It's amazing how you can do that," he said.

"Do what?"

"Put music on paper like that."

"Doesn't mean it doesn't stink," I said.

"Hey, Miranda. Don't be so hard on yerself. Yer too hard on yerself."

"It's a competitive business. And it's a man's business."

Lyle roughed up his hair and looked at the ceiling, bemused. "Hey, ya know, it's hard to be a man. And it's hard to be a father."

"What are we talking about?"

"I just wanna say, don't be so hard on him, either, eh? You know you can have kids of yer own and feel like a kid inside, kinda helpless. And sometimes when ya see how good yer wife is at doin' all that stuff that kids need, ya figure you're like a fifth wheel, eh, and that they don't maybe need ya so much as you thought, that if somethin' happened to ya, they'd get by okay. It can be real depressing for some guys."

"Is that how you feel?"

"I'm not talkin' about me. I'm just tryin' to say, yer father was human, eh? Ya might wanna think about…like…forgivin' him? Forgivin' them both. Yer mom and yer dad."

I stared at Lyle. I'd been looking at him for years but had never really seen him. He shrugged and left the room.

By the time I was ready to leave Cold Shanks, it was on everybody's tongue.

I don't know how it got around. My mother said the only person she told was Lyle.

I tried to picture Lyle, down at his auto shop, saying, "Could you pass me the spanner, Bud? And by the way, Miranda's writing an opera." And his brother, Bud, might say, "No shit, Lyle, would that be in the style of Puccini, with all the romantic screamings of verismo, or some horrific serial music, exemplary Bing Bang Bong, or can we look forward to something more refined and Belliniana, in the bel canto style perhaps? I can't wait to get home and tell Sal." Then he'd take a big swig of his beer and belch.

Because they all knew about it. The whole town knew about it.

I was just preparing to leave for the bus station, getting my stuff together in the front hall, the beautiful crimson dress in its garment bag and draped over my arm, when Bud's wife, Sal, pulled up in front of the house. She came running up the front steps, the entire blond burly bulk of her, and blocked me in the open doorway.

The first thing she said to me was, "So, Miranda, I hear you're writing an opera." And she said it to me the way you might say to a person with no legs, "So, I hear you're going to compete in the triathlon in next year's Olympics."

Then the twins, who were in the living room testing the couch springs, started to shriek, "Miranda's writing an opera, Miranda's writing an opera," which had about the same meaning for them as "Miranda is a rotten egg."

But then they surprised me. They suddenly stopped bouncing and asked, "Can we be in it?"

So let's put it this way. The challenge had been set. I had the whole of Cold Shanks to contend with. I had to be a warrior. There would be no turning back.

Chapter 25

Patrick's place didn't smell like rotten fish at all. I put his keys down on the table and looked around. He'd made it spotless, blissfully clean, neutral, and devoid of all traces of Evie. Dan the Sasquatch struggled in behind me carrying my computer. Caroline followed with my keyboard and a big suitcase full of my clothes. She'd managed to coerce Dan into using the brewery truck to help me move the most important things over to Pat's place.

"Where do you want it, Your Ladyship?" asked Dan.

"Over there, Jeeves." I pointed to the long table and told him where to put the computer down. He made an exaggerated bow and backed toward the door. My relationship with the Sasquatch had developed into this playful mock master/slave routine. I'd always known that he thought me frivolous and stuck up, but now we were acting on it.

He had started to say things like "Let me lie in that puddle, Your Ladyship, so that you may walk on my kidneys and not get your dainty feet wet."

And I would reply, "Lower, serf, lower. I can still see your brutish face." We got quite Shakespearean at times.

Caroline said, "I'm really sorry about the screwup. Just consider it a holiday, Miranda. I'll get Cassie out of there somehow. I'll negotiate something with her. Consider it your place still. Your stuff's in the locker and not going anywhere, right? Your furniture's still there. Come round whenever you like."

"Sure," I said. But actually, I was really looking forward to having Patrick's big space to myself. For the next few weeks, I had a very long list of "Things to Do."

The first and most important thing to do was write to Madame Klein. It turned out to be a long apologetic letter of the begging and groveling type, telling her that she was right and I was wrong, and that my singing voice was irrecoverable and that I needed her help for a special project that she might find interesting. I put the first half of my score into a big envelope and also put in a cover page:

City of Dreams
An Opera in Two Acts
by
Miranda Lyme
Cast

John Boldright, a police detective—bass baritone

Blossom Sanchez, a jazz singer—lyric spinto soprano

Julia Lau, John Boldright's wife—dramatic soprano

Gypsy girl, the messenger—coloratura soprano

Vanessa, an actress—mezzo-soprano

Kevin, a hairdresser—tenor

The Homeless Man—bass

The Woman—mezzo-soprano

Two boys—sopranos

Dancers and mime artists

Chorus

Chorus of mixed adult voices—SATB

Chorus of children's voices—soprano and alto

Orchestra

Violin, Viola, Cello, Bass, Clarinet, Saxophone, Percussion, Piano/keyboard

Numbers and variety of instruments are not fixed—they may be adjusted according to preferences and type of instruments available. The work may also be performed with only keyboard/piano in small environments. One of the composer's aims is to give space to a minimum of improvisation. Most of the score is written out, but there are sections where the singers and musicians are allowed and encouraged to break away musically.

Staging Notes

The work is best staged in an open theater rather than on a proscenium stage. In certain moments chorus members should mingle with the audience. The sets are minimal.

The opera is extremely chorus heavy, as the chorus voices are in demand for most of the opera, double as instrumental backing and are often required to use experimental vocal techniques, speech and chanting. Apart from acting as a type of Greek chorus, commenting on the action and supplying background noise such as wind and waves, the chorus singers are also required to play a variety of found percussion instruments such as stones banged together, sticks and tin cans, etcetera. For these purposes, they should be equipped with chairs and multipocketed aprons to hold their instruments. At certain times they will break formation, add a piece of costume and become part of the stage action.

Inside the envelope, I also put Patrick's video of *The Other Street,* with a special note to play close attention to Biba's interview.

I got up early each day and worked hard on my composition. My crimson velvet evening gown hung on a wall hook in its transparent garment bag. Every time I looked up and saw it, the dress made me think of blood, of a wound, a reminder of what I'd lost. I knew I'd wear it one day, but I wouldn't be the first person to wear it. Tina and I had already set a plan in motion. Every day at four o'clock, after a full day's work, I showed up at Tina's door, along with her accompanist, Rita, and we went to work.

The ad that I put up all over town read: "Professional singing teacher available for all singing styles. Reasonable rates." Tina told me what to write and to put her phone number on it, that she would take the calls since she already handled lots of students. I didn't want to do it, but Tina said she'd teach me to teach, that it was easy.

The chorus rehearsals for *Carmen,* my only source of income at that moment, were under way. It was a catfight. The women were scrapping over who got to be an aristocrat in lace and jewelry and who got to be a cigarette girl in bare feet and cleavage. Marian was in the front line desperate to get her tits out there where no one could flee from the sight of them.

I had considered quitting the chorus but it would have been an act of bad faith. It would have been like admitting that I was never going to get my voice back. And I was going to get it back. It was only a matter of time. So I pretended to be invisible, staying in the shadows as much as possible. Once, Marian turned and glared at me then whispered, "You're not singing. I haven't heard you sing a note all night."

"It's an acoustic thing," I waffled. "We studied this effect at university. Certain frequencies seem to disappear when they're combined with certain kinds of harmonies. It's a mirage effect. This section of *Carmen* is notorious for it.

You're actually hearing something you think you're not hearing. It's just hard to perceive, that's all. You know, like dog whistles?"

But she continued to stare at me all night, as though I were a serial killer disguised as a chorus singer.

When each section was called on to sing their parts separately, I used my voice. It was pure torture. But I needed the paycheck. I was beginning to understand my father's despair.

Michelangelo and Belinda's wedding was a big Catholic blowout of yellow roses and cream silk moiré and lace. As the bride and groom marched down the aisle, looking like a couple of really bad hangovers, Tina sang a wonderfully tear-jerking "Ave Maria." There were a hundred and fifty guests and not a dry eye in the place.

The day culminated in a lavish reception on a private ship moored in the harbor. Even Mike's granny was there. When we were all finally aboard, the crew cast off and the ship motored out in the direction of English Bay. Tina and I started in on the rivers of champagne that were flowing everywhere. After I'd had a few, I got up and went over to say hello to Nonna. The old woman asked me if I knew how many more days we'd be on board before we docked in America and then she grabbed my hand and flattened my fingers to examine my palm one more time. I shuddered. It was sure to be another black prophesy. But instead of bursting into tears she began to chuckle and cluck like an old hen.

"What do you see in there?" I asked her, but she just kept on chuckling.

Later, as Tina and I were making a third round of the dessert table and homing in on the white-chocolate mousse with the mango topping, Tina grabbed my arm and said, "Well, beat my time, Shostakovich, take a lookie over there at who's stuffing his face with seafood pasta, the sexy oink."

She pointed through the crowd.

"As I live and breathe. Wayne," I said.

Tina straightened her tight black cocktail dress and said, "I got him the invitation but I really didn't think he'd come. I'll see you later." She marched straight up to Wayne, who was looking as wonderful as ever. They both drained another glass of champagne then headed arm in arm toward a staircase that led belowdecks to the staterooms. I sighed heavily. Oh, for someone to rock *my* boat.

It was eight o'clock in the evening in early March. I'd been at Pat's place for three and a half weeks, when I heard a key in the lock. The door opened and Patrick was in the doorway, struggling to bring in a large carryall.

He stopped and said, "Hi, Miranda. Hope I didn't scare you."

Then he put down his bag and pulled off his jacket. A wave of relief went through me at the sight of him. He looked like some kind of modern Eurasian gladiator. His eyes were blacker and shinier than usual, his black hair loose and long, his face a mix of pride, candor and intelligence.

And then there was the muscular build I knew was hidden under all those clothes, the physique I'd mapped faster than the world's fastest cartographer that day in the sauna.

"I was wondering when you'd get here," I said.

"So, how's the opera going?"

"It's…uh…" I ran my hand through my hair. "It's not going. It's at an impasse."

"Do you feel like talking about it?"

"I don't want to bore you with my petty attempts at composition."

"Well, here's a miscellaneous news bulletin for you—I happen to be an opera buff. Don't look so surprised. Let's have a coffee and we can talk about it. I always find it helps to bounce your ideas off any old Tom, Dick or Harry who happens to be sitting on the bar stool next to you. If you want to, that is."

"I guess so. I think I'm probably better at doing music than explaining it. But if you want to hear about it anyway…"

"What are you doing for a libretto?"

"I'm not really doing anything for it. The characters have been in my head for a while. They speak and I write it down. So obviously the prose is fairly modern and natural but sometimes it glitches up because it's too modern or awkward and the words just don't fit the music."

"That's really interesting. Most composers don't write their own libretto."

"It's just that I think I can do this thing. I *have* to do this thing. I spent so much time on the stage when I was studying, especially when we produced the Bing Bang Bong efforts of novice composers, imagining how I would do a modern opera if I had my way. I'm a megalomaniac. I want it to be the way I want it, and I don't want to fight with anyone. This thing is born out of pure frustration."

"I know exactly what you mean, Miranda." He lightly ran his hand along my cheek. His fingers felt cold, but then my cheek was very, very hot.

He went into the kitchen and I could hear him taking down cups and running water. He shouted out to me, "Jeeez, I haven't seen this kitchen so clean in ages. Evie was a woman of leisure in that respect. Afraid she'd break a fingernail, I guess."

He came back into the main area and sat down on the edge of the bed.

"Are you staying a while?" I asked.

"Don't look so worried when you say that," he laughed. "I know what it's like to have no home. I won't get in your way. Yeah, I'm staying for a few days, then I'm off to L.A. again. They're slippery sons of bitches down there. You have to catch them on the run. They change jobs faster than they change their underwear and your financing's gone as fast as it came."

"Listen, if you want me to go, I can stay over at my friend Tina's, or sleep on the couch at my old place."

"Don't you move. I've got a neat little system. Just you watch."

At the far end of the big space was a lot of junk of the kind you find in attics and basements. There was a bicycle, some furniture, planks and boards and trunks. Patrick shifted some of the boards and hauled out something that turned out to be a long folding wooden screen. He dragged it over to the bed and placed it so that it formed a private bedroom area. Then he brought out a roll-away mattress and dropped it right in the middle of the open space.

"My period of incarceration." He grinned. "I can sleep anywhere. This is what I do when my parents are here."

"I can't take your bed. That's not fair."

"Well, it's a big bed. You could share it with me. You might have to handcuff me to the box spring so that I don't accidentally end up on your side. Awake, I can promise not to sneak over and pester you, but asleep, my subconscious might make me rove too far."

I didn't say anything. I was having trouble swallowing.

Then he said very matter-of-factly, "If it gives you any idea of how well things were going with Evie, I haven't been with a woman in over six months. Hey, don't look at me like that."

"What about Mary? From your e-mails it sounded like you'd sort of found each other again."

He grinned again. "Mary's a sister."

"Oh, I see. That's always nice. To have someone who's not actually a sibling be like a sister."

He shook his head. "No, she's a sister. She's a lesbian now. I can't tell you what that does for my fragile male ego, thinking that I may be in some way responsible." But he was still smiling and didn't seem fragile at all. He was exuding pure, strong, exuberant maleness.

"How did I miss that?" I said.

"Mary's quite the girl. I guess I should say Chi Narnia. Now, let's see this impasse you've reached," said Patrick. He rummaged in his carryall and produced a video camera. He aimed it straight at me, then said, "Ignore the camera."

It was hard to do with the lens staring straight at me, but I did as he said and went back to the music. "It's a problem with an aria. I don't know if it'll make any sense to you..." But he was already shooting over my shoulder. I had my computer on, the music-writing program I'd stolen from Kurt open, and the virtual manuscript in front of me. The handwritten score was laid out across the table, and my keyboard set up to fiddle around with and try out ideas.

I said, "Here's the vocal line. The computer can play the lines but it can't sing the words, so I'll try to give you an idea, but I don't have much of a voice left." I started the piece and sang along to the end. "The thing is, I'm stuck on a phrase. Just one word is mucking it up. I need a synonym for ghost but the other words sound stupid—phantom, spirit, shade— they just don't work. I've been stuck on the one word all day."

"What if you tried a different emphasis with those words there, take it off the first beat and put it on the second? Like this."

He set the camera down on a couple of books on the long table, went to my keyboard and played and sang the section I'd shown him.

"Oh my God, Patrick. You know music. I mean, you *really* know music. You played that after one read-through. No. One glimpse."

"You don't think that any child growing up in Cold Shanks would escape the gnarly clutches and musical chin hairs of Agnes Krucker, do you?"

"You took lessons with Agnes Krucker?"

"Agonizing Agnes had some very rigorous exercises for her students. We did a lot of listening and dictation and sight-reading."

"They all said she was the best around for miles. I wanted to study with her but my mother didn't have the money. God, I envied all those kids who could afford her piano lessons. I used to beat them up on the playground whenever I got the chance. Them and the kids who got more singing lessons than me."

He raised his eyebrows. "If it would make you feel better to beat me up, go right ahead." He stretched his arms out wide, ready to become a passive punching bag.

I laughed. "Naw. I've outgrown the habit."

He looked at my score again. "Look. If you just syncopate this section here, you don't need to change the word, and it keeps the strange quality that you want. It is a strange quality that you want?"

I nodded.

"Listen." He played it again.

"That might work," I said.

"Sure it might."

"I feel so embarrassed. Pretending to write an opera and you know music."

"Miranda. It's hard for anyone who's going out into unfamiliar territory. Being the creator is a different discipline from being the actor or performer. You end up turning yourself inside out and back again. But it can be so good. It can be the most depressing thing in the world and also the most elating." He came over to me and rested a hand on my shoulder. "This little tune you've been working on is really quite haunting. I'm not sure I could come up with a musical idea like this. It gave me goose bumps. That's always a good sign. Courage and phlegm, as my mentor used to say." Then he picked up the camera and put it back in front of his face again.

I said to the lens, "It's new territory for me. I'm floundering. I haven't had enough instruction."

"Sometimes instruction can squash the inspiration right out of you." He looked toward the kitchen. "Coffeemaker's stopped burbling. Let's get a good dose of caffeine. We're going to need it. We're going to be up pretty late tonight."

I flashed him a surprised look.

"Didn't you say you wanted to meet Biba?" said Patrick.

Patrick made me put some of his old clothes on top of my clothes before he could declare me ready for the Biba mission. He didn't want to tell me anything beforehand and just before we set out at around 9:00 p.m., he said to me with great earnest, "Whatever you see tonight is confidential. It's already a big breach of some people's trust that I'm taking you to Biba. You'll see what I mean when we get there. Miranda, I want you to promise that you'll keep to yourself anything you see tonight."

He was starting to scare me a little.

"I'm lousy at keeping secrets. If you want to keep a secret, don't tell me," I said.

"I'm serious. If you want to talk to Biba, you have to promise."

"Yeah, okay. I promise."

Why Biba had this secret-agent status was beyond me. But I didn't feel like waiting around on street corners hoping she'd show up.

I slopped along beside Pat in clothes that made me look like someone who grubbed around in garbage cans to nourish themselves. Pat had a knapsack on his back and carried the video camera in his hand. He was dressed the way he usually dressed, which wasn't fair at all, since he looked much better than me.

We were walking away from the center of the town toward Stanley Park, and when we reached the beginning of the greenery, I said, "The park, Patrick?"

"Yup, that's right."

The park at night. Highly unadvisable.

We walked for quite a while in darkness along the main road that led into its heart, and then suddenly Patrick veered off into the dense bush and whispered, "Be careful where you step. Stay close behind me." Now I was grateful for the clothes, which kept me from getting scratched to bits by the bushes and brambles. We struggled through the dark undergrowth for at least half an hour making almost no progress until finally, I could see the dimmest glimmers of orange light through the wintry brush.

The forest and underbrush became thinner and Patrick and I stepped into the edge of a tiny clearing. He held out a hand, motioning me to stop, then he grabbed my arm and pulled me in close to him. In a low voice, he said, "Don't move. Don't say anything."

The only thing I was able to make out at first was a black forest punctuated with tiny fires. As my vision adjusted, I could distinguish the forms. Some were covered in tattered rags hiding dirty faces, faces encrusted with filth from years of living rough. Some of the other people appeared normal, clean, in regular street clothes, tracksuits, windbreakers and jeans, but from their expressions, eerie in the firelight, I could see that it was definitely a them-and-us situation. Each small group had their little camp set up with all their belongings. Some of the people were quite young. There was even a young woman with two grimy toddlers hugging her knees.

Patrick took off his knapsack very slowly and knelt down on the ground to open it. Every one of his movements was tortuously drawn out. The darkened faces watched him without reaction, mesmerized by months and years of starvation and living out under the elements. He pulled out tinned meats, tin openers, condensed milk, protein snacks, fruit bars and cigarettes, and spread them out like a floor mosaic in the clearing, then stepped back.

"I'm looking for Biba," he said.

No one moved or replied, but after several minutes of standing and exchanging solemn stares with these people, Biba appeared soundlessly out of the blackness. When she realized it was Patrick, she smiled and said, "Pat. I was thinking about you." Then she looked at me and said, "I've seen you around. Downtown."

Patrick explained, "This is my friend Miranda. She'd like to talk to you. About singing."

Biba looked back over her shoulder at the other campers and said, "Not here."

Then she led us down a trail that must have been a secret to most of the world. We emerged near the sea walk and walked a little farther along. When we came to a bench, Patrick said, "Let's sit down here."

Then he asked Biba if she minded him filming us while we talked. He pulled a strong light out of his knapsack and trained the camera on us.

I told Biba all about my seeing her in *The Other Street* and then put my idea forward. She seemed interested and asked me a million questions with an enthusiasm that was almost childlike. We talked for over an hour and when we'd finished, we had an understanding.

As we were leaving, Patrick whispered, "They figure that there are a couple of hundred people camped out in Stanley Park. I knew you were going to take that approach to Biba. A good thing, too. Let's hope it works out."

Chapter 26

Tina and I got dressed at her place. We had two hours before leaving for the single orchestral rehearsal of Kurt's song cycle. Dressing up was Tina's idea. She had talked a friend in the opera costume department into finding her two wigs. One was blond with long straight hair and the other was brunette with short curly hair. She put on the blond wig and I put on the dark wig. I'd brought some of my clothes for her to choose from and she put on my outfit with the lace patchwork skirt and the V-neck cream cashmere sweater that I'd worn in London.

"You need extra stuffing in your bra," I told Tina. We were more or less the same height and weight, but Tina was flat-chested. She dutifully went off to enlarge her bust, and when she came back, she had a grin on her face and these two enormous watermelon-like boobs.

"Now I'm insulted. Jeez, you don't need to go that far. You look like a porn star," I said.

She pulled a couple of socks from each cup and tossed them in the air. "How about this?"

"Yeah. That's better. I guess."

I worried that those clothes might be hexed and bring her bad luck because they were associated with Kurt. But Tina said, "It doesn't work that way. By having me wear these cursed clothes of yours for an important event, I'm giving them back the good luck that they lost."

After that we exchanged coats. She took my camel hair and I took her long black leather coat. We surprised even ourselves. As a finishing touch, Tina put on dark glasses.

We took a taxi to the theater. Tina was in form. This was just the kind of challenge that Tina, fearless as always, thrived on. I, on the other had, was nervous to the point of nausea, and when we got there, my first stop was the gilt-and-marble bathroom.

As we were going into the main part of the theater, we were stopped by a large jowly woman with bright copper highlights and a diamond ring that could only be described as a "rock." She blocked our path and said, "I'm sorry, girls, but the rehearsals are closed to the public."

"This is no girl," I said, indicating Tina. "This is your soloist, Miranda Lyme, and I'm her agent. She goes nowhere without me."

"Oh, go right on in," the woman gushed.

I may have mentioned before that Tina was a good singer, but I had no idea until that afternoon just how good she was. Even though her theory was as scarce as mine, she had perfect pitch, a photographic memory and no fear of the stage whatsoever. But the other, most important thing, was that she had the voice, the rich dark ringing mezzo voice, evenly distributed sound all the way through her range, and great high notes.

All through university, it had made me furious to see how lightly she took her talent. But isn't that always the way? People taking their greatest talent for granted and preferring to waste their time in something else that is equivalent to running upward on a down escalator.

Like Miranda Lyme and music composition, you might be saying?

But, hey, it's a free world.

The concertmaster was conducting the rehearsals that afternoon and Kurt wouldn't be arriving until two days later, the actual day of the first performance. By the time he got to the theater and met Tina, it would be too late to withdraw. He'd have to let her perform.

The first part of the program was Vivaldi and Beethoven, to keep the audience sweet before the huge overdose of Bing Bang Bong they'd be receiving after the intermission. We sat in the theater and listened, and then when it was time to perform the song cycle, Tina walked up onto the stage. She left on the dark glasses and camel coat and I have to say, she looked like a real diva, a Maria Callas without the nose.

"Are you ready, Miss Lyme?" asked the concertmaster.

Tina nodded.

He raised his baton and the music began, complete with my corrections.

Tina was more than ready. She was in control. I sat back in the plush seat and listened.

When Tina held the final note, provoking a few raised eyebrows and nods of appreciation among orchestra players, I knew everything was going to be all right. The concertmaster was falling all over her, oh Miss Lyme here, oh Miss Lyme there, Miss Lyme the Sublime. And I have to confess, I had more than a few pangs of jealousy. But I consoled myself with the fact that the score of *Città di Pietra* was now a little sunnier, a little sweeter and less bleak.

Tina and I left the theater together and went out for Chinese, Tina offering. What really irked me was that she didn't even realize what a huge success she had been, and was going to be.

She elbowed me violently and said, "So. You and Patrick Tibeau, eh? Nice going."

"Whoa, Nelly. We're just friends."

"In your own words...I may look stupid but I'm just slow."

"Excuse me. What about you and Wayne?"

"It's physiotherapy. That's all."

I didn't want to tell Tina that I was in a new state of total confusion. After our trip to Stanley Park, Patrick took me out to eat in a little tapas bar near Robson. We talked about this and that and before I could stop myself, I was telling him all about my opera, every last damn thing right down to the eighth rests. We talked hard-core shop, pausing only long enough to take bites of the food. We could have been eating sponge rubber and drinking turpentine for all it mattered to me. I didn't taste a bite of what was set down in front of us.

Pat made a few suggestions that, I have to confess, solved some problems I couldn't have solved on my own. They were mostly to do with the dramatic turn of things, and I realized how easy it is to play the solitary hunchback poet lurching around in an empty villa, or a deaf composer falling into destitution, and think that your revenge-steeped mind can handle the whole business of giving birth to your little masterpiece. But after I talked to Pat, I realized I couldn't see the forest for the trees half the time and that some of my problems could be simply resolved. We were still talking when the waiters started to sweep and mop around our feet and put chairs up on top of tables, and we were still talking, talking, talking as we walked home.

When we got back to Pat's place, he looked drained. Slowly, he took off his clothes and tossed them on a chair. He wasn't the slightest bit inhibited, or aware that it might have an effect on me. Naked seemed to be a natural state for him. He could probably have stood in front of a crowd and given a speech just as he was, and it wouldn't have fazed him in the least.

He sank down onto the bed. I thought he was going to say something but he'd fallen asleep. He slept without a sound, no directing in his sleep, no hiring and firing of actors and cameramen. I covered him up, took off my clothes and put on the big T-shirt I usually slept in. I crawled into the other side of the bed, and didn't close my eyes all night.

The next day, the day of Tina's big performance, the concert that would have been my professional debut, I took the crimson velvet dress over to her house. She was concentrating on the score when I got there, looking over the trouble spots again. Although, if you asked me, the piece was one long trouble spot. For the first time in my life, I had the sensation that it was better her than me, that I was happy to be out of the big ring on that occasion.

I was apprehensive about seeing Kurt again. I would have preferred to stick to disguises and tricks, but Tina said anyone could have seen through it. She wanted to be taken seriously.

Patrick was attending, too, but would be coming to the theater at the last minute. Tina had given him one of her comps. I had the other one. We'd talked about calling her mom and mine and getting them to come down from Cold Shanks for the concert, but in the end decided that Kurt's music would be too weird for them, that it didn't merit the trip.

We got Tina made up and her hair pulled back into a very divaesque knot at the back of her head. Then we got her into the dress. She'd bought a stuffed strapless bra and with that and some two-sided tape, we got the dress to stay up. It looked much more dramatic on her than on me. I wore my old black Levi's flares and coral T-shirt. All my clothes were stuffed away in the basement of my old apartment and I just didn't have the energy to dig them out and dress up.

We arrived at the theater a half hour before concert time

and made our way to the greenroom downstairs, and the moment I dreaded.

"C'mon, let's get this over with," I said.

As we approached the conductor's dressing room, Kurt stuck his head into the hallway. I froze in my tracks, but Tina dragged me forward.

Kurt came out. It hurt me to look at him. He was still attractive to me.

When he saw me, he became all warmth and largesse, spreading his arms wide, as if he hadn't taken my heart and danced an evil mazurka on it with steel-toed boots. He rushed toward me and said, "Miranda, Miranda, it's so lovely to...good Lord. You're not dressed, Miranda. You're not going on like that? Where's your concert dress? The one you told me about. I want to see it."

I pointed to Tina. "There's my dress. It's beautiful, isn't it? My mother really outdid herself."

I swallowed and stared hard at Kurt, as though I might discover some new detail about him, something that would redeem him.

"Miranda," said Kurt, looking befuddled. "Why aren't you dressed?"

"Kurt, let's all go into your dressing room."

We all went inside and I shut the door. "Why aren't you bloody well dressed?" he asked again.

"I won't be singing tonight, Kurt."

"You won't *what?*" I could see that apoplectic purple color filling up his veins, swelling him to bursting.

I said, "I have this little...tickle...in my throat. Actually, it's a permanent tickle. I haven't been able to use my voice properly since Christmas, but let's not cry over spilt milk, shall we?"

"I don't see that *I* could possibly have anything to do with the fact that your voice—"

I interrupted him. "This is my good friend, the mezzo-soprano Tina Browning. She'll be singing your piece tonight. She's very good and she's ready and if you don't be-lieve me, go and ask the concertmaster about the rehearsal."

"I've already spoken to the concertmaster. He told me that the rehearsal went very well indeed, that Miranda Lyme did a wonderful job."

"*Tina Browning* did a wonderful job. She was posing as me. But tonight she'll be herself. She wants her own name to be announced before she sings. It's easy. The general manager gets up on the stage and announces to the public that there will be a change of program, that Tina Brown-ing will be performing in the place of Miranda Lyme. Oh, don't worry, Kurt. I know about the grant money. You have to use some unknown local singer under the age of thirty to fulfill the stipulations. Guido told me."

Kurt's eyes burrowed into me. "I'll deal with *you* later, Mi-randa."

He barked at Tina, "You, whatever your name is, come with me." Then he gathered up his score and led her into a room with a piano at the end of the hall. I followed them and listened outside the door. He launched into the open-ing of the piece and Tina was right there, teeth sharpened and glittering, ready to meet the Bing Bang Bong challenge. It must have crossed her mind that he was using his original score and that she had rehearsed the "Girls Just Want to Have Fun" version. But she was still able to hold her own because I hadn't altered the vocal line. Kurt bounced from one dif-ficult section to another at lightning speed. When he'd fin-ished testing her, he said, "I suppose I don't actually have a choice at this point, do I? I want to see *you* after the concert, Miranda Lyme. And if you try to escape, I'll hunt you down."

"Certainly, Kurt. No reason why we can't be civil. How's Olivia, by the way?"

"Er, she's pregnant. In her third month," he said proudly.

"Really?" I squealed. "How great for you."

"Triplets," he said pompously. "One of those fertility treatments, as it turns out."

I knew a little something about multiple births and the minityrants they spawned. His pomp would soon lose its puff, and fizzle off into the stratosphere like a punctured balloon.

I stayed downstairs during the first half. I couldn't bear to watch Kurt. It was all too fresh still. During the intermission, I stepped outside. When the announcement was made for people to return to their seats, I went back into the theater. I was shown to my seat. Patrick was there in the seat next to mine.

"I wondered where you'd disappeared to," he said.

I had a brief violent lapse into self-pity. "I can't believe that I was supposed to be singing tonight. And now Tina's taking my place. My emotion's are a mess."

Patrick pointed to Kurt's name on the program and said, "So he's the one, eh?"

I nodded. The musicians were returning to the pit. The members of the audience were shushing each other. Kurt stepped up to the podium accompanied by thunderous applause. And then Tina walked onstage and bowed. The moment I'd visualized for so long, the moment that had consumed all my passion, was passing me by. I was on the verge of nervous tears but I strained to keep them back. Patrick must have sensed it. Without looking at me, he reached over and took hold of my hand.

After the last notes had sounded, and the applause and the gazillion ovations had finally ended, I turned to Patrick and said, "I have to go backstage. I've got one more big piece of music to face tonight."

"Would you like me to come with you?"

I hadn't thought of it. Kurt was going to be livid. A bodyguard wouldn't be a bad idea. But I was already getting enough help from Patrick. I said, "No. I better do this alone. Thanks for the offer."

"You'll have my place to yourself tonight, Miranda. A friend of mine, he's a commercial pilot, got his own plane, he's flying down to L.A., said he'd take me down. I'm spending the night at his place because we leave at six. He doesn't like to fly light. I'll see you when I come back."

"Okay. When will that be?"

"In about four days if all goes well."

"Then have a good trip, Pat."

It was just as well that he was leaving again. I couldn't handle another sleepless night. I was too eager to see him now, starting to miss him when he wasn't around. The same old pattern was forming. And I was afraid of getting too close to him, being too distracted to work, and all those dead male composers would laugh from their graves, victorious by sheer default.

Backstage, everyone was crowded around Kurt and Tina. From a distance, I gave Tina a big thumbs-up. We both knew we'd get together for the postmortem once all the fuss had died down. But it was her night, and it was only right that she enjoy it without me wrecking it for her. I had thought that I'd be able to face up to the whole *Città di Pietra* ordeal, but the truth was, I was slammed with exhaustion and disappointment in myself. I sat down on one of the greenroom sofas, closed my eyes and waited for all the people to go away.

I was jolted out of a half sleep when a cool, almost clinical voice in my ear said, "Miranda. You tampered with my work."

Kurt was seated beside me on the sofa, pressed up tight against me. An onlooker might have thought that we were the best of friends having a cozy little gossip together. They might even have thought we were lovers.

I opened my eyes very slowly and stared straight ahead for a second then closed them again as I said, "I noticed the critics were crawling all over you, loving you to death over there, licking the underside of every single nether region they could get close to. What did they think of the piece? What did they think of *Città di Pietra?* Did they tell you?"

"Oh, yes. They did. Indeed, they did. They couldn't say enough good things about it. They're saying I've mellowed, that I've found my feminine side, my anima." Kurt started to laugh.

I opened my eyes and stared at him. His laughter was such an unexpected sound that I started to laugh, too. I couldn't help myself. His charm was still contagious.

"You really are *something,* Miranda Lyme."

"Well, if it's taken you all this time to realize it, you're a little slow on the uptake, Maestro Hancock."

"A great deal of time and patience is required for people to understand one another. To find each other on both a spiritual *and* physical level."

Now he was running his index finger up and down, up and down my bare arm. "You know, Miranda, my love, I'll be here for another four days. Now that Olivia's broodier instincts have been quenched, the situation between us has changed somewhat. She's loosened the leash. We have an understanding now. She's otherwise engaged with her hormones, as well as her morning sickness, which, I'm afraid to say, doesn't seem to be limited just to mornings. It goes without saying that she's rather gone off sex. I thought you and I might just pick up where we left off. You know. Have another go. And not the concert version this time. No. The complete, unedited, fully staged opus. You know, I *do* love you, Miranda."

I closed my eyes again and let the sleepy sensation envelope me.

"Miranda? Miranda, are you still with us?"

"No, Kurt. I'm not with you at all."

Chapter 27

I began to collect voice students. I still had my old key to the university practise rooms and I met some of my new students there, where we could have access to a piano and the occasional stray student accompanist who happened to be wandering by.

There was the forty-five-year-old Bulgarian man who always wore a formal black suit with a diamond pin and presented me with a single red rose at every lesson. He sounded like a caricature of Pavarotti, but who was I to rain on his parade? His family thought he was a star and his exaggerated gallantry and roses always made my day. There was also the skinny nasal-sounding girl whose main ambition was to be able to get up at the office party and wow them with a Celine Dion song. She was cheerful and had an endless supply of the dirtiest jokes I'd ever heard. And there's the kid I like to call Metallica Boy. He was the vocalist in a small-time heavy-metal band but wanted to be sure he'd have a solid vocal technique for the day when fame and the big tours arrived.

And then there was Martha.

Martha made it all worthwhile. She was a tall mountain of a woman, a thirty-two-year-old divorced mother of three, and she had a glorious paint-peeling Wagnerian voice and no idea that she had it. I mean Brunhilde right down to her toenails. When I asked her why she wanted to take lessons, she told me that singing made her feel good and she wanted to learn some new tunes. Most of her tunes came from AM radio.

With the power of her voice, she could have straightened the hair of everyone in the back row of the Queen Elizabeth. And that's a big theater. She had the kind of voice you're always shushing up, the kind of voice that makes the crystal glasses vibrate in the house three doors down. I got so excited when I first heard her I made Tina come up and listen to her second lesson.

After Martha had gone, Tina said, "Holy shit, she's one of the beasts."

By this, Tina meant the opera beast, the person whose physique alone guarantees the wonderful effortless freak voice that appears once in a decade.

Tina went on, "You won't be able to keep her. You're going to have to bombard her with information, throw a lot of music and a lot of listening her way, then hand her on to somebody who really knows what to do with her."

"I know. I know. I'll do it eventually. But just let me enjoy being her teacher a while longer."

"Okay, Dr. Frankenstein."

I wrote a part into my opera for Martha. At first I thought of making it a big role but then changed my mind. Start small. She was going to be a solo voice in my chorus. It was such a demanding chorus already. It had to behave as an orchestra and create color and atmosphere, and Martha's voice alone was a one-woman storm.

The opera was growing. Between lessons, up at the university, I sometimes collared music students and begged them to read through a fragment I'd written, just to see how they felt about it and whether it was doable. Because I knew from experience; you could write whatever you wanted on that manuscript paper, but if your musicians weren't comfortable playing and singing it, it would only be an obstacle to the final production and its drama.

I kept a tiny tape recorder with me so that if an idea came to me, I could catch it right away. Wherever I went, walking down the street, buying my groceries, paying my bills, I was humming to myself, and thinking.

Four days after his expected return, there was no sign of Patrick. Detained by what? Business? Or someone, maybe? Although I was tempted to phone my mother to ask her to phone Pat's mother to find out if he was all right, that he wasn't lying half-dead in a hospital in the Hollywood hills, I resisted.

Instead, two weeks after the official debut of *Città di Pietra,* I got the phone call I'd been waiting for.

Madame Klein's voice was so well placed it nearly pierced my eardrum. "Fräulein Lyme, I don't know vhat to do viz you. I received your package. You haff become a big problem for me again. Come for dinner at six next Saturday. I am an old voman vis a tricky stomach and must eat precisely at six, so do not be late. Und bring ze girl soprano. Der is de possibility dat I can vork vis her." And then as a thoughtful aside, she added, "I tink maybe her childhood and mine are not so different."

Madame Klein spent part of her childhood in the ghetto at Theresienstadt and later, Auschwitz. I didn't know whether it was possible for an elderly woman and a teenage girl to form a useful relationship on the basis of their common ground—discrimination, torture and music—but I hoped with all my heart that it was.

Since Pat wasn't there, I decided to set out to look for Biba by myself.

I waited until dark then followed the same road into Stanley Park that we'd taken that night. I turned off at what seemed like the same point, pushing uncertainly into the forest, shoving my way through the underbrush and trying to ignore the ghoulish shapes evoked by the enormous waving boughs of Douglas fir and cedar. With each step I took, it seemed as though I was getting more deeply entangled and going nowhere. I could hear other sounds, crunching and crackling and breathing, animal sounds, human sounds, that all became more menacing as my hearing grew more sensitive.

There was a moon that night and as I crashed my way through all the undergrowth, the sense of living things moving everywhere in the forest turned a tiny suggestion of terror into a concrete fear that I could taste in my mouth. I could feel myself moving into panic mode, just short of a whimper. I had no idea where I was or how to get out of there. I kept thrashing my way forward, becoming more and more reckless until finally, I burst onto a small gap in the foliage. Everything I saw, the Douglas firs, the maples, cedars, ferns and salal, were both plant and human. I couldn't distinguish one from the other because my imagination was going wild. I crossed the gap in the undergrowth and was face-to-face with a stumpy-looking broken-off tree trunk. When the tree trunk shifted to reveal a man's features, toothless mouth and filthy skin, my bubble of terror burst and filled the air. I stammered, "I— I'm looking for Biba."

The man raised a filthy claw of a finger, pointed to the sky and said, "The moon is my lover."

I turned and ran. I must have crashed through every bush, fern and small tree that got in my path. I don't remember any of it, nothing between the moon man and finding myself gasping for breath at the door of my Bute Street apartment, my clothing torn and my skin covered with bleeding scratches.

Caroline opened the door. "What happened to you?"

"I was in the woods," I said.

"Jeez, d'ya run into a Sasquatch or something?" asked Dan, which I thought was funny coming from him. His focus shifted to something over my shoulder and he raised his eyebrows. I turned around. There in the hallway behind me was Biba, loaded down with all her possessions.

"I followed you," she said. "You were running so fast I almost couldn't keep up. I figured you'd come to tell me it was time."

"You figured right," I said.

I didn't need to introduce Biba to anybody. Caroline and Dan had both seen her singing around town. I explained about Madame Klein and was on the verge of taking Biba back to Pat's place with me when Caroline said, "She can stay here. You got work to do, Miranda."

I led Caroline into the kitchen. "It would be good if somebody would just keep an eye on her. I'd hate to have her slip away into the night again."

"Keep her prisoner, eh? Sure. What's one more person? Dan's got an air mattress somewhere."

Cassie arrived just after that. She looked at Biba, said, "What is this? A youth hostel?" and retreated to her room.

After Biba had had a bath and something to eat, we sat at the kitchen table and I told her what she could expect. "If Madame Klein takes you on, you won't be able to sleep out or live like a nomad. She won't want you exposing your body, your voice, to too much fresh air. You have to treat yourself with kid gloves."

"But I'll be singing," said Biba.

"Yes. But she'll make you study. Did you go to school in Alberta?"

"I know how to read and write if that's what you want to know. My Gaj parents made me learn."

"Good. You'll have to study piano, theory, sight-singing— Kodaly and solfeggio, dictation, composition, music history,

French, Spanish, Russian, German—Madame Klein will probably teach you German and Italian."

"I speak Italian," said Biba. "I was born in Italy."

"That's right. You were. I forgot. Now, are you sure you want to do this? Because Madame Klein will kill us both if you don't do what she tells you to do. She doesn't tolerate people wasting her time."

"I'll be singing, won't I?"

"A lot of the time."

"That's okay then. But I want Patrick."

"Sorry?"

"I want Patrick to come with us to meet her on Saturday."

"If he comes back in time, Biba."

The way things had been going, it was a big if.

But on Friday night, a key turned in the lock and Patrick came through the doorway.

I rushed up to him and said, "Guess what? Madame Klein wants to see Biba. Tomorrow night. And you have to come, too."

He raised his eyebrows then smiled broadly. "We can take my van. Way to go, Miranda. So, now tell me about you."

"I've been working."

"Good. And now for the really important question, the cultural clincher of this decade."

"Yes?"

"What do you like on your pizza?"

"Anything but pineapple."

"My sentiments exactly."

"So how was Los Angeles?"

"Schizoid."

"I'll bet you saw a lot of starlets, eh?" I prodded.

"Yeah, but you don't want to touch any of them. You never know if some body part is going to come off in your hand."

"Did it work out then? The financing?"

"Yeah, it did. But as you can see, I had to bullshit with those people for an extra week and a half. God, it's good to be home. Hey…what's this?"

He pointed to the dark end of the room where I'd arranged the roll-away mattress and opened the screen fully to form a private corner.

"My bedroom," I said.

He cocked his head to one side and bit his lip, scrutinizing me the way one might scrutinize an abstract painting that defied understanding. I thought we would have to verbally tussle, each offering the other the big bed, but after a long pause, he said, "Okay," cheerfully, and didn't pursue it any further. "I've got a lot of work to do on the camera script, so don't mind me if I'm not sociable tonight." Then he sat at his desk and got to work, and when the pizza was delivered, he continued to work, utterly concentrated, munching and scribbling at the same time.

I said, "'Night," and tiptoed off to my mattress in the corner.

I dreamt I was up onstage at a long table reminiscent of The Last Supper. I was sharing pizzas with the composers.

Lully was there again wearing the beautiful black-and-gold brocade coat, but he'd dribbled tomato sauce on the ample sleeve and kept trying to wipe it off with a large lacy handkerchief and the tomato stain was spreading.

Arnold Schoenberg was there, seated at the end of the table. But he wasn't eating. He had his back to me and was deliberately pouting. I couldn't blame him. After all, he had a right to be angry with me. I never lost an opportunity to trash his music.

And Mahler was there, too, huddled over his food and feeling sorry for himself. *Brust, O, Brust,* he moaned over and over, his hand on his heart.

Mozart came in suddenly and skipped around the set,

climbing up onto the table, kicking over glasses and stepping onto plates.

"Would you please get your foot out of my pizza, Wolfgang?" I asked. "I love your music but you have the worst table manners I've ever seen."

Then Beethoven, who was really tucking into his food, put down his fork and said, "Eh? What did you say?"

"Table manners," I repeated.

"Eh?" said Beethoven again.

And then Kurt's voice, out of nowhere, like God's voice-over, said, "Stupid cow, Miranda. Everybody and his dog knows that Ludwig is deaf."

Mozart continued to skip around the table maniacally and sing at the top of his lungs a shrill falsetto version of the Queen of the Night's aria from *The Magic Flute*.

"Stop it," I shouted.

Verdi came up behind me, gray-bearded and authoritarian, and said, "Leave the little man alone. He's a genius. *Lui è bravissimo.*" And then he grabbed my ass.

Puccini jumped up and shouted, "*Mascalzone.* Don't touch that buttock. It's mine." Verdi shrugged and walked off into the wings, leaving room for Puccini, who came over and swaggered around me in his long cape and hat. He looked like a mafioso don. "I like blondes," he said to me. "And you've got good breeding hips, too, I see."

"Respect," I shouted. "Is it too much to ask for a little respect?"

Beethoven waved his empty glass toward me and boomed, "Waitress! More wine!"

And then suddenly my double was there at the edge of the stage. It was me, and I was wearing a beautiful, long, green-and-gold brocade coat, far nicer than Lully's. As soon as the composers saw my double, they clammed up.

The other Miranda said, "Composers, off the stage, all of you. This is not your cue."

The composers began to grumble and protest. Verdi

yelled, "I have a lot of friends in the music business. You'll never work in this town again."

Beethoven began frantically stuffing bread rolls into his pockets.

"Is this or is this not Miranda's dream and am I or am I not the director of this dream?" asked my double, calmly.

They all nodded.

"Then, all of you, off the stage immediately." And so off they all shuffled, mumbling, swearing, grumbling and protesting.

When the stage was empty, the other Miranda made a low bow in my direction then floated away.

In Madame Klein's steamy little kitchen, Patrick was filming our dinner. Madame Klein spoke straight to the camera. She seemed to be giving it a piece of her mind. She was elegant in a black Chanel knit suit with white edging, one she'd had since 1959, she informed us, because she took care of herself by not dieting and her figure had always been the same. She was shaped like a small block, her legendary breath control and expanded diaphragm having pushed her waistline to the disappearing point.

She served us roast beef, insisting that people who had their own teeth (hers were made to measure, she said, and had cost her a bomb) should eat meat while they still could, with brussels sprouts, boiled potatoes and crème caramel for dessert.

After dinner, she turned to Biba and began to speak to her in Italian. Both of them spoke so fast that I could only get the gist of about half of what was being said, but the basic translation was that if she wanted to work with Madame Klein, there was a whole long list of things that Biba was forbidden to do, including stealing from her teacher, and that foolish and irresponsible behavior would bring her to the same end as that little fluff-head Miranda

Lyme, who had been an idiot in the extreme, and had lost her voice as a consequence.

Madame Klein looked at me, and at Pat behind the camera and said, "And ze girl vill live here vis me. She vill eat, drink, breaze, dream und excrete music. She vill be my protégée."

I wanted to yelp.

Madame Klein paused and looked at Biba again, as if Biba were off at a great distance, and in a strange sad voice, she said, *"Mein kleines Zigeuner'l."* My little Gypsy.

And then Madame Klein stood up and said, "Und as for you, Fräulein Lyme, I do not know if you are talented or vhat. Dere is a little bit of stuff in your vierd little opera dat is pretty good, and a lot of stuff dat is pretty bad. So ve vill take a look at it now. *Ja?"*

Be still, my pounding heart.

After that, we all went into the music room where Madame Klein tore my work to shreds. For three hours. Biba sat on the couch and listened, devouring it all, and Pat continued to film.

By the time she'd finished with me, I had a pounding headache and an ego the size of a flea. All I wanted to do was go home and sob. She snapped at me, "Oh, don't look so miserable. You vill finish your opera and it vill be gut. Und remember, Fräulein Lyme, tings are not really bad until zey are taking you avay in a cattle cart."

Madame Klein saw us all off at the door. "I'll zee *you* tomorrow, Biba."

Patrick kissed her hand and said, "Madame Klein, it's been an honor."

Patrick, Biba and I finished off the evening with ice cream in Shaughnessy. Pat and Biba were having a strange conversation about the "colleagues," the homeless people who had appeared in *The Other Street* along with Biba. Some of them had died since the making of the film, and this line of conversation was making my headache and mood worse. I would have preferred to apply the ice cream to my head rather than eat it, but I kept working away at the sweet cold vanilla mound, bringing it to my mouth with the spoon and not tasting it.

I was relieved to be learning from Madame Klein again, but she was too demanding. She wanted the kinds of revisions that required real brainpower and uninterrupted concentration. Maybe women were just constitutionally unfit to write big compositions. How many women in history had actually composed?

Well. A few. But many of the women, like the one who married Mahler, for example, were told to stop composing when they got married, or were forbidden to do it by their families. In those days, being a female musician or composer was about the same thing as being a prostitute.

In the past, there was Ethel Smyth, born 1858. When she first submitted some songs to a publisher, she was told, "No women composers have ever been successful except Clara Schumann, whose work was published with her husband's work, and Fanny Mendelssohn, whose work had been published with her brother's." They went ahead and published Ethel's work anyway, but Ethel was so disheartened by their comments that she didn't ask for a royalty. How's that for an inferiority complex?

She wrote two operas in German, her biggest success *The Wreckers* in French, and a fourth opera, *The Boatswain's Mate* in English. It was no surprise to learn that she eventually went to bat for women's rights.

And there was Francesca Caccini, born 1587. But she was a *figlia d'arte,* the daughter of the composer Giulio Caccini (how else could you get ahead in those days?) and the first woman to write an opera, *La Liberazione di Ruggiero,* to celebrate a visit by the prince of Poland to the Medici Court. Francesca sang, directed, composed, and played the harpsichord and lute. And unlike me, she had the Florentine Medici to support her efforts.

Maybe Guido Castracani had a point. I needed a wealthy patron.

Either that or I needed a sex change.

Patrick talked to Biba but he looked over at me often, his features softening each time he did. When we'd finished our ice cream, he said, "You're tired, Miranda. Let's go home."

After we'd pulled up to the Bute Street apartment and dropped off Biba, he told me, "I'll be heading East in a couple of days. We've got some location shoots to do in Montreal. I'll be away for about six weeks, but when I get back, your opera should be in rehearsal, right? Mid–June? You said you wanted it performed by mid-July. A month of rehearsals is about right for an opera, or am I wrong?"

"No. You have a lot of confidence in a piece that isn't even halfway to being finished. I wish I did, too."

"I'm really looking forward to filming the rehearsals, Miranda, and then the performances. You're just lucky I happen to have so much free time this year. So count on it, because I'm like Madame Klein. I don't like people to waste my time."

"You make a lousy authoritarian, Patrick. People do what you ask them because they love you and they love your work. Being tall doesn't hurt, either."

"Listen, Miranda. Keep my extra set of keys. The place is going to be empty and I'd really appreciate it if you'd stay on there."

I nodded.

"I'll see you in June," he said, then he leaned across and kissed me on the cheek.

Chapter 28

It was the last week of April and *Carmen* was in full swing. I'd managed to live through it all by giving it voice whenever we sang in easy registers. It was a now-you-hear-it-now-you-don't effect kind of like turning the volume on and off with a radio dial, but it convinced the people around me, and particularly Marian, that I was pulling my weight.

Tina and I sat at our makeup desks after opening night. We were the only ones left in the dressing room.

"What's eating you, Miranda?"

"I don't know."

"Are you mad at me? Is it about next fall?"

"Partly. But don't worry about it, Tina, I'll get used to the idea. I have to, don't I?"

Since Tina's performance of *Città di Pietra,* she was the woman of the year. Everyone wanted her. She would be singing Ravel's *Sheherazade Songs* with the Seattle symphony next fall, Kurt conducting. I had the sensation of being left in the dirt.

And I'd listened in on some of Biba's lessons, and she

was thriving, too, singing difficult pieces with a seeming lack of effort.

No. It wasn't like being left in the dirt. It was like having a huge fast expensive limousine full of your friends and acquaintances roar by and splash you in the face with oily puddle water.

Composing was a lonely business, but now it had become the life raft in my big empty ocean. I sat at the trestle table in Pat's apartment, put on Grace's rainbow pom-pom sweater and worked into the nights, hoping a little of Grace was watching over me, helping me out. I poured myself into the work and by the end of April, Madame Klein had given her approval. It wasn't the kind of approval I had imagined it was going to be, with fanfares, and back-patting and champagne. It was considerably more reserved. She said, "It's a vierd opera, maybe a little scary even, but not so bad. It vill pass for you first effort. It is musical. Now you haff ze big problem of mounting it."

"I thought Biba could sing the messenger," I said meekly.

"I know you did. Ze music is written for her. I'm not so dumb. Dat's okay. She can do it. She is a better singer zan you ever vere. Don't look so miserable. It's a physical ting. You can see by looking inside her mout at her troat, at her palate. You haff a lazy soft palate. She doesn't. You vould alvays haff to vork much much harder. Dese tings count in ze long run."

No. Not a big fancy limousine roaring by and splashing me with mud. A double-decker bus.

But in the end, she enlisted some of the singers I needed, threatening them, and I could only be grateful. She wouldn't have bothered if she didn't think it was worthwhile, and that was something. I didn't have to hold auditions for the principals. Tina was going to sing The Woman. One of Madame Klein's sopranos would do Julia Lau, another Vanessa the actress, and her one star baritone,

Martin, would sing John Boldright, which was perfect, because Martin's beautiful voice but wooden personality suited the role. John Boldright was a character who was always three steps behind everybody else.

The Meow Sisters, George and Brandon, agreed to do The Homeless Man and The Hairdresser.

I found an Anglican church hall for rehearsals and practically had to sell my soul to the devil to have it because you wouldn't believe what a little mafia it was, how hard it was trying to get a toehold between the box teas, the Bible study meeting and the Alcoholics Anon. Okay, so I told the minister that the church choir could sing in my opera chorus as long as they stayed in the background. This was a professional endeavor after all.

Then I booked the Vancouver East Cultural Centre for two nights in mid-July, a Thursday and the following Saturday, and paid for it in advance with the last of my savings.

The best news was that Rosie would do Blossom Sanchez, Morris would conduct from the piano, and Clint would rehearse the adults, children and chorus. The Pemmicans were coming to town.

At the beginning of May, the scent of blossoms and cut grass made me feel like a prisoner. When I wasn't locked in the tiny airless practice rooms with singing students, or being mentally whipped by Madame Klein at her boxy overheated little house, or running around helping Caroline with publicity, or gathering the used fabrics my mother had asked me to put together for costumes and set, I was spending my spare hours tweaking at the opera, trapped in Pat's place. There was no time for long walks and spring epiphanies.

And I had bad dreams every night. In one, I was frantically writing down notations to find that it was in invisible ink; no sooner had I scribbled down a melody than it disappeared. Or I would finally finish a section of music and when I tried playing it back with the software, a series of terrible atonal squawking noises came through the speakers. In one dream, I was admiring my new set (a few tables and chairs) when thick lurid green vines and creepers began to grow up out of nowhere, twining and curling around everything and obscuring the stage completely.

I got so claustrophobic by the middle of May that I called Tina at midnight one night and cried into the phone. "It isn't natural, Tina. I'm shut up in here while the whole world's out having fun. I can't miss the spring. I can't do it. I want to go dancing."

"Oh, yeah? Belly dancing maybe?"

"Christ, don't remind me."

"It's almost finished, Miranda. It's going to be great. It feels lousy now because it's hard work but it'll feel good later."

I hiccupped.

"Hey, Miranda. Have you ever noticed that in a lot of cartoons that the girl is always a human girl and the guys are all animals? You ever notice that?"

"Well, no…I don't know…maybe."

"Think about it. Oh, and listen." I could hear her rustling a newspaper. "This'll really cheer you up. It was in Around Town in today's paper. It reads like this—Evie Marcelle of *Silent Heart* fame has been charged with breaking and entering and with being a public nuisance. Miss Marcelle, it would seem, could not accept le fin with most recent producer boyfriend Ray Suarez and forced her way into their once-shared residence, damaging thousands of dollars' worth of property, as well as personal belongings. Around Town's question is—Miss Marcelle, has your star grown dim?"

"Thanks, Tina."

"You're welcome."

Over the six weeks that Patrick was away, he e-mailed me with short messages:

How's the opera coming? Sure. The Pemmicans can stay at my place. No problem.

I hated to admit it, but Patrick Tibeau quickly became my biggest card for reeling in the other musicians, and singers for the chorus. At first, I tried everybody I knew and simply asked them if they'd like to be in my opera. I went to the university. I went to the conservatory. I approached every musical group I could think of. Most of them, especially the people I worked with in the real chorus, looked at me as though I'd suggested we go hunting rattlesnakes in bare feet. I could understand their reaction. Opera makes you vulnerable.

And then by accident—I was trying to talk an elementary-school teacher into lending me some of her children's choir—I mentioned that Patrick Tibeau was filming the opera-making process. The woman perked up and sucked up. She couldn't do enough for me.

So I made the rounds all over again, this time using Patrick's name. I would have liked to do it all alone, but it was impossible. Nobody was interested until I mentioned him. Because, of course, I couldn't afford to pay anybody. The price of the tickets wasn't going to begin covering my expenses. I had already started to pawn my few pieces of jewelry.

But there were people with a loyal streak. Like Caroline. She and Dan were taking care of advertising. They'd publicized rock concerts, so an opera was a mere bagatelle. And Betty down at Little Ladies got wind of my project, too, I don't know how, and tracked me down. She appeared at my door, loomed over me while flexing her muscles and said, "I done some stage-managing work with Gold Rush Glory, eh? That's the big show they run up in the Yukon for all them tourists. Yup, I done it eleven years running. And…ah…Fern says she can do props." Then she looked at me as though her life depended on it, and she'd murder me if I didn't say yes, so how could I say no?

And my mother agreed to come down with the twins.

The nice part about homeschooling, she said, was that they had a flexible schedule. Tina said she would put them up at her place. When I told my mother what I needed her for, she didn't hesitate, and when I told her I'd run out of money, she laughed hard. I didn't think it was funny at all. I asked her why she was laughing and she said, "All parents wait for their kids to tell them they've run out of money. I've been waiting for years for you to ask me for a loan. Your high-school graduation was the last time you actually came out and asked for money. That's not bad, Miranda, not bad at all."

In the third week of May, the Pemmicans arrived with their instruments. They had gigs lined up before they even touched Vancouver soil.

The first musical rehearsal was held in the church base-ment. I got a terrible shock when I saw Martin, the lead bar-itone, come through the door with Madame Klein on his arm.

"Madame, what are you doing here?" I gasped.

She said, "I don't get out much. I vas tinking dis vas a gut opportunity. Don't vorry. I von't spoil your party."

"No. No, I'm thrilled."

I made them get Madame a chair.

When Morris entered the hall wearing light makeup, one large gold earring, a psychedelic sixties flowered shirt, his long sheepskin vest and gray suede bell-bottom pants, everybody stepped aside. Madame whipped her bifocals out, straightened them on her nose and peered.

Brandon turned to me and whispered, "What is *that?*"

"*That,*" I replied, "is Morris, the music director."

George said, "But Miranda, his fashion sense…"

"…is courageous and wonderful," I said. "And wait until you work with him. You'll encourage him to wear what-ever he wants—chiffon, sackcloth, sequins, anything, as long as he still wants to make music with you…"

George and Brandon looked at each other conspiratorially but I knew Morris would wipe the smirk off both their faces in no time.

Clint had worked with the children's chorus before everyone else arrived for the rehearsal and he had them so engrossed in fooling around and playing armpit symphonies that they didn't notice Morris at first, and when they did, they equated him with any other flamboyant musician with a colorful image to uphold.

I invited the fifty-two cast and chorus members to sit down, then launched into my speech. "I really want to thank you all for coming and helping me out with my project. You've seen the music by now. I've tried to be kind to all you singers, make it melodic enough so that you can have some enjoyment, too."

A lone voice said, "Amen," and there were a few chuckles.

"And you should know that Clint, Rosie and Morris—" I indicated each of them "—have come all the way from England to work on this with us. They were there at the birth of the piece and we went over it together last night, and I trust them a hundred and fifty percent with it so please listen to them. They may look like a bunch of dead-end kids, but they're geniuses." Rosie and Clint took exaggerated bows and Morris blushed heavily. "Rosie will be doing some acting coaching, so you soloists can set up appointments to work with her on your own time. Morris will be conducting from the piano and will want to work with all the soloists, so make your appointments with him also. And Clint…well, you kids have already met Clint. We don't have a dramatic director just yet. I'll be doing some of the staging, but as you know, Patrick Tibeau will be filming the rehearsals and performances."

There was a ripple of excited murmurs.

I smiled, then continued. "This is my first time composing an opera. Composing anything really. As you may have noticed, I'm a woman…"

"No kidding," said a jocular male voice from the chorus.

"...and uh, I know you're going to do a wonderful job. Morris, do you want to add something?"

He nodded bashfully, and in a strained voice, said, "Each time we work on the piece, I want you to forget the world you came from, the problems outside, your little aches and pains. I want you to enter into the story and the score and give it all the energy and intelligence and musicality and drop-dead voluptuousness that you would give it if you were going to die tomorrow and never get another chance at it. I don't feel that I'm asking too much."

The singers and chorus all exchanged looks. Everything, the light, people's faces, colors, sounds, seemed sharp and crystalline, focused.

"Well then," said Morris, "let's sing this baby."

I answered Patrick's e-mails with reports on the rehearsals.

Dear Pat,
The first read-through went very well but the second was mayhem. Our Julia Lau ate peanuts before she came and it threw her high notes all to shit. Biba knew all her music by heart, and so did Martin, the baritone lead, but Tina didn't and she was in a rotten mood too. Good thing she doesn't have a huge role. Did I make a mistake using my best friend?

Rosie knew her music too. She helped develop some of it back in London. You'll really like Rosie. She's a big fan of yours. I still don't know if it's going to be good or horrible, but I'm starting to get excited.

What was I thinking when I wrote kids into the opera though? It's hard to shut them all up and get started. I've never really been religious, but now all I can say is, pray for me.
Love, Miranda

Dear Patrick,
Biba's got a cold and now all the other kids in the choir are getting it. Brandon didn't look well either. We have to make

tapes of all the accompaniment and send it home so the sick people can study on their own. I'm directing the stage action myself. I thought it would be easy, but it looks like the big army-and-navy designer sale on a Saturday morning. I wish you were here.
Love, Miranda

Dear Pat,
It was better tonight. The music is starting to gel. Morris, who's conducting, is a big surprise. I told you about him. I thought he was so timid. He's not timid at all when he's working. He's brilliant. I'm just a bit worried about what he's going to wear on opening night.
Love, Miranda

Dear Pat,
My mother came today with the fabric bolts, the gauzes and costumes. But they're more like props than costumes and the chorus has to learn how to work with them. The dancers are helping out with that a bit. The cast is starting to get a sense of what it's all about. Morris has found another piano and is taking people aside and going over everything with them. Boy, you should have seen him and Madame Klein together. It was like old home week. Nobody could understand it. It was like you and Mary. Heads together and talking in a secret language.
See you soon.
Love, Miranda

It was the beginning of June when I was at Pat's place with Caroline, Dan and the Pemmicans, and Pat arrived home. We were pooling our money for yet another rice-and-bean meal when he came in. Our finances were so tight that we were getting creative. Dandelion greens. Day-old bread. Sauces made from the crates of tomatoes that the supermarket was throwing out. My mother chipped in to buy us real food once a week. And when one of us got paid, it was a feast. That's how it is when you go out on a limb for something you believe in. You eat stone soup and nasturtium salad.

Pat looked tired but he was very gracious about having his place overrun. That night, he came in with us on the meal and we were able to buy enough for four courses and lots of beer. Rosie stuck herself to Patrick like flypaper and dominated his attention the whole evening. But then Pat brought out his camera and started to film, and Morris started to play the keyboard, with Clint and Rosie joining in, and Caroline and Dan grooving on the sidelines.

By midnight, Morris was playing and the rest of us were dancing. I took a break, gathered up plates and went into the kitchen to tidy up.

Patrick followed me. "I like your friends," he said.

I turned and looked up at him. "I like them, too. They saved my skin in London. Emotionally, I mean."

"I meant to say before, Miranda, how sorry I am about your father. I downloaded some of his arias from the Internet…"

"Don't get caught."

"No. Listening to a voice like that, it would be impossible not to dream about meeting him, especially if you're a singer, and his daughter."

"I feel cheated. I'm sure we would have had so much to talk about, so many things in common, but now it's a lost opportunity and there's nothing I can do."

"There's one thing," said Pat.

"What's that?"

"The fact that he's remained a mystery will make you create. Creating will be a way to work it all out. Maybe you don't think so now, but it will."

"I hadn't thought of it that way. It's sort of happily cynical."

"You're a composer now. Don't go into therapy. It'll take

the steam out of your work. But I didn't come in here to talk about this."

"No? What did you come in here for?"

"To…um…what did I come in here for? To compliment you on your…um…clothes?"

I laughed. "Oh, really? On my filthy lovely sloppy jeans and sweaty T-shirt?"

"Exactly."

Patrick slid one arm around my waist and pressed up against me. He was bending his head down toward mine when Dan the Sasquatch rushed into the kitchen holding up a glass.

"Gotta hydrate," he said, and pushed between the two of us to turn on the tap. "Only way to avoid that bad hangover." He drank the glass of water in one gulp then wiped his mouth on his sleeve. Only then did Dan realize that something was going on. "Hey, what's going on in here? Is Her Ladyship about to get hot and heavy on the kitchen table? Or did I already miss it?"

Patrick leaned back against the opposite counter but kept his gaze fixed on me, unfazed.

I stared hard at the floor and said, "No, Dan, you didn't miss a thing."

That was when I realized that Patrick and I had been colliding ever since that day in the Super Value. The big body crash seemed inevitable. But would I be ready?

Chapter 29

Patrick was at the next rehearsal, filming. We were at the awkward stage of trying to bring music and action together and sometimes it was so chaotic that it reminded me of a day-care center. Patrick's presence and camera brought a glue to the rehearsals that had been missing. People realized they might be appearing on national TV and better get it right. He quietly made little directing suggestions and I took them. I'd have been crazy not to. My biggest worry was Martin, the baritone lead. He was so rigid onstage. But whatever Patrick said when he took him aside must have been the right thing, because Martin improved drastically.

By the time opening night in mid-July rolled around, we were almost overrehearsed.

I put on the crimson dress and looked in the full-length mirror in the Bute Street apartment. Miracle of miracles, Cassie had met a man who adored cleanliness and having his tins of food in alphabetical order. So I had my room back. My mother stood behind me, pulling and adjusting the dress's fabric. She said, "I'm so proud of you, Miranda."

Choked up, I held back the tears.

The whole thing had blown up a little. Caroline had brought the media in and made a big deal about Patrick filming the process and performances. I'd only seen him at rehearsals because both of us had been so busy. *City of Dreams* had been publicized on TV and radio, and there had been a long article in the paper, and now both nights were sold out.

My mother drove us to the theater an hour before curtain. I went backstage and said toi, toi to everyone. Patrick and some cameramen were set up at three points inside the theater. My mother and I had been planning to sit at the back of the theater, but we ended up not, because it was standing room only by then. And Lyle—Lyle was part of the backstage crew.

Morris came on, dressed in a black satin shirt, black pants and full makeup, turned to the audience and nodded. The houselights went down and the music started. No overture, just right into the action.

So here's what the opera's about.

There's this police detective, John Boldright, whose Chinese wife wakes him up one night to tell him that she's had the strangest dream. He tells her he always thought he'd married a sensible person and now he finds out he's married to a hysterical neurotic.

She sings an aria about all the women in her family in China who have always been able to predict floods and fires. The scene is stylistically acted out to one side by her and the chorus, the music influenced by the Beijing clapper opera–style and the chorus participating with singing, cries, whispers, water, wind and other percussion sounds. Julia Lau warns her husband that her dream is an omen.

Boldright asks her what she saw in the dream. Then we,

too, see in her mind's eye a Gypsy girl, a messenger, sent to tell her that the two little boys are about to go home.

Boys? What boys? Boldright wants to know. Has there been a kidnapping?

The boys, says his wife. The Babes in the Woods.

Next scene—John Boldright is at his desk in the police station, a single stark light above him. He remembers the Babes in the Woods case in an aria and he can't help being a little intrigued. But then he reflects on what a busy guy he is, dealing with the scum of the earth. A comic moment, the chorus men and women form lines of suspects and sing an ensemble piece about crime.

Then another woman comes into the office to report to Boldright that she's had a dream and a Gypsy messenger told her to go and see Boldright and tell him the boys were about to go home.

Boldright's reaction is, "Not another hysterical woman?"

But the woman, Blossom Sanchez, defends herself. Boldright asks her the standard questions, who she is, what she does, and she answers that she's a jazz singer, and the chorus stylistically creates the scene that she draws Boldright into. We're shown the nightclub scene. The music is jazzy, and there is a guest artist who improvises something (we had Clint play the sax on opening night) and a big chorus blowout with dancing as well.

Then he's back in his office.

A third woman, Vanessa, an actress, approaches Boldright with the same story and he's getting more and more defensive.

He grills the actress and she tells her story. She already hears voices, she's on the brink of madness. The chorus stylistically enacts the strange scenes in her paranoid mind.

Boldright wonders what's going on.

The last complaint is made by a woman who reports that her neighbor, an elderly woman, has gone missing.

Scene—the three women, Julia Lau, Vanessa and Blossom Sanchez, all at the hairdresser's, compare stories. Each one has a tragic background involving a baby they lost or couldn't have. Then they learn that they have all had the same dream. The hairdresser claims he has had it, too, that maybe the whole city is having it, just that we don't know it. They also realize that the Gypsy girl is real, they've seen her around town.

That night, Boldright dreams the Gypsy messenger himself, he sees her clearly, and she says the same thing, that the boys are about to come home. His wife wakes up and says the girl is real. She accuses him, saying he's a policeman, he should find her.

John Boldright takes to the streets, trying to find the Gypsy girl. This is a big chorus scene with everyone participating. The Gypsy girl darts in and out. Now you see her, now you don't. The chorus have big flashlights to achieve this effect (the Pemmicans found amazing street drummers for this scene and there's a building tension).

The chorus members transform themselves with costumes and strips of fabric that act as props to make them like trees and then like the Woods People. Boldright walks the city streets and ends up in the deep forest of Stanley Park, and he's surrounded by the Woods People who have an eerie supernatural appearance. The girl is still darting in and out like a dangerous sprite or erlking, leading him deeper and deeper into the forest. The Woods People clear and there's an old woman lying at the foot of the tree.

The Homeless Man explains how she wandered into the woods and went down on her knees and began to dig in the earth and weep and call, "My boys, my boys." The Woman who has been immobile as though dead on the ground, sheds all her gray rags and wig and slowly stands up to show herself as a young woman. She picks up a fur coat that is lying on the ground, puts on a missing high heel and calls John Boldright by name. The chorus have brown and green bolts of gauze waving in the background to create the woods effect and as The Woman tells her story, that she was John Boldright's grandfather's mistress, and that when she realized he would never leave his wife, she lost her mind and committed her crime. Boldright sinks to the ground. In the background we hear the sound of children laughing and playing, and they come closer until we see them, in their little WWII flying caps (my brothers, the twins, of course). They sing a little duet, take their mother's hand and all three disappear into the gauziness. The chorus turns the scene back into an urban street, and little by little the music rises then disintegrates into the individual thoughts of the pedestrians, and John Boldright comes to his senses and walks along with them as if nothing has happened. The music decreases and ends on a single long cello note.

Okay, I know. It's a little strange. But you have to consider that people have written serious vocal works about lichen.

There was a long silence after the lights went down, and then applause, thin at first, then growing louder. I didn't make too much of it. It was a rigged performance. Half of Cold Shanks was there for both me and Patrick. Cold Shanksians were so generous with people from their own town that they would have applauded a fly buzzing across the stage. But when they called me up on stage to hold hands with the cast, it was all I could do to hold back the tears.

When the audience had started to trickle out, I heard a familiar voice. "Miranda Lyme."

"Lance."

"Miranda, let me introduce you to Steve, my roommate." A nice-looking and very gay-looking man stood beside Lance.

I shook Steve's hand. "Hi, Steve. So, Lance. What did you think?"

He gave me a hug. "It was great. Weird but great. Biba is

amazing. You made something happen here." Over Lance's shoulder, Patrick signaled to me that he was leaving, taking his little crew home to see what they had bagged. I waved and mouthed, "See you on Saturday."

Chapter 30

At the second performance, Saturday, we were all a little nervous. There was more of the Vancouver brass-ass crowd attending. The important critics had finally decided to come, too. But we'd done the opera once already, and the cast was more confident. Everyone knew it was the last chance they'd get, so they gave it everything: performances that made every hair bristle.

I took my bow again, imagining the future of my opera, the good paper and stiff binding of the edition that would be registered at the Canadian Music Centre, then stuffed away on some shelf to collect dust.

I made my way around the entire cast, crew and all the musicians, thanking each one. Then I went to the dressing rooms and changed into my old jeans to help strike the set and clean up. As I emerged from the dressing room, I almost ran headlong into Kurt. Behind him were Guido, Peter and Ellie.

"Howay, Miranda," said Ellie, and gave my arm a squeeze.

I looked at Peter, wincing, but he just winked, as if to say the ENO audition had never happened and there were no prisoners taken.

"Hello, Ellie. Peter. And Guido. And you," I said to Kurt. He looked better than ever.

"And you, Miranda," he said. "Curious little piece you've written. Some interesting voices, too."

Over Kurt's shoulder, Guido mouthed the word, "Brava."

"What are you all doing here, Kurt?"

"We bought tickets."

"That's not what I meant. In Vancouver."

"We have a *Butterfly* in Seattle, and your chatty woman in the opera office mentioned you were up to something, so I decided to come and see for myself."

I was squirming. I didn't know how to deal with him. I wondered if Kurt would always have such a disturbing effect on me.

And then Patrick came striding up behind him, saw the expression on my face, and realized who I was talking to.

He was about to turn around and walk away when I said, "Patrick."

He stopped.

"Patrick Tibeau, this is Kurt Hancock. And this is Guido Castracani, the person who wrote the text for *Città di Pietra*. And this is Ellie Watson, and Peter Drake, soprano and tenor."

He shook everyone's hand.

As Kurt shook Patrick's hand, he said, "I've seen your work. It's good."

Patrick smiled a fast, tight-lipped smile.

"Well, Miranda..." said Kurt. And I waited. But nothing else came.

"How's Olivia?" I asked.

"Enormously pregnant and off her feet. But it's all proceeding as it should."

"Good. Good. And she's due when?"

"Mid-September, they think."

And I was about to ask Patrick what he'd be doing after,

if he wanted to go out for a drink when we'd struck the set, but he'd already gone.

Then Kurt blurted, "Take care, Miranda."

"You, too," I replied.

"I'll be in the lobby when you're ready," he said to the rest of the group.

Guido, Peter and Ellie didn't budge. They all grinned at me.

"Isn't Kurt Hancock just so full of his own bollocks," said Ellie.

Guido grabbed me by both shoulders and gave me a kiss on each cheek. "I never would have thought that you could be both beautiful and talented in this way. Bravissima, Miranda. You know, you have made Kurt jealous. I could hear him stewing in the seat next to me. It will do him good. He needed to come down a notch or two." He threw back his head and roared with laughter.

"Guido…" I stuttered.

"I have just written the notes for the review of your opera for one of the English papers. The *Guardian* might take it. I made up my mind about your opera in the first half and started the review in the intermission. Sneak preview?" He thrust a small notepad into my hand. I could only make out some of the words but the review looked promising. New name on the music scene. A return to sweet tonality and dramatic plot. Innovative use of voices and vocal techniques. Popular- and world-music influences. Much to look forward to from this young composer.

"Thank you so much, Guido. Thank you," I said. "I feel so…flattered…and relieved."

"I understand," he said. "I have been in your position. When I was younger."

"We were thinking…" said Peter in a sly little voice.

Ellie joined in. "Yes, we were thinking…a little piece for me and Petie, perhaps? Ooo, it was a loovlay opera, Miranda. And loovlay in a way only us women can make it. So how about it? Something small for the Edinburgh Festival? Some songs perhaps? Soprano and tenor duets?"

I felt dizzy. My first sort-of commission?

"Oooo, she's cryin'. The poor lass," said Ellie, and she gave me another squeeze.

A week later, Patrick appeared at my door. We hadn't seen each other since closing night but I'd heard from the others that he'd been hard at work on his new project.

He held a tape in his hand. "Here it is," he said. *"The Making of an Opera."*

"Come right on in." I snatched the tape from him and said, "I'd offer you a coffee or something but I just can't wait to look at this." I nodded in the direction of the bedroom. He hesitated.

"C'mon, don't just stand there," I said.

He followed me in, looked around my room and said, "Miranda's inner sanctum."

"It's not much, but it's home." I put the tape in the machine and pressed Play, then I threw myself down on the bed. He sat down carefully on the edge.

There I was, full face shots of Miranda Lyme sputtering on about how insecure she felt about an idea for a new opera and writing music.

I covered my face with my hands. "Oh, God."

Pat stood up again and sat down a little closer. "No, it's sweet. You see the whole process, the transformation. Your vulnerability makes it edgier. The chaotic beginning makes us wonder if it's going to work out and that creates a nice tension."

Then there was the meeting with Biba, the session with Madame Klein (who came across as astoundingly lively and gracious in front of the camera—who would have thought it?), and then the rehearsals, Caroline and her crew plastering the town with posters and organizing publicity, and the Pemmicans sleeping on Pat's floor complaining about working conditions and eating nasturtium salad, and my mother at her sewing machine, and then at the dye vats, working her magic with all the fabrics, and then the children's choir practicing and then rapping afterward, and all through it, this mounting sense of anticipation. Looking at the film, even *I* wondered how it was all going to turn out.

Just as the camera cut to the opening night of the opera, my door burst open. Tina stood there, huge and noisy, her face puffy and blotchy with crying.

"Tina, what is it?" I asked.

"Wayne!" announced Tina.

I was impatient. The film was slipping by and I was missing it. But I could see that Tina was too upset to ignore.

"What's he done?" I asked.

"What an asshole. I knew what he was like so why did I go ahead and do it anyway? It's like walking head-on into a moving train. He doesn't just have a couple of girlfriends. He's got a different one after every meal. Like a different flavor of toothpaste. Tina Browning, you are such an idiot," she said to my ceiling.

"Hi, Tina," said Patrick.

"You're so obvious," she cried. She was in orbit. "Men are such bastards. Every single goddamn one of them. Bastards, bastards, bastards."

I said, "I agree that they can sometimes be pretty..."

"Evil selfish egotistical cretins, every single one of them. I mean, the only way you'll ever know what they're really like is by getting involved with them. That's when you see their true colors. But by then it's too late. The damage is done and you're screwed. I mean, now, you, Miranda, for example. Is there a single guy in your whole history of relationships that hasn't been shit, that hasn't let you down?"

"Tina..." I protested.

"Go on. Can you name one?"

"Well, actually, I...ah..."

"You can't, can you?"

"I…ah…"

She crossed her arms.

"No, I guess not," I said.

"See," said Tina, triumphant.

"I've never thought about it much before but my record kind of sucks up till now."

"See? They've been disasters. And why?"

I said, "I guess the problem was that if they weren't screwing around on me, then they just didn't love me enough. Somewhere along the line, they just got bored, I guess. I'd go nuts finding ways to keep them, but they didn't love me enough to stay with me."

It was a horrible thing to have to realize.

"You see? That's exactly what I mean," said Tina. "Men are incapable of being in a relationship. They're just a bunch of ambulating sperm-providers. With them it's all wham bam, and thank you for the slam but now you're spam. I hate them all. I hate them…"

"So Wayne lived up to your expectations?"

Tina nodded. "Or else they're like Patrick here. Mr. Door-mat of the Year." She pointed at him. "Mr. We Have to Have an Open Relationship Because My Girlfriend Screws Around on Me. They're just as bad. They spend the whole of their next relationship whining about the last girlfriend."

"Now wait a minute, Tina…" I said.

Patrick stood up abruptly. "You gotta be kidding me with this."

Tina was about to start again but Patrick interrupted her. "You girls, you *women,* seem to think it's so easy to be around you all. We knock ourselves out to try and understand your next move, but let me tell you, it's not a transparent thing, it's like trying to figure out Machiavelli's next move. We're *human.* We're a bunch of poor, imperfectly made, sloppy, *lonely* human beings just trying to survive on a shrinking hos-tile planet. We don't know what we're feeling half the time or why we're feeling it…and we haven't got the time to analyze it because we're working. Some of *us* are working to pay for some of *you*. But let's not get into that.

"And then there's women and sex. You all complain because you're not having sex, then when you're having sex, it's not the right kind of sex, then when it's better, you complain that the guy is an animal, that the only thing he ever thinks about is sex so you shut him out and he doesn't know what he's done wrong, then if he tries to be considerate and sensitive, he's a wimp, he's gay, he's impotent…you don't know when somebody cares about you, you don't know when somebody might want to share more than just a bed with you. You don't know when he's trying to be honest with you so that you'll never hold his silences against him.

"You know what I think? I think that a lot of you women don't really like or want us men, let alone love us. I get the feeling some of you wouldn't know love if it came up and slapped you in the face. I think you only like the *idea* of us. And you know what else? It's exhausting. I've had enough. You can keep the tape, Miranda. See you around." He strode out of the room, then we heard the front door slam.

Tina and I stared at each other, incredulous, then both of us burst into tears.

Chapter 31

At first, Patrick and I are talking together face-to-face about words in a song. I'm wearing my green-and-gold brocade coat. He keeps touching me and running his hand up and down my sleeve, feeling the fabric. Then suddenly, he yanks the coat off me, puts it on and walks away. He's hurrying along a corridor. I follow him, anxious to get my coat back. I run after him but each time I get close, he turns a corner and disappears.

I woke up stiff and aching in my bus seat and angry at him. Even though I knew it was ridiculous, the dream felt so real. He had stolen my beautiful coat and I wanted it back.

Later on, in my mother's car, I bounced recklessly over the bad mountain road, sending up huge clouds of dust, giving the engine a dubious workout. If there had ever been a speed limit on that road, I was way over it. The afternoon sun sent warm golden shafts driving through the tall evergreens, and the July sky was that shade of electric purplish blue that suggested infinity.

I pulled into the clearing and parked so fast that there was a screech of tires and gravel flying. I jumped out and marched to the front door where I raised the iron mermaid knocker and brought it down hard and loud. After a long wait and no answer, I tried again.

A voice behind me made me jump. "I thought it was Nora, but it's you, Miranda. You're so much alike in some ways," said Jeanette. She was wearing gardening clothes, a scarf on her head and had a basket of raspberries over her arm. "Come inside and have some of my raspberry vinegar. It's hot out here."

"No, I can't stop," I said, trying to keep the desperation out of my voice. "I'm looking for Pat."

Jeanette scrutinized me, now looking like a concerned mother. "Are you okay, Miranda? Your face is awfully pale."

"Please. Can you tell me where Pat is?"

"I'm not sure, dear. I think he was planning to go for a swim. He might be out on the raft, or down on the far side of the lake…there's a path that goes all around…he has his rock…he likes to go there when he's trying to think through a problem. Or you could try looking down by the little dock…"

"Thanks, Jeanette. I'll find him." I didn't wait for her to finish.

I was running. Past the gardens, the kitchen garden of scarlet runners, lettuces, cherry tomatoes and Swiss chard, past the flower beds of sweet pea, hollyhocks, roses, fuchsia, rhododendrons, past the smooth green lawn that stretched to the lake's edge, along the path that cut deep into the woods. I was gasping when I finally reached the place where the woods gave way to a small flat rocky outcrop beside the lake. On top of the flattest rock, Patrick was stretched out, his brown body glistening under the sun. One hand trailed back and forth in the water.

Quickly and quietly I took off my shoes and left them on the ground. Then I padded up onto the hot rock. He heard me and opened his eyes. He slowly pulled himself up to a sitting position, shaded his eyes against the sun and said, "Miranda Lyme. I'm overwhelmed. I really didn't expect to see you here. What can I do for you?"

Methodically, I took off my clothes with Patrick looking on. His expression was deeply serious, almost studious.

I turned, walked to the rock's edge and plunged into the lake, letting the bubbling rush of cool water flood away all my thoughts, all my worries. I swam farther into the center of the lake. Patrick stood up and dived in after me. I was treading water as he began to swim wide circles around me. I rotated to follow his movements.

"What do you want from me, Miranda Lyme?"

Across the stretch of shimmering water that lay between us, I said, "I want you to make love to me, Patrick."

He swam up and wrapped himself around me, effortlessly taking my weight on his like a floating chair, under and around me. He put his forehead against mine, closed his eyes and said, "You only had to ask."

We were still intertwined when the sun disappeared and the stars and mosquitoes started to come out. There was the rich scent of the earthy-sweet grass we had lain on all afternoon, the smell of pine bark and needles from the trees surrounding us, the clicking of cicadas, and there was another sound—a rising, wild, free, singing, animal sound that would have made even Matilde envious, and it was coming from me.

Lucy's Launderette

Betsy Burke

Ever had the feeling that your life is spinning
out of control? Lucy has! Despite her degree in
fine arts, she is working as a professional gofer
for an intolerable art gallery owner, her
free-spirited grandfather has just passed away,
leaving behind his pregnant girlfriend, and she is
the only sane member in her eccentric family.
Read LUCY'S LAUNDERETTE to find out what
finally puts Lucy back on the road to happiness.